Praise for
An Ex to Grind

"*An Ex to Grind* is the perfect battle-of-the-sexes tale for today's world. Every woman reading this book will empathize with the heroine and revel in the fresh take Jane Heller provides on marriage and the rules of dis-engagement."

—Karen McCullah Lutz, author of *The Bachelorette Party*

"Lively, warm, and wise. Melanie Banks is a heroine to root for, and I couldn't put this book down! I really loved it!"

—Amanda Brown, author of *Legally Blonde* and *Family Trust*

"What's so great about Heller's writing is her wit. Not one chapter is a sleeper; the plot and characters lock the reader in. The twists continuously tempt us to skip to the final page. *An Ex to Grind* deserves a sequel. Please, Jane Heller, give us more."

—*Cleveland Plain Dealer*

"Come along for a witty, fast-paced and clever ride! Jane Heller is at the top of her game."

—*New York Times* bestselling author Carly Phillips

By Jane Heller

An Ex to Grind

Coming Soon in Hardcover

Some Nerve

Jane Heller

An Imprint of HarperCollins*Publishers*

This title was originally published in hardcover by William Morrow in July 2005.

This book is a work of fiction. References to real people, events, establishments, organizations, or locales are intended only to provide a sense of authenticity, and are used fictitiously. All other characters, and all incidents and dialogue, are drawn from the author's imagination and are not to be construed as real.

HarperCollins books may be purchased for educational, business, or sales promotional use. For information please write: Special Markets Department, HarperCollins Publishers Inc., 10 East 53rd Street, New York, NY 10022.

FIRST EDITION

ISBN-13: 978-0-06-089930-1
ISBN-10: 0-06-089930-1

Interior text designed by Chris Welch

The William Morrow hardcover contained the following Library of Congress Cataloging-in-Publication Data

Heller, Jane.
An ex to grind / Jane Heller.— 1st ed.
p. cm.
1. Divorced women—Fiction. 2. Investment advisers—Fiction.
3. Football players—Fiction. 4. Dating services—Fiction.
5. Unemployed—Fiction. 6. Alimony—Fiction.
I. Title

PS3558.E4757E97 2005
823'.914—dc22 2004053648

06 07 08 09 10 RRD 10 9 8 7 6 5 4 3 2 1

For Marty Bell,
whose belief in this book early on
carried me through

Acknowledgments

I sought the advice of several people well before I began writing this novel and would probably not have written it if not for them. So thanks to Rhonda Friedman for the inspiration, Amy L. Reiss, Esq., for the legal expertise, and Kathy Sulkes for putting me in touch with Amy. Thanks to Bruce Gelfand for the hours of brainstorming on the phone, and to Brad Schreiber and Ciji Ware for the ideas and encouragement they contributed. A huge thanks to my editor, Carrie Feron, whose astute notes on the first draft made the finished book much stronger, and thanks to her capable assistant, Selina McLemore, for getting all the details right. As always, my deepest thanks and love to Ellen Levine, agent extraordinaire, and her team at Trident Media Group.

Thanks to Amy Schiffman at Gersh for continuing to fight the good fight in Hollywood with her customary caring and decency. Thanks to Kristen Powers for keeping my website up and running, even though she's a Red Sox fan and I'm a Yankees fan and we can't bear to speak to each other while our teams are going at it. Thanks to the Santa Clara Valley chapter of the Brandeis University National Women's Committee for inviting me to participate in their contest—and to good sport Lynda Fox, who won a walk-on part in this book at their fund-raiser luncheon. And finally, thanks to my husband, Michael Forester, who, despite his own challenges while I was writing the book, never wavered in his moral support for me.

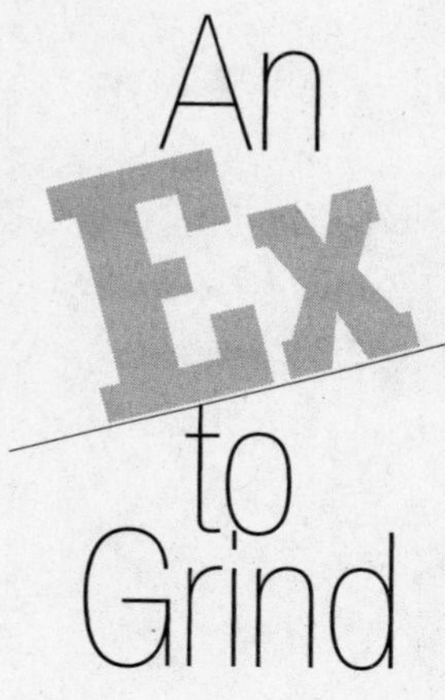
An
Ex
to
Grind

Chapter 1

Let me begin with a few words of caution for women in their thirties and younger: if you think sexual equality is a nonissue, a relic from your mother's or grandmother's bra-burning past, a subject that's *so yesterday,* think again. The debate over it is back in a new and particularly insidious form, and I need to warn you about it. Please don't groan and say, "Sexual equality? She must be an alarmist." I know what I'm talking about.

You see, this isn't about whether women can succeed in the workplace. That's a given. It's about whether our success has cost us; about whether the fact that we're running companies and winning Senate seats and performing delicate brain surgeries has made us vulnerable to men who will glom onto us for our bucks, not our boobs.

I'll be specific. I was a thirty-four-year-old woman in the once-male-dominated field of financial planning, pulling in a high six figures as a vice president at the Manhattan-based investment firm of Pierce, Shelley and Steinberg. I was well regarded and well compensated, because I was good at helping my already wealthy clients become more wealthy. The sexual equality thing never crossed my mind.

But then something snapped me out of my complacence. I began to notice that with women grabbing more and more of the big-ticket jobs, men were being relegated to the so-called pink-collar ones. Suddenly, women were the doctors, the lawyers, and the college presidents, and men were the nurses, the paralegals, and the librarians. We were undergoing a seismic shift in our culture, and I realized there had to be a consequence.

Well, there *has* been a consequence. Men, discouraged by our growing dominance, are starting to shrug their shoulders and drop out of the workforce altogether, leaving it to us to support them. Take a look around if you don't believe me. Ask your friends. It's happening, and it's throwing off the balance, impacting both the way we hook up and the way we break up.

This still isn't hitting home for you? To be honest, it didn't hit home for me until it hit *my* home.

In the early years of my thirteen-year marriage, my ex-husband was the breadwinner. Then his career ended abruptly, and I became the breadwinner. At first I wasn't concerned about our change in roles. A study had just been released reporting that wives were outearning their spouses in over a third of households, so I knew I wasn't the only woman bringing home the bacon. I accepted the fact that if you're the partner who's up, you should assume responsibility for the partner who's down, no matter which gender you are.

But then my ex-husband's bout with unemployment became chronic, which is to say that he didn't lift a finger to find himself a new career. The marriage unraveled. We couldn't handle the role changes after all. But as distressing as that was, the divorce was worse. Why? Because I got stuck assuming responsibility for the partner who was down, even though we were no longer partners!

I was forced not only to hand over a huge chunk of my assets to my ex but to pay him alimony too. "Maintenance" they call it in New York state. Whatever. We're talking about me having to write checks to the guy every month for eight years. I was a good and generous person who gave to numerous charities and never cheated anybody out of anything. But this? Well, I balked, to put it mildly.

Maybe you're thinking that if we're the big achievers now, we should stop whining and just fork over the cash in the divorce. But here's the thing: when it's your turn, you won't want to fork over the cash any more than men did when they were hogging the power seat.

Did I go to extremes in my effort to wriggle out of my legal obligation to my ex? Sure. Do I regret what I did to him? Deeply. But I was caught up in that nutty fantasy about men—that even as we're out there conquering the world, they're supposed to be the strong ones, capable of rescuing us, or, at the very least, providing for us.

It's all so confusing, isn't it? Well, maybe this little story of mine will help sort things out.

Or maybe it'll simply confirm that equality, like beauty, is in the eye of the beholden.

Sign here," said my divorce attorney, Robin Baylor, a fortysomething black woman with impeccable credentials. Harvard for her undergraduate degree. Yale for law school. Louis Licari for the auburn highlights that were expertly woven through her short, spiky hair. The two of us were sitting in her elegantly appointed, wood-paneled conference room at a table the length of a city block. She had just passed me the gazillionth document pertaining to *Melanie Banks* (me) *vs. Dan Swain* (my ex). "It's the last one," she announced.

"Promise?" I said with pleading eyes as I glanced at the huge file she had on Dan and me. So much paper. Such a waste of trees.

"Trust me, yours wasn't as complicated as some," she said, and she wasn't kidding. She'd handled my friend Karen's divorce, which became a truly unsavory affair after it was revealed that Karen's ex was not only an insider trader with the SEC breathing down his neck but also a bigamist with two families on opposite coasts. "You've waited out the year of legal separation, and now you're just signing the conversion documents. Once these are filed, you're divorced. Case closed."

"Closed?" I said. "I wish. Thanks to this settlement, I'm tied to Dan for seven more years. Having to pay him while we were separated was no picnic, but having to write him checks for the next . . . Well, the whole thing makes me sick."

"We had no choice. If we'd gone to trial, the judge could have awarded him more, given the disparity in your incomes and the duration of the marriage. I explained that to you."

"I know." I nodded dejectedly at Robin, who, despite having a conference room that reminded me of one of those men-only grill rooms at country clubs and practically cried out for cigars to be passed out and smoked, wasn't a shark. She was compassionate as well as conscientious. She baked little sweets and brought them to the office for her clients, if you can believe that. How women with demanding careers found the time, not to mention the motivation, to actually turn on their ovens was a mystery to me, not being a multitasker myself. But at that very moment, there was a plate full of homemade cookies on the table—chocolate chip and oatmeal raisin—and over the course of our meeting, I scarfed down several of each. And I didn't even like raisins. But "like" had nothing to do with it. I'd gained fifteen pounds since Dan and I split up, and while I wasn't a tub of guts by anyone's standards, I'd discovered that eating, along with plotting his death, had become enormously satisfying. "I'm not blaming you at all, Robin," I added between bites. "It's the situation I can't stomach." I avoided looking down at mine. I was sure that fourteen of those fifteen pounds had settled there.

"Whether it makes you sick or not, he's entitled to the spousal support," she said. "This is the new millennium, Melanie. Things have changed. It's not a symbol of weakness anymore for men to take money from women if they need it to maintain their lifestyle."

"*If they need it.* Those are the operative words. Dan could maintain his lifestyle by himself if he went out and got a decent job."

"He had a decent job. He was a wide receiver for the Giants."

"Yes, and now he's gone from being a wide receiver to a wife receiver. I throw him money; he catches it."

She laughed. "Come on. He didn't blow out his knee on purpose."

No, the injury wasn't Dan's fault. It had happened in a game against the Redskins in only his third season as a starting receiver, and it extinguished the shining light he'd become. Before the accident, he'd been a hero in New York, the fans chanting his nickname—"Traffic! Traffic!"—wherever he went. But then came cruel disappointment. He was in the act of making a spectacular catch when he was clobbered by two defensive backs. One climbed on his shoulders, the other wrapped himself around his legs, and the result was a horrifying tackle, sending the top half of his body one way, the bottom half another. I could hear the snap of the cartilage all the way up in the wives' box. When you're married to a professional athlete, you're supposed to steel yourself every time he gets hurt, reassure yourself that your guy is doing what he loves and be grateful for all the money he's making. But then came the diagnosis, the surgery, and the end to his promising career as well as the nullification of his lucrative contract. He was lost and stayed lost. "What *is* his fault is that he didn't try to do anything after he blew out his knee," I said.

"That's not true," she said. "He did try sports broadcasting."

"Don't remind me."

"He wasn't that bad."

We both laughed then, knowing he stunk. On the two NFL broadcasts for which he'd been hired to provide color commentary, he stammered, forgot to smile, seemed confused by the directions coming at him from his headset, wasn't clear which camera was on him. He was devastated by his performance, but he was even more devastated when the phone stopped ringing and similar gigs were not forthcoming. I did what I could to prop up his spirits and boost his self-confidence. I adored him and hated to see him so miserable. But he couldn't get over that he had failed. "He should have taken lessons," I said. "They have communication specialists who train people to be on television, but he was too macho to ask for help."

"I wonder if he might have improved with a few more chances," said Robin.

"They gave him another chance, remember? He went on the air after four scotches and referred to a female reporter as 'sweetcakes.' And that was before he threatened to moon his coanchors."

She winced at the memory. "He was so out of it that night. I actually felt sorry for him. Why didn't he ever go into coaching?"

"A good question. I kept telling him, 'You love the game. Coach a high school or college team. There are schools in the Tri-State area that would be thrilled to have you.' And every single time, he shook me off and grumbled, 'I'll never be one of those losers.' Instead, he became a loser. Now, except for the occasional ribbon cuttings and collectors' shows, *he* parties while *I* work. How is it fair that I have to pay him?"

"As fair as when men pay their ex-wives who don't work."

"Hey, aren't you supposed to be on my side?"

She smiled. "I am on your side, but I have a lot of male clients, so I have to see things from their perspective too."

"Lucky you." I reached for another cookie. As I chewed the first mouthful, I decided to try to see the situation from Dan's perspective, just to prove to myself that I could be as fair-minded as Robin. But I couldn't do it, couldn't get past the twin images of writing him a check and then watching my bank balance shrink, couldn't take the sight of those disappearing zeroes. The mere thought of losing money gave me nightmares, and it had been that way since I was a kid. My mother died when I was two, leaving me with a father who was only marginally employed, was often in a drunken stupor on the couch covered in empty beer cans, and was constantly moving us from one crappy place to another—sometimes in the middle of the night—just so we could beat the eviction notices. I made a decision at a very young age that money meant security, stability, and happiness, and that my goal in life was to accumulate a lot of it. How could I surrender even a piece of that security to a man who seemed capable only of frittering it away?

"Mel, you okay?" asked Robin.

"Fine," I said, not fine at all.

She patted my shoulder with her perfectly manicured fingers—the same fingers that baked cookies. I guessed she was one of those women who wore rubber gloves in the kitchen. "Before I send you out into the world," she said, "I want you to stop resisting and start accepting."

I laughed. "You sound like a therapist. Do you charge extra for that?"

"No, and you should take my free advice. Stop making Dan the enemy. He may not have a high-profile job anymore, but his celebrity made it easier for you to do yours. He put you through business school, introduced you to his jock buddies, got you your first big clients. He was the ideal husband in some respects, and the eight years of spousal support is the court's acknowledgment of that."

"Ideal husband?" I scoffed. "He was the one who trashed the marriage. Not only did he give up on himself, but he also got on my back about my long hours at the office and my—what did he call it?—*corporate attitude*. That's the irony of all this. He wanted me to cut back at work and then didn't think twice about helping himself to the spoils of that work. He lives like a prince now, thanks to me, and it's disgusting. He's disgusting." I slumped down in the chair and played with the ends of my hair, which was light brown, shoulder length, and wavy. Winding it around my index finger had become my other nervous tic, besides eating.

"Let it go, Mel. Let *him* go. Move on with your life and find somebody else."

"I don't want somebody else after this fiasco," I mumbled.

"Then pray that he finds somebody else," she said.

"Why would I want him to be happy?" I said, twirling my hair with even more gusto.

She shook her head at me, as if I were missing her point. "Didn't you read this agreement?"

"Oh, right. If he remarries, I get to stop writing him checks. Like that'll happen." I forced myself to leave my hair alone and placed my hands in my lap. "After the way things turned out he's as down on the institution of marriage as I am."

Robin shook her head again. "I'm talking about the cohabitation clause, stipulating that if Dan lives with another woman for a period of ninety days, the spousal support is terminated."

I sat up straighter. "Right, right," I said, remembering now. "He doesn't have to remarry. He just has to shack up with someone."

"For 'ninety substantially continuous days.' That's how it's worded. Which means that he can take a break from her every once in a while, but once he reaches ninety days total, he invalidates the agreement."

I blinked at her, feeling a glimmer of an emotion I couldn't identify. Hope? Glee? Something. "How awesome would that be if he had a three-month fling and I didn't have to pay him anymore."

"You'd be off the hook, it's true," she said. "But if he's so turned off to relationships, I wouldn't count on him entering into one. And let's face it: he may be unemployed, but he's not stupid. He's not going to risk losing that monthly maintenance unless he falls madly in love, and what are the chances of that?"

"Slim to none," I conceded and felt the hope, glee, or whatever it was evaporate.

"Okay, then. Back to business. Sign this last document and we're through here."

I scribbled my signature in between all the *Whereas*'s and *Heretofore*'s, put down the pen, and exhaled noisily. "That's it. I'm officially divorced."

No sooner was that pronouncement out of my mouth than I was overcome by melancholy—sort of a heavy, invasive sadness. Sad because I had loved Dan once. Sad because our marriage was the only period of my life when I'd felt the stability I'd craved as a child. And sad because it was now final and irrevocable that I was forced to share custody of Buster, my sweet pug, the dog Dan had *given* me for our fifth anniversary. That's right: Buster was supposed to be mine. But the minute we started negotiating the settlement, Dan claimed that my twelve-hour workdays made me unfit to be the dog's sole guardian. After months of haggling—he said *he* should get Buster and *I* should be granted visitation and I said *I* should get Buster and *he* should be granted a visit to hell—we agreed on the shared custody bit. We alternated weeks. Every other Monday morning, I would hop in a cab with Buster and drop him off at Dan's on my way to the office. And the next Monday morning, Dan would hop in a cab and drop Buster off at my place on his way to—well—wherever it was he went on Monday mornings. To the gym, probably, followed by lunch with the boys, followed by a game of poker, followed by a massage and/or nap, followed by a hot night on the town. All of it with my money, mind you.

On second thought, *sad* didn't begin to describe my feelings that cold December day. *Pained* was more accurate.

"Mel?" said Robin as she stood up and regarded me. "Are you crying?"

"Don't be ridiculous. I never cry." I rose from my chair. As I did, a cascade of cookie crumbs fell from my skirt onto the carpet. "Sorry about the mess," I said. "I'd offer to pay for a cleaning crew, but all my spare change goes to you-know-who now."

She sighed, frustrated that she'd failed to bring me around. "You weren't listening when I said it was time to let go and move on, were you?"

"Yes, yes, I was listening." I forced a big smile. "And I'll try to follow your advice, Robin. I will."

Forced smile aside, I meant what I'd said. I really didn't want to become one of those bitter divorcées who can't go five minutes without bashing her ex—women who poison all their relationships with their vitriol, bore everyone to death with the same twisted stories, and end up miserable and alone, a pathetic victim. No, I would suck it up, act like the sort of gutsy dame I fantasized my mother would have been if she'd lived, and move on. That was the plan, anyway.

Robin and I said good-bye and gave each other a professional career woman hug—i.e., we held each other for a nanosecond, making sure not to smudge our lipstick.

As I walked out of the conference room, I felt her eyes on me, and I sensed that she hadn't bought my declaration of goodwill;

that she had deemed me yet another client who'd been freed from the bonds of matrimony only to become entangled in the bonds of acrimony.

She had me pegged, all right. Yes, I left her office with the best intentions, but I'm sorry to report that the case of *Melanie Banks vs. Dan Swain* wasn't closed, despite all the pieces of paper we'd signed. On the contrary. The acrimony—the madness—was just getting started.

Chapter 2

I spent the weekend working, chained to the computer at home. Well, at my temporary home. Since my separation from Dan, I'd been renting a dark, thoroughly charmless, furnished studio on the third floor of a five-story walk-up on West Forty-sixth Street between Eighth and Ninth avenues—an area known alternately as Hell's Kitchen for its gangland past, Clinton for its later association with DeWitt Clinton, the city's former mayor, and Midtown West, a bland name conceived by real estate agents hoping to attract people who'd been priced out of fancier neighborhoods. Just west of the theater district and not far from Times Square, Hell's Kitchen wasn't my idea of heaven, with its topless bars and mom-and-pop ethnic restaurants. (My building was next door to a Hungarian restaurant where they put paprika on everything, even the desserts.) You could walk by a stripper in a G-string, a grandma in a babushka, or a drag queen in a ball gown. It was all too bohemian for me, but I was on a tight budget since the split. My dreary, tiny place was all I could afford if I wanted to stay in Manhattan.

And I did want to stay, needed to stay. For one thing I needed to be near my dog, who, when he wasn't with me, was with Dan in our old apartment—a sunny, thoroughly charming, professionally decorated three-bedroom on the thirty-second floor of a thirty-six-story building on Seventy-eighth and Madison on the very civilized Upper East Side. For another, I needed to be near my office, which was at Forty-eighth and Park. And for a third thing, I needed to stay in the city because I just couldn't bring myself to go back to Brooklyn or Queens. Not after spending my childhood in the outer boroughs, dreaming of crossing the bridge into Manhattan where someday I would become a success and escape my gloomy past. No, my walk-up in Hell's Kitchen wasn't paradise, but it allowed me to hang on to my dream—being made a partner at Pierce, Shelley and Steinberg and then buying myself a drop-dead apartment that would put Dan's to shame.

In the meantime I was camping out in my closet of a home in a building the landlord called the Heartbreak Hotel, because nearly all of its occupants were divorced or separated and in transition. An upbeat place it wasn't.

Since it was December, there were year-end tax documents to be reviewed for my clients—all of whom had been enriched by the decisions I'd made for them, even in a down market. If it was a sound investment, I was all over it, researching, making calls, grinding out the numbers, doing whatever it took to manage the assets of the people who'd put their trust in me. Yeah, that was my MO—the woman who never let up—which is why my boss had dubbed me his "top gun."

In addition to the year-end stuff, I was also going over the file on Jed Ornbacher, a seventy-year-old Texas widower who'd made a fortune in oil and was considering Pierce, Shelley as the new custodian of his millions. I was flattered that I'd been asked to make the presentation to him, because it meant I'd been charged with reeling him in. I was good at reeling them in. Maybe if I reeled Jed in, I'd get that partnership I'd been hoping for. A nice bonus, at least.

"Look who's here to check out Mr. Ornbacher's file with me," I said with a laugh when Buster jumped down off the sofa where he'd been lounging, trotted over to the makeshift desk I'd set up on my bed, and leapt up next to me.

I put aside my paperwork. I was nearing the end of my week with Buster, so I tried to take advantage of our time together. Maybe you only know pugs from the movie *Men in Black,* but let me tell you: they're cute little clowns. That flat, black, wrinkled face is enough to make anybody smile—even a depressed divorcée.

"Are you hungry?" I asked him. While my appetite had increased following my breakup with Dan, Buster's had decreased. According to the vet, he was suffering from a psychological disorder that was becoming all too prevalent in New York City: pet separation anxiety brought about by custody disputes. Not only did Buster have to be shuttled back and forth every other week between my poor excuse for an apartment and Dan's *Architectural Digest*–worthy residence; he had to get used to two sets of crates and toys and food bowls. It had to be extremely disorienting for him.

I went and got him a biscuit and played with him for a while. At one point he looked up at me with those eyes—big, round, dark, expressive eyes—and I could almost hear him saying: "Where's Daddy?" Yeah, laugh all you want, but when you love a dog, you're convinced you know what they're thinking.

"He's at our old house," I said. "He and Mommy aren't living together anymore, remember? But it has nothing to do with you, and there's no reason for you to feel guilty."

Okay, yes. That's what you tell a little kid whose parents split up. But it's the same thing with a pet. Really.

Buster snorted loudly, as if to demand more details.

"Why aren't Mommy and Daddy living together anymore?" I said. "Well, the short answer is that Daddy doesn't like it that Mommy is doing better at her job than he is at his. Daddy's very macho except when it comes to taking Mommy's money."

Buster passed gas. Luckily, I wasn't downwind.

"Okay. I won't say anything negative about Daddy." Buster called us on it whenever Dan was nasty about me and vice versa. What a loyal, sweet dog. Besides, I had promised Robin I would try to lose the attitude. "It's hard to explain what went wrong, but essentially Mommy told Daddy that he wasn't the person he used to be, then Daddy told Mommy that she wasn't the person she used to be either. You can't have a marriage between strangers."

He appeared to give that one some thought. Then he shot me the inquisitive eyes again.

"How did we change into different people?" I shrugged. "How does any couple drift apart, especially when they were so right for each other in the beginning. You should have seen us then,

Buster. When Mommy met Daddy, it was the happiest day of her life."

I was twenty when I met Dan Swain, and happiness wasn't on my agenda; working my way through school was. I'd been working ever since I could remember. While my father did nothing to put food on the table, I had a paper route, babysat for anyone who asked, ran errands for people. Once, when he was drunk, he told me we'd end up in debtors' prison if I didn't "hustle ass," and since I was too young to know that there was no such thing as debtors' prison, I spent my entire childhood petrified of being locked up in it.

My plan at age twenty was to finish up my undergraduate degree at N.Y.U. as a scholarship student, get my MBA, and start climbing the corporate ladder. One of my part-time jobs at the time was waitressing at a restaurant that was frequented by professional athletes. I didn't know a thing about sports and couldn't care less about them, but I was very pretty, with my dark, wavy hair and curvy figure, so I was popular with the male patrons.

"Hi. What can I get for you?" I said to the table of four, large college-age men to whom I'd brought menus five minutes earlier. It was nine-thirty that Sunday night, and I was dead tired after having worked the lunch shift too, but I put on a perky smile, hoping to nail a perky tip.

"A room," one of them said, staring longingly at my breasts. "You and me and a king-size bed, and I'm so there, baby."

The others thought this was a riot. Well, except the blond one with the bluest eyes I'd ever seen. He was gloriously handsome in his yellow cable-knit sweater and chinos, like one of those radiant golden boys from the Ralph Lauren ads. He leaned toward me and smiled apologetically, exposing big, straight, white teeth, and said, in a twang that suggested somewhere south of the Mason-Dixon line, "Please pardon my friends. They left their manners at home."

Suddenly, I was charmed. Maybe it was the "please." Maybe it was the respectful tone. Maybe it was the fact that he wasn't just gorgeous but polite too, and the combination was so unexpected. "Not a problem," I said, noticing he had a little scar to the left of his right eye. It only added to his appeal, because it humanized his otherwise too perfect face. "We keep a cage in the back for animals who haven't had their obedience training."

It was the blond who laughed this time. "Score one for the lovely lady."

A compliment. I was oddly thrilled. "How about something to eat?" I said, getting back to business.

"Yeah, you and me can order room service and eat naked," said the jerk.

I sighed. "I'm sure you're a work of art without your clothes on, but the museum's down the street, okay?"

"Yeah, enough, Ernie," said the blond, with authority. "You're lucky she has a sense of humor."

Did I have a sense of humor? No one had ever mentioned it.

After the blond silenced his buddy for the moment, he asked me if I had any specials to recommend.

"The pasta special is excellent tonight," I said, aware now that he was the leader of the group.

"Then four pasta specials it is," he said. "And four glasses of water."

"Water?" Ernie griped.

"Water," he said. "We've celebrated too much already."

"What are you celebrating?" I asked.

"Our first trip to the Big Apple," said the blond, who then flushed slightly and added, "I must sound like an idiot. Nobody who lives here actually calls it the Big Apple, right?"

Gorgeous, polite, *and* self-deprecating? Yeah, I was charmed. "Not usually, but welcome to New York anyway," I said, little Miss Chamber of Commerce. "I hope you enjoy your stay."

"Are you gonna ask us why we're here, or do you just want to kiss me?" said Ernie.

Jeez. The guy didn't quit. I was about to respond with another put-down but restrained myself. I'd discovered that when you're dealing with alcoholically impaired jocks, it's best not to antagonize them. "Okay, tell me," I said. "Why are you here?"

"For the Heisman ceremony last night," he said.

He acted as if I was supposed to understand what he was talking about, but the only Heisman I knew was Sophie Heisman, the old lady who lived upstairs from us in Queens. She was always letting her bathtub overflow, which caused mold to breed in our ceiling.

"Our hero was the runner-up for the trophy," he went on, pounding the blond on the back. "Voted the second-best college football player in the country."

"No kidding?" I looked at the blond and thought how refreshing it was that he hadn't bragged about himself but instead left it to someone else to tout his accomplishment.

"No kidding," he acknowledged. "I was the bridesmaid."

"Bridesmaid or not, you deserve congratulations," I said, duly impressed. "I'll probably read about you in the newspaper. What's your name?"

"Dan Swain," he said.

"But everybody calls him Traffic," said Ernie.

"Traffic?" I said.

"That's his nickname. He's the best receiver in the game because he can catch the ball even with ten guys charging him. Like, when he's *in traffic.*"

"Ah, I get it," I said as I studied this Dan Swain person and found myself drooling a little. I mean, I just couldn't find anything not to like about him.

"You think it's dumb, don't you?" he said.

"Not at all," I said. "If you can be the calm one in the middle of chaos, I think that's a gift."

"Thank you."

"You're welcome."

No, it wasn't poetry, but we were connecting in a way that made me sweat. I'm serious, my armpits were leaking.

"So what's your name?" He pointed at me. "I'll probably read about *you* in the newspaper someday."

"Because I'll be voted second-best waitress in the country?" I said.

"Something tells me you'd never settle for second best," he said, then gently removed the pencil and pad from my hands, took my right hand in his, and shook it. "Your name?"

"Melanie Banks," I said as he held on to me seconds longer than was necessary and my insides started to turn over.

By the time he finally released me I had forgotten what I was supposed to be doing there, until Ernie mouthed off that he was hungry.

"Four pasta specials coming right up," I said, writing down the orders, forcing myself to do my job.

"See you soon," said Dan as I headed for the kitchen. "*Melanie.*" When I glanced back at him, he smiled at me, and I felt truly off balance—wobbly, a little nauseated, wonderful. I wasn't the type to get derailed by silly infatuations. I had a plan for myself, as I've stated, and it didn't involve love. And yet there I was, falling. Fast and out of nowhere.

I went off and waited on the other tables in my station but was mainly counting the minutes until the pasta dinners were ready so I could get back to Dan. After what seemed like an eternity, I carried the tray over to his table and served everybody. When I placed his plate in front of him, I asked him where he was from.

"Minco, Oklahoma," he said. "Bet you've never heard of it."

"You'd win that bet," I said. "What's the population? The four of you and your relatives?"

"We've got about sixteen hundred people living there—only fifteen hundred of them being relatives," he said with a sly grin. "It's a sweet little town. You oughta come visit."

"Is that an invitation?" I said, humiliated that I was flirting with him. I'd never been a flirter.

"Sure is," he said. "You should come for the Minco Fair, our biggest event of the year. Maybe they'll let you judge the cake contest."

His eyes held mine, and I had the crazy notion that I would have followed him to Minco or the moon. I was about to ask him how long he'd be in New York when he was surrounded by three fawning young men who'd watched the Heisman ceremony on television the night before and wanted his autograph.

I disappeared and busied myself with other tables, watching from a distance how effortlessly Dan handled the starstruck sucker-uppers. Most of the athletes I'd waited on at the restaurant had monstrous egos and a sense of entitlement, but Dan didn't seem to. He simply accepted the meeting-and-greeting, shaking hands, answering questions, allowing his space to be invaded, without the revolting me-me-me attitude. What he had wasn't poise exactly, because that implies sophistication. It was more a genuineness, an ease. Since I'd always been such a striver, who pushed and pursued and persevered, I marveled at him, at how laid-back he was, at how everything seemed to come naturally to him. Yeah, we were opposites—I was a hustling New Yorker and he was an Oklahoma country boy—but, improbable or not, practical or not, ready or not, I was enthralled by him.

"Anyone care for dessert?" I said after I'd cleared their table. "The lemon meringue pie is the best in the city, according to *New York* magazine."

The others declined, but Dan asked if he could get a slice to go.

"Go?" I said, and realized my heart was breaking. Perky, I told myself. Stay perky. "Absolutely. I'll have it wrapped up for you."

I presented them with the check and dashed off to get the piece of pie. When I returned, I handed Dan the dessert in its Styrofoam container, took the cash off the table, and said I'd be back with their change.

"Keep it," said Dan. "It's all yours."

"Thanks," I said, stuffing the bills into the pocket of the dopey black apron they made us wear. That was the whole reason I was waitressing—to pocket tips—but when I watched Dan and his friends get up, put on their jackets, and start to leave, I didn't give a crap about the money. I only wanted him. How insane was that?

"See ya, Melanie," he said with a little salute as he trailed after the others.

I faked perky again. "Yeah," I called out. "The next time I'm in Minco."

He nodded and walked toward the door. He was about to push

it open when he stopped. Literally. He just stood there, getting jostled by the crush of people waiting for a table. Just stood there with his back to me, head down, staring at the floor. Just stood there. I think I actually held my breath as I watched him and wondered what was going on. Did he forget his wallet or his keys? Did he feel sick? Was I supposed to rush over and help?

I was frantically debating the above when he turned in my direction, slowly, very slowly, and picked his head up. Instead of continuing out the door, in pursuit of his pals, he walked straight back inside the restaurant, his eyes lasered on mine. I remember emitting sort of a gasp as he strode toward me. *Please don't let this be about nothing,* I prayed, as he kept coming. *Please don't let this be that he has to use the men's room or make a phone call or buy another slice of pie for the girl back in his hotel room. Please let this be a miracle happening, something I didn't have to work for just this once. Oh, please—*

He was face-to-face with me then, and my brain shut down.

"What?" I managed. "Did you leave your—"

"Look," he cut me off. "I know I didn't exactly sweep you off your feet while you were bringing my buddies and me dinner, but—"

"You were the only one who didn't treat me like I *was* dinner," I said, cutting him off this time.

"I ordered the pie just to hang around you a little longer," he admitted.

"Did you?" I asked.

He nodded. "Do you have a boyfriend?"

"No," I said, my pulse thumping in my ears. "No."

"Good," he said. "I'm not leaving for two days, and I was thinking maybe we could see—"

"Yes," I said. More thumping. "Yes."

He reached up and touched my cheek. "I want you to know that I'm not like Ernie," he said. "I don't go around hitting on waitresses."

"Then what do you do?"

"I follow my instincts."

He lowered his head and kissed me. Right there in the middle of the restaurant. It was a fabulous kiss that was interrupted only when one of the other waitresses bumped us as she passed.

"It's okay," said Dan. "I don't drop the ball in traffic, remember? I'm the calm one in the middle of chaos." And then he kissed me again.

Chapter 3

"Hi, Ricardo," I said to the doorman at my old building. It was Monday morning at eight-fifteen and I had to get to the office by eight-forty-five for the Jed Ornbacher meeting at nine. I needed to hurry upstairs, deliver Buster to Dan, and beat it.

I tightened my grip on the dog's leash and was about to rush toward the elevator when Ricardo stopped me. "I'll have to buzz Mr. Swain before I can let you up, Melanie."

Of all the indignities. It had always rankled me that Dan was "Mr. Swain" while I was "Melanie," even though *Mr. Swain* wasn't the celebrity he used to be and I was the one paying for the damn place. But what really got me was that I had to be buzzed up to my own apartment whenever I brought Buster over. Like I was a dog walker.

I stood there, insides churning, while Ricardo, a short, burly Latino with a thin mustache, called Dan on the house phone, spoke to him in this totally ass-kissy voice, laughed at whatever he said, then hung up. Ricardo was the opposite of the surly, I'd-rather-be-doing-anything-but-this doormen you hear about. He took his job seriously, which I used to appreciate when I lived there, but now I found it insufferable.

I smiled sweetly. "So? Do I get security clearance?"

"Mr. Swain says it's fine to go up," he said, seemingly unaware that it was mortifying for me to have to stand there in my former lobby, being snubbed by my former neighbors, being *buzzed up* by my former husband.

"Thank you," I said. Buster chose that moment to fart in Ricardo's face. I reminded myself to give him an extra biscuit for good behavior.

We rode up in the elevator to the thirty-second floor, where Dan was standing at the threshold of 32G. He was wearing a velvety navy blue robe with what appeared to be a Polo logo on it and a pair of buttery brown leather moccasins with Gucci *G*s on them. Only the best for our Danny. God, did it gall me that while I could no longer afford to spend freely on my wardrobe, his had become the stuff of *GQ* layouts.

And then there was the fact that he was wearing a robe, instead of a business suit, on a weekday morning. My guess was that Ricardo had woken him up. The right side of his face had pillow dents.

Did he bear any resemblance to the golden boy who'd swept me off my feet at the restaurant thirteen years ago? Sure. A handsome guy is a handsome guy. But there were shortcomings. His hair was still blond but longer and more straggly now, the bangs falling across his forehead, the ends curling around his ears. His body was still muscular but not nearly as tight as it was in his playing days. He'd gained weight and grown a gut, and his face had filled out, which, together with the puffiness around his eyes, gave him sort of a doughy, dissolute look.

"Did somebody die or are you just glad to see me?" he said as I ushered myself and Buster inside the apartment.

"Somebody died." I eyed his feet. "The poor calf whose hide made those shoes. They're new, aren't they, Imelda?"

"Maybe. I'd lend them to you, but they wouldn't go with your getup."

Getup. Please. I was wearing my investment banker gray pinstripe. It was a little on the mannish side, but so what?

"How's Buster?" he said, bending down to play with the dog.

"He's great," I said, glancing around the living room, where not a single piece of furniture had been rearranged or replaced since I'd moved out. He hadn't even repainted. (I was in my colorful period when we'd decorated the apartment. The living room was robin's egg blue, the dining room forest green, the master a deep burgundy.) Everything was just as I'd left it, including photos of us in happier times, which rested on various surfaces in their lovely silver frames. When I'd asked why he continued to display them, he'd shrugged and said he liked them. Typical Dan. Stuck in the glory days.

I also noticed two glasses on the coffee table, next to an empty bottle of champagne. But it wasn't just any champagne, mind you. It was Cristal, which is, like, three hundred dollars a pop. *Now* do you understand why I resented him? Wouldn't a less extravagantly priced bubbly have been festive enough? No, of course not.

"Listen, don't forget to take him for his checkup," I said. "It's Wednesday at four-thirty."

"You've reminded me six times."

"I'm just making sure. Also, he really seems to like the rope toy I bought him last week, so I think he should have one here too."

"I'll buy him one on the way to the park this afternoon."

"The park? You're taking him to the park?"

"Yeah, what's the problem?"

"It's unseasonably warm for December, Dan. They predicted it might go up to fifty degrees. I don't want him to overheat while he's chasing a football around."

He tugged on his earlobe, which is what he always did when he found me exasperating. "I'll be the one chasing the football around. It's my regular pickup game with Ernie and the guys."

"It must be nice to spend your afternoons in Central Park," I said with a little sigh.

"Where I spend my afternoons—or mornings or evenings, for that matter—is none of your business anymore," he said as he let Buster wander around.

"It *is* my business where you take Buster," I said. "For all I know, he goes with you to those lap dance clubs."

He laughed. "You're welcome to come too."

"My point is, I don't want Buster exposed to naked women."

"He's been exposed to you, hasn't he?"

"Yes, but I don't wear pasties on my nipples."

"I guess they frown on that at Pierce, Shelley and Steinberg?"

"Can we change the subject?"

"You brought it up."

I counted to ten, mindful of my promise to Robin. "All I ask is that you remember to take Buster to the vet on Wednesday."

"And all I ask is that you remember to stay out of my business. We're divorced now, which is how you wanted it, Mel."

I moved closer to him, stood face-to-face with him. I could see every pore of his skin, every bit of stubble along his jawline, every broken capillary on his nose and, yeah, he had a few now. "So I opted out and you're punishing me for it by getting alimony."

"I'm not getting alimony. I'm getting combat pay—for thirteen years of having to put up with you, darlin'."

"Put up with *me*?" I counted to ten again, but only made it to five. I was being provoked! I had to stick up for myself, didn't I? "I was the one who watched you sit around with Ernie, reminiscing about the good old days instead of trying to figure out what to do with the rest of your life. You think that was fun?"

"Ernie accepts me for who I am."

"Ernie's a hanger-on."

"It's not such a bad thing to have someone who hangs on."

"What's that supposed to mean? That I should have hung on even though you made absolutely no attempt to—"

I was in the middle of my counter when Buster started barking. Pugs aren't barkers, normally, but he was definitely letting us know he wanted us to cut out the fighting.

"Okay. Not in front of the dog," I said.

"Right," said Dan. "And now that you've brought him over, there's nothing keeping you. So why don't you hop back on your broomstick and fly off to work."

"You know what?" I said, stung by the implication that I was anything other than a kind, patient woman who'd been pushed to her limit. "I came over here determined to be nice, determined to show restraint. But you're baiting me and I refuse to be baited."

"Fine. I apologize." He tried to wipe off his smirk and look serious. "How is work, by the way?"

"Actually, I have a presentation this morning. If I land the client, I'll be very happy."

"Me too. In fact, I'll celebrate. Ernie and I will break open another bottle of Cristal."

You see that? He was incorrigible! "What are you thinking, Dan? Cristal costs a fortune."

"Yeah, but it'll be in honor of your latest success. You wouldn't want us to drink the cheap stuff while we're toasting you. Would you, darlin'?"

That did it. I didn't even bother to count to ten. "You're a selfish jerk, pissing my money away like that, not to mention your own. It's not bad enough that I have to scrimp and save and live in a place that's a pit compared to this palace? You have to rub my nose in the world's most expensive champagne too?"

"So much for your restraint, huh?" Back came the smirk.

"Because you make me crazy!"

He winked. "That's what all the girls tell me."

Too angry to muster an intelligent response, I gave Buster a hug and Dan the finger and left.

During the entire cab ride to my office, I replayed this latest war of words between my ex and me, and I thought, How did it come to this? He was always goading me now, getting me to lose it even when I vowed not to. Was it his way of paying me back for leaving him? And if so, why had he expected me to stay? He had given up on football, on himself, on life. What was left to stay for?

As I rode down Park Avenue, I marveled at how two people who were so much in love could have ended up the way we had. But, as any woman who's ever been in a failed relationship with a man can attest, things change. Circumstances bring about change. First, there's a setback, or maybe a series of setbacks, and suddenly our hero's other self is revealed, and it's not what we anticipated. We find ourselves shaking our heads and muttering, "This is how he copes with problems? This is how he handles adversity? This is who he turns out to be?"

In the early years, Dan and I were in a perpetual state of bliss, and adversity wasn't on our radar. We were young, invincible, confident that together we could do anything. Each of us lived up to our advance billing—I was the feisty, street-smart one who was always coming up with strategies for getting ahead; he was the talented, all-American athlete who didn't need strategies for getting ahead because everything came easily. We were perfectly matched, perfect together.

Even the night Dan proposed was perfect. It was in Minco, on the back porch of his house overlooking his family's cornfields, about a week after we each graduated from college. There was a moon in the sky—not full, but almost—and the air was clean and fragrant following a late-afternoon rain. I'd come out on the porch feeling as if I'd already been designated a member of the Swains; they were the hokey, close-knit family I never had, and I couldn't get over how warm and welcoming they were to an outsider.

"We'll live here in Minco," Dan said after he'd popped the question and I'd said yes. "Buy a farm, like Mom and Dad did. Grow corn, wheat, peanuts. Whatever we want."

At first I was stunned. "Wait a second, honey," I said. "You're Traffic, remember? The guy who's about to be drafted in the first round by a professional football team."

"Oh, that." He shrugged. "I'd rather grow peanuts. Be with my girl in peace and quiet, away from the bright lights. You in?"

"I—" Yikes. I loved Dan more than anything, but a farmer's wife?

"Minco may not be a thriving metropolis," he said, watching my face fall, "but it's got four restaurants, two gas stations, a flower shop, a beauty salon, even a video/tanning place."

I was speechless. Completely floored. All my dreams of an MBA, a job in finance, a beautiful apartment . . . gone?

"Mel?" he said.

"Yes?" I said.

"It's a joke."

"What?"

He grabbed me and hugged me hard. "I'm about to be drafted by the Giants, and you and I are gonna live in the Big Apple!"

I shrieked with excitement and shrieked again when he told me he'd be able to pay my way through business school, thanks to his hefty contract.

"Before you know it, I'll be the team's starting wide receiver," he said, "and you'll be hired by my rich teammates to tell them how to invest their money. How does that sound?"

"It sounds so—well—easy."

"It will be."

"But it's never been that way. Not for me."

He kissed me. "Everything's gonna change now, Melanie."

He was right, as it turned out. Everything did. He got injured, couldn't play football, flopped on TV, and stopped living. I continued to suggest a coaching job, but he said he'd never stoop that low. As if sleeping until noon, then dusting himself off for an evening of glad-handing and ass grabbing wasn't stooping low enough.

We started to drift apart. I was spending more time with clients; he was spending more time with Ernie, an even bigger slacker than his buddy. We stopped making love. He claimed I didn't respect him anymore; I claimed he didn't respect himself anymore. We were both right.

Eventually, I'd had it. I'd concluded that the differences in our personalities, once so complementary, were now liabilities. I was the go-getter who couldn't make him go and get. He was The Natural to whom nothing came naturally anymore.

Although something *was* coming naturally to him now: the alimony. God, did it stick in my craw. How could he throw my money away on champagne and shoes and—

"Hey, lady. For the third time, this is it," snapped the cabdriver, interrupting my trip down memory lane. "You want to sit here forever or what?" We had arrived at my office on Forty-eighth Street and had, apparently, been parked at the curb long enough for the cars around us to start honking. It took me a second or two to shake off my reverie, but after the driver shouted at me to pay up and get out, I paid up and got out.

As he tore away, tires squealing, I stood on the sidewalk for a few minutes to straighten my skirt, smooth my hair, and banish all thoughts of Dan, past and present. I had a show to put on, and I had to be at my best. No distractions.

I gathered myself up to my full height of five feet six, took one more deep breath and strode into the building, Jed Ornbacher's millions dancing in my head.

Chapter 4

"Has he shown up yet?" I asked Steffi Strauss, my twenty-six-year-old assistant, as soon as I got off the elevator and spotted her in the hall. She was carrying a stapler in one hand and a package of legal pads in the other, and if she'd had more hands she would have found useful jobs for them too. She was the most organized person I'd ever met, always prepared, always on top of things. The day human resources sent her to me was a lucky day indeed. She wasn't just a bright kid who'd aced all her courses in business school. She was also what is commonly referred to as a "self-starter" and had an uncanny knack for anticipating my every need.

"No," she said, with a shake of her head that made her blonde ponytail whip across the back of her neck. She was tall and sturdy and plain-looking in her sensible clothes and sensible shoes, but she projected a positive energy that made you forget she wasn't pretty. Maybe it was the size of her mouth that threw her face off-kilter. It was too big—i.e., not in proportion to her other features—and when she smiled you got the impression she had seventy-five teeth. "He's due any minute." She checked her watch. "In five minutes, to be exact. Will you need me to sit in during the meeting?"

I smiled. She was so devoted to me, and in turn, I tried to do all I could to mentor her, involve her in my work at the company so that someday she would rise up the ranks as I had. "You're sweet to ask, but no. I'll be fine. I've got the speech down pat at this point."

"Nobody reels in new clients the way you do, Mel." She nodded and hurried off to answer my phones, my e-mails, and whatever else needed answering while I took a quick look at the messages on my desk, grabbed Ornbacher's file, and headed for Bernie Shelley's office, where the meeting was to take place. Bernie was sitting behind his throne—a Louis the Something antique table—scribbling notes to himself when I walked in.

"Mel, glad you made it," he said.

"When did I ever not make it?" I said with a laugh. I hadn't missed a meeting or even been late for one since the day I'd joined the company, but then Bernie was a worrywart. A worrywart and a notorious sacker of people who *were* late and *did* miss meetings. The managing partner of Pierce, Shelley and Steinberg, he was a thin, wiry guy in his forties with a fair complexion and tons of red hair. I say "tons" because the red hair on his head was thick and coarse and because he had a red goatee and a red mustache too. And if you looked really closely, there was red hair on his fingers and red hair on the tops of his hands and still more red hair on his upper chest, which was visible when he wore open-collared shirts on casual Fridays. He'd asked me out shortly after my separation, but I'd begged off, saying I didn't think it was a good idea to mix business and romance. The truth is, I wasn't attracted to Bernie any more than I was attracted to Carrot Top.

"I guess I'm a little overeager," he said, gnawing on a fingernail to prove it. "Would I ever love to have Jed Ornbacher as a client. If he comes on board, he just might bring along his oil-rich friends."

"You can count on me," I said.

"I know I can. You're my top gun, so I'm just gonna sit back and let you fire away."

A few minutes later Ornbacher arrived. He was a portly man with a leathery tan, and he was dressed like a cowboy—the hat, the boots, the blue jeans, the string tie. As Bernie introduced me, I kept thinking, Where's the rodeo? And what is it with Texans anyway? People from other parts of the country don't show up for business meetings in costumes that announce where they're from. I had a client from Maine, for example, and he wasn't wearing a checked flannel shirt, overalls, and a lobster bib when he came to the office.

But then Ornbacher had a reputation as a bit of an eccentric. He'd been a professional singer in his youth—a crooner of minor-key love ballads that didn't go over well with the public because they were too morbid. His most famous song was a ditty he wrote himself called "Don't You Go Dying on Me." Later, before moving into oil, he ran a company that manufactured the cord that's used to hold Venetian blinds together. Word was, he had many pursuits, another of which was the female species. While he'd never remarried, he had a slew of girlfriends. "He's supposed to be a horny bastard," Bernie had warned me. "A real toucher. But you'll have to ignore it." Easy for him to say, I thought. He wasn't the one the guy would be touching.

"So nice to meet you, Mr. Ornbacher," I said as we shook hands.

As he held on to mine for about an eternity, he gave me a big smile and his lips receded, making him look sort of predatory.

"Call me Jed," he said in a too-loud Texas twang. It was as if he had bellowed through a bullhorn. I wondered if he might be a little deaf as well as horny.

"Jed it is," I said, gesturing for him to sit. "Can we get you anything to drink? Coffee? Tea? Water?"

"What's that?" he yelled, cupping his hand to his ear.

I stood closer and repeated the offer.

"A shot of bourbon would be swell," he said and laughed one of those phlegmy smoker's laughs that morphs into a death rattle. "Water's good," he said when he recovered.

We got him his water. I sat in the chair next to his and began my routine.

"So," I said, "Bernie tells me you're in the market for new financial management, Jed."

"New what?" he said.

"New financial management," I repeated. He probably gets away with a lot of touching, I figured. Women tell him to buzz off and he can't hear them.

"Yes, ma'am. I decided it was time for a change," he said. "Can't let other people get too comfortable with your money, you know what I mean?"

Did I ever. If Dan hadn't gotten so comfortable with my money, I wouldn't be living at the Heartbreak Hotel in a—"I know exactly what you mean," I said, blinking away the intrusive thought. Where had it come from? No matter how angry I'd been at my ex earlier, I couldn't let him get to me now. Not in the middle of a client presentation. "And you've come to the right place," I went on. "Pierce, Shelley's excellent reputation speaks for itself, but it's the personal attention we give our clients that separates us from the pack. Our experts are the best in their respective fields, but we're not a money mall."

"A what?" he said.

"A money mall," I repeated. "Like a shopping mall."

"A money mall. I get it," he said, then laughed-coughed-wheezed for several long, excruciating seconds.

"I'm saying that while we have CPAs, insurance agents, retirement specialists, and stockbrokers under our roof, we're not just a one-stop-shopping experience. You won't be passed around from department to department. You'll be assigned to a qualified account executive who will work closely with you, overseeing all your assets. A person you can trust. Someone you can depend on day or night."

I caught Bernie's eye. He was grinning at me, pleased with me. So far, so good.

"I like the sound of that," said Jed. "With the kind of money we're talking about, I should be able to call you people whenever I damn well feel like it."

"Yes, you should," I agreed. "Our job doesn't end when the markets close. If I'm the lucky one who gets to oversee your account, you can be sure I'll be available to you twenty-four/seven."

He tipped his hat, revealing a head with exactly two strands of gray hair on it—strands that went straight across his scalp in a do I would come to call his cowboy comb-over. "I admire a gal who doesn't mind long hours," he said. "If you sign me up, you've gotta be willing to roll up your sleeves."

Sleeves. Yes. Dan's plush bathrobe was definitely Polo and definitely worth twice the price of the old terry cloth number that was hanging in my—Oh, God. Why was I even thinking—"Long hours aren't a problem at all," I said, furious with myself for allowing the distraction.

"Good. Getting back to the markets," said Jed, "what's the word on the Dow? We're at the end of the year. What does next year look like to you?"

"My opinion is that while there will be opportunities next year, there will be challenges too," I said. "It's a very bifurcated market. The recovery has been tech-centric and risk-oriented. Last year everybody jumped on safe, quality stocks as the place to be, but they turned out to be the place *not* to be."

"I'm betting that interest rates will spike, dragging everything else down the tubes," he said.

I didn't answer. Instead, I was picturing Dan's new moccasins and wondering how much he'd spent on them. The leather reminded me of—

"Interest rates, Melanie?" Bernie prodded.

"Right," I said, berating myself yet again for my lapse in concentration. It must have been my ex's crack about the champagne that was making me nuts. I wanted to bash him over the head with the bottle every time I thought about him toasting me with it. "The Fed will probably tighten later as opposed to earlier. They have tremendous fears about moving too fast. They don't want to re-create the deflationary atmosphere of the nineties in

Asia, so they'll probably take baby steps. We, on the other hand, will take huge steps with your assets, Jed."

"Damn right," he said, pumping his fist at Bernie. "How about the bond market?"

And he's playing catch in Central Park this afternoon, I thought. Isn't that special? I'm sitting here with this randy blowhard, busting my butt to pay my bills, and he'll be tossing around a football with—

"Melanie?" said Bernie, who had resumed his fingernail chewing. "Jed asked about the bond market."

"Right. My guess is it'll be a low-return world," I said. "Not just next year, but beyond." I leaned forward, met Jed's eyes underneath the brow of his hat, and prepared to deliver my signature line. It always got a laugh. "You know, Jed, Will Rogers once remarked, 'I'm not looking so much for the return on my money, but the return *of* my money.' "

On cue, Jed Ornbacher chuckled. We spent another hour or so on the details of his financial picture, and when it was all over he reached for my hand, stroked it suggestively, and declared that he wanted not only to move his money over to Pierce, Shelley and Steinberg but also to have me watch over it personally. He felt comfortable with the fact that I would be so accessible, he said, staring unapologetically at my breasts, as if he'd never heard of manners, much less appropriate behavior in the workplace.

After he left, Bernie congratulated me and went on and on about how I was still his top gun and always would be. He did ask me if anything was wrong, however.

"If you're talking about Jed, his hand-holding didn't faze me."

"I wasn't talking about Jed," said Bernie as he escorted me out of his office. "You didn't seem yourself during the presentation.

There were a few minutes when I wasn't sure we had your full attention."

"Are you kidding? I was totally engaged," I said with a laugh. "We got his account, didn't we?"

I waved away his concern. What I couldn't wave away was my own. I did zone out a couple of times during the presentation. It had never happened before, and it worried me. I would have to see to it that it never happened again.

Despite my victory at the office, I felt glummer than usual when I stepped into my apartment that night, mostly because Buster wasn't around, but also because there was sobbing coming from the unit next door. Patty, my neighbor, was the owner of Letsmakeup.com, a company that sold high-end cosmetics online. She'd recently been dumped by her photographer husband and was extremely despondent about it. Normally, I kept to myself after a long, hard day at the office, but it would have been inhuman of me not to extend myself and try to comfort her.

"Patty?" I said as I knocked on her door. "It's Melanie Banks from 3B."

When she didn't answer right away, I pressed my ear to the door to listen. The sobbing had stopped, and there was silence—until the loud crash. A china plate? A glass vase? Definitely something shattering.

"Patty?" I said, pounding on the door with my fist now. "Let me in, okay?"

A few seconds later she appeared, her eyes flooded with tears, her mascara running down her cheeks in black streaks and sticking to them like tar. I made a mental note not to purchase the mascara on Letsmakeup.com.

She was about my age and very "done." Hair professionally blonded. Nose professionally bobbed. Chest professionally boobed. She'd even had a couple of toes shortened so she didn't have to cram her feet into her stilettos. And she was clearly a guinea pig for the products she peddled. In addition to the mascara, there was evidence of three different shades of eye shadow, a heavy eyebrow pencil, lipstick and lip liner, and enough foundation to replaster the walls of the Heartbreak Hotel.

"Melanie, hi," she said between sniffs. "Wanna come in?"

"Is it safe?" I said as I entered her studio, which was furnished identically to mine. All the units at the Heartbreak Hotel were set up with the same cheesy tables, chairs, and lamps, which looked like they were held together with Krazy Glue and produced in some third-world country. I guess you'd call the decor "outsourced chic."

"Sure," she said and pointed to the photograph of the studly guy she'd taped to the wall. Shards of a crystal champagne flute were lying on the floor below it. "I was just taking target practice." She grabbed another glass off a tray of about a dozen glasses and flung it at the photo. I feared it would be a long night if I didn't intervene.

I held her elbow and guided her away from the weapons of mass destruction, toward the sofa.

"That's your ex?" I said, nodding at the photo as we sat.

"Yeah, that's Jason. He shot his picture with one of those self-timers. It was probably the last time he used the camera." She dabbed at her eyes with a tissue. "He was too busy with the hundred-and-fifty-dollars-a-session shrink appointments."

"So he didn't really work as a photographer?"

"Jason didn't really work, period. He didn't have to. He lived off me." She blew her nose, causing a fissure in the foundation underneath her left eye.

"I'm sorry," I said. "What attracted you to him in the first place? Other than his good looks, I mean."

"I thought he was an artistic type. Who knew he'd turn out to be a freeloading type. A total bumbo."

"Bumbo?"

"Yeah. That's what you call a male bimbo who doesn't have a job." She started to cry again. "And now I have to pay him alimony. How much does that suck?"

"A lot," I said. "I'll never understand how the lawyers come up with these settlements."

"It's all about the math," she said. "If you're the one who earns it, you're the one who pays it. Such a joke, huh?"

"I hear you," I said with a sigh and told her about Dan.

"I think a lot about killing mine," she said with a faraway look.

"I think about killing mine too, but I'd never go through with it," I said. "We have a dog together."

She nodded. "Jason and I talked about getting a dog, but I figured I'd be the one who'd have to do everything. Housebreak it. Train it. Walk it."

"Actually, Dan did all that. He may be a bumbo, but he loves our Buster."

"Let's get back to killing our exes," she said, rubbing her hands together with entirely too much enthusiasm.

"I wasn't serious about that, Patty."

"Okay, forget killing. But Jason's just begging me to smack him around. Last week he took his girlfriend to Australia. To the outback." She started crying again in earnest. "The only outback he ever took me to was the steakhouse. And *I* paid."

"It's torture to watch them piss away our money, I know." I patted her. "But you say Jason has a girlfriend?"

"Yeah, the little bitch he left me for."

"Is he living with her?"

"Don't I wish. Then I could nail him on the cohabitation provision and terminate the support payments. Another joke, huh? The guy's too dumb to get a job, but he's not dumb enough to lose his meal ticket."

I then remembered my conversation with Robin—the part about the terms of the agreement. "So you have a cohabitation clause too?"

She shrugged, as if I'd asked a dumb question. "Everybody has one. Is your ex living with somebody?"

"No," I said. "I mean, no one I know about."

"No one you *know* about?" Her jaw dropped. "Like, you're not keeping tabs on the women he sees?"

"Why should I? I'm trying to get him out of my life. The last thing I want to do is involve myself in his affairs."

"Hellooo? If he lives with somebody for ninety days, you'll get him out of your life. No more chest pain every time you add up what you're paying him. No more headache every time you see him wearing something stupidly expensive. No more irritable bowel every time you realize you've been thinking about him in the middle of an important business meeting."

That last one got my attention. I'd do anything not to repeat my lapses in Bernie's office, minor though they were. And all it would take to get Dan out of my mind and out of my bank account was ninety days with a woman? It sounded so simple, but how could it be? Robin and I had already concluded that he wouldn't fall for it, wouldn't let me off the hook. Nobody in their right mind would forfeit their support payments unless . . .

"If Jason really loved his girlfriend—I mean, really loved her, in spite of the negative experience he had with you—he'd want to be with her every night," I said, testing out what was just a vague notion, a harmless line of reasoning. "He'd decide that the money isn't nearly as important as waking up next to her in the morning."

Patty gave me another look that suggested I was out of touch. "That's very romantic, Melanie, but you've been reading too many Danielle Steel novels. Men aren't wired that way. They've always got an agenda."

"I'm not sure you can generalize. There must be some men who'd rebound from a bad marriage, find new love, and put it ahead of money." I was grasping, I suppose. Hoping. Nothing serious. It was only Patty's next response that bumped up the hoping a notch—to something more akin to wondering if maybe, possibly, conceivably the hope could become a reality.

"You think so, huh?" She rolled her eyes. "Yeah. Like maybe if they—I don't know—grew up in the middle of a cornfield or something. I bet those farm boys have different values than guys from New York. All that corn probably stays with them."

Hopeful, yes. But still just that.

Chapter 5

I spent Christmas Eve at my best friend Louise's. She and her husband, Leonard, hosted a lovely, spirited, very traditional dinner at their 1810 colonial house in Westport every year—a house with hardwood floors and crown moldings and an actual white picket fence. Along with their two precocious children, an eight-year-old boy who played the bassoon, and a ten-year-old girl who spoke Japanese, which, she informed me, was essential in the global economy, they invited her parents and his parents and various strays. I, of course, was one of the strays—the only stray that year.

It hadn't snowed, and the front lawn was a sad, wintry brownish gray. But inside, standing in the foyer so you saw it the minute you walked in the door, was a shimmering Christmas tree decorated with green-and-gold lights and ornaments handed down from generations. When I was a kid, my father said we couldn't afford a tree, so we never had one. Not that we would have had a place to put it, given our cramped quarters. After he died and I married Dan, I made a point of buying a huge tree every year. I would weigh it down with lights, ornaments, tinsel, popcorn, and anything else I could think of. It was a gaudy, nouveau riche Christmas tree that some might have sneered at, but I hated when it was time to take it out to the street for the garbage truck.

As I entered my friend's house that night, I realized that it was my first Christmas as an officially divorced person. Oh, joy. Oh, rapture. There's nothing worse than being the only single woman at a party, eliciting everybody's pity, but I would try to act festive. Besides, I was doing just fine. Okay, not so fine.

"Mel! Come on in!" said Louise as she gave me a big hug. She was wearing a no-nonsense pair of slacks and a sweater, as was her custom, no matter what the occasion. In fact, I'd never seen her in a skirt, just as I'd never seen her with a stitch of makeup. She wasn't unfeminine, just more interested in comfort than fashion. One of the reasons I adored her was that she didn't spend hours critiquing herself in the mirror, like most women I knew.

When I'd first met her, an athletic, freckle-faced, sandy-haired New Englander who'd attended the best schools and went by the name of Weezie, she was a colleague of mine at Pierce, Shelley and Steinberg. She came from money and I came from none, but despite our different backgrounds, we hit it off immediately. We were both scrappers, both on the career fast track, both get-it-done types who didn't sit around crossing our fingers. We made things happen.

One of the things Weezie was trying to make happen was marriage. I was happily married to Dan back then, but she was still single and determined to remedy the situation. After enduring numerous failed fix-ups arranged by Boppy, which is what everybody called her father Bob, and by Els, which is what everybody called her mother Eleanor, she began advertising herself in personal columns, offering herself up on Internet dating sites, signing herself up for singles weekends on cruise ships—with no groom to show for any of it. Undaunted, she hired Desiree Klein, a professional matchmaker who had appeared on *20/20*, and finally hit the jackpot. Through Desiree, who catered to upscale lonelyhearts and charged a five-thousand-dollar fee, she met Leonard, an ear, nose, and throat specialist who was from a similarly WASPy background and, therefore, went by the name of Nards. They fell for each other, had a tasteful Park Avenue wedding, and settled in Westport, not far from Boppy and Els in Darien. Soon after, Weezie got pregnant and gave up investment banking for full-time motherhood. When she first quit her job, I wondered if she'd be bored up there in Connecticut, away from the action, but she loved it, loved her life with Nards and the kids, and applied her go-getter attitude to the PTA, the historical society, and her tennis game. Her marriage thrived while mine disintegrated. Luckily, I got custody of her and Nards after I split from Dan. While they'd always liked him, they were in the same boat as most friends of divorced couples: they felt obligated to choose. As I said, I was lucky they chose me.

"Thanks for having me," I said after admiring her tree.

"I wouldn't have this party without you," she said. "Now, go mingle, and we'll catch up later."

And off she went.

The menu that Christmas Eve was roasted goose with all the trimmings. It was delicious, and I, newly voracious, not only cleaned my plate but helped myself to seconds. I forced myself to join in the conversation too. Wasn't it oddly mild for this time of year? Wasn't the housing market softening just a little? Didn't the Giants need a good quarterback if they had hopes of making the playoffs?

Naturally, I clammed up on that last subject, and Weezie shrugged apologetically at me when her father raised it.

Dan, Dan, Dan. It was always about Dan. I'd spent the entire ride up to Connecticut obsessing about his latest stunt. Not only had he taken Buster to Puerto Rico for the holidays to attend some big-deal reunion of former Giants players. He had chartered a private plane to get them there! Really! Every time I calculated what that little adventure must have cost, I went crazy. It wasn't fair. It just wasn't fair. That money should have been in the bank—*my* bank—earning interest, making *my* life more secure.

After the meal, when the kids were in bed, and Boppy, Els, and the rest of the family had gone home, I sat in Weezie's den, sipping tawny port with her and Nards. There was a fire in the fireplace and Diana Krall on the stereo, and I should have felt mellow but didn't.

"So," said Weezie. "Tell us how you're doing, Mel."

"I'm hanging in there." I swallowed the port the wrong way and it came back through my nose. "Trying to 'move on,' as my lawyer says. Unfortunately, Dan chartered a private plane to Puerto Rico and took Buster with him, so I'm stuck in resentment mode."

"A private plane? That's how he's spending your money?" she said. "You need a grown-up man in your life."

"I've got this doctor friend. A gastroenterologist," said Nards, who was extremely tall with a large, bobbing Adam's apple. He was on the chatty side and tended to pontificate, so there were times when I tuned him out, but he meant well. "His wife committed suicide a few years ago. I think he's ready to start dating again."

"I appreciate it," I said, "but the truth is, I'm not ready to start dating again."

"And we don't know why his wife offed herself," said Weezie. "Maybe he drove her to it."

"Women." He sighed. "Always assuming the worst about men."

"I'm sure he's nice if he's a friend of yours, Nards," I said charitably. "I'm just not interested in being in a relationship. I may never be interested in it."

"Don't be ridiculous," said Weezie, who, like other married people, encouraged her single friends to be married too. "Give it time. You'll meet someone wonderful like I did." She winked at Nards.

"I don't want someone," I reiterated. "I just want Dan to find someone."

"So he'll remarry and let you out of the alimony?" she asked.

"He doesn't even have to marry her," I said, thinking of the cohabitation provision. "He just has to live with her for ninety days."

"That could happen," said Nards. "He's a celebrity. Women love celebrities."

"Nah. They love the kind of celebrities that open movies, not supermarkets," I said. "I think his most recent performance was at a Winn-Dixie in Florida."

"It's hard to believe he's fallen so far," said Weezie.

"He was a hell of a ballplayer," Nards reminisced. "Not just great hands, but quick. And graceful. He could dart in and out of oncoming traffic like nobody else."

"He did earn the nickname," I conceded. "That day they carried him off the field on the stretcher broke him. And he broke again when they nullified his contract. He never had the patience to read the damn contract, so he was shocked that it was no-play, no-pay."

"Must have been rougher on him than we realized," said Nards.

"Yes, but I really thought he'd get back on his feet and do something else, something great. I mean, there *are* people who come back from a loss with even more motivation to succeed. Besides, we had my salary to live on during the transition. I figured, I love him and he loves me and we can get through anything. Was I ever naive."

"And now you have to support him even though you're divorced," said Weezie with a disapproving shake of her head.

"You weren't upset that your uncle Wally supported your aunt Bootsie after they got divorced," Nards reminded her. "Or do you think alimony should only be for women?"

"Of course I don't," said Weezie. "But Aunt Bootsie deserved every penny. She gave Uncle Wally the best years of her life."

"Maybe Dan gave Mel the best years of his life," said Nards. "He certainly gave her his most productive years."

"He could still be productive if he tried," I said.

"Right," said Weezie. "He's still young, and he has his whole future ahead of him. But why should you have to subsidize him if he sits on his ass?"

"Because the justice system can't be gender biased," said

Nards. "There have to be laws that protect men, just as there are laws that protect women. No double standards."

"That's very noble, Nards," I said, "and I agree with you in principle. It's just that—"

"It's just that it's hard when you're the one having to part with the money," he said. "I get it. But we're living in the twenty-first century, and if women want to be the hunter-gatherers, they have to accept the burdens that come with it. They also have to accept that men are feeling shaky these days."

Weezie and I looked at each other and groaned.

"I'm serious," he said. "The whole definition of what it means to be a man has changed, and it's not easy for us to keep up. Look at Dan. Once he stopped being the provider, he didn't know how to cope."

"Dan didn't know how to cope because he never had to," I said. "When the road is smooth for your entire life, you don't develop any skills for when it gets bumpy."

"True, but the same can be said for a lot of guys," Nards went on. "You should see some of my male patients, the ones who've lost their jobs. They're the walking wounded. They don't realize that they're still human beings even without the fat wallet."

"And can my speech-making husband, who loves the sound of his own voice, tell us why?" Weezie teased.

"Because men today have a terrible case of performance anxiety," he said, "and I'm not just talking about the bedroom. Women are a force to be reckoned with. The more empowered *you* feel, the more inferior *we* feel. We don't know who we are anymore."

"*I* know who you are, and I'm wild about you," she said, then made kissing noises at him.

I smiled at my friends. "I think it's time for me to head back to the city."

She shook her head. "We haven't solved your problem yet. I may have left Wall Street for Westport, but that doesn't mean I still don't strategize everything to death."

"What's to strategize?" I said. "The divorce is final, and I'm writing checks to a jobless ex who charters planes. The scary part is that my resentment about it is creeping into my work. I was in the middle of an important client presentation last week when I started fixating on Dan's new bathrobe, among his other purchases. I'm living in a one-room dump because of him, wearing the same clothes I've worn for years, and he's living in the lap of luxury, buying himself bathrobes! It's obscene!"

"Calm down, calm down," Weezie soothed. "Did you land the client?"

"Yes, thank God. But Bernie noticed that I was a little distracted and asked me about it."

"Wow. Not good," she said. "We've got to get you out of that alimony, no question about it."

"Get me out of it?" I said, still pure of heart at this point, merely indulging in the occasional orgy of wishful thinking.

"You mentioned the cohabitation thing. Tell us the rest."

"There isn't any 'rest.' The provision states that if Dan lives with a woman for ninety days, the support terminates."

"He must be having his share of dates," said Nards, "but he'd really have to fall for someone to risk forfeiting the alimony."

"Or be sneaky about the arrangement," said Weezie. "He could live with the woman and make sure you don't find out about it, Mel."

"Far be it from me to defend Dan, but he's not sneaky," I said. "He's a lot of things, but not that."

"Then you just have to find him the perfect woman," she said. "A woman who's turned on by the sports star he used to be and who's pushy enough to start hanging her clothes in his closet. Oh, and she has to have more money than you do."

"You're forgetting the crucial element, hon," said Nards. "She has to be a knockout."

"Right," said Weezie. "She has to be a total babe, so he'll be powerless to resist her."

"Okay," I said with a laugh. "Where do I find this goddess? On eBay?"

Weezie and Nards said simultaneously and as if it were obvious: "Desiree."

"Your matchmaker?" I said.

"Well? How else?" Weezie challenged. "You have specific requirements here. You can't just go surfing on the Web, as you just pointed out. You can't put an ad in the classifieds either. You're dealing with a delicate situation, and it requires a professional."

"A professional who charges five grand," I said. "To fix up a man who doesn't know he's being fixed up. You guys have had too much port."

Nards poured us all another glass, then sat on the arm of his wife's chair and nuzzled her ear. "Don't be hasty, Mel," he said. "Desiree is a genius. Look what she did for us."

"Maybe so," I said, "but if I had five grand to throw around, I'd lose the Heartbreak Hotel and install myself in a decent apartment."

"You get a lot for your money with Desiree," said Weezie. "Dan will be guaranteed one date per month for a year."

"Sort of like the Book-of-the-Month Club," I said.

"A whole year of dates," she said, ignoring my sarcasm. "Dan's bound to find a woman to live with. And once he does, you won't have to support him ever again. You'll be saving money, Mel."

"It's a brilliant plan," said Nards, applauding. He turned to me. "And you'll get a big kick out of Desiree. What a character."

Weezie nodded. "I feel better now that we've settled this."

"Settled this?" I said, my head spinning.

"Before you leave, I'll give you her number," she said. "You should wait until after the holidays to call her, but don't wait too long. It could take her a few months to find your Ms. Right-for-Ninety-Days, and you want to stop writing those alimony checks sooner rather than later, right?"

"Thanks for trying to help, but there's no way I'm calling her," I said wearily. "Even if I approved of the idea, which I don't, I already told you: I can't afford to hire her."

"You can't afford not to, from the sound of that client meeting," she said ominously. "You've always been a take-charge person, Mel. You need to take charge of this or you'll find yourself out of a job."

"Out of a job? I'm planning on making partner one of these days. So I flaked out for a second or two in the meeting. It was only—"

"You don't want Bernie thinking you're not a hundred percent. He can be a mean little shit, remember? He canned Roberta Chapman when she started losing it after her divorce."

"I'm not losing it, Weezie. I'm just—"

"Call Desiree," she said.

"Yes. Call her," said Nards.

Before I could say another word, my hosts had turned their attention to another subject: whether the goose had been cooked properly.

As I drove back to the city that night, I grew closer to cooking my own goose. No, I didn't make the fateful decision to call Desiree Klein during the trip, but I did mull it over.

What I wondered was this: did I actually have the nerve, not to mention the motivation, to hire her to solve my Dan problem? It was true that she was a matchmaker, not a hit woman, and I'd be committing no crime by engaging her services. Still, to set Dan up with someone—someone to whom he would be forming an attachment, sexual and/or emotional—without his knowledge or permission seemed, well, snarky. I had my issues with the guy, God knows, but he'd always been a straight shooter who hated deception in others. Not a sneak, as I said. Could I really go behind his back and meddle in his personal life simply because I was pissed off about having to scale back my lifestyle while he was scaling up his? Could I justify manipulating him into a three-month relationship so I'd be relieved of the financial burden he'd saddled me with? Did I have it in me to toy with his feelings—his and the woman's—to avoid having to pick up his tab for seven more years? Was my poverty complex that severe? Was my sense of fair play that skewed?

Apparently, the answer to all of the above questions would be yes. Condemn me if you must, but hear me out first. Please.

Chapter 6

Dan was late bringing Buster back the Monday morning after New Year's. I was expecting him at eight-thirty. It was eight-forty-five, and there was no sign of him. I called him at the apartment. No answer. I called him on his cell phone. No answer there. I even called him at the dreaded Ernie's, figuring they'd been out together the night before and might be sleeping it off at his place, but no answer there either.

Straining to keep the hysteria out of my voice, I called Steffi, asking her to make my apologies to Jed Ornbacher, whom I was supposed to meet in our conference room at nine-thirty so I could introduce him to our department heads, all of whom would be in attendance, as would Bernie. Even if Dan breezed in right that very second, I might not make it to the office with enough breathing space. I liked to prepare before meetings. That's what top guns do.

"In case I don't get there in time, just say I'm running a little behind schedule, due to a family emergency," I instructed her. She seemed surprised, and why not? As I've indicated, I was never late. But now Dan was causing me to be late. I hoped he had a good reason.

At five after nine—I was having a flat-out panic attack by then—Dan finally put in an appearance at my apartment. Since the Heartbreak Hotel did not have a doorman, he simply materialized at my door.

"Where in the world have you been?" I demanded, fanning my sweaty face with the newspaper. Actually, my whole body was sweaty. I was sure the black silk blouse underneath my wool tweed suit jacket had pit stains. And I'd taken such pains getting dressed that morning. I'd wanted to look smart, neat, and professional for the meeting.

"Should I stand here while you read me the riot act or would you rather say hello to your dog?"

God, he made me nuts. And not just because he'd shown up late. Because he'd shown up late without looking the least bit repentant. In fact, he was looking resplendent. Along with the creamy new white cashmere sweater he wore with his jeans, he had a shiny new watch on his wrist that was the size of my head.

But I would not, could not, let him goad me. Not again.

I bent down and folded Buster into my arms. "Here's my sweetie boy," I said as he licked me. "Such a sweetie boy. Mommy missed you so much." I glanced up at my ex. "Was he okay in Puerto Rico?"

"He was great. I was the one who took the hit."

I studied his face. No bruises that I could detect. No swelling. "What hit?"

"In the casino. A bunch of us stunk it up at the blackjack table."

"You were gambling?" I said, feeling my fury bubble back up. I know, I know. I needed to stay cool and calm, but gambling? Come on.

"That's what people generally do in a casino, yeah," he said. "I was winning there for a while, but then my luck went down the toilet."

What was he thinking? He wasn't in a position to gamble. He wasn't in a position to take an expensive trip. He was in a position to stay home and redo his résumé!

As I stared at him with a mix of disdain and disbelief, there was an instant when I wished he were still the unspoiled, idealistic young man I'd married instead of this . . . this . . . child. But I quickly came to my senses and reminded myself that this was the same man who'd allowed himself to self-destruct in front of a national television audience; the man who was convinced that coaches were losers; the man who was draining my bank account.

"Just curious," I said. "How much did you lose at the blackjack table?"

"Too much."

"But you were still able to afford a new watch?"

"Uh-uh-uh," he said, wagging a finger at me. "Not Melanie's business anymore."

"Just tell me this, Dan: does the watch keep good time?"

"Perfect time. It's a Rolex."

"*Then why were you late this morning?* You were supposed to be here at eight-thirty." Of course I shouldn't have stayed and nagged him. I should have dashed out of there and rushed to my meeting as soon as he'd dropped off Buster, but, as usual, he'd managed to suck me in. There was something about him that *always* sucked me in.

"I got a slow start," he said.

"Lame excuse," I said.

"Fine. I was coming all the way from Ninety-second and York, not from my place. I spent the night at a lady friend's. She worked the flight back from San Juan, we hit it off, and she invited me home with her."

My brain exploded. He'd kept me waiting because he was banging the flight attendant he'd picked up on the way back from Puerto Rico? I was turning over *half* of my salary every month to a person who actually banged flight attendants?

"What? Are you jealous?" he said, smirking at me.

"Oh, please. Did it ever occur to you that it might be healthier for Buster if he didn't have to wake up in strange settings all the time? Even a steady girlfriend would be preferable to your one-nighters."

You know what? I wasn't thinking about Desiree Klein at that moment, I swear. I really did have our dog's well-being at heart.

"A steady girlfriend, huh?" he said, full of skepticism.

"So Buster would be able to sleep in the same bed for a couple of nights in a row."

He found this hilarious. "I know you want out of the alimony," he said between guffaws, "but I'm not about to do you a favor by getting married again. I'm on top of that little loophole, so nice try."

Getting married again? He thought *that* was the loophole? Had he forgotten all about the cohabitation clause?

"Okay, I do want out of the alimony," I said, fishing. "But you're right, Dan; that won't happen unless you take another walk down the aisle." Maybe he really didn't remember what was in our agreement. I was suddenly transfixed by this possibility.

"Then I guess you're stuck with me, because I'm done with marriage," he said.

Well, how about that. The ninety-days thing *had* slipped his mind. I should have known. He'd never paid attention to the fine print of his football contracts, so why should he pay attention to the fine print of his divorce papers? My God, this was incredible news! There was a chance, remote though it was, that I could be off the hook for the alimony forever! No more worries about money. No more living in a fleabag. No more distractions at work.

Of course, the chance of his cohabitating with a woman for ninety days would be a lot less remote if I hired Desiree to find her for him.

No. I couldn't do something as down and dirty as that. Not unless I had no choice.

"Look, I've really got to get going," I said. "Could you please leave, so I can lock up?"

"You're the one who seems to want to talk, darlin'."

He didn't move a muscle. He just stood there with this annoying grin on his face, flustering me.

"Dan. I asked you to leave. I have an important meeting this morning. I'm late enough as it is."

He cocked his head at me. "Do you ever take a day off for no reason? Just to have fun?"

"You're having enough fun for both of us," I said. "Now *go*!"

I literally started shooing him out of the apartment with my hands, like some woman in an old western movie shooing varmints off her land.

Finally taking the hint, he left, but I was so frazzled by then that as I turned to grab my briefcase, my right hand clipped the side of the "I ♡ the Giants" coffee mug that was resting on the little table near the door. The mug was three-quarters full, and I reached for it in midair, hoping to catch it before it crashed and broke, spilling the coffee all over the floor. What I succeeded in doing was to redirect its path; the mug did break as it fell to the ground, but the coffee splashed onto my black silk blouse before it did. And I was worried about sweat stains.

"I don't believe this!" I wailed, gazing down at myself as Buster snorted and sniffed and wondered what all the ruckus was about. I was soaked with Folger's Instant. Yes, Instant. I wasn't a fan of spending time in the kitchen and that included learning how to operate some high-tech brewing contraption. Wasn't making coffee Starbucks's job anyway?

As for the mug, I cursed myself for having saved it. I'd thrown out the rest of my Giants memorabilia when I moved and couldn't imagine why I'd hung on to a stupid cup. But now it was in pieces, just like my sanity.

Frantic that I would miss the meeting entirely, I raced into my closet, found another suit to wear, changed clothes, blew Buster a kiss, and flew out of the Heartbreak Hotel.

Everyone was already in the conference room when I got to the office. The door was closed, but the room was decorated with glass block panels, so I was able to see inside. The four department heads were all accounted for; Bernie was there, nibbling on one of his fingernails as if it were a chicken wing; Steffi was sitting in the chair that was meant for me, covering for me, bless her heart; and Jed was laughing and coughing and winking lasciviously at Steffi.

I nearly died as I watched them. Where were my priorities? Why hadn't I left my apartment the second Dan had shown up with Buster? He was the one who was always late, not me. Where was my head? Up my ass, apparently.

I paced back and forth outside the door, trying to decide if I should go in and face the music or let the meeting proceed without me. I had to at least put in an appearance, I decided. I couldn't just slink away and pretend they weren't all wondering where I was.

I gulped some air, let it out, and opened the door. Everybody turned.

"Hi. Hi. So sorry," I said, sweeping into the room and walking directly over to Jed. "Family emergency. Couldn't be helped. Please forgive me."

He cupped his ear. "Say it again?"

"I had a family emergency! Please forgive me!" I shouted, feeling like a fool and a fraud.

While Bernie shot me a less-than-thrilled look—he knew there was no family emergency because he also knew I had no family—I debated whether I should have just shown up wearing the coffee-stained blouse instead of changing clothes. The blouse would have been easier to explain.

"Of course I forgive you," Jed bellowed at me, much to everybody's relief. "I'm a Christian."

"I appreciate that," I said, figuring it wasn't the best time to tell him I was half-Jewish.

"Why don't you pull up a chair, Melanie?" Bernie suggested from between pursed lips. His expression made it clear that he was less forgiving. "We're almost finished here, but you might as well listen in."

"My pleasure," I said as I sat between him and Steffi, to whom I mouthed a silent thank-you.

When the meeting was over and everyone had left, I took Bernie aside and apologized profusely for being late.

"The divorce is getting off to a bumpy start," I told him. Well, why not be honest. Yes, he'd fired Roberta Chapman for losing it after her divorce. But I wanted to prove to him that I was dealing with my problems, not flipping out about them the way she did.

"You and Dan have been apart for over a year," he said, scratching his red goatee. "Shouldn't you have adjusted to the separation by now?"

"Yes, yes," I said. "But it's not the separation that needs adjusting to. It's that I'm paying Dan spousal support and it's causing me a lot of aggravation."

He nodded as if he understood, even though he was single and had never paid an ex-spouse anything. "What are you doing about the situation?"

"Doing?" I asked.

"I'm behind you, Mel. You know that. You're important to this company, and one missed meeting isn't the end of the world. But . . ."

"But what?" I thought of Roberta Chapman again and how

quickly she'd fallen out of favor with Bernie. Despite his words of assurance, I felt a sudden shudder of fear.

"If the spousal support is creating a distraction, then you'd better get yourself some professional help," said my boss.

So. In the end, I was only following orders by calling Desiree to assist me. You can see that, can't you?

Chapter 7

"Desiree Klein Heart Hunting. This is Taylor speaking," announced a voice with the seriousness of a suicide hotline operator. Very professional. And heart hunting instead of head hunting. Clever marketing gimmick.

"Hi, Taylor," I said. "I'd like to make an appointment with Ms. Klein as soon as possible." I was speaking softly, so no one lurking outside my office would hear me. I had closed the door and made sure that Steffi was out to lunch before I called. Despite my decision to move forward with the plan to hire Desiree, I wasn't entirely proud of it.

"You're a first-time client?" she asked.

"Yes," I said. "I was referred by Louise and Leonard Chester."

"Oh, cool. One of Desiree's many success stories," she said, the serious tone giving way to a girlish enthusiasm. "When would you like to come in?"

"Preferably early in the morning or at the end of the day. I have a busy schedule."

"How's Wednesday morning at eight-thirty?" she offered.

"Perfect," I said.

She asked me for my name, address, and phone number, then told me where they were located. "You'll need to bring the five-thousand-dollar fee with you," she added.

"Already? Doesn't Desiree have to do anything to earn it first?" I was still very queasy about spending so much money, but Weezie had reminded me how much I'd be saving if things worked out.

"We refund it if she doesn't make a match for you."

I started to explain that I wasn't looking for a match for me but decided to save the speech for her boss, since the situation was fairly complicated.

"You'll also need to bring a recent photo," she said, "as well as a one-page biography detailing your educational, financial, and marital histories; an essay of any length describing your hopes, dreams, desires, and dating patterns; and a complete medical history, including a list of current medications, particularly antidepressants or antipsychotics, and any sexually transmitted diseases. If you've had herpes or genital warts, for example, you'll need an accompanying note from your doctor indicating the date of your last outbreak."

Gee, did she want to know about the regularity of my periods too?

"Melanie?" she said. "Did you get all that down?"

"Yes," I said. "It's just that—"

"You're a little embarrassed about the STD query?"

"No, it's not—"

"Because you shouldn't be. It's just part of the background check, and if you've been sexually active, you've probably had something, right?"

"Right. But I—"

"Oh, I know. You don't think you'll be able to pull all the info together in two days. Because of that busy schedule you mentioned."

"Exactly." This was crazy. I was crazy.

"Not to worry. Everyone feels overwhelmed by the paperwork, but it'll be easier than you think. And it's all for your benefit, don't forget. The more Desiree knows about you, the easier it'll be for her to find you your special someone."

Nope. This wasn't such a hot idea. I would find another way to deal with Dan, a way that didn't involve special someones. "Oh, gosh. I just remembered I have a meeting Wednesday morning so I won't be able to make it," I said.

Taylor giggled. "Everybody does that too."

"Does what?"

"Try to chicken out. It's normal." She took a breath. "The consultation will last about an hour, so plan accordingly. And when you start getting butterflies, keep telling yourself that Desiree is all about bringing you a lifetime of happiness. She really is a magician when it comes to putting people together."

It was that last line that roped me back in. If Desiree Klein could put Dan together with a woman for ninety days, she'd be bringing me a lifetime of happiness all right. I just had to fill her in on the game plan and hope like hell she was a sports fan.

■ ■ ■

Her office was off the living room of her apartment, a glitzy affair on Fifth Avenue with a spectacular view of Central Park. Its message to all visitors was: "You can never have enough gold." There were gold silk draperies and gold-leaf mirrors, and wood tables inlaid with—what else?—gold. There was also a zebra skin rug and a grand piano and a gilded cage in which a parrot rested on a swing chirping a ribald Eminem lyric. Well, Nards had warned me that Desiree was a character. As I sat in the chair opposite her desk and waited, I noticed that the only reading material available were articles about her.

"Hey there," she said, waddling into her office, an overdose of sickly sweet perfume wafting after her. She was in her fifties and plump as well as short—a dumpling, except for her chin, which was pointy in the manner of, say, Maria Shriver. She was wearing a purple caftan and matching fuzzy slippers with little pom-poms on them and a long, platinum blond wig with bangs. Oh, and there was jewelry—rings, bracelets, earrings, a necklace. Surely enough gold to ransom a kidnap victim. Yes, I remembered her from the wedding now. I just hadn't made the connection between the woman I'd assumed was one of Weezie's wacky aunts and this person, who appeared to have a thriving business.

She approached my chair and shook my hand. "Melanie?" she said in heavy New York–ese. It came out "Malanay."

"Yes, and you must be Desiree," I said.

"It's really Donna," she said in a conspiratorial, between-us-girls whisper. "I changed it when I got into this heart-hunting gig. Desiree works better for people, you know what I mean?"

A character and a hustler?

"So. You brought the info?" she asked.

"Yes." I handed her the folder containing all the goodies her assistant had asked for.

"Is the check in here?" she said.

"It's paper-clipped to my cover letter," I said.

"Bee-uteeful." She sat behind her desk, the folder in front of her. "Not that I'm about money, you understand. I'm about *love*."

Yes, I'm afraid she pronounced it "luv." I took a quick look around the room, making a mental note of my evacuation route. What the hell was I doing there?

"I hear you're a friend of Louise and Leonard's," she said.

I nodded, squirming in my seat. I would make my apologies and scram. It probably wouldn't be the first time one of her first-timers did that. "Louise and I met at Pierce, Shelley and Steinberg."

"Class acts, Louise and Leonard," she said. "They capped off a good year for me. I think I married over fifty clients."

"Fifty?" I said, amazed. It seemed as if there were hardly any weddings anymore, unless you counted the civil unions in Sunday's *New York Times* Styles section.

"You got it," she said. "But I've had hundreds of couples get married in the fifteen years I've been a heart hunter. Without any divorces, knock on wood." She knocked on the side of her head.

"You must be very adept at what you do," I said. Well? Maybe matchmaking was a talent, just like ice-skating, and Desiree had it. I reconsidered my initial impulse to bolt.

"I'm the best," she said without a hint of modesty. "And not a single complaint from the Better Business Bureau, which is unusual for a matchmaking service. There are plenty of shady organizations out there, taking people's money and then pairing them with ex-cons. I'm strictly on the up-and-up. I don't pull any shenanigans."

"What's the secret of your success as a matchmaker?" I said, deciding I'd stick around after all and see if it made sense to pull my own shenanigans.

"Part of it is that finding matches for people is my passion." She pressed her hands together in the prayer position. "I consider what I do a mission from God."

"That's very spiritual," I said.

"And my background checks contribute to my success," she said, returning to earth. "I prescreen my clients so that there are no surprises." She patted the folder on her desk, the one that would be full of surprises.

"And I make a special effort to recruit men," she said.

"Why men?"

"Because they're in short supply, compared to all the available women on the prowl. If there's an eligible bachelor out there, I'll bag him."

I smiled. I had an eligible bachelor she could bag. He didn't have a job, but he wasn't an ex-con.

"Oh, and there's one other reason I'm successful," she said. "I understand what makes a good relationship."

Blah blah blah, I thought. Here comes the Dr. Phil crap. Just sit there and listen politely.

"It doesn't begin with the first date," she said. "It begins with two people who are well adjusted. When a match is truly a match, it's because each person has faced up to something that scarred them—some baggage—and gotten past it, before they came together. Like, if you're still caught up in the bitterness of a breakup, you're not match material."

"No?" So I wasn't match material. Big deal. I wasn't there for myself.

"No. Being overly critical of an ex during your first meeting with the new person isn't exactly a turn-on. Besides, the critical ones are usually the people who have low self-esteem. I can set them up on a million dates, but they'll never be satisfied until they look in the mirror, take stock, and learn to love that reflection shining back at them."

Okay, yeah. I was critical of my ex to anyone who would listen, but who wouldn't be? He was a jerk.

"That's very interesting," I lied. "I'm also curious about the financial terms. You charge five thousand for a year's worth of dates?"

"Right. You become a client, you're guaranteed a minimum of one date per month for twelve months. But a pretty girl like you? The odds are you're gonna meet your dream man within the first six, Melanie." She opened my folder and started reading my biography.

"Actually, Desiree," I said as her eyes widened, "I should probably clarify—"

She held up a finger to silence me—a finger with a two-inch-long, acrylic, fire-engine-red nail that curled downward at the tip and looked like it could hurt somebody. "What's with this? I'm a little confused," she said. "Who's Dan Swain and why is this a biography of him?"

"That's what I wanted to clarify." I cleared my throat. "I came to you so you'd find a match for Dan, my ex-husband, who deserves the kind of happiness I wasn't able to give him."

"I still don't get it."

"Let me explain." I assumed a Mother Teresa look, a look that would appeal to Desiree's delusions of sainthood. "Dan is a wonderful human being. We had our problems, but we parted amicably. And now that he's newly single, *my* mission from God is to find him a woman to replace me in his heart."

She looked skeptical. "If he's such a wonderful human being, why'd you divorce him?"

It was time to launch into my act. I lowered my head and fake-cried for a few seconds. She asked me if I wanted a glass of water. I told her I just needed to be able to tell my story to someone with her vast experience and gift for empathy. "Oh, Desiree," I said. "Sometimes people just aren't meant to be together. Dan and I were very young when we got married—too young to make such a commitment. As time went on, it became all too clear that he was the caring one and I was the workaholic who cared only about climbing the corporate ladder. I wasn't cut out to be the kind of wife Dan needed, so I made the ultimate sacrifice: I set him free so he could find a woman more suited to the nurturing individual he is."

"Now that's a switch," she said. "Most women would rather see their exes dead than happy."

"Maybe, but Dan is a decent, loving guy and I really want you to find him someone equally decent and loving—the kind of quality person you seek out for your clientele; the kind that doesn't have to take antipsychotic medication, for instance."

"Why can't I just meet Dan and discuss this with him directly?"

"Because he was a professional football player, Desiree. With the New York Giants." I nodded at the folder. "It's in there."

She gave the biography a cursory reading. "I thought his name sounded familiar."

"Yes, well he's got a lot of macho pride, like most athletes," I said. "He would never in a million years seek the services of a matchmaker. The idea of confiding his innermost feelings to a stranger would be mortifying to him. When we were married, he wouldn't even do couples therapy."

"Then what do you expect me to do?" she said.

"I want you to set Dan up with Ms. Right without his knowing about it. We'll arrange for her to meet him and see what happens." She started to protest, but I plowed ahead. "You just told me there's a shortage of single men out there, right? Well, I'm delivering you one. He's very handsome, as you'll see from the photo in the folder, and he's not even forty yet, which puts him in the most desirable demographic category. And here's another thing that makes him desirable: he's a celebrity. We all know how women love celebrities."

"I can't argue with that," she said.

I was getting to her. I knew I was. "After a knee injury ended his playing days, he remained in the public eye by transitioning into broadcasting and doing on-air reporting for several networks."

A lightbulb went on then. She started nodding sourly. "Yeah. I remember him now. He was drunk on live television and insulted a female reporter. Not my kind of client, sorry."

She was about to get up when I fake-cried even harder—hard enough to get her to sit back down.

"Wait, Desiree. You don't know the whole story."

"What whole story?"

"He wasn't drunk that night. He had a stomach virus. An hour before he went on the air, the doctor gave him something to stop the nausea, and it made him a little punchy. It wasn't booze, really. It was a pill so he wouldn't puke all over his coanchors. You have to believe me!"

"All right, all right. Don't have a cow."

Sure, I'd gone overboard. Desperation does that to people. But

I still had her attention. "And now he has a very active career as a goodwill ambassador for his sport," I continued. Goodwill ambassador, my ass. Right before we split up, he'd been paid twenty-five hundred dollars to appear at the bar mitzvah of a kid whose father was a Giants fan. He stood next to the rabbi and made a little speech about how life was like a football game and becoming a man was like scoring a touchdown. Then he drank a few glasses of Manischewitz and beat it. "But being famous has made him cautious about women. Where can he meet them? He can't go out with a groupie. And he can't log on to some Internet dating chat room. He needs someone discreet to help him find a good woman, Desiree. Someone of your professional caliber."

"So he's got money?" she asked. "That's a big issue with my female clients."

"A lot of it," I said, willing my eyes not to roll. "Just recently he chartered a private jet and flew off to Puerto Rico. He dresses beautifully, loves to dine at fine restaurants, and lives in one of the nicest apartments in Manhattan." Yeah, so what if I was footing the bill for all of it? His dream date wouldn't know that. Dan certainly wouldn't tell her.

"He does sound like a catch," she said. "Almost too good to be true. But what kind of a person is he? You know, deep down."

I beamed. "The real deal, that's what kind of a person. He was born and raised in Minco, Oklahoma, a small town where everybody knows everybody. His family lives on a farm and grows corn. It doesn't get much more real than that, does it?"

"It does if your ideal man has a family with a castle in Scotland," she said. "A lot of women want a guy who comes from money."

"How shallow," I said with an ostentatious shrug. "Dan is for the woman who wants sincerity, genuineness, and honesty. I'll take that over family money any day of the week."

"But you didn't take it," she pointed out. "You divorced him."

"I explained that. We had lifestyle differences."

She went back to reading the biography. "It says here he has a dog. A pug."

"Actually, he and I share custody of Buster," I said. "Dan has him every other week and on alternate holidays."

" 'Client must not have allergies to or phobias of dogs,' " she read aloud.

"Correct," I said. "We keep Buster very clean, but pugs do shed."

She put aside the biography and went for the essay about Dan's hopes and dreams. I'd had fun writing that one. I'd loaded it up with the same drivel you see in personal ads—how Dan wanted a woman who enjoyed walks on the beach at sunset and mugs of hot cider beside a roaring fire and black-and-white movies on rainy Sunday afternoons when there wasn't a football game on TV. I added that he preferred a woman who was independent (i.e., had her own money), affectionate (was good in bed), witty (would tolerate jock jokes), and adventurous (would be up for expensive trips and paying for them too). Not bad, right?

"So, will you help?" I begged. "Will you find Dan his soul mate?"

She shook her head. "I could set him up with dozens of my clients, but I'd feel guilty about involving them in something as iffy as this. Like I told you, my business is on the up-and-up."

"This *is* on the up-and-up," I maintained. "You'll be offering these women a chance at ninety days of happiness."

"Ninety days?" said a justifiably puzzled Desiree.

"Forgive me." Talk about almost blowing it. Talk about tipping my hand! "It's just an old saying of my mother's: ninety days of happiness guarantees a hundred years of good health."

She chuckled. "Who makes those up, huh?"

"Yes, well about the women. Just tell them about Dan and his celebrity and how he was too proud to sign up with a professional matchmaker. Explain that you heard from a close friend of his that he's lonely and eager to be in a lasting relationship. They'll understand, especially after they meet him and find out how great he is."

"But how am I supposed to set them up with him if he doesn't know he's being set up?"

"No problem," I said. "You and I will sort through your client list and pick out the women we want to set him up with. Then for each date we'll send the client where we know he's going to be at the appointed hour. We'll put them in the same place at the same time and let nature take its course."

"So the client is supposed to—what?—pick him up? My girls aren't sluts."

"Of course they're not. They'd just be making the first move. This *is* the twenty-first century, Desiree. Women are allowed to go after what they want. It wouldn't be all that different from your usual way of doing things."

"My usual way of doing things doesn't involve tricking somebody's ex."

"Tricking? Hardly!" I feigned indignation. "You would be putting the smile back on his face, putting the light back in his eyes, putting the glow back in his cheeks, putting the—" Yeah, I was overdoing it again, but it was amazing how quickly I'd gone from a reluctant participant in this scam to an eager one. I suppose it was Desiree's success rate that had me revved up. I was a numbers person. Her numbers spoke to me. I became a believer once I'd heard how many couples she'd put together. "You can't *not* do this," I begged her. "You'd be depriving two exemplary people of what could be the romance of their lives!"

She pondered a bit, then shook her head. "Can't do it, sorry. It doesn't feel right."

Okay, I thought. Don't give up. You're not a quitter. You've always got a strategy, so come up with a new one—fast.

I remembered her living room, remembered the velvet chaise and the crystal chandelier and the enormous oil painting of two large mythical animals having sex, and it struck me. The new strategy. The last shot at reeling her in.

Desiree had expensive taste. Bad expensive taste, but expensive taste nonetheless. Maybe it was time to put the emphasis on the money and forget the hearts and flowers stuff.

"What if I doubled your fee?" I said. "Five thousand up front and another five after you've found the right woman for Dan." Of course it pained me to offer her ten grand. It was a ridiculous amount. But I'd still be saving money in the long run if I could put an end to the support payments. "That's a lot of money to turn down, Desiree. If I walk out of here, it walks out with me."

She was stunned. "Maybe you'd better tell me what's really going on here."

Yes, I thought. I should tell her what's really going on. I should also tell her how she could use it to her own advantage. She likes gold? I would suggest a way for her to strike gold. I hadn't gone to business school for nothing.

"Fine. I'll level with you," I said. "I'm proposing a brand-new division of Desiree Klein Heart Hunting."

"What are you talking about?"

"You just said you didn't want to trick my ex. But there's a huge market for tricking exes, and you'd be the first to tap into it."

"Tricking them how?"

"Finding them new partners, so former spouses like me won't have to pay them alimony anymore."

"I—" She stopped, letting the notion sink in. "This is about alimony?"

I smiled. "And the start of a profitable new venture for you."

She sat there for a minute, looking a little dazed. Then: "You want me to get him remarried, so you'll be off the hook?"

"We could go that route, but we don't have to," I said. "I have a cohabitation clause in my divorce settlement—he only has to live with a woman for 'ninety substantially continuous days' for the alimony to terminate—and there are plenty of others in New York with similar clauses. You could make a fortune off people like me, Desiree."

Next came a few more minutes of back and forth. She appeared to recoil from the idea at first. (There was her supposed guilt over the exploitation of her unsuspecting clients. There was her supposed standing with the Better Business Bureau. There was her supposed belief that love made the world go around, not money.) But gradually she warmed to it, especially after I made the pitch that liberating alimony payers could be another kind of mission from God.

"You're a tough cookie, Melanie," she said.

"Thanks," I said, assuming she meant it as a compliment. "Do we have a deal then?"

We had a deal. I leaned across her desk to shake her hand,

careful not to get scratched by her talons. “You won’t be sorry,” I promised her.

“Let’s hope *you* won’t be sorry.”

I laughed. “Why would I be sorry?”

“Buyer’s remorse.”

It was an odd thing to say, I thought, but then Desiree Klein was an odd person. Oh, well. The good news was that progress had finally been made. I had taken action instead of sitting passively by while my life fell apart. I felt optimistic for the first time in a long time.

Chapter 8

"Good morning, Ricardo," I said to the doorman. I was dropping Buster off at Dan's the Monday after my appointment with Desiree. She and I had agreed to speak again once she had compiled a portfolio of potential girlfriends for him and I had nailed down his schedule. He had become quite the creature of habit since we'd split up, so I expected my part of the assignment to be easy.

"Hi, Melanie," said Ricardo. "I'll buzz Mr. Swain and see if he's up for visitors."

"You do that," I said, trying to keep my annoyance in check.

After the usual humiliating wait in the lobby, I was finally permitted to go up to my own apartment. Dan was waiting in his bathrobe and moccasins, half-asleep.

"Is there any chance you could stop dropping Buster off in the middle of the night?" he said, wiping the crud out of his eyes.

"It's eight o'clock in the morning," I said as I brushed past him, Buster trailing after me. "Some of us have places to go, people to meet, salaries to earn."

"And some of us need our rest," he said. "Being a single man in New York takes a lot of energy these days. Women have become very aggressive." He shook his head in mock consternation. "They don't understand that 'no' means 'no.' "

"That must be quite a burden," I said, unhooking Buster's leash so he could hop onto the sofa and, hopefully, drool all over it. "I'd love to hear more about your sex life, but there's serious business I need to discuss with you."

The smirky attitude vanished. "You're not sick, are you, Mel?"

Weird. Just when I thought Dan had no redeeming qualities, he showed his concern for my health. Maybe I hadn't been completely wrong about him in the early years. Maybe there *was* a decent, caring person hiding inside the jerk he'd turned into. And maybe I wasn't lying when I'd told Desiree he would make one of her clients very happy. "No, I'm fine, thanks. This is about our schedules. I've decided that in the event of an emergency we should be accessible to each other at all times."

Back came the jerk. "You really can't stand being without me, can you, darlin'?"

"This is about Buster, Dan. If something were to happen to him, God forbid, you would know where to reach me, since I'm almost always at the office, but I wouldn't know where to reach you."

"You've got my cell number."

"Yeah, but your cell isn't always turned on. Or you're not in an area where there's a good signal. Or you leave it in a taxi."

"I did that exactly once," he said defensively. "Four years ago."

"I'm just saying I'd like to have your schedule, in case I need to get in touch with you quickly. I know you have your familiar haunts now, spots where you hang out on a regular basis. I promise I won't make any cracks about them or give you any lectures. I just want a list, okay?"

"You're not yanking my chain? This is really about Buster?"

"Why else would I care what you do with your time?"

"You tell me. You're the one who's always got an angle."

I stood very straight, trying my best to appear upright, dignified, beyond reproach, anything but the architect of . . . an angle. "It's strictly about Buster, Dan. As I said."

He shrugged and went into the kitchen for a pen and paper. While I waited for him to return, I took a little stroll around the living room, stopping to run my hands along the chenille fabric on the club chair. I recalled picking it out and thinking how lush and soft it was, never imagining that I wouldn't be the one sitting on it anymore, much less owning it.

I continued to move throughout the room, gazing with greater and greater yearning at each piece that I—okay, Dan and I—had purchased, allowing myself to dwell on the memory each evoked: the antique-brass wall sconces we'd discovered at an estate sale; the mahogany side table that had been hand-carved for us by craftsmen we'd met while vacationing in Montego Bay; the fringed Turkish rug on which we'd made love the night Dan had returned from a road trip to San Francisco.

And then I came upon a grouping of framed photos, including

one of him and me at my graduation from business school. I was positively beaming into the camera as I clutched my diploma to my chest. I had achieved my goal, but it was Dan who'd made it possible, and the expression on my face reflected both my excitement and my gratitude. He'd paid my way, taken care of me, sheltered me. I'd tried to do the same for him when he needed me, but those days were over. I was not taking care of a person whose only goal in life was to torture me. He was Desiree's problem now, not mine.

He came back a few minutes later with his list and handed it to me. I stuffed it into my briefcase, kissed Buster good-bye, and left.

"Don't do anything criminal at work," he called out after me.

I ignored him and walked down the hall, toward the elevator.

"I'd hate to read about you in the business section of the *Times,* with all those corporate crooks and their legal hassles," he added.

"That shouldn't be a problem," I said as I hit the elevator's Down button. "You never read the business section of the *Times.* The classifieds either."

If he had a comeback, I was too far away to hear it.

I studied Dan's schedule in the taxi on the way to the office. It wasn't exactly a page-turner, but I hoped it would be useful. I tried to call Desiree from my cell phone to get her thinking about which client to send out to which of his hangouts, but the cab-driver had his radio on. A pulsating, repetitious song was playing, and I couldn't compete with the Middle East's equivalent of Justin Timberlake. Might as well wait for a land line, I decided.

"Ornbacher called about fifteen minutes ago," said Steffi as

I arrived at work. She was seated at her desk with her headset on, her neatly recorded call sheet in front of her. "Do you want me to get him at his hotel? He said he'd be there a little longer."

"Did it sound urgent?" I said.

"It always sounds urgent with him. Why does he have to yell at everyone?"

I smiled. "Don't be intimidated by him." Despite how poised Steffi was, I had to remind myself that she was still inexperienced with clients, most of whom believed that their money entitled them to push people around. Ornbacher may have been a lecher, but he was actually pretty easy to deal with, relative to the others. "He yells because he's got a hearing problem, that's all," I said. "I'll call him in a few minutes."

"But—"

"There's something I need to deal with first."

She blinked in surprise.

"I'll call him before he leaves his hotel, Steffi. Not to worry."

I hurried into my office, closed the door, and dialed Desiree's number. I was dying to get started on our "project." I figured our conversation would be quick—just an exchange of information—leaving plenty of time for me to get back to Jed.

"Hi. It's Melanie checking in," I said after Taylor put me through.

"So soon?" she said.

"I'm a doer," I said. "You told me to find out Dan's schedule? I found out his schedule." I pulled the piece of paper out of my briefcase and spread it out on my desk. "Now, he doesn't account for every minute of the day and night, but there are definite areas to exploit. Like the gym. He goes to Manhattan Body and Fitness on Sixty-fourth and Second on Tuesdays, Thursdays, and Fridays from ten to noon. I've already confirmed that they take walk-ins, so your clients can pop in there any time. On those same days, he has lunch at the Post House, the steak place on Sixty-third between Park and Madison in the Lowell Hotel. He likes to sit in the back, so he can avoid the legions of people he's deluded himself into thinking will still recognize him. Late in the day he plays poker at his friend Ernie's apartment at 201 East Seventy-second, which isn't a public place, of course, but maybe your clients could—"

"What? Pose as the UPS delivery person?"

"Fine. Forget that one. On Wednesday afternoons he plays football in Central Park, in the North Meadow at Ninety-seventh Street. He's there from two to five—lots of time for that special someone to stroll by and get his attention."

"Melanie?"

"Yes?"

"Dan goes to the gym, eats lunch, and plays games. I knew he wasn't out there finding a cure for cancer, but you didn't tell me he did nothing."

"Why do you think I'm trying to shed him like a bad cold?" I said.

She sighed. "I don't know who's going to jump at the chance to meet him. Not my clients. Not even my really desperate ones."

"He does have a certain kind of charm," I said. "Maybe when he finds the right woman, he'll be motivated to change."

"Maybe, but in the meantime he's no catch."

That's why *you're* getting paid the big bucks, I wanted to say. Instead I tried flattery, which is always a good motivator, I've learned. "You'll find the perfect person for him, Desiree, because you're the best matchmaker in the city."

"In the country," she corrected me. "I'm opening branches in Miami and Beverly Hills as soon as I pull my financing together."

"The financing won't be a problem once you get your Heart Hunting for Exes division off the ground," I said. "You'll make a fortune off people like me."

"Yeah, well right now I've gotta find somebody for your ex, like you said. I just don't know which girl to put with him."

"I'll go through your files with you if you want," I said. "I know what type of woman he likes."

"Hey, be my guest if you've got the time," she said.

"I'll make the time." I checked my calendar. "How's five-thirty tomorrow afternoon?"

"You're in a big hurry about this, huh?" she said.

Just then, Steffi knocked softly on my door, opened it a crack, and stuck her head in. "Sorry to interrupt, but I took the liberty of getting Ornbacher on the phone for you. I checked my watch and thought he might be leaving his hotel, so I placed the call. You'll talk to him, right?"

How could I not love Steffi? She really did anticipate my every need. I was just about to finish up with Desiree anyway.

I mouthed to her that I'd be right with him.

"Yes, I'm in a big hurry," I told Desiree. "See you tomorrow."

She hung up. I hung up. Then I closed my eyes, took a deep breath, and picked up the other line.

"Jed," I said, full of confidence. It was incredible how much better I felt about things since making the decision to hire Desiree to solve my Dan problem. It was as if the proverbial weight had been lifted off my shoulders. "I was just about to call you. What's up?" I chuckled. "Besides the stock market, I mean."

"Nothing," he boomed. I had to hold the phone away from my ear to avoid permanent damage.

"But you called me earlier," I reminded him.

"I sure did, but I got hold of Bernie when I couldn't reach you, and he already answered my question," he said. "I told him you must have had another one of those family emergencies."

Okay, so I'd made a poor choice by trying to slip in a call to Desiree first. I wouldn't make it again.

That night I was back at the Heartbreak Hotel, sharing some wine and cheese with Patty. She'd resumed her unfortunate habit of hurling breakable objects at the picture of her ex-husband that was taped to the wall. In the interest of peace and quiet, I'd pleaded my way into her apartment and wrestled a small hurricane lamp out of her hand.

"Have you seen the hottie who just moved into 3F?" she said, having calmed down considerably after her second glass of merlot.

"No," I said. "And I thought you were off men after your experience with Jason."

"I am, but that doesn't mean I can't appreciate a hunk when I see him." She sipped more wine while I went for another helping of cheese. "This one's very Viggo Mortensen."

I shrugged, drawing a blank.

"The actor from *Lord of the Rings,*" she said as if I were a complete blockhead.

I never went to the movies anymore, so the reference was lost on me. I'd been too busy working. Even as a kid I didn't take up movies or any other activity that would qualify as a hobby. There wasn't time. Not with debtors' prison looming.

"He's got these deeply set eyes," she said, "and wild dark hair, and a body that's lean and mean and—"

"Are we talking about the guy in 3F or this Viggo person?" I said.

"Both," said Patty. "There's one big difference though. Viggo's rich. The guy in 3F is hurting for cash, judging by the torn jeans and the cracked leather jacket."

"Dan paid thousands for his cracked leather jacket. It was Ralph Lauren."

"Yeah, well this guy's not buying designer clothes any time soon. When he was moving in, he hardly had any cartons. Just a bunch of canvases."

I rolled my eyes. "Painter?"

"Laid-off-book-editor-turned-painter. His name's Evan Gillespie and he specializes in water."

"You mean he's a watercolorist?"

"No, I mean he paints oceans, rivers, streams, whatever."

"Don't tell me. His wife kicked him out because his 'art' wasn't paying the bills."

"Bingo. They just separated, and he's camping out here until the divorce comes through and he finds a place of his own. He told me when we were down in the laundry room."

"He's probably waiting for the alimony checks to start coming in."

She nodded. "What is it with these men? Didn't they used to be able to support *themselves,* never mind *us*? Is there an epidemic out there? Something in the air? Some odorless, colorless toxin that renders them incapable of earning a living?"

"My friend Nards says it's our fault."

"Oh, you mean the whole bit about if we hadn't stolen their jobs and performed as well as they did, the natural order of things would be restored? What a crock."

"I know. What's wrong with us being on top?"

"Amen to that. Who needs the missionary position?"

"Yeah. Why should we shrink just to make them feel bigger?"

"Some women are doing that, you know."

"Doing what, Patty?"

"Having vaginal reduction surgery. To shrink, so the guy will feel bigger."

"I wasn't talking about sex." Were women really doing that? "I was talking about how men are paralyzed by our success. Look at Jason. He's a photographer who stopped taking photographs because he couldn't compete with you. And this Evan is probably a painter who's—"

"Different. I'm not interested in him, trust me, but he's a painter who actually paints. I saw his stuff."

I rolled my eyes again. "Just what the world needs. Another masterpiece of a sunset over the Gulf of Mexico."

At that moment, there was a knock at the door. Patty wiped the red wine off her mouth with the back of her hand and got up to answer it while I dove for more cheese. God, food was wonderful.

"Who's there?" she said, peering through the peephole.

"Evan Gillespie from 3F," said a male voice. "I just wanted to return the Tide you lent me in the laundry room. I bought you a new box."

I stood up to leave. "And they say chivalry isn't dead."

"Don't you want to meet him?" said Patty, who had already opened the door.

There, in the threshold, was a tall, lanky, shaggy-haired man in his thirties with the aforementioned deeply set eyes, plus the jeans and the leather jacket. He had a long face and thin lips and cheekbones so prominent he looked as if he was sucking on something. Patty was right: he was striking. Dan had swept me off my feet with his golden, all-American, comic-book-hero beauty, but this guy was handsome in a darker, more subtle way.

"Hey, sorry to barge in," he said to Patty, ducking a little as he entered her apartment. His voice was raspy, whispery, soft. "Here's the detergent. Much appreciated."

"Thanks," she said, taking the Tide. "Melanie and I were having some wine and cheese. Want to join us?"

He glanced at me and gave me a friendly smile. "I'm Evan Gillespie."

"Melanie Banks," I said, walking around him so I could make my escape out the door. The last thing I needed was to get trapped having to make conversation with another bumbo. The one I was forced to make conversation with every other Monday morning was more than enough. "Welcome to the Heartbreak Hotel."

"Melanie's ex-husband is Dan Swain," Patty blurted out for a reason known only to her. Maybe she thought that dropping the name would impress Evan.

"Traffic Dan Swain?" he said. So he was impressed.

"Yes," I said. "Let me guess. You're a Giants fan."

"To be honest, I hate football," he said with a shrug. "But if you live in New York, you know the city's sports heroes. Your ex-husband was one of them."

"Ah, so true," I said, hoping to avoid having to listen to Dan's accomplishments on the gridiron, entertaining though they were. I wasn't in the mood. I stepped closer to the door and found myself wedged between Evan and a chair. His eyes, now that I could see them up close, weren't just dark. They looked black, thanks to pupils that were huge.

"Sorry about what happened," he said, surprising me by not going the highlight-reel route after all. "Tough break for him. For both of you."

"Are you referring to the injury or the aborted TV career?" I asked. It was always interesting to me which aspect of the Traffic Dan Swain legend people remembered.

"I was referring to his current situation. Being a former jock with no other identity," he said. "He's in the newspapers now and then—when he's at a nightclub shaking hands with fans and stuff like that. He looks pretty lost. I feel kind of sorry for him."

Now that was a switch. Most people would do anything to trade places with the golden boy. "He's living very well," I said. "I wouldn't get out my violin on his account."

"Melanie supports him," Patty volunteered, continuing to serve as the provider of information that wasn't hers to provide.

"That's a big responsibility," Evan said, nodding at me. "You must be a very generous person to help him out like that. Especially since you're not married to him anymore."

Well, now that was downright odd. He had completely misunderstood Patty. Surely, he didn't think I was writing Dan checks because I wanted to. Surely his own wife was about to get stuck writing him checks, and it wouldn't be because she wanted to either. Still, his eyes were kind as they took me in, his expression one of admiration. I glanced at Patty and willed her to keep her mouth shut. There was no reason to disabuse this nice man of his good opinion of me.

"Well, I guess I'd better get moving," I said, my hand on the doorknob now. "I've got work to do."

"What sort of work?" asked Evan.

The sort of work that enables me to support that ex-husband you're feeling sorry for, I thought. "I'm a financial planner at Pierce, Shelley and Steinberg."

"She's a vice president," Patty chimed in.

"Great. I wish I could hire you, but I don't have any investments to manage," said Evan with a laugh.

"That'll change," I said, wondering how his wife would handle the burden of making the support payments every month. I made a mental note to get her name and pass it along to Desiree. Another potential client for the new division of Desiree Klein Heart Hunting.

"I hope you're right," he said. "I'm certainly putting in the effort."

"I bet you are." He probably had a good lawyer. They all had good lawyers, and we got stuck paying their legal bills, as if the alimony wasn't enough.

"You really can't stay, Mel?" said Patty, pouring herself another glass of merlot.

"Thanks, but duty calls," I said. Duty always called. Every night. That's how it was. Ever since the separation and even before it.

"Maybe you'll stop by my place sometime and take a look at my paintings," said Evan. "I'm just down the hall."

"I'm pretty busy," I said. I had both feet out the door at this point. I needed to go home. He was sweet, but my mind was elsewhere. I had paperwork to go over and memos to write, especially since I'd be leaving the office early the next day to meet with Desiree.

"No interest in making a new friend?" he asked in that low, soft voice of his. It was sexy, the way it drew you in and made you listen harder. But he was penniless, for God's sake. I didn't need another drain. What I needed was a ninety-day wonder woman for Dan.

"Look, Evan," I said, backing out now, "I don't mean to be rude, and I did enjoy meeting you, but I'm really focused on a special project these days. I don't have a lot of time to look at paintings or anything else. Okay?"

He held his hands up in surrender. "Your loss."

I waved good night to both of them and went back to my place, thrilled to be alone. I closed and locked the door, kicked off my shoes, then dumped my keys, purse, and briefcase onto the foyer table, pausing to give myself a cursory glance in the fake-pewter mirror that hung there. I was about to walk away when I noticed there was something on my—

I leaned in, took a closer look at my face. Yes, there was a piece of—

I planted myself even closer and squinted at my reflection to try and figure out what—

Great. It was a small crumble of the blue cheese I'd been wolfing down at Patty's, and it was clinging to my skin, right underneath my left nostril. How the hell it had landed near my nose instead of in my mouth I can't tell you, but it looked exactly like a booger. I stood there staring at it for a second or two, then flicked it off in disgust.

No, of course I didn't care what Evan Gillespie thought of me. I'd probably never run into him again, and I certainly wasn't planning on seeking him out.

Chapter 9

"Jelly? That's her name?" I said as I studied an eight-by-ten glossy of an extremely pretty young woman whose brown hair was a mop of corkscrews.

"It's Jill, but people started calling her Jelly when she was a kid and it stuck," said Desiree, who was wearing another wig—a short dark one that curled under her pointy chin. She was in another caftan too—purple again but with black stripes—and the same fuzz ball slippers as before. I couldn't decide if she was one of those people who enjoys being different or if she didn't get that she was.

"Dan's not a fan of women with ringlets," I said. He likes long, wavy hair, I thought, remembering how tenderly he used to comb mine with his fingers after we made love.

"Don't be ridiculous. She's a beauty," Desiree said, the way you'd say it about a boat or a racehorse or a piece of salmon fillet. "She jogs, goes hiking, all that outdoorsy stuff. He'll love her."

"How about her personality?"

"Friendly. Upbeat. Lots of energy. She won't have any problem making the first move with him. She's the type who marches right up to people and tells them to have a nice day."

I rolled my eyes. "What about her job? Or is she too busy spreading good cheer to work?"

"She's a massage therapist."

I flung the photo onto the coffee table. "Come on. We need one who can support Dan, not just knead his sore muscles."

"Why? *You're* supporting Dan."

"Yeah, but I was hoping I wouldn't have to support both of them for three months."

"What's three months of supporting *them* compared to seven years of supporting *him*?"

She had a point.

"I know my business," said Desiree. "The fact that Jelly's even heard of Dan is a plus. Some of the others didn't have a clue."

I picked up the photo and looked at it again. "Dan and Jelly, huh? Sounds like a sandwich a child would eat."

She checked her watch and sighed heavily. "We've been at this an hour. What's the holdup?"

I didn't know why I was hesitating. I wanted to get this show on the road more than anything, but for some reason I was having trouble making a decision. "Swear to me that she was never in a loony bin."

"I swear."

"Now swear that she doesn't have any jilted boyfriends who were in a loony bin."

"I swear. Look, it's your call, but I'd give her a shot."

The following Tuesday morning at ten, Jelly bounced over to the reception desk at Manhattan Body and Fitness, signed up to use the treadmill, and watched for Dan to make his entrance. I know this because I was hovering outside, on the street, my nose pressed against the wall-to-wall window. Yeah, I felt pathetic, but less pathetic than if I'd gone there in disguise, which is what I'd contemplated and then dismissed as being utterly out of character. (I was the killjoy who would never even wear costumes to Halloween parties.) What was I doing there when Desiree promised she'd call me with all the details after she spoke to Jelly? I was dying to witness the very first of our fix-ups for myself, that's what. Wouldn't you feel the same way if you were in my situation?

What I could make out from my post outside the gym—my breath kept fogging up the window and I had to keep wiping it clear with the sleeve of my coat—was that as soon as Dan walked into the room in his gym shorts and Giants T-shirt, Jelly hopped off the treadmill and zoomed over to him.

I couldn't hear their conversation, obviously, but she said something and he said something and she smiled and he smiled. Then she said something and he laughed, like it was the funniest thing he'd ever heard, and I thought, Wow, wouldn't it be wild if I nailed him with the first one? I know, I know. A two-minute exchange wasn't the stuff of long-term relationships, but it was better than a total kiss-off.

I continued to play the stalker until my cell phone blared the "William Tell Overture."

I reached into my purse and grabbed it, irritated by the interruption.

"What?" I hissed into the phone.

"It's Steffi," said my assistant. "I'm standing outside Ornbacher's suite at the Waldorf. Did you forget that Gary's here to meet with him about his taxes?"

"Oh, God." I hadn't forgotten about the meeting exactly. I'd spent the previous night preparing for it, even calling Gary, our top CPA, at home to discuss it. I'd assumed I would simply pop over to the gym, take a quick look at Dan and Jelly to see if they were clicking, and be at the hotel before the meeting started.

"When they called to ask where you were, I figured I should run over here myself. I saw your folder on your desk when I came in this morning, so I brought it with me. I can refer to your notes."

"Great. But I really should be there too," I said, my stomach in knots. "Can you stall them a little?"

"I'll try," she said.

"You're a lifesaver," I said. "I'll get there as fast as I can, I promise."

"Don't stress about it," she said, always my steady backup. "Where are you, by the way?"

"I'm—" I trusted Steffi, as I've said. She was more than my right hand. She was the young woman I'd once been—smart and industrious and willing to do whatever it took to advance within the company, no matter how menial the task. Still, I couldn't possibly explain to her that I was spying on my ex-husband and the woman I was trying to shove down his throat. "I'm—coming," I said vaguely and hung up.

I lingered for a few seconds, unable to tear myself away from Dan and Jelly, before finally getting into a cab. As I was leaving, they were still chatting up a storm, smiling and laughing, laughing and smiling.

My God, I thought. If he really liked her—

Well, the mere prospect made me so giddy I tipped the cab driver an extra five dollars.

I got out at the Waldorf and told the front desk clerk at the exclusive Towers wing of the hotel that I needed the suite number for Mr. Ornbacher.

"Name?" asked the clerk, a handsome young blond man who looked eerily like Dan. Or was I just having a psychotic break?

"Melanie Banks," I said. "I'm late and they're expecting me up there, so could you just—"

"I see your name on the list, Ms. Banks, but the meeting's over," he said.

I dropped my briefcase onto the marble floor. "Over?"

"There's nobody up there. I saw Mr. Ornbacher leave about five minutes ago."

I just stood at the desk staring at the guy. Not speaking. Not moving. Not breathing.

"Ms. Banks?" he said, snapping me out of my stupor.

"Yes. Right. The meeting's over," I said.

I picked up my briefcase. It felt heavy suddenly, as if there were weights in it. How could a morning that had gotten off to such a promising start go so terribly wrong?

When I arrived at the office, I thanked Steffi for saving my ass by going to the meeting in my place.

"You're very welcome," she said. "But Jed was upset that you weren't there."

"How upset?"

"He said to tell you he was beginning to think—and I quote—'that gal's twenty-four/seven speech was bullshit.' "

"Oh, God. I should have called him on my cell and given him the family emergency story again."

"Was there a family emergency?" she asked tentatively, as if she didn't want to accuse me of lying. She was so respectful.

"I'm trying very hard to settle a sticking point in my divorce" was how I phrased my answer.

She nodded. "I'm here if you need me. But *please* be on time for your eleven-thirty with Bernie."

Bernie. Oh. Normally, I looked forward to my Tuesday meetings with him. It was my weekly opportunity for a one-on-one with him, my chance to tout my accomplishments without interruption. But on this particular Tuesday, I didn't have much to tout, except the possible match between my ex and Desiree's client, and I doubted he'd want to hear about that.

Nevertheless, the meeting got under way in his office at eleven-thirty on the dot. He'd heard about the Waldorf incident, and instead of launching into his usual diatribe about interest rates and the tyranny of Alan Greenspan, he reiterated how concerned he was about my recent distractions.

"You were the one who made the pitch to Jed that sealed the deal," he said, "so I'm inclined to keep you on his account."

"Keep me—" How could there be any doubt that Jed was mine? I was Pierce, Shelley's top gun. Of course I would stay on the account. Yes, I'd screwed up a couple of times, but I'd do better. As soon as Dan was no longer a drain on my—

"Did you find a professional to help you deal with the alimony thing?" said Bernie.

"Yes," I said.

"How's it going?" he asked.

"It's still early, but I'm giving it everything I've got."

To prove the point, I dashed out of his office right after the meeting and called Dan on his cell. Perhaps he and Jelly were still at the gym. Perhaps they were sipping power juices and exchanging phone numbers. Perhaps they were making plans to live together for ninety days. I had to know, had to stay on top of the situation.

"Hello?" he said.

"Hi, it's Melanie," I said.

"What did I do this time?" he said.

"Do?" I had to think of a reason for the call. A good reason, not necessarily an honest reason. "Buster's been itching and scratching since you dropped him off yesterday," I lied, buying time until he dropped a clue about Jelly. "Did you give him his flea and tick medicine?"

"Same as always. Maybe he's got an allergy to you, darlin'."

"Very funny." Pause. "Gosh, have I caught you at the gym?"

"I gave you my schedule, Mel. You know exactly where I am."

"It must have slipped my mind. Are you, um, with a trainer?"

"Nope," he said.

"All by yourself?"

"Nope."

"So you're with someone?"

"Is that why you called? To play Twenty Questions?"

"I was just curious, because of Buster. Maybe the person you're with knows about dogs and why they scratch themselves if there's no flea and tick problem."

"Hang on, I'll ask her."

Her! Be still, my heart!

And then I heard him ask his companion, "Are you a dog person, Jelly?"

Well, I nearly did a cartwheel right there in the hall. So he liked her enough to still be talking to her! What a great, great start!

"Hey, Dan?" I said.

"Just a second. I'm asking her—"

"Never mind. I'm in the middle of my workday, so I've gotta run."

I hung up beaming. I stuck the phone in my pocket, picked my head up, and swaggered down the hall, to my office. My mood change must have been obvious because Steffi remarked that I looked more relaxed than I had in a while.

"Things have taken a favorable turn," I said, because I really thought they had.

Chapter 10

The next morning I called Desiree.

"Did she stay over?" I asked breathlessly, having tossed and turned the entire night, imagining Dan sharing his bed—my old bed—with Jelly. No, I didn't picture them in graphic sexual detail. I wasn't a complete psycho. I just sort of envisioned them in this gauzy, dreamy, wish-fulfillment scenario that ended with his begging her to pack her bags and move in with him and her jumping for joy and saying yes and me ratting him out to some family law judge and then buying myself a nifty apartment, maybe even my old apartment. Totally unrealistic, I know, but I wasn't at my realistic best.

"I told you before. My girls aren't sluts," said Desiree. "When they sign up with me, the first thing I tell them is: don't give away the store until the third date."

"Why the third date?"

"Because it's the Desiree Klein Heart Hunting way of doing things, that's why, and it works."

"Right." If memory served, Weezie and Nards did it on the second date, and it hadn't affected their relationship adversely. But whatever. "I was just eager for some feedback from Jelly."

"I spoke to her a few minutes ago."

"And?"

"She liked Dan."

"That's wonderful!"

"She thought he was very handsome."

"She should have seen him ten years ago."

"And she enjoyed listening to the stories about his playing days."

"They're great if you haven't heard them a million times."

"And she said he wasn't an egomaniac like a lot of professional athletes."

"You have to have an actual job to be an egomaniac."

"But here's the bad news: he didn't ask for her number. He just said, 'See you again sometime,' and went to take a shower. She was really disappointed."

"She's not the only one." Crap. "It must have been the hair."

"What?"

"I warned you. Dan's not attracted to women with ringlets."

"She says it was her remark about her brother."

"What's her brother got to do with this?"

"They were talking about their families and she mentioned that she had a brother who was always borrowing money from her and spending it on things like clothes and cars and trips. She said to Dan, 'He has absolutely no shame when it comes to taking from me. What kind of a man acts like that?' She could tell by the look on his face that something was wrong. I guess he soured on her right then."

"You think?"

"Hey, it's not her fault. We were the ones who didn't tip her off about Dan's situation."

"Dan's situation," I muttered. "It's my situation, and I need to get out of it. I hired you to help me get out of it, Desiree."

"Relax, would you? I've got plenty of other girls. All shapes and sizes. Later in the month I'll go through my files and you can come—"

"Later in the month? I don't think you're getting the urgency here."

"And I don't think you're getting that your five grand only buys you one date per month."

"I doubled your fee. I'm entitled to as many dates as you can scare up."

I needed to calm down. Acting all pushy wasn't a smart move. If I really pissed her off, she could tell Dan what I was up to and blow the whole deal. "I'd really appreciate it if we could pick another client right away," I said sweetly. "Are you free this afternoon, by any chance?"

"I suppose."

Contestant number two was Rochelle, a former ballet dancer who currently designed websites. Desiree maintained that dance and football were both sports and that the two of them were bound to find common ground. I had my doubts, given Dan's antipathy for anything with cultural significance. Besides, Rochelle looked awfully skinny in her photo, and he had always liked that I had meat on my bones. But Desiree kept promoting her, so I finally agreed.

Rochelle and Dan met at the Post House, the restaurant where he ate lunch after the gym. She reserved a table for herself, sat in the back right next to him, caught his attention, and eventually got herself invited over to his table. I know this, not because I was peering at them through the window, but because I stopped by the restaurant earlier that day and paid the maître d' to spy for me. I was a busy executive, and it would be a much more efficient use of my time, I'd decided.

The maître d's name was Fred, and he was one of those brusque, old-style maître d's who work at the same place forever and have no aspirations of being, like, a screenwriter. At first he was protective of Dan and nearly took my head off about what a loyal customer he was. But within five minutes, the guy was in my pocket.

"Will this cover it?" I said, sliding a twenty across the table.

"A hundred will cover it."

"How's fifty?"

He shook his head. "A hundred bucks and I'll squeal like a pig."

So I paid him his hundred. He promised to call me at the office with a full report about Dan and Rochelle the minute they left. We also agreed that, should there be future occasions where I required his assistance, he'd be available. At the same price.

It amazed me how quickly he was willing to sell out his "loyal customer," but such was life. As for that wad of cash, no, I wasn't crazy about parting with it, but I cleaved to the dictum I'd learned in business school: there are times when you've got to spend money to make money.

Fred checked in about three o'clock. Apparently, Dan bought Rochelle a Bloody Mary, which she barely touched. He bought her a steak, and she didn't touch that either. Nor did she touch the baked potato with sour cream and chives, the creamed spinach with minced onions, or the cheesecake with fresh strawberries. Fred was clearly more interested in who ate what than in who liked whom.

"She's a ballet dancer," I said. "She probably eats lettuce for lunch."

"Nope," he said. "He bought her a salad, and she hardly touched that."

"Did they seem to have good chemistry?" I asked. "I mean, was there any physical contact?"

"He had his hands on her blouse."

"He was pawing her in public?" I said with a mixture of excitement and revulsion.

"Nah, he was mopping her up. She spilled the Bloody Mary on herself. It was the one sip she took, and it ended up all over her."

"Not very coordinated for a dancer," I said. "Did you notice anything else?"

"I heard her say she'd love to."

"Love to what, Fred?"

"I didn't catch that part."

"This is what I get for my hundred dollars? Fragments of sentences?"

"You wanted the whole conversation, you should have paid me more. I would have put a bug under the table."

Later, I called Desiree to see if she'd heard from Rochelle.

"Good news," she clucked. "They're going out tomorrow night."

"He asked her out?" I said, practically leaping out of my chair. It was late and I was the only one left in the office. My voice echoed through the empty corridors.

"She was the one who asked him out, but a date's a date."

The night of the date was a nerve-wracking one for me. As I sat on my bed with Buster on my lap, my back propped up against the fake-walnut headboard, I was fixated on whether Dan held Rochelle's arm when they crossed the street, whether he kissed her good night when he brought her home, whether he brought her home at all and instead took her to his place.

Or should I say our place. I sighed as I looked around my bleak, impersonal studio in the Heartbreak Hotel with its I'm-only-living-here-temporarily vibe. It was fine, sure. Not a total rat hole. It's just that our old apartment was special. It was a home. The only one I'd ever known. Instead of facing a dark alley, it had sweeping views of the city that used to make Dan shake his head and say, "I'm definitely not in Minco anymore." It was dated and tired when we'd bought it, but after our renovation it was spectacular. I remember standing in the threshold and thinking, This apartment will be my security. I'll hold on tight and never let it go.

What a fool, huh? Who would have guessed that not only would my ex get to keep it but that I'd get to pay him to keep it.

"Well, we'll just see about that, Buster," I said, rubbing my face up against my dog's. "We're not giving up without a fight."

Buster snorted, jumped down from the bed, and trotted off to the tiny alcove that was my kitchen with its miniature appliances. They reminded me of the ones Weezie gave her daughter as toys, so she could "pretend cook."

I got up and followed my dog to make sure there was enough water in his bowl in case he was thirsty. While I was there, I decided it was time to throw out the stack of newspapers I'd allowed to pile up on the floor. I bundled them up, told Buster I'd be right back, and headed for the trash room at the end of my floor—locking myself out of the apartment in the process. As soon as I heard the door slam behind me, I realized I was in trouble. I'm serious. I was wearing only a T-shirt over my underpants. That was it. Not exactly the appropriate attire for prancing around the building in search of the super.

Oh, and did I mention it was 10 P.M.?

I might as well have been stark naked the way I skulked over to Patty's apartment, praying no one would see me.

I rang her bell, put my mouth right up to her door and whispered, "It's me. Melanie. Let me in, okay?"

Nothing. I pressed my ear to the door. No target practice. Not even the hum of the TV. Patty was either out or out cold.

Now what? I thought, sliding down onto the floor, so I could cover my tush with the T-shirt while I tried to get a handle on my predicament. I couldn't just go knocking on my neighbors' doors. They were all strangers. Well, except for Evan Gillespie, who was practically a stranger. What's more, the last time he'd seen me, I'd rejected his overture to come over and look at his paintings. And then there was that piece of cheese/snot dangling from my nose, which had rendered me unappetizing as well as unfriendly.

God, how could I possibly show up on his doorstep half-dressed and ask for his help?

Because I had nobody else. The realization of how alone I was—not just in the hall that night, but in general—depressed me. There were a couple of colleagues at work whom I saw socially, when we made a conscious effort to clear our schedules, and there was Weezie, although she had a full life with Nards and the kids and lived an hour away in Connecticut. But no big, boisterous circle of buddies. Dan had been my best friend once, which was only natural. A husband is supposed to be your best friend, but then what happens when he falls away?

You're stuck in the dimly lit hallway of the Heartbreak Hotel, that's what, wishing you could crawl into the carpet.

I allowed myself a few more minutes of self-pity then picked myself up. I yanked on the bottom of the T-shirt, stretching it, stretching it, stretching it so that it just covered my privates. And then I padded in my bare feet and bare legs over to Apartment 3F.

Please let him be by himself, I thought as I rang the bell. If there's a party in progress and ten people rush out to have a look at the wacko from 3A, I'll die.

Just then, the door opened.

Evan was alone, it appeared, and understandably surprised to see me. He was wearing a smock over his jeans, and it was splattered with paint. Even his finely etched face had paint splotches here and there. I must have interrupted Picasso at work.

"Uh, hi," I said, continuing to pull on the T-shirt. The only problem there was that, while pulling on it made it longer around my crotch, it also made it sheerer around my chest. A no-win situation.

"Hi," he said, looking me up and down. His expression was sort of a cross between squelching a laugh and trying to figure out what was going on. "Melanie, right?"

"Right." I started winding a lock of my hair around my finger and twirling it.

He nodded, continuing to eye me. "I remember inviting you over to see my work. I just don't remember you saying yes."

"I'm sorry. I didn't come to look at paintings," I said, utterly mortified but relieved that he was home.

"No paintings, huh?" He checked out my state of undress again and smiled. "Then you must have liked me more than you let on."

I felt my face flush deeply. It had been so long since a man flirted with me, let alone ran his eyes over my body (not counting Jed Ornbacher) that I found it extremely unsettling. "I hate to bother you, but the reason I'm here is because I locked myself out of my apartment and I can't really go asking the super for his key like this. I was wondering if you'd help me."

He crossed his arms over his chest and didn't even try to conceal his amusement. "You want me to lend you some pants?"

"No."

"A longer shirt than the one you've got on?"

"No. I would appreciate it if you'd go downstairs and ask the super of this fine establishment to give you the key to my apartment."

"Supers don't hand out keys to anybody who asks for them. At least, they shouldn't."

"But you're not anybody. You're my neighbor. You could explain the situation to him."

I was desperate, and he could see that, so he toned down the teasing and offered his solution.

"Come." He motioned me inside 3F. "First you'll call him and explain it to him yourself. And then I'll go downstairs and get your key. It'll all work out just fine if we do it that way."

"Okay." Despite the awkwardness of the situation, I liked listening to him. Whether it was the unique cadence of his voice or the reassuring way he spoke to me, I liked it.

He took off the smock he'd been wearing over his turtleneck and handed it to me. "Why don't you cover yourself with this while I find the man's number. You're probably cold."

I liked that he cared if I was cold too. I thanked him and put on the smock, paint and all. While he went rummaging around in his backpack to look for the phone number, I glanced around his apartment. It was supposed to be furnished just like mine, Patty's, and all the others, but he must have moved some pieces out because all I saw in that studio was the sofa, the coffee table, and the bed. The rest of the space was filled with art stuff—bins of brushes, piles of drawings and photographs, and canvases in various states of completion, one of which was propped up on an easel.

Intrigued, I walked over to take a closer look.

It was a colorful oil painting of the sea during a storm, on a Caribbean island, possibly. Along with the blues and greens and even pinks of the water and sky, there were a couple of fishing boats in the scene, their crews struggling to stay afloat. The painting was amazingly three-dimensional—as accurate and realistic as a photograph but so much more vivid. I was entranced.

"It's called *Summer Squall*," said Evan when he came back and caught me appraising his work. "I painted it in the Bahamas last summer after I got fired. I'm just doing some touch-ups now."

"It's beautiful," I said. "I feel as if I'm right there."

"Glad you weren't. We all got soaked that day."

"But nobody drowned or anything?"

"Not a soul. It was one of those five-minute thunder boomers. They have them almost every afternoon." His dark eyes shone at the memory. Obviously, he was a man who enjoyed the outdoors. An adventurer.

"Do you sell in galleries or is this just something to fill your time while you look for another publishing job?"

"I'm not looking for another publishing job," he said. "Not after I was replaced by a woman barely out of college whose only work experience was at MTV. I met her once, and she actually confused Thomas Pynchon with Monty Python."

"Why do you think she got your job?"

"Because she's the right demographic—young and female and a reader of chick lit. Haven't you noticed that men are becoming obsolete in this society? It's all about what women want now."

His speech sounded like Nards's. "Do you really believe that? Women are doing well, but men are still running the world."

"For now. Meanwhile, those of us who aren't running it are getting nudged aside. I'm lucky I have my paintings to fall back on. And yes, I do sell them—to private collectors through word of mouth. Galleries are for people who want trophy art."

In other words, he was talented but clueless about how to market himself. Another Dan, for God's sake. No wonder his wife got fed up and threw him out. Still, he was awfully attractive.

"Here's the super's number," he said, passing along a business card. "Give him a call, and I'll run down and get your key."

"I appreciate it." I called the super, arranged everything, hung up. "It's all set."

"Then off I go."

"You sure you don't mind?"

"Not at all." He smiled, little creases forming around his eyes. "Now that I've vented about how mighty women are, I think I'll relish the thought of rescuing a damsel in distress."

As he headed out the door, it occurred to me that no one had ever referred to me as a damsel in distress. I was Melanie Banks. I was accomplished. I was empowered. I had always fended for myself. I wasn't in the habit of being rescued. What I didn't expect, as I watched Evan go out the door, was that it felt kind of nice to be rescued for a change, to depend on someone else to do the heavy lifting.

I'll have Steffi send him one of those delicious fruit baskets to show my gratitude, I thought. Since he's a bumbo, he'll be thrilled with some free food. Of course, as soon as his ex starts sending the checks, he won't be the starving artist anymore. He'll probably move to the Bahamas and buy a place right on the water—with her money.

I sighed, sank onto his sofa, and resumed my obsessing about my ex's date with the ballerina/Web designer. It was nearly eleven now. Maybe they had already gone back to Dan's and were making out on my old living room sofa right that very minute. Maybe they were getting so carried away with each other that Rochelle would be powerless in the face of her lust, blow off Desiree's third-date rule, and decide to sleep with him after all.

I allowed myself a smile. If they did spend the night together, that would only leave eighty-nine nights to go.

Chapter 11

Evan returned with the key and insisted on walking me back to my apartment. After all that gallantry, I figured that the least I could do was invite him in for a minute. He'd been very decent, and while my focus was on Dan and whether he was or wasn't having a good time with Rochelle that night, I wasn't completely without manners.

"I'd love to, but I've got the painting to finish up," he said.

"It's almost midnight," I said. "Do you always work so late?"

I laughed when I heard myself. Like I didn't work late nearly every night of the week?

"I told you, painting's my passion," he said. "My wife would give you an earful on that subject. She's a successful real estate agent, and even she keeps more reasonable hours."

I bet she'd give me an earful, I thought, picturing a woman at the end of her rope after enduring her husband's layoff, his affair with his paintbrush, and his financial dependence on her. "Patty told me you're recently separated," I said.

"True," he said. "Kaitlin and I are hammering out the details of the divorce now, but I have a feeling it'll go smoothly."

Yeah, smoothly from your perspective. You'll get everything while Kaitlin, the one with the misfortune of having the bank account, will get zilch. "And then I guess you'll be moving out of the Heartbreak Hotel?"

"That's the plan. But then I don't see you staying here forever, Melanie." His eyes locked onto mine with such intensity that I had to look away. Yeah, he was cute, but so what? They were all cute and look what good it did anybody?

"Right you are," I said. "As a matter of fact, I'm hammering out a plan of my own. It should have me out of here in a little over three months."

"Maybe you'll tell me about it sometime."

"Maybe. Anyhow, thanks again for the help with the key."

He bowed at the waist. "Just being a good neighbor."

"I owe you one."

"I'll remember that. The next time I lock myself out of my place, I'll come knocking."

"And I'll try to be fully dressed for the occasion."

I looked down at myself and realized I was still wearing Evan's smock. I started to whip it over my head so I could give it back to him, but as I did, the T-shirt that was underneath it stuck to it—we're talking about major static cling—so that I nearly whipped them both off at the same time. What I'm saying is that I flashed the guy. In one extremely ungraceful move, I managed to expose both my tits *and* my ass. I'd never been so thoroughly embarrassed in my life. Normally, I was a buttoned-up type, cloaked in my armor of business suits, the last woman in the world to go around showing skin. Now Evan had seen my skin.

"Gotta go," I said, practically slamming the door in his face, then opening it a crack, passing him the smock, and slamming it again.

"I've seen breasts before, Melanie," he whispered out in the hall, "and they're nothing to be ashamed of."

"You haven't seen mine before!" I called back. "And I wouldn't count on ever seeing them again!"

There was a chuckle, then footsteps, then he was gone.

They went to a Knicks game," said Desiree. It was the next day, about one-thirty in the afternoon, and she was only just getting back to me after I'd called her office three times.

"And?" I said.

"Rochelle raved about the seats. They were right down in front, where all the big shots sit."

"I know all about those seats," I said. "They're season tickets and guess who paid for them."

"Well, she was impressed."

"Was she impressed with Dan too?" Oh, please God.

"She said he was a lot of fun. Easygoing, quick with the jokes, knowledgeable about the game. Oh, and he made sure to introduce her whenever somebody came over to talk to him."

"What a guy. How did it go after the game? Did they stop somewhere for a nightcap? Or did they just head back to her place?"

"She wishes. He put her in a cab, gave the driver a twenty, and sent her home by herself."

"No!" I was crushed. We were 0 for 2.

"He told her he had a headache."

"That's what Advil's for. Why didn't she drag him over to a drugstore and buy him some?"

"He said it was a migraine."

"Dan doesn't get migraines, Desiree. He was ditching *your* client." Weezie and Nards had promised that Desiree Klein was a matchmaking genius. So far, I wasn't seeing evidence of that.

"You're blaming me?" she said, her voice getting all screechy.

"Well, you're the one who's supposed to come up with women he'll be attracted to, not repelled by."

"I thought he'd be attracted to Rochelle."

"She was too skinny for him. He likes them not to look like they'll blow away in a light breeze." I sighed, deflated. "I get the feeling you're holding out on me, Desiree. You're not giving me the cream of the crop here. Where are the ones with the looks and the personality and the careers? Why aren't we fixing Dan up with one of them?"

"Because I pair my A-list women with my A-list men, and Dan isn't even a C-lister."

"Then how come both Jelly and Rochelle were disappointed that he wasn't interested? Obviously, there are women out there who want to spend time with him. Can't we at least try him out on one of your best ones?"

"I don't know."

"Come on, Desiree," I pleaded. "I really need this to happen."

"Fine. Pay me an extra thousand and I'll give him Leah."

"An extra thousand? What makes her worth that?" I sounded like a john bargaining with a madam, didn't I?

"She's a prize, that's what. She's only been a client for a month, and I don't expect her to be on the singles market long."

"How old is she?"

"Thirty-one."

"Pretty?"

"She has the face of an angel and the body of a stripper. A knockout in anyone's book, but she doesn't flaunt it. Not even the silky brown hair, the kind you see in those shampoo commercials. Trust me, she's as bee-uteeful on the inside as she is on the outside."

"What does this paragon do for a living?"

"She's a veterinarian with her own practice, so your dog will love her."

"Buster doesn't have to love her. Dan does."

"How could he not? She's independent but also nurturing, carefree but also sensible, sexy but also—"

"As pure as the driven snow. I get the point. But if she's so perfect, how come she needs you to find her a man?"

"Because she's picky, like all my A-listers. So if you want me to set her up with Dan, it's gonna cost you."

What could I say? Leah sounded so great I was ready to move in with her myself.

That night Weezie came into the city and met me for dinner at the Hungarian place next to the Heartbreak Hotel. It was sweet of her to drive all the way down to Hell's Kitchen, and she could certainly have afforded to eat at a fancier place, but she insisted that she found my neighborhood "exciting and eclectic." I promised that I'd meet her closer to her neighborhood the next time.

I was surprised that Nards wasn't with her—they were one of those couples who are so compatible that they do everything together—but she explained that he was home nursing a bad back and wailing about it.

"You know doctors," she said. "They're the worst patients."

"Otherwise, life is good?" I said as we sipped martinis. I never drank martinis except when I was with Weezie, next to whom I always felt like such a wimp. She could handle anything, even a drink that tasted like kerosene.

"Better than good," she said. "The kids are doing well in school. My parents are healthy—they're off on a cruise, in fact. I'm chairing the historical society fund-raiser this spring. And Nards has so much business that he's decided to bring another doctor into the practice."

" 'Better than good' is right and I couldn't be more envious, but do you ever feel—I don't know—ambivalent about not having a career anymore?"

"I have a career," she said with a hearty laugh. "It's called being a wife and mother."

"Of course," I said. "I didn't mean to imply that you weren't working as hard as you did at Pierce, Shelley."

"Harder. *You* try juggling everything I juggle. And no, I don't feel ambivalent about it at all. Why the question?"

"I guess I've been thinking about men lately."

She smiled. "That's a positive sign. Anybody in particular?"

"God, no. Nothing like that. It's just that I had this conversation with a new neighbor—his name is Evan—and it stirred me up."

"He stirred you up?" she said with a twinkle in her eye.

"The conversation did," I said with emphasis. "He was talking about how men are being nudged aside in our culture, while women are zooming ahead. Sort of the same thing Nards was talking about on Christmas Eve. It was interesting hearing it from someone else's point of view."

"Did he lose his job?"

I nodded. "He said it was reverse sexism."

"Sour grapes."

"Maybe. But I can sort of see how it must drive men crazy when they're told they're not the 'right demographic.' "

"Come on. Women of past generations had to listen to that for years."

"But those same women waged a battle to get into the best business schools and law schools and medical schools. Now we get into them without even having to think about it. We land the top jobs and then we give it all up to raise children. Well, you did. Lots of women do. I'm just saying that if I were a guy, I might hate us."

"They can hate us all they want, but that's no excuse for curling up in the fetal position and sucking their thumb. Some of the mothers at my kids' school—the mothers of boys—were complaining the other day that the educational system favors girls and that their sons are failing as a result. So ridiculous."

"Is it, Weezie? Then why *are* so many boys falling behind and dropping out of the system?"

"Because when the going gets tough, they sit on their asses

playing video games instead of putting themselves out there. They lack our survival instinct, which is why they die before we do."

I laughed. "Dan won't die before I do. He exists just to torment me."

"This alimony thing has really shaken you up, hasn't it?"

"More than I realized. Instead of getting on with my life, I spend much too much time obsessing about it. It's unhealthy and I know it, but I can't help myself."

"Hey, you got a raw deal—especially since you stayed with Dan longer than most women would have."

"I loved him, Weezie."

"I know you did. I liked him a lot myself, until he turned into someone who couldn't handle not being the big man on campus anymore." She sipped her drink. She'd ordered the restaurant's house martini, which, of course, had paprika in it. "It was painful watching how the two of you went in opposite directions. The higher you rose, the lower he sank, speaking of boys who drop out."

"So you understand why I'm crazed?"

"Who wouldn't be?" she said. "But now you're in Desiree's capable hands. How's it going with her?"

"Her capable hands weren't so capable with her first two clients."

"Maybe Dan's not ready for a new woman. Maybe he's still hot for you."

"Yeah, right. We wouldn't even be speaking to each other if it weren't for Buster." Still hot for me. That was a joke. He couldn't stand the sight of me, and the feeling was mutual. "No, he just didn't click with the two she set him up with. But now she's bringing out the heavy artillery. Tomorrow afternoon, a woman named Leah Purcell will take a walk in Central Park, where he'll just happen to be playing football. She's one of Desiree's A-list clients, whatever that means, so I'm cautiously optimistic."

"Dan doesn't have a clue what's going on?"

"None. Neither do the women. Desiree just tells them that he's a former pro athlete with too much pride to be fixed up by a professional matchmaker. She sells them a line about how a dear friend of his came to her instead, begging her to find him someone. Since there are so few eligible bachelors around, these women are desperate enough to actually buy it."

"Desiree can sell anyone anything."

"So I'm learning. How well did you get to know her when you were a client?"

"Not very well. Who can penetrate those wigs?"

I laughed. "Any idea if there's a Mr. Klein?"

"There was a Mr. Klein and three other husbands."

"She was married to four men?"

"And divorced each one."

"Great. So this four-time loser is giving everybody else advice about love?" And I had put my life in her hands?

"You know the expression: 'Those who can, do; those who can't, teach.' Look at the smart advice she gave me. Nards isn't the most ambitious guy in the world or even the handsomest, but she convinced me that he was a better catch than all the rest because he's hardworking and dependable—qualities that are scarce in men, as we've established. I told you, she's a matchmaking genius."

"An expensive matchmaking genius."

"If she gets you out of the alimony, she deserves whatever you're paying her."

"Okay. I'll drink to that."

We raised our glasses in anticipation of a toast.

"To Desiree," said Weezie.

"To Leah," I said. "May she be the woman of Dan's dreams."

"And the answer to your prayers," she added.

We clinked glasses and downed the martinis.

Chapter 12

You've heard of wishing on a star? Well, I'd wished on a martini, and it worked. Leah showed up in Central Park, struck up a conversation with Dan, and lit his fire in a way that no woman—well, no woman since yours truly—had in years.

"Desiree Klein delivers!" said the engineer of this wondrous pairing when she called me at the office with the news.

Usually, my eyes glaze over when people start speaking of themselves in the third person, but I bolted straight up in my chair. "Leah and Dan liked each other?"

"An understatement," she said. "I think they're in love."

"Give me a break, Desiree," I said. "Nobody falls in love that fast."

As soon as I said it, I realized it wasn't true. *I* had fallen in love that fast. With Dan. But we were young and naive back then. Mere children.

"I'm telling you, Melanie, they clicked big time. Do I know my business or do I know my business?"

"Why don't you slow down and take me through this," I said, conscious of not wanting to get my hopes up. Maybe they did flip for each other, but what good would it do if their attraction only lasted one night?

"It all started after Leah showed up in the park toward the end of Dan's game yesterday," said Desiree. "She introduced herself to him and mentioned that she was a Giants fan. He asked her to stick around so he could buy her a drink."

"Go on," I said, pleased that it was Dan who'd initiated the date this time.

"The drink turned into dinner, which turned into a marathon yak session at her apartment. She said they talked until two o'clock in the morning!"

This information totally stopped me in my tracks. Sure, Dan could be charming when he wanted to be, but talkative? By the end of our marriage, the best he could grunt out was: "Do I have any clean underwear?"

"You mean he trotted out all his football stories and Leah was a good listener," I said.

"They didn't even bother with that stuff," said Desiree. "They got right into heavy issues—politics, the environment, the challenges they've each faced in life."

I laughed. "Dan's biggest challenge is getting up in the morning. His second biggest challenge is deciding what to have for breakfast."

"Speaking of that, the two of them had breakfast together. At seven-thirty."

"Now I know you're kidding. The only time Dan sees seven-thirty is when he's coming home from an all-nighter."

"According to Leah, the time was his idea. He knew she had to be at her office at nine, and he was respectful of that. The breakfast was his idea too. He said he felt so stimulated by their late-night conversation, he wanted to keep it going."

I was speechless. Dan getting up early? Dan discussing world peace? Dan doing anything other than sitting around feeling sorry for himself? This was downright bizarre.

"There's more," Desiree went on. "They're seeing each other again tonight. She's making him dinner."

"My, my. With all those other delightful qualities, she manages to be a cook too?"

"She's A-list, all right. They're doing construction in her kitchen—she's having a new double oven installed—so she's making them dinner at his place."

I bit my lip as I thought of my old kitchen. It had lovely glass-paned white cabinets and dark green granite countertops, along with gleaming, state-of-the-art stainless-steel appliances that I'd never used but appreciated nonetheless. Someday it would all be mine again. As soon as I didn't have to pay Dan anymore.

"Did Leah tell you what she found so mesmerizing about my ex?" I asked. "You didn't think he'd be good enough for her."

"She said he reminded her of a yellow Lab that had been neglected."

"Neglected? He takes better care of himself than anybody. His dry cleaning bills equal the gross national product of small countries."

"I guess she meant emotionally. She said Labs are her favorite breed, because they thrive with just a little tender loving care and become loyal to you forever."

"Please. Dan becomes loyal to you the minute he senses you'll keep him in Hugo Boss suits."

"Look, I know it's only the beginning, but right now she's crazy about him and he's crazy about her, so don't look a gift horse in the mouth."

Desiree was right. It was all good.

Of course, a lingering question was this: would Leah stay over at Dan's after playing chef? Technically, it would be her third date with him, if you counted dinner the night before as her first and breakfast the next morning as her second. So if she bought Desiree's dumb rule about not giving away the store, she'd be in the clear for a legitimate sleepover and I could start the clock on their cohabitation.

But even if she did spend the night at Dan's as well as the next eighty-nine nights after that, how would I document it? My lawyer would need proof of any breach in our settlement. I had to have a concrete plan for getting that proof, a strategy for trapping my ex. Was I jumping the gun by trying to trap him so soon in his relationship with Leah? He had literally just met her after all, and it was more than remotely possible that their "love" would fizzle out before it had time to work to my advantage. But what if it didn't fizzle out and they did move in together and, because I was overly cautious, I missed even a day? I couldn't. I wouldn't.

An idea came to me as I arrived home that breezy, chilly night in January. I was standing in front of the Heartbreak Hotel, juggling my groceries, my mail, my briefcase, and my purse and feeling like a total klutz as they all came spilling out of my arms, when Evan appeared. My first thought was: does this man always have to see me when I'm at my most awkward?

"Hey," he said. "Looks like you could use a hand there, little lady." He was wearing his cracked leather jacket and jeans, and his hair was windblown, flying in all directions. He looked very appealing with his lanky body and dark eyes, but it was how nice he was that struck me most.

"I hate to bother you again," I said as I bent down to pick everything up.

"No bother," he said and joined me on the ground.

As we both scrounged for my purse at the exact same second, our heads collided—ouch!—and we fell back onto the street, each rubbing the spot on our forehead where we'd made contact and laughing like a couple of silly kids.

"You could get hurt helping me," I said after catching my breath.

He smiled. "I'll take my chances."

I smiled too. I'd come home with a million things on my mind, including how to document Dan's sleeping arrangements with Leah, but for that brief, spontaneous moment on the street with Evan Gillespie, I didn't want to be anywhere else. I was glad that I'd run into him, glad to be in his company, and the realization surprised me. Yes, he was kind and considerate and handsome, but I hardly knew him. And what he knew of me wasn't even accurate. I wasn't supporting Dan out of the goodness of my heart, as he thought I was. Far from it. And then there was the fact that I had no interest—none whatsoever—in getting involved with another bumbo.

He continued to rescue me (he even invoked the "damsel in distress" label again). As he helped me gather up the assorted items that had fallen, my thoughts drifted back to Dan, as they always did. I began to refocus on the matter of who would keep track of whether or not Leah stayed over. Who would agree to be my spy? Who?

"Well, I guess that's everything," said Evan once we were upright, all my possessions safely back in my arms. "This is what we get for not living in a building with a doorman, right?"

"Doormen sure are handy," I agreed. "Except when you have to tip them at Christmas."

And then the solution to my latest Dan problem dawned on me: Ricardo.

"Want to stop by for a glass of wine once you get your stuff unpacked and put away?" Evan asked as we walked up the three flights together. He held my elbow as we mounted the stairs, was careful of me, protective. I noticed and I was grateful. "This very thoughtful neighbor of mine sent me an enormous basket with all kinds of fruit and cheese, so we won't go hungry."

"Oh," I said, remembering I'd asked Steffi to send it. "The basket. It's just a token of my appreciation for the other night." I felt my face turn as purple as one of Desiree's caftans as I relived the flashing incident.

"I got the basket and now I want to share it," he said. "How about coming over for an hour or so and I'll take a painting break?"

"Can't, sorry," I said. And I was sorry. I would have enjoyed spending more time with Evan, but I had pressing business to attend to.

"You can't or won't come over?" he said as we stood in front of my door.

"I can't," I said. "But I appreciate the offer. Really."

"Hot date?"

Well, yes. But why mention that it was Dan's hot date I was running off to? "Actually, it's that project I've been working on," I said. "It's taking up all my free time, but I think it'll be worth it in the end."

"Sounds mysterious." He arched an eyebrow at me. "You're not plotting a hostile takeover, are you? You can never tell with you financial types."

Since a hostile takeover of Dan was exactly what I was plotting, I simply said good night to Evan and hurried inside my apartment.

I arrived at my old building a few minutes before seven-thirty—late enough for Leah to have already fed Dan a few hors d'oeuvres but early enough for Ricardo to still be on duty. His shift ran from seven-thirty in the morning until seven-thirty in the evening, at which point the night doorman took over.

"Hi, Melanie," said Ricardo after he revolved me through the revolving door into the lobby. "No Buster?"

"No Buster," I said. "I'll be bringing him by on Monday morning."

"Then you came to see Mr. Swain?" He loosened his tie and

wiggled his neck around, the way men do when they're extremely uncomfortable. "He's already got company."

"I'm aware of that, Ricardo. I have no interest in going up there," I assured him. Well, I had *some* interest.

"So how can I help you tonight?"

I linked my arm through his and walked him a few steps away from his post. "Actually, I'm here to help you."

Ricardo and I had never been chummy, so he was understandably puzzled.

"I've been thinking about how well you do your job," I began. "I may not live here anymore, but there's no mistaking what a professional you are. I remember the first time I met you. I thought, Wow. This man gives his very best, day in and day out."

He puffed out his chest. "I try. Sometimes the people here don't appreciate what I do for them. Signing for their FedExes. Locking up their valuables in the storage room. Sending up their Chinese takeout deliveries and getting duck sauce on myself when the bag leaks."

"Who wouldn't appreciate all that?" I said with the proper outrage.

He shrugged. "But I'll tell you who does appreciate it: Mr. Swain. He'll say, 'Here, Ricardo,' and hand me a twenty. Just to be a good guy."

I gritted my teeth as I pictured Dan making similar Lord Bountiful gestures all over town. What fun it must be to be generous with someone else's money, I thought. "As I recall, you have five children to support, so every little bit counts, right?"

"I have six now," he said, clearly pleased to have spread his seed yet again. Never mind that he hadn't gotten around to marrying any of the children's mothers.

"Six, huh? Gosh, that's a lot of mouths to feed."

"You're telling me."

"All the more reason why it's high time I repaid you for all the Chinese takeout deliveries you sent up for *me.*"

"What do you mean?"

I dipped into my wallet, pulled out five hundred dollars, and greased his palm with it. "Buy your kids some toys."

I thought he'd pass out when he saw the amount.

Five hundred was a lot of money, but I figured that even if Leah was a bust, it could be applied to Dan's adventures with Desiree's next client. The main thing was to bond with Ricardo. "You deserve every penny," I said.

He looked at me with shimmering new respect and thanked me over and over. And then he uttered the magic words. "If there's anything I can ever do for you, Melanie, name it."

I feigned surprise, as if the idea of reciprocity had never occurred to me. "There's nothing I need at the moment." I sighed, let a beat go by. Then: "Although I'm worried about Mr. Swain."

"Worried about him? Why?"

"Well, ever since our divorce he's been horribly depressed," I said. "Okay, suicidal, if you want the truth." Ricardo didn't need the truth, so why bother him with it? "I can't sleep at night, knowing he's so down in the dumps that he might—" I instructed my lower lip to quiver.

"Kill himself?" said Ricardo.

I nodded, trying and failing to coax out a couple of tears. "His psychiatrist is very, very concerned."

Ricardo shook his head in amazement. "You could have fooled

me," he said. "He was whistling when he came in this morning, a big smile on his face."

I blinked through my nonexistent tears. "Part of that is the medication they've got him on now. It allows the depression to lift for short periods at a time."

"Like when he plays football in the park?"

"There you go. But his condition is still grave. So we've hired a caretaker for him, a woman named Leah who's supposed to stay with him at night, which is when he's most vulnerable, and prevent him from harming himself."

"You're talking about the babe who's up there now?"

The babe. So Desiree hadn't exaggerated when she'd described Leah. "Yes. The doctor is optimistic that if Leah spends every night with Mr. Swain for three months or so, he'll be free of his suicidal demons and begin to lead a normal life again."

"Man, oh man. This is wild. I had no clue. I'd hate it if something bad happened to him."

I resumed the lip quivering. "Nothing bad will happen if we can be sure that Leah stays up there with him at night."

"Why wouldn't she stay with him? You said she's the caretaker, so she's getting paid for it, right?"

"Right. But not everybody is as trustworthy as you are, Ricardo. Some people slack off on the job."

He looked at his watch and rolled his eyes. "Don't I know it. Donny, my replacement, should have shown up ten minutes ago for the night shift."

"I have to be certain that Leah shows up for the night shift and stays until morning. That's where you come in."

He nodded. "You want me to keep tabs on her?"

"Yes. Yes, I do. And Mr. Swain will be so much better for it."

"Anything for Traffic Dan Swain, Melanie. You too. You're both good people."

I thanked him and reached into my purse again, this time pulling out the small spiral-bound notebook I'd bought on the way over.

"I was planning to stop by here every morning, ask you if Leah had spent the night, and then enter her visitation record in this." I held up the notebook. "It was the doctor's idea. Apparently, Mr. Swain's insurance company requires proof of her consecutive dates of service. Seems like a lot of paperwork for nothing, but chalk it up to the crazy health care system we have in this country."

I know, I know. It's hard to believe I said all this with a straight face, but I did. I'm sorry. It's just that you have to size up the person you're trying to buy off and act accordingly.

"Hey, I've got an idea. Why don't you let me mark down the dates this Leah is taking care of Mr. Swain?" Ricardo offered. "I'm right here every morning. No point in you coming over."

I gasped, as if to show my delight at his suggestion. "Oh, Ricardo. You sure you wouldn't mind?"

"Mind? Nah. Like I said, Mr. Swain has always treated me real good. And now you gave me all that money for my kids. It's the least I can do."

I handed him the notebook. "Then we have a deal. Nothing about this to Mr. Swain or Leah or anyone else, okay? It has to be our secret. Ours and the doctor's. If even a whisper about this came out in the press, Mr. Swain's career would be over." Like it wasn't already.

"Don't even think about it."

I thanked Ricardo again, and he thanked me again, and we

both reiterated our mutual hope that three months under Leah's care would save Dan's life. There was no point in adding that it was mine we'd be saving.

As I walked away, wearing a self-satisfied grin, he called out to me.

"Melanie?"

I turned. "Yes?"

He hurried over to me, the spare change in his pocket jingling as he ran. "We forgot something," he said. "I'm off on weekends, so you'll have to find another way to keep an eye on the caretaker while I'm gone."

Damn. Damn! Ricardo had always seemed so ubiquitous that I really had forgotten he wasn't on duty Saturdays and Sundays. Now what? I needed backup!

"I'll figure it out," I said.

So I'd have to shell out more money. The question was: to whom?

Buster and I spent a quiet weekend together. He whiled away the hours thinking his happy doggie thoughts about food and water and comfy places to park himself, while I whiled away the hours thinking my obsessive human thoughts about Dan and Leah and the comfy place I hoped they were parking themselves. Desiree had gone to Chicago to visit her mother and new stepfather (she'd fixed them up, she was proud to tell me, adding that she'd only charged her mother half her usual fee), so I wouldn't be getting any feedback from her for a few days. And, of course, Ricardo wasn't around to spy for me until Monday. I felt totally frustrated that the lovebirds might be shacking up on both Friday and Saturday nights but that

I wouldn't be able to count those days. My frustration was only heightened by a chance meeting on Sunday.

Eager to get away from my neighborhood, where some sort of street fair was going on and it was so crowded and noisy that I couldn't concentrate on my paperwork, I decided to take Buster uptown, to my old neighborhood. We were walking along Fifth Avenue when I bumped into Wendy Winger, a semifriend because she used to be married to Ken Winger, the Giants quarterback when Dan was with the team.

Wendy, one of those people who not only gets too close to you when she talks and invades your personal space but who unwittingly spits on you, especially when she's pronouncing words beginning with *p*, came right up to me and said, "Melanie! Just the *p*erson I was thinking about!"

I was dying to wipe my cheek where the spit had landed, but you can't really do that, can you? "You were thinking about me?" I said.

She bent down to pet Buster, and even he flinched when she said to him, "Such a *p*retty, *p*retty *p*uppy dog." She stood back up and said to me, "I ran into Dan last night."

"Did you?" I said. "Was he ordering beluga caviar at some overpriced restaurant?"

"I didn't notice his meal, but I did notice his date."

I felt my pulse jump. "I'd heard he was seeing someone," I said, trying to sound casual. "I'm not sure if it's serious though."

"It sure looked serious," said Wendy. "They were all over each other."

"Interesting," I said, understating it. Part of me wanted to leap in the air and cheer. The other part was cursing the fact that they *had* to be shacking up over the weekend and yet I had no way to prove it. Talk about a waste.

"He introduced me," said Wendy. "Her name is Linda or Lana or something like that."

"Well, whoever she is, I hope she makes Dan happy."

"Wow. You're a nicer *p*erson than I am," she said, wetting me again. On the other cheek this time. "I wish Ken nothing but *p*ain."

"You don't mean that," I said. I didn't wish Dan pain, not really. I just wished he'd stop confusing me with an ATM machine.

"As you must know, Ken left me for our children's *p*ediatrician," she said, her eyes moistening. "Do you have any idea how much it hurts that they feel more comfortable in her hands than in mine?"

"I'd be devastated if Buster felt more comfortable with Dan's girlfriend than with me," I commiserated.

"Then you'd better hope this Lana isn't a veterinarian," she said.

I nodded at the coincidental nature of her remark, feeling just the hint of something—a prick of concern, maybe—and then dismissed it.

Wendy and I vowed to get together, which, of course, we both understood we'd never do. We had only been in each other's worlds because of our husbands, and now that they were gone we had nothing in common. She was getting money from her ex. I was giving money to my ex. Old school. New school.

When I got home I was more motivated than ever to find someone to handle the spying duties on weekends, should Dan and Leah's romance continue at its torrid pace. I decided a good candidate would be Isa Johnson, Dan's cleaning lady, who used to be my cleaning lady too until I no longer had an apartment worth cleaning. She worked for him six days a week—not Sundays, but Saturdays, which was better than nothing. She came in at noon and spent a couple of hours tidying up his mess, doing his laundry and ironing, making sure he didn't trash the place. Yes, I thought. She'd be a good snitch, although she was not without her quirks.

In her forties, Haitian-born Isa claimed she was a witch. Dan and I used to refer to her behind her back as our voodoo housekeeper, because she put spells on tough-to-clean surfaces in addition to giving them a shot of Fantastik. "You want magic? You have to use magic," was her explanation when I once asked her why she was chanting with her head inside our oven. Yeah, she was a little bizarre, but nobody got rid of soap scum better than she did.

She'd been married once when she was very young—he'd left her, whoever he was—and the product of their union was her terrifying son Reggie. I say "terrifying" because he was only sixteen but was nearly seven feet tall. They'd had hopes of him being a professional basketball player and had asked Dan to intervene on the kid's behalf, but Reggie was as uncoordinated as I am and was told by NBA scouts that he needed to "grow into his legs." In the meantime, he was a giant boy who sat around their Bronx apartment smoking crack and eating copious amounts of food. In other words, everything Isa earned either went up his nose or down his throat.

Wait, correction: it also went to the voodoo church she belonged to near Yankee Stadium. She was devoted to the House of the Heavenly Spirits, where there was singing and praying and chanting and sacrificing of animal parts, and she was always asking Dan and me to make donations. How happy she would be, I figured, when I surprised her with a very large donation during my Sunday night visit with her.

I wasn't crazy about driving around in her neighborhood after dark, given that it was a known haven for car thieves. I had a Mercedes then (hang on, it was three years old and leased; I'd been forced to sell the spanking new one I used to own in order to pay Dan), and I feared for its stereo system, not to mention its hubcaps, but, as I said, I was motivated.

Reggie answered the door of their ground-floor unit in what was a run-down, four-story brownstone building. I tried not to look scared when I saw him, but, call me old-fashioned, there's something about dope-addled people—especially when they're manic and can't stay still, then suddenly their eyes roll back in their heads and they look like they might be dead—that unnerves me.

"Hi, Reggie. *Reggie.*" I snapped my fingers at him. Twice. Finally, his eyes opened. "It's Melanie Banks," I said. "Your mom used to work for me, remember? I called earlier and she invited me to stop by."

He peered down at me from his great height and said, "I don't like you now and I never did like you."

I laughed, guessing he was just being, you know, crackheadish. "It's nice to see you again too. May I come in?"

"Whatever." He let the door hang open while he lumbered off in search of his mother.

I stepped inside and waited. I couldn't help noticing the smell of something cooking. Something with pungent herbs and seasonings. A cauldron of boiling chicken heads, perhaps. Isa had once told me that their steam vaporized negative spirits. I hoped she would help me vaporize the negative spirit known as my ex-husband.

After a minute or two, she came bustling into the small sitting room, her face in a wide grin. She was very dark skinned and very pretty, and it was too bad she'd wasted her youth on some deadbeat husband, but I wasn't one to talk.

"Well, look at you," she said in her island-flavored accent, giving me a hug. "It's been a long time. You learn how to work a microwave yet, *chérie*?"

"I can heat up my instant coffee. That's about it."

"Pitiful. And how's my little Buster? I only get to see him every other week at Dan's these days. Last week, he told me to air out the rug in the master bathroom. He said there were ghosts in it."

"Dan said that?"

"No, Buster did. You didn't know he spoke to me?"

"No." Well, he spoke to me too. Just not about ghosts.

Isa motioned for me to sit, then she joined me. "So, what brings you all the way up here? Must be important."

"It's about Dan."

"Ah." She nodded. "You jealous?"

"Of what?"

"The new gal who's been staying over the last few nights." She winked. "Cleaning ladies know everything."

"I'm counting on that. You see, Isa—"

"You don't have to tell me. You split up with him because he lounged around on his sorry ass all day long, but now you don't want somebody else to have him."

"God, no. I do want somebody else to have him. Anybody else, in fact. At the moment, it looks like he's interested in Leah, so I want her to have him."

"Why do you care?"

"Because—" I was about to roll out the kind of extravagant lie I'd told Ricardo, then realized it made sense to be honest with

Isa. She was sort of psychic, so she would have mind-read me anyway. "When Dan and I got divorced, he decided it wasn't enough that he ended up with the apartment. He wanted alimony too, just to spite me."

"He doesn't seem like the spiteful type. He gives me nice big tips."

Nice big tips. Not only was my ex-husband squeezing me financially; he was sullying my reputation. By handing out my hard-earned cash to everybody on the planet, he was making me look like a cheapskate. Which I wasn't. Look at how much I was paying people to spy on him. I'm not saying I was an angel here, but I was practicing my own brand of trickle-down economics, wasn't I?

"He can be a very likable guy, no doubt about it," I conceded. "But for me to have to support a man who's more than capable of supporting himself—just because I happened to succeed at my job longer than he succeeded at his—isn't fair. He's taking, taking, taking, and I can't stand it."

"You want me to put a spell on him so he'll give the money back?"

"Thanks, but no." I pulled my chair closer to hers. "What I want is for him to live with his new girlfriend for ninety days. If he does, I won't have to support him anymore."

"So you want me to put a spell on her?"

"No, Isa. No spells." God. "This is a legal matter having to do with my divorce settlement. Dan just has to live with another woman for ninety days or so, and I'm off the hook for the alimony. The only catch is that I need someone to help me prove that they're cohabitating—and, if so, how often."

She shook her head vehemently. "I'm against all that pornography."

I smothered a laugh with my hand over my mouth. "Cohabitating isn't sexual. It has to do with their living arrangement. All I'm asking is that you help me prove she's staying there with him. You don't have to inspect their bed linens."

"If you want me to snoop for you, I'll have to say no."

No? I wasn't listening to *no*. "Let me understand this, Isa. Putting a spell on Dan is okay, but snooping on him isn't?"

"Spells are who I am, *chérie*. All members of the House of Heavenly Spirits are skilled in the art of spells. We do it to restore the balance between good and evil."

"I'm glad you brought that up," I said. "Your church, I mean. If you help me keep tabs on him and his girlfriend, I'm prepared to donate five hundred dollars to it."

"Five hundred dollars?" She jumped up, raised her arms in the air, and whirled around and around and around until she nearly fainted. I didn't know whether to revive her or give her a big round of applause. "This is wonderful," she said when she had composed herself. "You should have told me about the money in the beginning. I'll snoop or whatever else you want me to do."

"I was hoping you'd see it that way. Now, Ricardo, the doorman, says he'll tally up the days the girlfriend is there during the week, but that leaves Saturdays and Sundays."

"I don't work Sundays, *chérie*."

"I know, but when you get there on Monday afternoons, you'll be able to tell if she slept over. Just check to see if she left any clothes or makeup or other personal property. And maybe Dan will be there sometimes and you can ask him about her. In a casual way, of course."

"And then I'm supposed to call you with information?"

I reached into my purse, pulled out a tiny digital camera,

and handed it to her. I'd decided against another spiral-bound notebook, since Isa wasn't great about jotting things down—appropriate things, that is. I'd once asked her to make up a shopping list of cleaning supplies, and she'd included crab eyes and turtle essence along with the Pledge. "Not necessary. I'd like you to take pictures of the evidence. Those clothes we talked about. Her makeup. Anything she leaves there."

Isa held the camera tentatively, as if it might break.

"It's really easy," I said. "You just point and shoot. And you keep pointing and shooting as long as Leah sticks around."

"But I've never used one of these."

"You'll be fine. If you can work a microwave, you can definitely work that camera."

She pointed it at me, peered into the viewfinder, and clicked. "Like that?"

"Just like that."

I got up, gave her the five hundred bucks, and said I'd better head back to the city.

"Remember, the goal is to document that this woman is sleeping there for three months," I said. "It's possible that she and Dan won't last that long and we'll have to start all this up again with the next one."

"That's where spells come in," said Isa as she walked me to the door. "You don't really mind if I put one on them, do you?"

I smiled. "Of course not. As long as you take the photos, the rest is up to you."

As I left her apartment, I was feeling pretty good about things. Plans were shaping up. Systems were in place. People were in motion.

Unfortunately, when I reached my Mercedes, I discovered that people had been in motion and stolen the car's hood ornament, along with all four of its wheels.

Don't read too much into this, I cautioned myself as I dialed 911. It's only a slight setback.

Chapter 14

The caretaker left about fifteen minutes ago," said Ricardo after I arrived with Buster on Monday morning.

He fetched the notebook and showed me how he'd entered the date and time of Leah's departure. It was clear that he was very proud of playing a role in Mr. Swain's recovery from mental illness. I should have felt guilty but didn't. What I felt was giddy that she had stayed over and that I now had Isa to confirm it. All I needed was someone to cover Saturday nights, and I was set.

"I probably shouldn't say this, because of how serious the situation is," Ricardo went on, "but if I had a caretaker who looked like her, I wouldn't be depressed for a second."

"Why?" I said. "Is she that pretty?"

"Pretty?" He laughed. "Gorgeous. Your basic ten."

"Maybe that's why the doctor paired her with Mr. Swain," I said, pleased that Desiree hadn't oversold Leah. I *was* paying extra for her, after all. "If she's so beautiful, she's bound to lift his spirits."

"Oh, yeah. Sweet girl, too. Gives me a big smile whenever she walks by. And she's never in too much of a hurry to thank me for opening the door. Can't say that about most of the people here."

Okay, so I'd been one of those people. I was always in a hurry and I didn't thank Ricardo for opening the door, not every time, and it wasn't because I was a bad person. I was just—well—preoccupied.

"Let's hope she works out," I said, making an extra effort to *smile* as I said it. Then I asked Ricardo to *please* buzz me up to Dan's and *thanked* him after he did. Sure, I wanted Leah to get me out of the alimony, but I wasn't about to let her show me up in the process.

"Look who's here," said my ex, who was waiting for Buster and me at the elevator instead of inside the apartment, which surprised me. Oh, and he wasn't in his bathrobe either. He had on a pair of slacks and one of his eight-trillion-dollar cashmere sweaters. And I do believe he was clean for a change, scents of toothpaste, shampoo, and cologne floating in the air. Apparently, Leah managed to accomplish in a few days something I wasn't able to accomplish in a few years: get him to shower, shave, and dress in the morning.

Ignoring me completely, he knelt down and clapped his hands. "Come, Busty boy. Come to Daddy."

As Buster scampered over to Dan in yet another demonstration of canine loyalty and devotion, I felt the old lump in my throat. I really couldn't bear sharing custody. I wanted my dog with me all the time, the way it used to be, and if my ex hadn't screwed up so royally, we'd still be married and I wouldn't have to *share* anything.

"What's the occasion, Dan?" I said as the dog licked his face. "You're not wearing your pajamas."

He glanced up at me and smirked. "Melanie, darlin'. I forgot you were even there."

"Did you think Buster hailed his own cab over?"

"No, but you're sort of quiet today. You waited two whole seconds before firing off a criticism."

I was about to fire off another criticism when Mrs. Thornberg, Dan's next-door neighbor, stuck her head out of her apartment. She was a widow in her eighties with short, badly dyed (i.e., shoe polish) brown hair that had thinned out to the point of bald patches on top. She had beady eyes that were set too close together and an unsteady hand when it came to applying her lipstick, and she always wore a dress and pumps, as if she were going someplace fancy when, in fact, she rarely left the building. She was a woman with way too much time on her hands. A condo commando type. There's one in every homeowner's association, isn't there? They poke their nose in everybody's business to make sure no house rules are being broken (loud pets, loud music, loud construction, loud sex), when what they should be doing is getting a life. When I was a resident there, it was nearly impossible to host even a small, tasteful dinner party without Mrs. Thornberg pounding on the door and squawking, "Keep it down!"

"No dogs gallivanting in the common hallways," she squawked

right that very minute. "We installed new carpet last month. You'll be assessed if there's doody anywhere."

In response, Dan went down on all fours, ran his hands along the carpet, and then sniffed it. "All clear, Mrs. Thornberg. Want to get down here and check for yourself?" He loved calling her bluff. On those occasions when she'd rant about our parties, he'd invite her in, knowing she'd much rather barricade herself in her own apartment than socialize with us; that was the best way to get rid of her. The funniest was when we'd hire Isa to serve at our parties. Mrs. Thornberg would complain about the noise and Isa would threaten to put a spell on her, and Dan and I would have to mollify both of them before attending to our guests.

"No, I do not want to crawl on the floor, thank you very much," she said. "I just want you to take the dog inside his home where he belongs. Let him do his business in there."

Dan gathered Buster up in his arms and stood. "Right you are, Mrs. Thornberg." He turned to me. "You coming, darlin'? It's probably best that you do your business inside too."

I rolled my eyes, told Mrs. Thornberg to have a fine day, and followed my ex and my dog into the apartment.

"I guess she hasn't mellowed," I remarked when the three of us were alone.

"Like someone else I know," said Dan. "Which reminds me: don't you have to rush off to work? There's gotta be somebody at that office who needs abusing."

"Actually, I think I'll use the little girl's room first. So I can do my business."

I strutted into the master bathroom, not because nature called but because I hoped to find evidence of Leah. Yes, I already knew she'd stayed over, but I wanted to get a sense of her, get a sense of the woman who held my financial freedom in her hands.

I did a sweep of the medicine cabinet. No prescription drugs with her name on them yet, but then you probably don't start leaving your Xanax at your boyfriend's until you've revealed your fear of flying or your anxiety about work or your estrangement from your mother, and it was much too soon for any of that.

I opened the drawers of the vanity. No makeup, no hair dryer, no tampons. Must be too soon for all that too.

I checked the shower. No loofah sponge or girly girl products of any kind. Surely, she rinsed off after sex, didn't she?

Okay. Here we go, I thought, after I turned and spotted something at the bottom of the Jacuzzi tub. I walked over, bent down, and picked it up. It was a waterproof toy. Not just any toy, but a rubber mermaid with the words I HAVE A PUSSY *AND* A TAIL! written in script on its torso. Eueew.

I dropped it back into the tub. So Leah was a babe with a playful side.

As I emerged from the bathroom, Dan was sitting on the sofa grooming Buster and humming.

"Gosh, you're a happy camper today," I observed.

"Never felt better," he said, positively beaming now. I thought his cheeks would explode from the hugeness of that grin.

"New girlfriend?" I said, trying to sound casual.

He raised an eyebrow. "What makes you ask that?"

"You're as radiant as a bride." I'd meant it as a jab—Dan was so macho that even implying that he had a feminine characteristic or two made him jumpy—but as I looked at him closely, I saw that it was true. He was radiant. His blue eyes were bright and shining. His cheeks were rosy but not the florid red caused by too much booze. And he had more energy, not his usual ennui. He was behaving like a man who was, well, happy.

"No weddings for this guy, as I already told you," he said, then shook his head at me. "You still think I'm a dumb jock from Minco, but even I know that if I get married again, I lose the alimony."

I sighed heavily and pretended to look resigned. "Can't put one over on you," I said. "But you do have a girlfriend, am I right?"

Back came that big stupid smile. "I'm seeing someone, yeah."

"The flight attendant from the San Juan trip?" I asked innocently.

"No, she's a vet," he said.

"Iraq or Afghanistan?" I said.

"Not that kind of vet," he said. "She's got a veterinary practice on Eighty-eighth and Madison."

"Wow. Your very own Dr. Doolittle," I said. "If she happens to come by the apartment this week, she can give Buster a free checkup."

"Oh, she'll be coming by," he said, no doubt fantasizing about the bathtub mermaid. "We're having dinner here tonight. She's *cooking*, not that you'd know what that is."

I'm sure I was supposed to feel bad yet again about my ineptitude in the kitchen, but where is it written that women must be gourmet chefs?

"How nice for the two of you," I said, tallying up Leah's sleepovers. This one would make five. "But you're not the dinner-at-home type, Dan. Or are you planning to take her strip club–hopping after you eat?"

"What I'm planning is none of your concern."

"Fine. Just one more question," I said. "Does she mind that you're unemployed?"

"Leah doesn't judge," he said with the implication that I did.

"Leah, is it?" I said. "Lovely name."

"For a lovely lady. Inside and out." So Desiree had said. So Ricardo had said. I was dying to weigh in on this creature myself. "She's not dating me because I used to be famous or because I might be famous again in the future, and she's not staying away because I happen to be in between jobs."

In between jobs. Right. "Okay, I'll bite. Why is she dating you?"

"Because she likes me," he said, getting up from the sofa. "And you know what, Mel? It feels real good."

As he walked out of the room, I was oddly silent. I couldn't muster a counter. For some reason, it hadn't occurred to me that Leah would be so flat-out accepting. I'd hoped she'd fall for Dan, obviously, but what was it about him that had made her fall for him? Was she the sort of woman who liked to mother men who were down-and-out? Was it strictly a physical attraction she had for him? Or was she seeing something in him that I'd missed? I couldn't get a handle on their relationship, and I didn't like feeling out of the loop. And so I comforted myself by sitting next to my sweet doggie to give him some good-bye hugs and kisses.

"Thank God for you, Buster," I said, rubbing him behind the ears. "No matter what happens, you're my boy, right?"

He looked up at me with his big shining eyes, as if sensing exactly how hard it was for me to leave him, then ducked his head under my arm. We stayed that way for a second or two before I finally went on my way.

■ ■ ■

I was heading toward the elevator when Mrs. Thornberg popped her head out of her apartment again.

"Psst! What's with the girlfriend?" she said, waving me over. "I see he's got one."

It's none of your concern, I wanted to say, to quote Dan. But then—wait—I had an idea. I still needed someone to confirm Leah's Saturday night sleepovers, and who better to enlist than the most meddlesome person in the building? Plus, she was rich. Her garmento husband—his company made bras—had left her a fortune, so I wouldn't even have to pay her. And there was yet another plus: she was always home on Saturday nights.

"Why don't you invite me in and I'll tell you what I know, Mrs. Thornberg?" I said.

She nodded vigorously, giving me the impression that I was probably the first one in years not to blow her off.

"Come in, come in," she said, ushering me into her place, which stunk of mothballs. Oh, and all the furniture was covered in plastic. I didn't know people still did that. "Want a root beer?"

"No, thanks."

"Why? You driving?" She cackled.

"The truth is, I've got to get to the office, so I don't have long to chat," I said.

"You career girls." She sniffed. "In my day, we stayed home and cooked our husbands breakfast in the morning." See that? If you're a woman, everybody expects you to cook! "We didn't run off to work. We didn't 'do our own thing,' as you young people call it. And we certainly didn't get divorced at the drop of a hat."

I nodded politely, then lowered myself onto one of her living room chairs. When my butt made contact with the plastic, it sounded like I'd just sat on a whoopee cushion.

"In fact, I don't think there'd be all these divorces if you girls paid more—"

"Mrs. Thornberg," I interrupted. I really did have to get to work. I was late enough as it was. "You asked me about Dan's new girlfriend."

"I sure did. She's a looker, I'll give her that."

So it was unanimous. "You've met Leah?"

"Leah? What kind of a name is that? In my day, we had first names like Jane and Mary and Betty." Never mind that her own first name was Antoinette. Dan and I used to call her the Antster.

I tried again. "So you've met her?"

"What choice did I have? The two of them were carrying on the other night with the music turned up so loud I couldn't hear Larry King. I knocked on your ex-husband's door to remind him that we have a rule in this building: no loud noise after nine P.M. He said they were dancing and lost track of the time."

Dancing? Suddenly, Dan was Fred Astaire?

During the early years of our marriage, he used to dance with me quite often, and I loved it. But as we began to drift apart, our dancing days dwindled to zero. Have you ever noticed how it's one of the first things to go when a relationship sours? The intimate act of two people holding each other and moving in sync to music?

"And that's not all they were doing," she said, bringing me back to the present. "After my visit over there, I came home and started watching my program again. And wouldn't you know it, the noise got worse."

"The dancing?"

"No. The sex. My bedroom backs up to his, remember?"

I did remember. The Antster used to complain whenever Dan and I went at it a little too spiritedly.

"I'm not a prude, mind you," she continued, "but it says right in the building's bylaws: no resident shall infringe upon the peace and quiet of another. So I made my displeasure known to them."

"I bet they were thrilled," I said.

"Not my problem," she said. "If I have to police them every night of the week, that's exactly what I'm going to do."

Police them. Wow. I couldn't have put it better myself. She was stepping right into the job.

"You should definitely watch what's going on over there," I said, "especially on Saturday nights, when they'll probably have parties." I leaned toward her and added in a whisper, "Someone told me Leah's parents were very strict when she was growing up, so now she overcompensates by going wild and crazy on 'date night.' It's a shame how dysfunctional childhoods can cause trouble later in life."

She grabbed my arm. "Is this Leah a dope fiend?"

"I doubt it, although she does have access to drugs. She's a veterinarian."

Her nostrils flared. "Well, she'd better not bring any of her 'patients' over here. We have rules about that too. Only one pet per resident."

"Which is why I think it's crucial that you keep a close eye on her. On her and Dan. You're the enforcer, Mrs. Thornberg. Everybody looks to you to maintain order and decorum. If you don't monitor their every move, who will?"

The more I talked, the more I realized how perfect Antoinette Thornberg was for this assignment. As I've said, she stayed home on Saturday nights, loved snooping, and didn't need my money.

"Why do you care so much what they do?" she said a little suspiciously. "You're out of the picture."

"Because of Buster, of course," I replied, as if it were obvious. "I don't want him exposed to loud noise or any other unseemly behavior. This shared custody arrangement has been difficult enough for him. He doesn't need any additional stress."

"You said Leah's a vet. She won't hurt him."

"Not unless she's having one of her Saturday night orgies."

Antoinette's jaw dropped. "Orgies?"

I shrugged. "Anything's possible from what I hear."

"That's it! I'm going to watch them like a hawk," she vowed.

I smiled. "I'm very relieved. Feel free to call me if things get out of hand." I gave her my card.

She looked it over. "Vice president, huh? No wonder you got divorced."

"I don't—"

"In my day, if a woman made it in the business world, she had to be a man hater."

"That's ridiculous," I said. "Women can be just as successful as men—more successful than men—and still have a happy marriage."

"Oh, yeah? Then what happened with yours?"

"My divorce had more to do with Dan's failure than with my success."

"You sure about that?"

I checked my watch. "I really do have to go." I got up from the chair, peeled the plastic off the back of my legs, and shook her frail, limp hand. Imagine my surprise when that hand tightened around mine and locked me in a viselike grip. "Glad we talked," I said, extricating myself. "I feel better about leaving Buster next door."

Later that night at about eight, I was back at the Heartbreak

Hotel, eating a bowl of Cheerios and doing some paperwork, when my cell phone rang. It was Mrs. Thornberg. She was at Lenox Hill Hospital with a sprained left arm after having slipped and fallen on a wet spot in the building's lobby (they had washed the floor but hadn't mopped it properly and she intended to get to the bottom of it). She said the doctor discharged her, but she had nobody but me to call and pick her up.

"Don't you have any children?" I said.

"No children," she said. "Mr. Thornberg was sterile. His testicles didn't work the way they were supposed to."

Too much information. "How about friends?"

"All dead," she said. "When I saw your number on the card, I thought of you."

Well, of course, I went all the way uptown and crosstown and picked her up. I couldn't very well tell her to hop in a cab at her age and in her condition.

I brought her back to her apartment, got her undressed and into bed, dashed out to fill her prescriptions at the pharmacy, took care of her entire shopping list at the supermarket, bought her cold cuts and chicken soup at her favorite deli, and rented her a bunch of movies at the video place. The doctor said she'd be able to resume her normal activities in the morning, but I felt good knowing I'd helped her out.

"Is there anything else?" I said when I'd returned with the loot, the sum of which added up to five hundred dollars (painkillers are expensive, but it was the groceries that broke the bank, since she wanted one of everything).

"No, that's it," she said weakly. "For now."

Her eyelids were heavy, so I thought I'd hand her the receipts and her checkbook, let her reimburse me, and get going.

"Here, Mrs. Thornberg," I said when I'd pulled the receipts together. "Grand total for tonight—not counting the taxi fare, which I'm happy to pick up—is five seventy-two. Call it five, even."

No answer. The heavy eyelids were now shut.

"Mrs. Thornberg?"

Then came the snoring.

I left the receipts on her night table, tiptoed out, and made my way home, resisting the urge to barge in next door, get a good look at Leah, and spend a minute with my precious Buster. I was too tired.

No, it didn't escape me that I had paid Ricardo and Isa five hundred dollars each to spy on Dan and that I had now shelled out the very same amount on Antoinette. In my attempt to get richer, I was actually getting poorer, which was slightly anxiety producing and didn't seem like a sound business plan. But I was cheered by the fact that Leah was spending her nights at my ex's and that all my accomplices were lined up to get them on record. Yes, the project was moving forward more quickly and efficiently than I could ever have imagined.

Chapter 15

Miracle of miracles. You're right on time," I said after I opened the door for Dan. It was eight-thirty the next Monday morning and he was bringing Buster back after their week together. And what a week it was. According to my spies, Leah and Dan weren't apart for a single night. Especially exciting was Isa's news that Leah had moved some of her clothes into Dan's closet and that we had the photographs to prove it. Oh, and there was Desiree's report, which prompted me to pump my fist in the air. She had spoken to Leah, who said she'd never been so happy, and although she knew she was rushing things, she felt sure that *living with Dan* was the right direction for her. In my wildest dreams, I never expected my plan to proceed so smoothly, and I had to give Desiree the credit. Of course, the minute I did she demanded the rest of her fee. I had to remind her that the deal wasn't a deal for another seventy-something days. Still, we were both filled with optimism that we would each put money in our pockets as a result of our arrangement.

"I know you have to get to work early, so here I am," said Dan, releasing Buster from his leash.

"My needs never seemed to interest you before," I said offhandedly.

"Is that true, or are you just yanking my chain?" he asked.

"Is what true?" I said as I got down on the floor to hug my dog.

"That I've never been interested in your needs."

I glanced up. So he was serious about the question? How odd. He was dressed oddly too, now that I took a good look at him. No fancy duds, just jeans, sneakers, and a faded Giants sweatshirt. "I might have overstated it with the 'never,' because in the old days you bent over backward to accommodate me," I conceded. "But let's be real here: mostly, the person whose needs interest you is you. How often over the last year did I tell you I had to be at the office by a certain time and yet you brought Buster over whenever you damn pleased?"

He considered this, then: "Too often. I'm sorry."

He regarded me with his beautiful blue eyes and his eight-by-ten-glossy face, and I waited for the smirk, the punch line, the put-down. Instead, he just stood there. Silent. Even penitent. Was it possible that his apology was sincere? Nah. His sincerity may have drawn me to him in the beginning, but the only thing he'd been sincere about recently was refusing to grow up.

"The truth is," he went on, "I think it's amazing how hard you work. If I had your discipline and focus, I'd be a lot better off."

Now I was really confused. For the latter part of our marriage, this loafer, this moocher, this spendthrift, ridiculed me for being a workaholic. A "maniac," he'd once called me. All of a sudden he was wishing he could be more like me?

"Better off how?" I said, keeping the discussion going, just for argument's sake.

"By being fully invested in something," he said. He was taking a little stroll around my poor excuse for a living room, acting all deep in thought, which amused me. You have to be *deep* to be deep in thought. "I'm starting to realize that for a while now I've been kind of checked out."

"Kind of?" I scoffed.

"Okay. Completely. I guess what I'm trying to say is that you're passionate about your work, and I'm envious of people who are passionate about what they do. I'm passionate about football, but that hasn't done me much good. Not lately, anyway."

I was about to get on his case about how there were plenty of football-related jobs out there if he bothered to knock on doors, but why frustrate myself? We'd had that conversation a thousand times—my urging him to be a college coach, for example, and his insistence that former-pros-turned-coaches were losers—so what was the point? What did intrigue me, though, was why the subject was even coming up. Normally, my Monday morning exchanges with Dan were Buster-related and hostile at best.

"Where's all this soul searching coming from?" I said as I watched him pace then stop to stare at the ceiling.

"Leah," he said with the sigh of a lovesick teenager—the heaving shoulders, the faraway look, the whole business. "We talk about things like this."

"Leah? The woman you've been dating?" I said, trying to maintain a deadpan expression.

He nodded. "She's passionate about her work. She's a vet."

"Right. I remember now."

"She went into her field because she loved animals, not because she expected to make a lot of money. She's encouraging me to do the same thing."

"Become a vet?" I know, I know. I was being a smart-ass, but you've got to remember: my position was that the guy was stealing from me.

"No, follow my passion. She believes that I'll find a way to contribute to society if I just go with what I love."

"You mean she doesn't consider hanging out with Ernie a contribution to society?"

He couldn't help smirking at that one. "Fine. I'll shut up. But you'll be happy to know that Leah has the same opinion of Ernie as you always did. Since I've been seeing more of her, I've been seeing less of him."

"Let's hear it for Leah! She sounds like a good judge of character. Well, except where you're concerned."

He laughed. "No sense in trying to have a meaningful conversation with you, darlin'. I'll do us both a favor and let you get to the office."

He kissed Buster good-bye and left. And then I sort of snickered to myself. I mean, how funny would it be—funny, as in ironic—if Leah not only cohabitated with Dan for ninety days and relieved me of my financial burden, but also turned him into a decent human being who went on to lead a productive life? What a joke, huh? That's how I thought of it at the time. Honest to God.

■ ■ ■

That night I ran into Evan at the trash compactor, looking his scruffy but hunky self, his lanky but muscular body clothed in jeans and a turtleneck, his dark hair in boyish disarray. He smiled when he saw me, the crinkles forming around his eyes, and I found myself drawn to him again, drawn to his friendly, open face. He was more than a neighbor to me, I realized. If he were merely that, I wouldn't have been so glad to see him whenever we ran into each other.

Thankfully, I had all my clothes on this time, wasn't locked out of my apartment, and didn't need help with my belongings. None of those damsel in distress situations, in other words. I admit I liked the feeling of his coming to my aid, but I didn't want him to view me as *needy,* which men think is just about the worst thing a woman can be.

Well, I wasn't needy until the tall-size Hefty garbage bag I'd lugged into the compactor room sprang a leak and all its contents started tumbling onto the floor.

"Oh, no. Not again," I said, throwing up my hands in frustration. "You weren't sure before, but now you're convinced I'm this lonely divorcée trolling for attention."

"Nothing wrong with being lonely," he said matter-of-factly. "And you don't need to troll for my attention, Melanie. You've already got it."

I met his eyes. His pupils were so big that they completely eclipsed the irises, the effect of which was that you couldn't look away from them.

Still, I cleared my throat and refocused on the matter at hand. "I'd better put all this stuff back in the bag."

"Here, let me," he said as we both got down on the floor.

We didn't butt heads this time, but it was a little awkward, as I was feverishly trying to stick the balled-up tissues, the candy wrappers, the mail from advertisers of antiaging creams, and all my other embarrassing personal articles back into the smelly bag.

"I notice there are a lot of these," he said, tossing one of the tissues into the bag. "Have you been crying a lot?"

"I never cry," I said emphatically, tying the bag up and throwing it down the chute. "I use the tissues to clean my dog's face."

"Hey, I told you. It's not a sin to be lonely," he said.

"No, really," I said. "I use them on Buster. With pugs, you have to get the grungy stuff out from between their wrinkles or they can become infected."

"I love pugs," he said after it sunk in that I was serious about the reason for the tissues. "How about introducing me to yours?"

"Sure," I said. "My ex-husband and I share custody of him, but this is my week. You're in luck."

"It sounds like your divorce from Traffic Dan was amicable," he said. "The support. The shared custody. You're so cool about it all."

Yeah, cool. That's what I was. A cool customer, scheming and plotting to defraud my ex out of what was legally his. But Evan didn't have to know that.

We walked to my apartment, and I opened the door to find Buster standing inside waiting for me. As soon as he saw we had a guest, he went right into his Flying Wallenda act, leaping onto the sofa, leaping onto the nearby chair, leaping back onto the floor. If he could have curtsied, he would have. Such a show-off.

"Buster, this is Evan," I said. "He's a painter. Maybe he'll paint a picture of you someday."

Evan bent down and stroked Buster's back. "Hey, boy. I'm the guy from down the hall. Pleased to meet you."

Buster snorted.

"Don't take it personally," I said. "He does that even with people he likes."

Evan smiled. "So you think he likes me?"

"I think it's too soon to tell."

"Well, I'll just have to try and ingratiate myself with him. Why don't we take him for a walk?"

"Now?" I checked my watch. It was eight-thirty. Maybe Dan and Leah were finishing dinner and hopping into bed early, and I could log in another night of cohabitation.

"Melanie? Did I lose you?"

Yes. "No. It's just that I've got work to do and you've got your painting and—"

"Come on. We'll take a quick one, just around our neighborhood."

"Our neighborhood." I rolled my eyes. "The lovely Hell's Kitchen."

"Oh. Right," he said, heading for the door. "Patty told me you're a former Upper East Sider. Well, this neighborhood *is* lovely, if you know where to look. So grab your coat and let's go."

It was another breezy January night. Not bone chilling but cold. Smoke-coming-out-of-your-mouth-when-you-talk cold. I bundled up in a down coat and floppy wool hat. Not very glamorous, but Evan didn't seem to mind.

"You like to eat?" he asked as we strolled down Ninth Avenue, Buster trotting along on his leash.

I puffed out my cheeks to demonstrate what a piggy eater I'd become. "More than I ever thought possible."

"Then how can you take the Upper East Side over this?" He gestured at all the restaurants on the avenue. "It's the city's premier neighborhood for food."

"No way," I said. "The Upper East Side has some of the most famous places in the world."

"Famous, maybe. But does it have Hallo Berlin?" He pointed to a small, undistinguished-looking fast-food place. "Authentic German. More wursts than you knew existed."

I turned to look at him. He was smiling, and his smile was infectious. "Hallo Berlin, huh?" I laughed.

"One of many treasures in our neighborhood," he said.

We kept walking. Despite my cynicism, the blend of aromas from the various cuisines were definitely whetting my appetite, not that it needed whetting lately.

"Over there," said Evan, nodding at a storefront called Fatina. "Middle Eastern food, plus live music and—you'll love this—belly dancing."

I laughed again. "A definite must see."

"Or maybe you'd prefer Grigo, the Greek place that has flamenco dancing. Organic salads too. And at L'Allegria, the restaurant to your left, the waiters don't speak a word of English. When it's your birthday, they sing 'Happy Birthday' in Italian, and it's like being at the opera."

I looked at him, this time with a sly grin. "Something tells me you published a restaurant guide when you were an editor, and that's how you know all this."

"Nope," he said. "I just enjoy exploring. New sights. New smells. New *people.*"

I blushed as I felt his eyes on me. He wasn't at all shy about saying what was on his mind, and I found it refreshing. I found him refreshing.

"Speaking of which," he went on, "who are you really, Melanie Banks?"

"What do you mean?" I asked.

"You sort of flinched back at your place when I mentioned your support of your ex and your shared custody of Buster. You let me rave about how civilized it sounds, but it's not a rosy picture, is it? I misread the situation, and you didn't want to tell me for some reason."

Either he was very perceptive or I was a lousy actress. "Yes, you misread the situation," I admitted. He was hard to lie to. He had the air of someone who didn't run from the truth, wasn't scared away by it, and I responded by being as straightforward with him as my convoluted personal life allowed. "I hate sharing Buster, but the support issue has been the really contentious one. And the reason I didn't tell you was because I assume your divorce is headed in the same direction."

He seemed surprised by the remark. "You think my ex-wife and I will fight over alimony?"

"You will, believe me. She'll resent having to support you and you'll claim you're entitled to the money."

He stopped walking and looked at me. "What makes you think she's the one who'll be supporting me?"

"Oh. I just assumed that because you lost your job and she—"

"Has one?"

"Yes. You said she's a successful real estate agent."

"She is, but we haven't gotten around to the terms of our settlement yet."

"Then brace yourself. It isn't fun." I gave Evan the highlights and the lowlights of my marriage and divorce, and let loose about my feelings about the spousal support.

"I can see that Traffic Dan gets your motor going," he said. "There's a vein on the side of your head that popped out as soon as you started talking about him. It's still throbbing."

"What vein?"

He placed the tips of his fingers on my left temple and rubbed it gently. "Feel that?"

I felt it all right. His touch was soft and sensual, and it had been so long since anyone touched me that way that I nearly jumped.

"You okay?" he said.

"I don't know," I said. "Nobody's ever told me I had a throbbing vein before." I reached up to touch my face myself, and there *was* a lumpy area there.

"It's your Dan vein," he said. "Let's change the subject and see if it'll go away."

"Fine with me." My Dan vein. I hoped it wouldn't burst and kill me.

"Tell me about this big project of yours," he said as we resumed our walk. "The one that's keeping you so busy."

Okay, so he didn't know he wasn't changing the subject after all. "Actually, it's moving along nicely now," I said, imagining Ricardo making another entry in his notebook and Isa taking more photos and Mrs. Thornberg going next door to complain about the dancing. "In about two months, I'll know if it's a success."

"Is the project part of your job as a financial planner?"

"It's financial in nature," I said cryptically. "If I pull it off, it'll mean saving a fortune. I'll be able to move out of the Heartbreak Hotel, for one thing."

"A fortune, huh? You love money, don't you? Why else would you be in the profession you're in?"

"I love the effect of money," I said. "I love that if you've got it, you can pay your bills and your taxes, own a home and a car, have decent health insurance, sleep at night. Money is security. It keeps us safe."

He cocked his head at me, as if still trying to figure me out. "There's no such thing as safe, Melanie. People with money die just the same as people without it. They just have nicer flowers at their funeral."

"I'm speaking from experience, Evan," I said with more force than I intended. "My mother died when I was little, and my father spent more time on the unemployment line than he did with me. I never had enough. Not for clothes. Not for school. Not for anything."

"Sounds grim, but was it the money you were missing or the affection?"

"The money." I met his gaze. "It's the one thing that doesn't disappoint."

"Compared to people, you mean?"

"Maybe." He *was* perceptive. He seemed to know me better than I knew myself, and we'd only just met. I'd never been with a man who took the trouble to know me, who cared enough to probe below the surface so early in a friendship.

"May I ask you another question?" he said.

"You will anyway, so go ahead," I said with a laugh.

"You said before that you never cry. How come?"

"I just don't. Never did. You'll probably say I'm holding my emotions inside, but I just think I'm in better control of them than most people."

"And that's a good thing?" He looked doubtful.

"It works for me."

Just then, we came to a traffic light. "Are we crossing here?"

"You bet. We've been talking about food, but now it's time to eat some."

He took my elbow as we crossed to the other side of Ninth, Buster close by. I felt cared for, protected, the way I always did when he was around.

"Here?" I said when we stopped in front of a nondescript place called the Ninth Avenue Food Gallery.

"Best pastrami you'll ever have." He leaned over the counter and ordered a pastrami hero sandwich with lettuce, tomato, mayonnaise, and melted provolone. When the sandwich was ready, he held it in front of my mouth to tantalize me. "Just taste this and tell me this neighborhood isn't amazing."

I took a bite, and the flavors exploded in my mouth. God, it was delicious. I'd lived in Hell's Kitchen for a year and never set foot in the place. I'd had no idea what I was missing.

I was about to hand it back, but he insisted I take another bite.

"You may regret that," I said. "It could be gone before you get a crack at it." As I sank my teeth into the sandwich, the mayo squirted out and landed on my chin, a big white wet blob just sitting there. It seemed as if I was incapable of not embarrassing myself in front of this guy.

"Whoops," I said, grabbing a napkin from the counter and wiping myself off, then handing the hero over to him. "Obviously, this thing is too much for me to handle. It's all yours."

He smiled. But instead of taking his first bite, he stuck his finger into the sandwich and scooped out a dollop of mayonnaise, which he proceeded to spread on his own chin.

I roared with laughter as other patrons turned to look at him. "What in the world are you doing?"

"Keeping you company. One of the best ways not to feel silly is to have someone else feeling silly right along with you."

I stood there, staring at him for a few seconds, moved by his consideration for me. He hadn't wanted me to feel silly alone. And as a result, I no longer did.

I reached for another napkin and wiped the mayo off him. "Are you for real, Evan Gillespie?"

He nodded. "Very." He took a bite of the hero, chewed, swallowed. "So will you go out with me Saturday night?"

"What?" The question caught me completely off guard. I wasn't ready for a *date*. Friendship? Sure. Romance? No. I was still involved with Dan. Well, "involved" in the sense of thinking about him nonstop, about the project nonstop. Plus, I didn't want another romantic relationship after the crushing disappointment of the last one, not ever. "I like you, Evan. I do," I said. "But it's not a good idea. I've just gotten divorced and you've just gotten separated and—"

"And we both enjoy eating. So we'll have dinner together. My place. I'll cook."

"You cook? I can't even make decent coffee."

"Come over Saturday night and I'll teach you how."

That was the interesting thing about Evan. About Evan and me. When I was with Dan, I'd been the tour guide. Suddenly, I was the one doing the learning.

I accepted his dinner invitation against my better judgment.

"Great," he said. "Saturday night. Seven o'clock. Apartment 3F. Leave the evening gown at home. This'll be a casual affair."

"Can I at least bring something?" I asked as we headed back to the Heartbreak Hotel.

"Yeah. Buster. He's more than welcome to join us. Unless, of course, he's got a date of his own."

"He's free. But he only eats premium kibble."

"Then that's what I'll cook."

"Seriously, Evan. Please don't go to a lot of trouble. Not for me." Not for a woman with no interest in anything more than friendship.

"Fine. I won't go to a lot of trouble. Is a little trouble okay?"

I laughed. "It is."

Chapter 16

The week sped by—my time with Buster always seemed to go faster than my time without him—and before I knew it, I was confronting Saturday night and my "date" with Evan. I'd considered canceling, but ultimately it was just easier to show up, keep things light and chummy, and then leave. Also, the fact that the site of the date was just down the hall provided me with an easy escape route, should I start to feel trapped. Yes, he was a great guy. We've established that. And, yes, I hankered for companionship. We've established that too. But my emotions were directed elsewhere, as you know.

Still, I dressed up a little bit Saturday night. Or, should I say, I dressed down a little bit. My uniform—business suit—remained in the closet in favor of navy wool slacks and a white silk blouse. Much too formal for a casual dinner at a neighbor's apartment, but I had lost touch with "casual." I was just in my thirties, and yet I wore the clothes of a middle-aged matron. Only my long wavy hair, full lips, and a bust size other women go under the knife for suggested that there was a babe in there somewhere. I had long since covered her up.

Having said all that, I was in a festive mood as Buster and I trotted down to 3F that night. Desiree, Ricardo, Isa, and Antoinette had all checked in, confirming that Dan and Leah were still going strong. Amazing, right? I had managed to cut the three-month cohabitation hurdle down to nearly two months. A mere sixty days—the amount of time the DMV gives you for paying a parking ticket! Ninety days had seemed like forever, but a sixty-day deadline seemed within reach, totally doable. I practically salivated as I imagined calling Robin and declaring, "We're done! Dan's on his own! I don't owe him another cent for the rest of my life!" God, what a glorious moment that would be. And it was so close now I could almost smell it.

Actually, what I could smell was garlic, and it was coming from 3F. I looked down at Buster as we stood by Evan's door. "What could he be cooking, sweetie boy? He doesn't have much money."

He rubbed his body up against my leg in what I took to be a manifestation of his ambivalence—about Evan, not the dinner. "It's not a real date, and Evan's not trying to replace Daddy," I assured him. "He's just giving Mommy a chance to relax a little."

Buster perked up, so I rang the bell.

"Here you are," said Evan, looking mighty fine. He was in jeans and a body-hugging black sweater, and while he had kept his promise and not donned a tuxedo and tails for our evening together, he had definitely taken extra care with his grooming. His unruly hair was sort of slicked back off his face, like a choirboy's, save for the cowlick that wouldn't lay down, and he had a couple of cuts on his face where the razor had nicked his skin. All of which I found rather endearing. "Come on in. Both of you."

Buster hung back in a rare display of reticence until Evan produced a squeakie toy and tossed it at him.

"Did you buy that for him?" I asked as my dog started playing with the toy and wandered off with it.

"No. I bought it for you. So you wouldn't have to worry about him."

"Very thoughtful. Really." I handed him a bottle of dry rosé champagne, my favorite. "I didn't know which went better with kibble, red or white, so I split the difference."

"Good choice. The kibble special tonight is lamb shanks with mashed potatoes and string beans almondine."

"It smells fabulous," I said, grateful that we weren't having ketchup sandwiches or Spam. I felt guilty that he'd spent so much on dinner when he obviously couldn't afford to. On the other hand, maybe his wife had started coming through with the checks by then. My eyes crossed as I thought about the likelihood of her paying for my meal. At that very moment, Leah was probably at Dan's, eating off *his* ex, and there I was at Evan's, eating off *his* ex. Talk about a circle jerk.

I followed him into the tiny kitchen, which was identical to mine except that his miniature appliances were hopping with activity. There were pots on the stove and pans in the oven, and it all felt homey and warm.

"Can I help with anything?" I asked as he stirred the potatoes with a big wooden spoon. I was just being polite. I hoped he'd say no, obviously, given my ineptitude in the culinary arts.

"You bet. I told you I would teach you to cook." He let go of the spoon and nodded at it. "Keep stirring until they get thick and creamy."

I panicked. "How about the lumps? Are they supposed to disappear?"

"Not completely. I'd leave a few in, just to keep it real."

He patted me on the back and left me to my stirring. I must tell you, I got a vague thrill from working those potatoes and watching them thicken and smooth. A satisfaction. A sense of having control over something. Yeah, the Leah/Dan thing was very promising, but I didn't know for certain if it would go my way in the end. The potatoes, on the other hand, were easily manipulated and much more predictable. Perhaps I had underestimated the joy of cooking.

Since Evan had moved out a lot of the apartment's furniture to make room for his canvases, there was no dining room table. So we ate on our laps as we sat on the sofa, Buster eating nearby. (Evan had bought him a food bowl too—a big, sturdy steel one—and filled it with lamb morsels.)

"This is so good," I said, licking my lips. "As professional as any of the restaurants on Ninth Avenue. Who taught you how to cook?"

"My wife," he said. "Kaitlin grew up in a large family, and she and all her sisters are naturals in the kitchen."

"How long were you two together?" I asked, since, unlike me, he never flinched when he mentioned his marriage.

"Five years," he said. "Funny how you expect these things to last a lifetime, in spite of the depressing statistics."

"Were you very traumatized when she told you she wanted a divorce?"

He shook his head in puzzlement. "You and all these assumptions of yours. What makes you think she was the one who wanted the divorce?"

"I think Patty said something. Or maybe I just figured that when you lost your job and took up painting instead of finding another . . . Well, I thought your wife—"

"Dumped me?"

I nodded sheepishly.

"Is that what happened with you and Traffic Dan? He lost his job with the Giants, so you dumped him?"

"No, of course not. I'm not that callous. There were other factors."

"Such as?"

"Such as: Dan didn't just stop working; he stopped trying to work." I was about to do my usual number on my ex, but I thought it might be awkward for my host, since he too was a bumbo, albeit not as flamboyantly.

"It's an interesting phenomenon," I said instead, hoping that if I spoke in general terms, I could avoid bashing Dan. "Men like to have it both ways. They want women to do well financially—or, at least, they say they do—but only if they're doing well too. The minute the balance of power shifts away from them, they can't handle it."

He looked skeptical. "What about you? Can women handle it when their man goes down? You act very enlightened and say it doesn't matter who's earning the money, but I think it does matter. I think you women don't respect a man if he's got less in the bank than you do."

"No, what I don't respect is a man who takes advantage of a woman he claims to love. Dan went on and on about how much he loved me and didn't want the divorce and wouldn't I reconsider, and now here he is hoarding what's mine, what *I* worked hard for."

"And you're hoarding a grudge."

"Wouldn't you?"

"Maybe in the beginning, but grudges use up a lot of space in here," he said, pointing to his heart. "I'm not pretending that life is fair, but sometimes things are what they are and you have to let them go."

Easy for him to say. He was about to be on the receiving end of the monthly checks. "Getting back to you, Evan, be honest: did Kaitlin give up on the marriage when you flew off to the Bahamas to paint? Was it the lifestyle change that prompted her decision to leave?"

"Assumptions again." He sighed, exasperated. "I was the one who left her, Melanie."

"Really? Why?"

"She had an affair."

"Oh." I put down my knife and fork.

"I told you she's a real estate agent. What I didn't tell you is that she sold this guy a loft in SoHo, then slept with him the day he closed on it. Some people celebrate closings with a bang, huh?"

"You're making a joke about it? You must have been devastated."

"Sure I was. But it happened during the third year we were married. We spent the next two trying to get past it, and we couldn't, so we broke up. Now I'm at the stage where I'm making jokes about it. It's called moving on. You should give it a shot."

"Okay, okay. I get it that you think I haven't moved on from Dan."

He set his plate on the side table and inched closer to me. "It's obvious that part of you is still in that relationship. You should hear yourself. If you didn't care about him, you wouldn't foam at the mouth every time his name comes up."

"I don't foam at the mouth." I wiped away the spittle that had formed in the corners.

"Right," he said. "Just like you don't have that vein popping out."

I reached up to feel my temple. There it was. The Dan vein. "Okay, so I get a little riled up, but it's not Dan I care about," I said. "It's the idea of giving him half of my income and then having to watch him piss it away. But I'm about to put a stop to his nights out on the town and all the rest."

Evan laughed. "He's probably too old to be grounded."

"I'm serious. I shouldn't be saying this to you, but the legal system has its loopholes."

"Why not to me?"

"Because you're about to battle it out with Kaitlin for alimony and whatever assets you have."

He leaned over and cupped my chin in his hand. "I like you," he said in his soft, raspy voice. "And I hope you like me too. I hope you like me regardless of the terms of my divorce settlement. I hope you like me in spite of your preconceptions about men who lose their jobs and become full-time artists. I hope you like me because you find me fun to be with or easy to be with or challenging to be with or a combination of all three. I know money's a huge issue for you, but it's irrelevant to me, so I really don't want to hear any more about it. Are you following?" Like a puppeteer, he moved my chin up and down so I would nod yes, then took his hand away and resumed eating. "Good. Now let's talk about something else. Tell me about your job, your friends, your position on global warming, anything but Dan."

Anything but Dan. Suddenly, I remembered my first conversation with Desiree. She said that a divorcée who goes on a first date and talks about her ex is a big turnoff to the new guy. Obviously, she was right.

Fine. It wouldn't do me any harm to stop obsessing about Dan and Leah for the rest of the evening, to forget the plotting and planning and strategizing just for a couple of hours. Things were going well in that department, so I deserved a night off, I told myself.

For the rest of the meal Evan and I talked and joked and scraped our plates clean. And when he brought out the dessert he'd made—fudgy brownies with pecans—we gobbled them up too. We even made faces at each other with the chocolate smeared across our front teeth and giggled like a couple of kids. It certainly wasn't the kind of evening I was used to, and I enjoyed myself more than I expected to.

"Want to take a walk with Buster or should we stay here?" he said after we'd fought over the last brownie and ended up splitting it. "We could talk some more or"—he reached for my hand and squeezed it—"just veg."

I wasn't inclined to go anywhere. I felt weightless, despite all the food I'd consumed, relaxed and loose. Buster was happy with his new squeakie toy, and Leah and Dan were on track to spend another blissful Saturday night together, and everything was right with the world.

"I guess we could stay here," I said sort of shyly, not sure of what would happen if we did.

He moved closer. I could swear he was about to kiss me, and I could also swear I would have let him. Then—damn!—my cell phone rang, startling us both.

"Why'd you even bring it?" he said as I got up to fish it out of my purse. "Your clients don't have financial emergencies on Saturday nights, do they?"

"Not usually, but there's this oil tycoon from Texas and I promised him access any time, day or night. Stupid me." I found the phone and answered it, prepared to have to suck up to Jed.

But it was Antoinette Thornberg on the line. She'd reinjured her arm trying to open a can of sardines and couldn't think of anybody else to call.

"Do you need a doctor?" I said while Evan played with Buster.

"I'm not going to that awful hospital again, if that's what you're asking," she said. "They'll just stick a thermometer in my mouth and send me home. What I need is someone to help me fix dinner, get me undressed and into bed, and make sure I don't end up like my friend Rose. First, her arm. Then, her hip. Then, she died."

"But your hip's okay, isn't it?" After the last medical episode, I had reached the conclusion that Antoinette was a hypochondriac *and* a condo commando.

"For the time being," she said. "Are you coming over or not?"

"Mrs. Thornberg, I'd be glad to come over, but I'm busy right now," I said. "A neighbor made me a quiet dinner at his—"

"A quiet dinner?" She sighed. "I should be so lucky. Your ex-husband and the party girl are having such a loud argument that their door slamming practically knocked my pictures off the wall."

I felt my throat dry up. "What?"

"You heard me. They must be on the outs."

"What are they fighting about?"

"How should I know?"

"You would know if you went over there and complained about the noise."

"How can I go over there and complain about the noise if nobody helps me with my arm? It's killing me!" She moaned. "Maybe they'll break up and he'll pick one that doesn't take dope next time."

Next time? No way. Leah was not moving out. I was *not* letting her move out!

"Okay, Mrs. Thornberg," I said, trying to stave off panic. "I'll be over as soon as I can."

"Good, but hurry. I'm starving."

I hung up and told Evan he was right: a client did have an emergency, although not investment related.

"She's a housebound elderly woman with no family or friends," I said. "She relies on me and"—I shrugged modestly—"I do my best to be there for her, even at odd hours."

He looked at me with a hint of suspicion in his eyes. "Are you being straight with me? You can be, you know."

"Absolutely."

"Well, then. I'm impressed. When you're not focusing on Dan and the alimony, you can be one terrific person. Very unselfish."

Yes, of course I felt like a lying sack of shit, but what was I supposed to do? It was one thing to admit I was bitter about the alimony. It was quite another to tell him I was so bitter that I'd rounded up a posse of accomplices to frame Dan into losing the alimony.

I clapped for Buster to come.

"Do you want me to watch him while you're gone?" said Evan.

"He'll be fine at my apartment," I said. "He's used to hanging out by himself."

I thanked him for the dinner and the doggie treats and said we should get together again soon, and then Buster and I left.

As I cabbed it over to Mrs. Thornberg's, I scolded myself for smelling victory too soon where Dan and Leah were concerned. I'd been foolish to think I was nearly out of the woods on the cohabitation. And I'd been equally foolish to think I could have a new man in my life when I still had unfinished business with the old one.

Chapter 17

They are yelling, aren't they?" I said as I was icing Mrs. Thornberg's arm and listening to the racket next door. We were sitting on her bed. She was stretched out like a dying person, although robust enough to wear one of her pretty dresses, and I was perched at her side, a regular Florence Nightingale. The arm wasn't the least bit swollen, and I suspected she was just looking for a little attention, but I wrapped it in a cold pack. The mere act of tending to her seemed to calm her down.

"You should have heard them an hour ago," she said. "Such lungs on those two."

"It's weird, because Dan never raised his voice with me."

"Probably because he was afraid of you."

"He was not."

"Well, then maybe he really loves this one. I think the more they care, the more they yell."

That remark really threw me until I realized she was probably just loopier than usual from all the extra-strength Tylenol I'd given her. I wanted Dan to adore Leah, don't get me wrong, but not in greater proportion to how much he'd adored me.

"She must have done something to provoke him," I said. "Maybe when you knock on their door to complain, you'll find out what."

"I'm not knocking on any doors until I eat my dinner," said Mrs. Thornberg, who had managed to get the can of sardines halfway open before succumbing to injury. As a result, her apartment now stunk of mothballs *and* fish oil.

"I'll bring you a sandwich and some tea," I offered.

"Good," she said. "Mash up the sardines, add a teaspoon of mustard, and a couple of squirts of lemon juice, and put it on some rye bread, with the crusts cut off."

Reminding myself not to feel put upon, since involving her in this drama had been my idea, I smiled and said, "Anything else?"

"Yeah. Make sure the tea's hot. There's nothing worse than tea that's not hot."

I could think of a lot worse things, and one of them was right next door. If Leah walked out on Dan, I was back to square one and much poorer for all my efforts.

I fed Mrs. Thornberg, watched a rerun of *Law & Order* with her, and, after more loud voices from her neighbors, encouraged her to go next door and see what was up.

"I'll remind them about the bylaws," she agreed. "No noise after nine P.M."

"You do that," I said, adding a "you go, girl" or some other inappropriate exhortation.

While she was gone, I pressed my ear to the wall, paced, sat on the bed, pressed my ear to the wall again, then abandoned the bedroom for the kitchen and scarfed down Mrs. Thornberg's discarded bread crusts.

Finally she returned. "So?" I said.

"Leah was crying." Oh, God. "But I told both of them in no uncertain terms that they'd better keep it down or else."

"Did it seem like she might leave?" I said, trying not to sound as desperate as I felt.

"What's it to you if she does?" She regarded me with her beady eyes. "I still don't understand why this is such a big deal for you. You don't even live here anymore."

"Because of Buster!" I said much too adamantly. "I want him living in a stable environment when he spends his time at Dan's. He's very sensitive, and his whole system will be upset if there's turmoil and strife over there." Turmoil and strife. Now there were words I hadn't used in, well, ever.

"Come, come," she said, waving me back into the bedroom with her "good arm." She asked me to help her undress and put on her nightgown and get her under the covers. As I filled all of her requests, I peppered her with questions. Was Dan crying too? (No.) Were they cursing at each other? (No.) Did she overhear any specifics of their argument? (Yes. Leah accused Dan of being afraid of commitment. Dan accused Leah of pushing him too hard too soon.)

"But she didn't threaten to move out," I confirmed again after tucking Mrs. Thornberg in.

"Not that I could tell," she mumbled. Oh, perhaps I forgot to mention that Mrs. Thornberg wore dentures. In addition to my other duties, I was charged with removing them from her mouth and dropping them into their fizzy cleanser for the night and then having to listen to her communicate with me through her gums. "I suppose it's possible that the fighting could escalate and she could move out during the night."

I panicked. How would I be able to verify if Leah stayed or left? Ricardo and Isa weren't around, and Mrs. Thornberg had taken an Ambien on top of the Tylenol. Within minutes, she'd be comatose. Dan and Leah could have a twelve-piece orchestra playing next door and she'd be too zonked out to hear it.

Which left only one thing for me to do: keep vigil myself.

"You'd have to put clean sheets on the bed," she said when I asked if I could spend the night in her guest room. "Nobody's used it in ages."

Poor Mrs. Thornberg. She was as lonely as I was.

As I watched her drift off to sleep, I felt sort of a kinship with her. She wasn't a mother figure, because mothers are supposed to take care of their daughters, and I was the one making her sandwiches and putting her to bed and soaking her dentures, but she no longer felt to me like the caricature of the brittle, meddling neighbor. She'd become more human with each intimate task she'd asked me to perform for her. I guess what I'm saying is that, while my motives for spending the night at her apartment were hardly pure, I wasn't totally heartless.

Once she was asleep, I called Evan and told him that my "client" wanted me to stay over and asked him to get my key from the super and check on Buster. Then I played solitaire with the old deck of cards I found on the dresser. But mostly I listened for movement from next door, and there wasn't any. The guest room was right off the foyer, so I would have heard if Leah had left in a huff, and she hadn't.

By the time the sun rose on Sunday morning, I was exhausted beyond belief but also relieved that the lovers had hung in. Whatever had caused their dust-up had either been resolved or at least tabled for the night.

I made Mrs. Thornberg breakfast and helped her bathe and dress before telling her I had to get home to my dog.

"You look tired," she said, tracing the dark circles under my left eye with her arthritic index finger. "You didn't like the mattress in the guest room?"

"It was fine," I said, surprised by her tenderness. "I was worried about leaving Buster alone, I guess."

"It's hard to be left alone," she said, casting her eyes over at the nearby photograph of the late Mr. Thornberg. He was a large man with a bad toupee. Perhaps if he'd lived longer, he could have bought one of those newer, more natural-looking hairpieces that give you an actual part on the side of the head, instead of a seam.

"I'll come see you again soon," I said.

"Who knew you were such a good girl?" she said, making me feel even more like a con artist than I already did. The fact is, I used to be a good girl—the one who did her homework and met every deadline and told the truth—but now I was somebody else, someone I didn't recognize.

I was supposed to drive up to Connecticut to visit Weezie on Sunday afternoon, but I told her there was a development in the

Dan-Leah situation that required my immediate attention. She wasn't happy that I was canceling—"If I didn't know better, I'd think you cared more about your ex-husband than you do about your best friend" was how she guilted me—but eventually she said she understood, and we rescheduled.

What I did instead was to show up at Desiree's without an appointment. Yes, it was a Sunday, but Desiree Klein Heart Hunting was a seven-day-a-week operation, so I went straight to her apartment from Mrs. Thornberg's.

"She's in with a client," said Taylor, her assistant. "She's not expecting you, is she?"

"No," I said, "but it's an emergency."

Taylor smiled sympathetically. "Bad date last night?"

"Uh, yeah," I said, realizing that Desiree hadn't shared the details of our arrangement. "Really bad."

She handed me the box of tissues on her desk. "In case you need them."

"Thanks, but I never cry," I said and took a seat in the living room.

Since I didn't bring anything to read while I waited, I closed my eyes and prayed for Dan and Leah to kiss and make up. I even pictured them kissing and making up. Well, as much as you can picture your ex-husband kissing a woman you've never met.

I was in midvisualization when an attractive woman in her fifties emerged from Desiree's office. She had short dark hair, a lightly tanned complexion, and the buffed, sturdy body of an athlete. There was something vaguely familiar about her—I wondered if she was a celebrity of some sort—but what was most noticeable about her were the tears. Her eyes were swollen from crying, her face blotchy with anguish. I assumed she'd been dumped by her husband of many years for a newly minted trophy wife and had now hired Desiree to ease her back into the dating world.

On her way out, she stopped at Taylor's desk, plucked one of the tissues from the box, and wiped her eyes with it.

"Feeling okay now, Lynda?" Taylor asked.

"Much better," said the woman. "Desiree gave me hope for the future. I have a reason to get up in the morning now."

Taylor nodded at her. "She's the best. I don't know your personal story, of course, since she keeps each case confidential, but I promise you she'll make your dreams come true, whatever they are."

"I'm counting on that," she said. "My friend Julie Marcus was a client of hers and not only ended up getting married again but had a late-in-life child. She used a surrogate—a nice young girl from Arkansas named Earlene, who needed the money and turned herself into a baby-making machine. Of course, this baby was born with a hole in its intestines and had to stay in the hospital for months after the delivery. Julie was such a wreck that she started shoplifting as a way of releasing the tension. Luckily, she got help before she got caught. Anyhow, thanks for the tissue." And she went on her way.

The instant she stopped nattering and left, I popped up and hurried over to Taylor's desk and bugged her about letting me see Desiree before the next client arrived. Two minutes later, I got my wish.

"Thanks for making the time," I said to Desiree, whose fuzzy slippers *du jour* had jingle bells on them. When she flexed her toes, it sounded like Christmas. She was also wearing the platinum blond wig, the one with the bangs. They were getting in her eyes and needed a trim. Either wigs grew or she had two blond ones.

"I'm booked solid today," she said, "so this better be good."

"It isn't good," I said. "Leah and Dan had a fight last night. You've gotta talk to her. They *cannot* break up."

"Hey. Chill, would you?" she said. "I don't know what you're getting so excited about."

"They were screaming at each other, that's what."

"So? Didn't you and Dan fight when you were together?"

"Yeah, and now we're divorced. Not only that, he never screamed at me."

"Probably because he was afraid of you."

"He was not!" What was it with everybody? "I think she's pushing him too hard to make a commitment. Maybe you went overboard during that last counseling session with her."

"You wanted her to move in there right away, didn't you?"

"Yes, but—"

" 'But' nothing. I convinced her that if she really liked the guy, she should throw caution to the wind and be the aggressor in the relationship."

"Well, now you've gotta tell her to back off a little. Just so she doesn't scare him off."

"Scare him off? He's crazy about her." She smiled proudly. "He bought her a necklace the other day. Amethyst, her birthstone. How many women get necklaces after just a few weeks, huh?"

I felt sick. "He's buying her expensive jewelry? With *my* money?"

"Melanie, Melanie." She shook her head. "You want them to stay together? It's gonna cost you."

"I know." I breathed deeply. "But you will call her, right?"

"Right."

"And you'll tell her to hang in there with Dan?"

"You got it."

"You'll say that men like him don't come along every day or something absurd like that?"

"Look, I know my business, okay?"

I rose from my chair. "You must know your business," I conceded. "You certainly made an impression on the woman who was just in here. She said you gave her hope for the future." I rolled my eyes. "She said a lot of other things too. God, the woman can talk. Her friend Julie had a baby by a surrogate and became a shoplifter. Did I need to know that? I mean, she's not very discreet."

She sighed. "Lynda Fox. A real yenta. Can't shut up about anybody. But she's been through hell and back."

"Lynda Fox? The professional golfer?" No wonder I'd recognized her.

"She had it all—LPGA championships, money, fame, houses all over the place—until her scumbag of a husband stuck it to her."

"He left her because she's such a big mouth?"

"No. She left him because she was hot for her caddie."

"Oh. Then what was she crying about?"

"What do you think? She's gotta pay the ex big bucks in spousal support now that they're history."

"Figures," I said. "I suppose he claimed he helped her become one of the best athletes in the country. I mean, really. She's the one with the talent."

"Ain't it the truth."

"Just one question though. If Lynda's in love with her caddie, why does she need a matchmaker?"

Desiree laughed, her dumpling body shaking and jiggling. "Same reason you do. She's a client of Desiree Klein Heart Hunting for Exes, my new division. I'm finding her a woman for the hubby so she doesn't have to pay him anymore." She laughed again. "You were right, Melanie. There are a gazillion women out there who are dying to unload their exes, and I'm just the one to help them do it. It's a mission from God."

I watched her lean her head back and laugh some more, and there was something about the laughter that nagged at me. Yes, I'd been the architect of her new revenue source. Yes, I was depending on her to help me the way she had just promised to help Lynda Fox. And yes, I believed fervently that men like Dan should be stopped from grabbing women's assets. But there was a tiny voice inside me whispering, wondering, warning, and what it was telling me was this: you've created a monster.

Unfortunately, what it wasn't yet revealing was whether Desiree was the monster or I was.

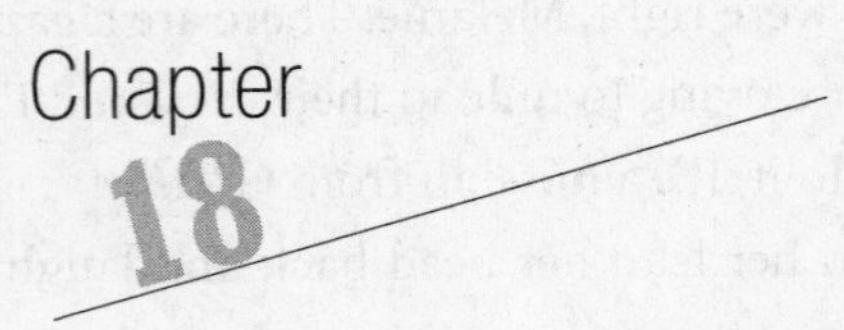

Chapter 18

Good morning, Melanie," said Ricardo. It was Monday at eight-thirty. I had come to deliver Buster to Dan—and to make sure Leah had lasted the weekend. "Mr. Swain's caretaker left about five minutes ago."

I sighed with relief. "So she's still staying with him."

"Every night. Got it written down right here for the insurance company." He pulled the notebook from the pocket of his uniform and held it up proudly. "If you'd been here sooner, you could have met her."

Did I want to meet her? Sure. Just not in front of Ricardo, who would inevitably launch into a discussion of Dan and his suicidal depression. "I'm just glad she's been looking after Mr. Swain so conscientiously."

"He does seem better. When he walks into the building with her, his whole face is lit up. If you didn't know about his mental problems, you'd think he was the happiest guy on earth. Happier than I've ever seen him anyway."

I thanked Ricardo for his commentary, but inside I was sort of taken aback. Dan was happier with Leah than he'd been with me? Not a chance. During our early years together, my ex was on top of the world—and not just because of his pro football career but because of how much in love we were. Well, no point in feeling competitive with a woman who was about to save me from years of financial hardship, I decided. I should be thrilled that everybody was loving everybody.

"Gosh, it's getting late," I said, checking my watch. "How about buzzing me up there so I can be on my way?"

After the usual song and dance, Buster and I rode up in the elevator, got off at Dan's floor, and rang his doorbell. When he didn't answer right away, I turned to Buster and muttered, "So much for what Daddy said last week about meeting my needs. He probably went back to sleep and forgot all about us."

I waited, tapped my foot on the floor, and waited some more. I was losing patience and was about to bang my fist on the door when it swung open. There was Dan, not in his bathrobe or even in his jeans but in an actual business suit. And he looked almost, well, fabulous. Over the past few weeks I'd noticed that he'd trimmed down a bit, but now that I really studied him, I could tell he'd dropped at least ten pounds. Was he taking better care of himself since he'd fallen for Leah? Paying more attention to his appearance? Watching those calories? Or was he so in love with her that he'd lost his considerable appetite? When he and I had first started dating, I couldn't eat a thing. "That's why they call it love*sick*," my college roommate had kidded me. Was it the same for him now? With her?

"Sorry. Sorry. Come in," he said, with a big smile for both me and Buster, which surprised me. Usually, I got his scowl. "I was on the phone confirming an appointment."

"Nice suit," I said, appraising him as I entered the apartment. "When did I buy us that one?"

"No pissing contests today, okay? I need to stay focused."

"On what?"

"A job interview." He crossed his fingers on both hands. "Think good thoughts around eleven o'clock."

I was so stupefied by this development I didn't answer immediately. *A job interview?*

"I know, I know. You don't believe it," he said with the sort of self-deprecating laugh he used to charm me with. "I heard that L.I.U. was in the market for a coach, so what the hell, huh?"

"Long Island University?" I said, still dumbfounded.

"The C. W. Post campus in Brookville. They're coming off their first undefeated regular season and their second-straight Northeast-Ten title, but the coach that got 'em there is retiring. They need somebody else to take over in the fall, so I tossed my name in the hat."

I shook my head, marveling at what he was saying. This was the same man who'd continually and contemptuously rejected the idea of coaching a local college football team? Now he was not only entertaining the idea but initiating it? Well, I couldn't help but be shocked by the one-eighty.

"Come on, darlin'," he coaxed. "Just tell me you're rooting for me today. You can go back to hating me tomorrow."

"I . . ." I stammered is what I did. Such was my surprise at this turn of events. Stammered, blinked my eyes, felt my upper lid twitch, started winding my finger around a lock of my hair. The usual nervous tics and then some. "I hope you get the job, Dan," I managed finally.

He nodded. "That means a lot. Thanks."

There was an awkward pause—we hadn't been polite to each other for so long that we were out of practice—until his phone rang. While he went to answer it, I strolled around the living room, processing this apparent and rather dramatic change in my ex. Was the old hackneyed expression true? That the love of a good woman can turn a man's life around? And was that what had happened to Dan? I'd tried to turn his life around but failed miserably. Hadn't I been a good woman? What did Leah have that I didn't? And why was I suddenly and irrationally so threatened by her?

I was standing next to the sofa table, staring vacantly at all the framed photos displayed there while trying to understand this new but nevertheless genuine negativity I was feeling toward her, when I realized with a jolt that the photos of me—of Dan and me—were missing.

I took another look. There was the one of Dan playing for Oklahoma. There was the one of him playing for the Giants. There was the one of him arm wrestling with his father and the one of him fly-fishing with his brothers and the one of him taking a bite out of his mother's apple pie. They were all accounted for, except those of him and me.

I know I said I thought it was weird that he'd left the photos of us around the apartment after we'd split up; that he was lazy and passive and clinging pathetically to his glory days by keeping them around. But now the absence of them threw me. Instead of being euphoric that he had obviously moved on, thanks to Leah, the woman *I'd* arranged for him to move on with, I was miffed. Who the hell did she think she was, coercing Dan into hiding, burying, even flinging into the trash those lovely memories of his past with me? She had no right! She was merely a temporary girlfriend! How dare she kick me and all traces of me out of *my* old place? I was hurt *and* roiled!

"You're still here," said Dan when he returned to the room. "You're usually in a big hurry to get to the office."

"And you're usually in a big hurry to get rid of me so you can have Buster all to yourself."

He smiled and extended his hand to me. "What do you say we call a truce, darlin'? You want to stay here and spend a little more time with Buster? It's more than fine with me. I don't have to leave right away."

He stood there with his hand out for a second or two and I thought, He really isn't goading me today. He's being incredibly human, for him. Why not follow his lead?

Warily, I took his hand and shook it.

"There. That wasn't so hard, was it?" he said, then sat on the arm of the sofa. "We don't have to be enemies. I'd like it better if we weren't."

"We're only enemies because you insist on taking—"

He placed his fingers across my lips. "Truce, remember?"

I nodded. It was all so unexpected, this courtesy he was showing me. I didn't know how to deal with it, so I got down on the floor to play with Buster.

"So how's it going?" Dan said, watching me, a great big smile on his face.

"How's what going?" I said.

"Work. Friends. Whatever. How's Weezie?"

Was he really on the level? Or was he setting me up for one of his stupid put-downs? I was completely off balance. "She's fine," I said, sure that he was just baiting me, letting me think things were different and then throwing a zinger at me. "Somehow she manages to have a happy life while the rest of us struggle along."

"Is it still a struggle for you, Mel?"

I gave him a look. Who was this guy anyway? The Dan I divorced never asked me questions like that. Reflectiveness was not a character trait I'd ever attributed to him. "*Still* a struggle? What are you talking about?"

"One of the first things you ever told me was how nothing came easily to you. I was just hoping that wasn't the case anymore."

His tone was so kind that I found my antagonism toward him dissipating, in spite of myself. "I'm having a tough time with the divorce," I admitted. "I've been angry about the alimony."

"You've made that clear," he said without even the hint of a smirk. Another surprise. "Tell me about the other ways the divorce has been tough for you."

"I hate sharing custody of Buster," I said. "I miss him when he's here with you."

"I feel the same way when he's with you," said Dan. "But we're both doing the best we can. He's got two parents who love him. They just don't happen to live together." There was a second or two, then: "Is it hard for you to be out there dating again?"

"Dating?" I laughed. "Talk about a low priority. I have zero interest."

"Don't you get lonely?"

There it was again—the kind voice, as opposed to the taunting, goading voice. I was as puzzled by it as I was entranced by it, by the change in his demeanor. Evan was the kind one, not my ex. Or at least he hadn't been in years. I couldn't remember the last time we'd had a conversation that didn't involve accusations and insults, so I didn't know how to respond. "Why on earth would you care if I get lonely?" I said.

"I'll always care, Mel," he said. "No matter what happens."

I regarded him the way you would a laboratory rat. He hadn't spoken of his feelings for me in a very long time, and while I didn't trust them—I was still fixated on the idea that a man who cares about you doesn't take money from you—I wasn't turned off by them. Once I let down my armor, I realized that there was something comforting about having a simple, honest give-and-take with my former spouse, the one who knew me best; the one who slept next to me and listened to me and confided in me; the one who was there in the beginning and there in the middle and, yes, there in the end. I had no parents and no siblings and no family to bolster my confidence in bad times. Dan had been and still was the most important person in my life. But the notion that we'd ever be able to sit in the same room and not only be civil to each other but compassionate seemed impossible.

" 'No matter what happens,' " I said, repeating his words. "That sounds a little mysterious. Are you referring to your own dating experience? Is your thing with the vet still going on?" Well, so much for the honesty part. You should have heard how innocently I posed the question.

"Very much so," he said, his face getting all "lit up," to quote

Ricardo. "Leah and I have been spending a lot of time together, and I think her good qualities might be rubbing off on me."

A *lot* of time together. And all of it fully documented. "In what way?" I nodded at the sofa table. "By convincing you to remove all evidence of me?"

"Oh. The photos." He shrugged. "Hey, she's a woman. She doesn't like coming here and seeing my ex-wife's face all over the place. You can't blame her."

Of course, I couldn't blame her. Of course, I did blame her. It made no sense to blame her, but even as I thanked God for her, I was building up a nice little resentment toward her.

"Was it Leah who suggested you go out on this job interview today?" I asked.

"Has she been encouraging me to embrace life instead of running from it? You bet. I know you tried to get through to me on that score, but she has a way of communicating with me that resonates."

Resonates. Like he'd ever used that or any other three-syllable word before. "Very interesting," I said, aware that I was now feeling outright hostility toward this woman. Not only did she make Dan happier than I made him, but she also communicated better with him than I did *and* improved his vocabulary! She was turning me into chopped liver.

"All I can say is that she doesn't judge or criticize when she talks to me," Dan rhapsodized. "She has an incredibly generous spirit."

No, *I* was the one with the generous spirit! She didn't pay for that amethyst necklace. I did! "So you two are getting pretty close. And in such a short time."

He wagged a finger at me. "We're close, but don't go pushing me down the aisle. I already told you: I'm not marrying anybody."

"What about living together?" I fished. "Is Leah thinking about moving in?"

"More than thinking," he said. "She's got some of her stuff here. We're testing the togetherness thing." He eyed me. "There's nothing in our divorce settlement against her staying here, right?"

How about that for a moment of truth? As I sat there staring into the baby blues of my ex-husband, the tarnished-but-still-golden Traffic Dan Swain, I asked myself: Can you really take advantage of him this way? This guy who seems to be trying to get his life on track but doesn't remember the terms of his own divorce settlement? Can you face yourself in the mirror every day if you sucker him out of the alimony? Can you do it? *Can you, Melanie?*

As I felt my enthusiasm for my plan weaken just a little, I reminded myself that it was Dan who'd suckered me. He was the one who'd had no compunction about going after every cent I earned and then frittering it away once he got it. He was the one who'd said, "I love you and I'm sorry you're leaving me, but I'll let you work your ass off so I can buy myself lots of shiny new toys." He was the one who was always flaunting the toys in my face and making me lose my concentration at work. He was the one who'd taken advantage of *me.*

So, yes, I could follow through with my plan. I *would* follow through with it.

"Nope," I said. "Nothing in our settlement about that. Leah can stay here and you'll still be in compliance. Happy?"

"Very." He smiled. "She's great, Mel. I don't know how long it'll last between us, but I feel like a new man since I met her. She reminds me of you in some ways."

"Really?"

"Yeah. She's beautiful, independent, good at her job." He paused. "Come to think of it, she's you without the wiseass." He laughed. "I bet you'd like her."

I wasn't so sure, but I was about to find out.

Chapter 19

I was still sitting on the floor, enjoying my extra time with Buster and shooting the breeze with the newly pleasant and professional-looking Dan, when I heard a key in the door.

"Doesn't Isa clean in the afternoons?" I said, since it was only nine o'clock—too early for our cleaning lady to put in an appearance.

Before he could answer, in walked a vision. A vision with a briefcase. Wearing a tight-fitting black skirt-and-sweater outfit under a nifty little black leather jacket, the woman had mile-long legs, a flat stomach, melon-shaped breasts, and thick, glossy, shoulder-length, chestnut brown hair, the kind that's so silky it should be made into a mink coat. Oh, and the face? Picture a flawless complexion, almond-shaped green eyes, and a nose and mouth in perfect proportion to the other features. Well, Desiree had promised me Leah was bee-uteeful, but this was ridiculous.

"Hey, honey," said Dan as she opened the door. Due to an odd sort of flashback, it actually took me a second before I realized he was not referring to me. "Did you forget something?"

"My checkbook," she said, hurrying inside with graceful little steps. Her voice was light and breathy and singsong, like the tinkling of a bell. "I must have left it—"

She stopped when she saw me on the floor with Buster, who, at that moment, bolted out of my arms so he could sniff her Manolo Blahniks. She bent down and stroked his head. "It's just me, Busty boy," she said. I watched with both horror and fascination as his tail wagged like an out-of-control windshield wiper. While she stroked him, he licked her, lifted his paws to her, and made purring noises at her like a goddamn cat. He was as besotted with her as his master was.

"Leah, this is Melanie," said Dan. "Melanie, Leah."

I did not get up. Let her stoop to my level, I thought. Well, you know what I mean. "Hi," I said. "Nice to meet you."

She gave me a little finger wave. "Same here. I've heard a lot about you. And I really, really love your dog."

"Looks like the feeling's really, really mutual," I said, not intending to mimic her but unable to help myself.

"I'd keep an eye out for cataracts though," she said. "Pugs his age can be prone to them, and I've noticed that his depth perception isn't always on the mark." She smiled. "In case Dan didn't tell you, I'm a vet."

"He told me," I said, "but we have our own vet for Buster, so we're all set. No cataracts, as of the most recent checkup. No problems of any kind, actually." You quack. You troublemaker. You stealer of my dog's affection.

"Okay, great," she said, then turned to Dan. "I'm gonna run and get my checkbook."

She took off for the bedroom, my traitorous Buster tagging along after her. She was gone a minute or two, during which my ex said, "As I told you, she's been staying over. It made sense to give her a key."

"No explanation necessary," I said, getting up off the floor. "But why would she need her checkbook at her office? Or does she have to pay people to bring their pets to her?"

"Mel."

"You used to think I was funny."

"And you used to make jokes that weren't mean-spirited. Leah's funny, but she manages to be sweet too."

"You just think that because she has nice tits."

"Mel."

"Fine. I'll stop."

Leah returned with Buster in tow. "Got it," she said, holding the checkbook. She kissed Dan on the mouth, then wiped her lipstick smudge off. "You nervous about the interview, Swainy?"

Swainy?

"Not yet, but I'm sure I will be as soon as I get in the car."

She took his hands in hers and pressed herself against him. I wished I'd averted my eyes. "Just remember what we said. Today is an adventure. You'll be meeting new people, learning about the school, hearing about their team, talking about a sport you love. Don't make it about how much they'll like you or whether you'll have the right answers to their questions. Make it about being yourself and letting whatever happens happen. There's no pressure to get this job, Swainy. If it's not this one, it'll be another one. Okay?"

No pressure to get this job? Sure, because he already had an income. Mine!

Dan winked at me. "Didn't I tell you she was sweet?"

"You did." So sweet my teeth were springing cavities.

"And didn't I tell you she has a way of communicating that resonates?"

"Yep," I said. "It resonates with me too. When I go to work today, I'll view it as an adventure."

"Dan told me what your job is, Melanie, but I forgot," said Leah. "Are you a stockbroker?"

"No, I have stockbrokers reporting to me," I said, throwing my shoulders back. "I'm a vice president at Pierce, Shelley and Steinberg, overseeing investment portfolios that cover a wide range of asset options, stocks included."

"Mel's their top gun," said Dan.

"Sounds really, really exciting," said Leah. "I've never been a numbers person. I put my heart and soul into living things."

"Living things are the ones who have investments," I pointed out. "My clients are mammals, for the most part."

Dan shot me a stern look. "I've got to get moving, you two," he said, ushering us both toward the door.

I said a quick good-bye to Buster and Leah said a quick good-bye to Swainy, and she and I ended up riding down in the elevator together.

"So," I said, feeling obligated to make conversation, the way you do in elevators. "How long have you been seeing Dan?"

"About a month," she said. "Not long by most people's standards, but we've grown very close very fast." She sighed a lovebird sigh. "He's the best thing that's ever happened to me."

What was the matter with her? Dan was the biggest slacker of all time, and she was beautiful and sweet, as advertised. Maybe she *was* a dope fiend, as Mrs. Thornberg would say.

"It's not just that he's the most gorgeous guy I've ever dated, although I can't deny I find him incredibly attractive, physically," she went on, without any encouragement on my part. "It's his goodness. His kindness. His decency."

"Then he hasn't taken you to any strip clubs yet?"

She laughed. "I know he's no angel, but he's really, really trying to improve himself."

"He told me you've had a positive influence on him."

"I think he just needed someone to support him."

Support him? Isn't that what *I* was doing? Every damn month?

"Well, here we are," I said when we arrived in the lobby. I was all set to shake hands and split, but she kept talking. And walking. And despite my efforts to break away, we were approaching Ricardo together.

"Ladies," he said. "Glad you got to meet each other." He turned to me. "She's some caretaker, huh?"

"Caretaker?" said Leah. "You make me sound like a nurse or something."

"Sorry. I don't know what you people call yourselves these days," he said before I could slap some duct tape over his mouth. "Caretakers, nurses, therapists, techies."

"We call ourselves veterinarians," she said with a look that suggested Dan's doorman was a little soft in the head.

Ricardo nodded. "Mr. Swain's an animal, all right. I'll never forget that game against the Dolphins when he took on four of their guys and still hung on to the ball."

I tugged on Leah's arm. "I've got to get to the office."

"So do I," she said.

Ricardo pushed open the revolving door for us. "Really happy about how well Mr. Swain's doing," he called out as we exited the building. "It would have been a tragedy if we'd lost him."

Leah's eyes widened. She did a complete revolution out the door, then revolved her way back inside, with me on her heels. " 'If we'd lost him?' " She glanced at me. "What's he talking about?"

"It's okay," said Ricardo, lowering his voice. "I know what's going on. Thanks to you, he's still with us."

"I don't understand," she said.

I linked my arm through hers and dragged her back through the revolving door, the two of us crammed in the same slot this time.

"Ricardo hasn't been able to deal with Dan's retirement from football," I told her once we were outside on the street. "He's a loyal fan, and he's afraid that, now that Dan and I are divorced, Dan will leave New York and move back to Oklahoma. That's what he meant by 'if we'd lost him'."

She relaxed into a smile. "Dan's not going anywhere. He'd never leave that apartment. In fact, last night he told me I could redecorate it. I know you and he lived there together, but it could use a bit of sprucing."

"Sprucing?" And Dan *was* leaving that apartment. As soon as the ninety days were up, he would no longer be able to afford it.

"Yes. The colors are a little, well, ten years ago. You don't mind, do you, Melanie?"

Those colors were my colors. Just like the photos on the sofa table were my photos. Just like the pug without the cataracts was my pug. I did not like this woman. But here's what I said in response to her question: "Whatever you and Dan decide is fine and dandy with me." Because the thing about sweet people is this: they can make the rest of us look bad if we're not careful.

"I'm so relieved that you feel that way," she said. "I didn't want to offend you."

"Offend me? Don't be silly." I chuckled at the very notion. "You and Dan are building a relationship together. The important thing is for you two to cohabitate continuously and substantially." I said it simply to keep myself on message, not to be facetious or smart-alecky.

She beamed then opened her arms and wrapped me in a squishy hug. "That was a lovely thing to say." She squeezed me again. "I've dated a lot of divorced men, and most of the time their ex-wives are bitter and vindictive. But you?" She hugged me a third time. "You're really, really great."

As I just indicated, the trouble with sweet people is that you can't tell them to go fuck themselves, no matter how much you might want to.

It was close to ten o'clock by the time I finally made it to the office. Late for me, yes. But I figured that after all the years and all the hours I'd logged in at that place, what was an hour here or there? Besides, there were no meetings scheduled, no presentations I was supposed to give. Just your run-of-the-mill day at Pierce, Shelley.

Steffi wasn't at her desk—she must have been foraging in the supplies room or making photocopies in the copy room—and my desk was piled high with messages. I went back out into the hall to look for her. There were other assistants milling around their cubicles gossiping, people who knew me well enough to at least greet me in the morning, but none of them did. In fact, they stopped talking when I passed by and lowered their eyes.

Something was definitely up, but what? Was there a juicy rumor circulating? Were we being acquired? Were we acquiring another company? Were we poaching a client from another company? Was some heavyweight getting canned?

I decided to stop by Bernie's office before getting down to work, hoping he'd fill me in. When I reached his office, Carla, his assistant, a large, pale woman with enormous nostrils, told me her boss was in a meeting. I said I'd wait, even though she seemed eager for me not to.

Two minutes later, Bernie's door opened, and he and Jed Ornbacher walked out together, slapping each other on the back and appearing to be in high spirits. They stopped in their tracks when they saw me standing there.

"Oh. Mel," said Bernie, looking uncomfortable. "I didn't think you'd come in yet."

"Who told you that?" I said with a big smile and an increasingly nervous stomach. "Of course I'm *in*." I turned to my client and shouted at him, so I wouldn't have to repeat myself. "Jed? Everything okay this morning? You're flying back to Dallas later, right?"

Jed removed his cowboy hat, revealing the cowboy comb-over, and moved closer to me. "You're a smart gal," he said, taking my hand and patting it, more grandfather than dirty old man for once. "I'm gonna pray for you, but I want you to do some praying yourself. You hear me, young lady?"

He was so loud they could hear him in Dallas. "Thanks, I need all the prayers I can get," I said. "We all do, right? Such a crazy world we live in."

He put his hat back on. "Put your faith in the Lord and it'll all be fine." He laughed-coughed-wheezed, then said he'd better run.

"Have a safe flight and I'll be in touch soon," I said, waving as Bernie walked him to the elevators.

How odd, I thought, as I watched them make their way down the hall. Why hadn't Jed set up an appointment to see me before he left town? And what was he doing in Bernie's office on the day of his departure? I was his account executive. I was the one who'd reeled him in. I was the one who'd impressed him during our very first encounter. Yes, I'd messed up a couple of times with the meetings and phone calls, but I'd come up with an excellent financial plan for him, and all I needed was some time to implement it.

Well, maybe he was just in a rush, I decided. Yes, he was only concerned about making his flight. But then, of course, I remembered that he had his own plane and it wasn't leaving until he was good and ready for it to leave.

My insecurities started to take on a life of their own, so I hung around until Bernie reappeared, just to reassure myself that nothing was amiss. Carla kept glancing at me with those nostrils in the air—they were so big you could stick hot dogs up them, rolls and all—but then this was no time to think about food, I reminded myself.

"Ah, good. I was hoping we could chat," Bernie said very gently, as if I were a mental patient about to go on a rampage.

"I'd like that," I said. We entered his office and sat down—he, behind his desk, I, in one of the chairs facing him. "Did my client offer to pray for you too?" I laughed. "The guy's too much, isn't he?"

"That's the thing I wanted to chat about," he said, continuing in this flat monotone he'd never used with me before. "Jed isn't your client anymore."

At first I didn't get it. Of course Jed was my client. He and Bernie hadn't been arguing when I saw them together, so there was no apparent rift with Pierce, Shelley. And I certainly hadn't received any notification that Jed was moving his account to another firm.

"*I'm* taking over his account," Bernie explained. "We worked out the details this morning, and I was planning to tell you as soon as he left."

I couldn't believe it. The news was like a punch in the gut. I'd never lost a client—well, not to another executive within the company—and I never envisioned that I would. I was counting on making partner, not getting demoted. How could this have happened? How could I have allowed it to happen?

"Why are you taking over Jed's account?" I said, trying to maintain my composure but hearing the plaintive tone in my voice. It was high and squeaky, like the toy Evan had bought for Buster. "Didn't he think I was competent?"

"Mel," said Bernie. "You and I both know you've lost your focus lately. You admitted as much."

So it was the whole business with Dan and the alimony. Well, sure, getting the project off the ground had appropriated a great deal of my energy, but as Desiree often said, matchmaking is a full-time proposition, even when you're not the one looking for love. Not for yourself, I mean. If I hadn't given the project my all, how else would I have been able to commandeer Ricardo, Isa, and Mrs. Thornberg to spy for me? How else would things have proceeded so smoothly? Because I was on top of every aspect of the project, that's how!

"It's that loss of focus that gave Jed the feeling that you weren't a hundred percent on the case," Bernie went on.

"But I promised you it was only temporary—"

"Let me finish," he said. "You're distracted. You're not coming to work prepared. You're not putting in the hours. You're not giving Jed the attention he needs."

"I'm not letting him grope me, you mean? Because if that's it, you can have him as a client," I said hotly.

"It isn't that and you know it. He just wants the full-time executive he thought he was getting."

"Did you tell him about the divorce? How it's complicated my life?" I said, feeling myself sink into the chair.

"I did. But he asked—and I have to confess that the possibility had occurred to me too, given how edgy and scattered you've been—whether it's drugs."

"*What?*"

"Are we looking, for example, at a cocaine issue?"

A dope fiend. That's what they suspected me of being. Well, what goes around comes around, I thought. My tall tale about Leah had come back to bite me.

"I don't do drugs, Bernie," I said, making myself sound incredibly sober, even though I already was.

"Normally, I would have sent you packing," he said, not committing to whether he believed me about the drugs or not. "But you've been an important member of our team, Mel. So I'm giving you another chance. I'll take Jed's account and you keep the smaller fish."

Yeah, great. How would I ever get a promotion and a raise with smaller fish? How would I escape the Heartbreak Hotel now?

There was only one way, and that was by *not* turning over half of my salary to my ex. I had to keep up the fight.

"It isn't drugs," I said again. "It's the divorce, and I'm getting a handle on it. In another couple of months, you won't even remember this conversation. I'll be my old self, Bernie. You'll put me back on the big fish, reeling them in the way I always have. You'll see."

He nodded. "Whatever the problem is, I'm rooting for you to get it under control."

Get *them* under control was more like it. And I was close. So close.

Chapter 20

When Dan came to drop off Buster the following Monday morning, he was not only right on time but also dressed for success. He was wearing an older suit that he'd been too heavy to squeeze into, but now there it was, fitting his trimmer body perfectly. He looked very handsome, but what was even more striking was how alert he was, how alive. It was as if his On switch had been activated. Each time I saw him I noticed subtle changes in him—in his expression, in his walk, in his attitude—and I wasn't sure how to react to them. Or to him. After all my bitching and moaning about how checked out he'd been, he was emerging from his fog and beginning to resemble a human being.

"I haven't heard yet about the L.I.U. job, but the interview went so well I figured I'd go on another one," he said, explaining the clothes.

"Another coaching job?" I said, amazed.

"Rutgers," he said. "And I've got Columbia lined up for later in the week. Their team is bad enough that they might even take a chance on me."

He laughed his self-effacing laugh, and I was suddenly transported back to the night we'd met at the restaurant when we were in college. He'd laughed that laugh then, when he'd told me it was his first time in the Big Apple, and I'd found him charming. But was I finding him charming now or was I merely grateful that he was no longer parading his extravagances in front of me? There was no question that he'd put a stop to the baiting, and as a result, I didn't go into every encounter with him prepared to do battle.

But the battle over the alimony was still raging. This was not the time for me to feel anything but an impending sense of victory as the ninety-day deadline approached. And yet, there I was, standing in my living room, smiling at him, and there he was, standing in my living room, smiling at me, and it was as if we were two people who actually liked each other.

"I'm impressed that you're putting yourself out there," I said, truly bewildered by these new/old feelings toward him.

"I appreciate that," he said.

"Well, you're making an effort, Dan. That's huge."

I looked at him, his golden hair gleaming under the light of the window, and was suddenly flooded with what-ifs. What if he'd made the effort sooner? What if he'd realized that all I ever wanted was for him to pursue a coaching job, instead of hiding in a bottle or a poker game or a night on the town? What if he'd understood that the reason I left him was because he wouldn't take the kind of risks he was willing to take now? Would we still be together? Would the divorce never have happened? Would I be the one sharing his bed, not Leah?

Leah. I'd actually forgotten about her for a second. Was it her sweet nature and kindergarten-level pep talks that were motivating Dan to improve himself? Or would he have changed on his own, given enough time and self-loathing?

I blinked, trying to cleanse myself of all the questions, because they were entirely inappropriate, given our current circumstances. But when Dan spoke next, it was as if he'd read my mind.

"Just thought you should know," he said. "I finally get what you wanted from me—and what I should have wanted from myself."

"You do?" I said, stunned that we were so in sync.

"Yeah. See, I don't blame you for walking out. Not anymore. I wasn't pulling my weight in the marriage. But more than that, I wasn't living my life. You tried to tell me that, but I was too terrified to listen."

So he *was* afraid of me, just as Mrs. Thornberg and Desiree had said he was, and the realization brought on another what-if. What if I'd been as sweet and uncritical as Leah? Would he have flourished back then? Was there a piece of our breakup that was *my* fault? "Are you ready to live your life now?" I asked.

He nodded. "I'm still a work in progress, but I'm gonna be okay." He nodded again. "I bet even you will be proud of me."

"Oh, Dan." I was completely flummoxed by his new self-awareness, his introspection. Finding myself tolerating him, much less being impressed by him, wasn't part of my plan, wasn't the point of "the project." He was supposed to fall into my trap, forfeit the alimony, and go his merry way. He wasn't supposed to remind me of the man I used to love.

"Why don't we have this conversation over a cup of coffee?" I suggested, because I didn't know what else to say. "Or do you have to run off to your interview?" Never mind that I had to run off to my job, for which I was already late. But since Jed Ornbacher wasn't my responsibility anymore, nobody seemed to care when I came and went.

"I've got a few minutes," he said. "Does your coffee still taste like water or have you graduated from instant?"

I poked him in the ribs, on the spot where he was ticklish, and he started poking me back. The poking was utterly spontaneous and the first remotely physical exchange we'd had in ages, but it felt right somehow. Familiar.

Dan stayed for coffee, played with Buster, and helped me replace a lightbulb that had gone out. And he talked to me, not like a man who was ducking my scrutiny, but like a man who was inviting it. He told me more about his interview at L.I.U. He told me he'd become a volunteer in an athletic program directed at inner-city kids. And he told me that he and Leah were repainting the apartment themselves, at night, both to save money and to give them an activity that they could do together.

"So you two are still going strong?" I asked, knowing the answer, of course. Isa had told me only the day before that she'd snapped a photograph of Leah's panties in their bed.

"Very," he said. "I never expected to get close to another woman again, but she and I have the kind of chemistry that—" He paused shyly. "Maybe I shouldn't."

"Go ahead. What were you about to say?"

"Just that she and I have the kind of chemistry that you and I had in the beginning."

Yet again, the comparison irked me. I resented the notion that the woman I'd schemed and plotted to bring into his life for only a brief stint was inspiring the same kind of devotion in him that I had. He'd married *me*. I'd been his *wife*. How could he even put her and me in the same category, let alone the same sentence?

"Remember when you came out to Minco for the first time?" he said.

"How could I forget?" I said. "You proposed to me during that trip."

"I sure did. But remember how we couldn't be apart for a second? We were like a couple of magnets."

"I remember," I said softly.

"And it wasn't just sexual. We each 'represented the other's missing half,' was how you put it. Once we got together the puzzle just fit, didn't it?"

I nodded, feeling a twinge of pain at the memory. I'd missed having a man to round me out, fill in my missing parts. I missed the way Dan and I used to be, plain and simple.

"Well, now Leah is my missing half," he said. "She completes the puzzle. Amazing, huh? I never thought it would happen again."

Okay. I'd heard enough about Leah and her many gifts. I'd much preferred the conversation about *my* gifts.

I looked at my watch, then Dan looked at his, and we realized we'd both better get moving. We said hasty good-byes.

"This was nice," he said, stopping in the doorway.

"My watery coffee?" I teased.

“Being with you and Buster without the tension.” He smiled. “Feels a little like old times, doesn’t it?”

“A little,” I agreed. A lot, I thought.

“Go get ’em today, darlin’.”

“You too. I hope the interviews go well.”

He nodded and closed the door, and as soon as he was gone I turned to Buster and said, “What the hell was that?”

Buster, being a very clever dog, remained silent, so that I’d have to answer my own question.

“Alimony aside, Daddy’s doing a very good imitation of a solid citizen.”

In response, Buster stuck his head under the sofa.

“I know,” I said. “Mommy doesn’t know what to make of it either.”

I spent the rest of the week in a state of confusion. Who was this ex-husband of mine with his job interviews, his volunteer work, and his steady girlfriend? And how was I supposed to relate to him? I was committed to terminating his support payments, committed to building back my assets, but as I sat at my desk, writing him his monthly check, filling in his name and the dollar amount and completing the deed with my signature, I’ve got to tell you: I felt ambivalent. Why? Because the guy was behaving like a mensch instead of a jerk. I didn’t understand the turnaround in him or in me, except to say that he’d changed and I’d noticed, and the pleasure of pulling the rug out from under him wasn’t quite there anymore. There was no pleasure in hearing him sing Leah’s praises either, and certainly no pleasure in listening to him give her the credit for shaping him up.

When the next Monday morning came around, I took extra care with my appearance before bringing Buster over to Dan's. I wouldn't admit it to myself, but I wanted to be more attractive to him than she was. Stupid, I know. Childish, I know. Competitive, I know that too. Nevertheless, I showered with the vanilla-scented body wash somebody at work swore by, and I tweezed my eyebrows so they'd be as ultrathin and stylish as hers. Unfortunately, I went overboard in the eyebrows department; they ended up with this dramatic arc in the middle of them, giving me the appearance of someone who's perpetually astonished. Which is sort of what I was, actually.

Just my luck, Leah was still hanging around the apartment when I arrived, and the scent of *her* body wash—a heady blend of lavender, rose, hibiscus, and every flower ever created—made my vanilla stuff smell like skunk oil in comparison. And then, of course, there was Buster. As soon as we walked in the door, he made a mad dash for her. As if he couldn't get away from me fast enough.

"Here you are, Busty boy," she said, folding him into her arms. "I missed you so much that I waited for you this morning instead of going straight to work. Yes, Busty. Yes, poochie poo. You are my really, really good boy."

My eyes bugged out when I heard/saw that one. And no. It wasn't the "really, really." It wasn't even the "poochie poo." It was the "my." I mean, come on. Buster wasn't hers. Dan wasn't hers either. Not really. She wouldn't be in the picture at all if I hadn't put her in it.

Okay, you can see where this was going.

"Hello, Leah," I said. Dan had greeted me, but she'd been too involved with *my* dog to acknowledge me.

"Morning, Melanie," she chirped. "It's a beautiful day, isn't it?"

It was February in New York. It wasn't snowing, granted, but how beautiful could it be? "Yes," I said. "It's brisk and invigorating." She was sweet? I'd be sweet.

She grabbed her briefcase. "I'd love to stay and chat, but I've got a waiting room full of animals." She started to move toward the door, then stopped and gestured at the living room. "Oh. I forgot to ask: how do you like our new color?"

Our new color. Oh. I'd been so distracted by Buster's defection that I hadn't noticed the paint job.

"You went with yellow," I said. During my occupancy, the room had been robin's egg blue.

"It's actually mustard," she said.

"Gulden's or French's?" I said.

"It's yellow," said Dan, laughing. "Leah thought it would be warmer than the blue, and I have to agree."

"It's very warm," I said, feeling the heat of resentment rising up into my neck and face. "Are you planning to do the whole apartment in it?"

"Variations of it," said Leah. "I think it's nice when there's a flow, as opposed to each room being a starkly different color."

Fine, I thought. Trash the blue in the living room and the green in the dining room and the burgundy in the master. Just remember, you're a temporary girlfriend and the second you're gone, your piss-color paint will be gone too. "Sounds lovely," I said with a broad grin.

She put her hand on my shoulder. "I'm really, really glad you approve."

And off she went. I turned to Dan to ask him how the job hunt was going, but he spoke first.

"Didn't I say she was great?"

"Who?" I said, as if I didn't know.

"Leah," he said. "Always so up. You couldn't be depressed around her if you wanted to be."

Ricardo would have been happy to hear that. "Yes," I said. "She's very up. But then she has a lot to be up about. Obviously, you and she aren't just dating anymore. You're actually living together, planning your future."

"She's been staying here, yeah," he admitted. Part of me wished I'd had his statement on tape. The other part wasn't as jubilant, the part that was causing this sudden conflict within me. "But it's still early. We aren't making anything permanent. I told you that, Mel. When my marital status is about to change, you and your lawyer will be among the first to know."

I nodded, feeling another stab of guilt about what I had perpetrated. What in the world was going on with me? Why was I wavering even the slightest bit?

I was so uncomfortable thinking about Desiree and the other cast of characters with whom I was colluding that I changed the subject. "Any news from the colleges?"

He pouted. "Columbia and Rutgers both passed."

"Oh, Dan. I'm sorry," I said.

His face exploded into a smile. "But L.I.U. called me back for a second meeting!"

Before I could demonstrate my excitement, he demonstrated his own. He took me in his arms and danced me around in a circle, and instead of recoiling or even pulling away diplomatically, I went with it. Just went with his joy and his eagerness to share it with me. In that moment, as he held me and I held him and we were magnets again, it was as if no time had passed since we were in Minco the night he'd proposed. There was no bitterness, no bad history. I was right back on his family's porch where he was proclaiming his love and telling me how our life would be easy and assuring me I'd never have to worry about money again.

When the dancing stopped, I stood there and wondered if I had lost my mind. I wasn't in Minco and Dan wasn't proclaiming his love. Not for me, anyway. It was Monday morning, and I had to get to the office.

"Want some coffee to celebrate?" he asked with such an imploring look I could hardly resist.

Making the excuse to myself that it wasn't every day that Dan was on somebody's short list for a job, I ended up staying for coffee. I ended up being late for work. I ended up calling Weezie during my lunch hour and telling her I had to see her as soon as possible. When she asked what was so urgent, I said, "I need an intervention."

"Are we talking about drugs?"

"No!" That again.

"You barely drink, so it's not alcohol," she mused. "Is it food? Gambling? Internet porn?"

"It's Dan, Weezie. I'm—well—thinking about him differently, more positively."

"Is that all?" She sounded relieved.

"You don't understand. I'm starting to wonder if I can go through with the whole Desiree project."

"Come on. You've been counting the days until you take away the boy's allowance."

"I know, but now I'm having second thoughts. You should see how he's changed. It's like Leah waved a magic wand over him.

The changes are all good, don't get me wrong, but I'm uncomfortable about how much influence she seems to exert."

"Wait. Now you're feeling protective of him?"

"I guess I am."

"Why? He's not your responsibility anymore." She paused. "I'm not getting this. Your problem is with Leah?"

"Yes! That's it. She's taken over everything—Dan, Buster, the apartment. She's painting it yellow, by the way."

"So you want her out of Dan's life?"

Was that what I wanted? Or did it just feel that way? It was all so bewildering.

"Or do you want Dan back in your life?" she said. "Is that what we're really talking about?"

"No," I said. Then, after a pause: "Maybe."

"Oh, Mel. This is crazy," she said. "You've been hating him for a long time."

"That's why I need the intervention," I said. "Right now, I'm not hating him nearly enough."

Chapter 21

I met Weezie halfway between Manhattan and Westport at the upscale restaurant of a Hilton hotel in Westchester County. It was one of those jackets-required places that attracts corporate types on weeknights and families on weekends and serves food that tries to be sophisticated but is merely overpriced.

"So Nards didn't mind being left out tonight?" I said while Weezie took the first sip of her martini.

"Not at all. He's working late anyway."

"I didn't know ENT guys worked late. Do people have emergency ear surgery?"

"He's not seeing patients," she said. "It's all the paperwork that's keeping him in the office."

"I thought bringing that new doctor into the practice was supposed to lighten his load."

"It was. But she's only created more paperwork."

"She?"

"Yeah. Her name's Molly Corbett. Great credentials. Very smart. Extremely dedicated." She took a bite of her thirty-dollar chicken, a similar version of which was six dollars at Boston Market. "Tell me about this Dan business. We didn't come to talk about boring old Nards and me."

I told her about the changes in my ex—the job interviews, the volunteer work, the conversations about our marriage, the new self-awareness, the rejuvenated cover-boy looks. "If he'd been like this a year ago, I might have stayed. I'll tell you one thing: the old chemistry between us isn't dead. When he touched me the other day, I actually wanted to jump him."

"That's because it's been forever since you've jumped anyone. You just need to get laid."

"I guess," I said with a sigh. I thought of Evan then, of the near-kiss we'd almost shared, of how much I enjoyed being with him, from walking around the neighborhood to stirring mashed potatoes at his stove. But no sooner did the image of his face appear before my eyes than it was displaced by Dan's. "I think I'm losing it, Weezie. I used to be so sure about my feelings about myself, men, work. But now?" I shrugged.

"It's Leah who's the cause of all this," she insisted. "Before she came along, you had Dan all to yourself—to love, to leave, to begrudge, whatever you wanted. Now that he's with her, your role in his life has diminished, and you're threatened. It's a normal reaction, and it'll pass."

I considered this possibility as I ate a fork full of my thirty-five-dollar shrimp, a similar version of which was ten dollars at Red Lobster. "I do feel muscled around by her," I admitted. "I don't like it that she found a way to pull him out of his funk when I couldn't. And I don't like that Buster adores her and that she has better hair than I do."

She laughed. "You asked Desiree for an A-lister. That means A-list hair."

"Desiree." I made a face. "You and your big ideas."

"Come on, Mel. You needed a way out of the alimony, and she hit the jackpot with Leah, who came to your rescue, in case you forgot. But by coming to your rescue, she also made Dan more attractive to you. Yes, he's trying to get his act together. Yes, he's looking great again. Yes, he's saying the things you've been waiting to hear. But your feelings for him aren't love, if that's what you're thinking. This is about her and how she's taken your place with him. We all want what we can't have."

I drank some of my five-dollar Evian, a similar version of which was free from my tap at home. "I'm sure you're right," I said.

"I am right," she said. "You hired Desiree to find someone for Dan and she did. She's a brilliant matchmaker."

No sooner were the words out of her mouth than I spotted Nards waltzing into the restaurant with a redhead. I did a double take, then watched openmouthed as he held her arm and pulled out a chair for her and sat down next to her at a cozy corner table-for-two.

I froze, not knowing what to do. It had never occurred to me that Nards was anything but a devoted and loving husband, but there he was, caught red-handed with a redhead.

"Mel? What's wrong?" said Weezie. "You look sick."

I had to tell her, didn't I? What choice did I have? I mean, all she had to do was get up to go to the ladies' room and she would have seen them herself.

"Maybe Desiree isn't such a hot matchmaker," was how I began. You can't just blurt these things out.

"Why do you say that? Consider how she brought Nards and me together and how happy we—"

"Nards isn't at the office." Oh, God. My heart was breaking for her. My poor, poor pal.

"He is so," she said, as if I were just being obstinate.

"No, he's here, Weezie. Over your left shoulder and to the right."

She whipped her head around, spotted the twosome in mid-embrace and turned back to me, her eyes as huge as our bread plates. "He's with Dr. Corbett!" And then she gulped down her entire martini, plus the olive and onion.

I reached for her hand and squeezed it. I felt so helpless. I wanted to comfort her, but how? "There must be an explanation," I tried.

"He's with Dr. Corbett!" she repeated, sounding like a robot. She was completely stunned, and who wouldn't be?

"You sure that's who the redhead is?"

She nodded, all the color drained from her face.

"Is it possible they're having a working dinner?" I said. "You know. Like maybe they needed a quiet place to discuss the latest techniques in throat cultures?"

She turned to look again. At that precise moment, Nards was taking a culture of Dr. Corbett's throat—with his tongue.

Weezie put her head on the table and started to sob. "I never in a million years thought he'd cheat on me," she said, although it was hard to hear her with her mouth buried in the tablecloth. "I married him because he was supposed to be honest and dependable. I can't believe this. I just can't believe it."

"Do you want me to go over there and talk to him?" I offered. "I bet he's just having a midlife crisis and needs to be reminded of his responsibilities."

"He's too young for a midlife crisis," she moaned. "What he's having is an affair. I hate him. And I hate Desiree for fixing me up with him."

It wasn't a good night for Desiree. "What are you going to do?" I asked.

She didn't answer for several long seconds, her chest heaving with sobs. Then all of a sudden, she picked her head up, wiped her eyes, straightened her posture, and stood, albeit wobbly. "I'm going to confront him. That's what I'm going to do."

With that, she marched over to Nards and the redhead. From my seat, all I could see was that he looked horrified, the redhead looked smug, and Weezie looked like a lady. She didn't throw a drink at anybody. She didn't throw a punch at anybody. She simply spoke a few words to them, wheeled around, and walked back to our table.

"What'd you say?" I asked, breathless with the melodrama—the total impossibility—of my best friend's husband, the least likely of men to stray, straying.

"I told them the chicken was rubbery and suggested they order the shrimp," she said. "And then I told Nards not to bother to come home."

"Oh, Weezie," I said, pained by the hurt in her eyes. "Do you want to stay at my apartment tonight? The sofa's a pullout."

"Thanks, but the kids need me." She paused, gathering her thoughts before continuing. "He fell in love with me when I was a big shot career woman. Then I became a full-time wife and mother, and he said he loved me even more. And now what? He's bored with the full-time wife and mother and is having a fling with a big shot career woman. What does that say about what men really want?"

"Only that we all want what we can't have," I said. "You told me the only reason I've been viewing Dan in a more flattering light is because I can't have him anymore. Maybe Nards will come to his senses just the way I will."

Only I didn't come to my senses. Not that week or the week after or the week after that. In fact, the revelation about Nards's infidelity only made Dan look better in my eyes and my respect for him stronger. I remembered how faithful he'd been to me when we were married. And it wasn't as if he didn't have opportunities. He was a sports god in a country that worships sports gods, and wherever the Giants traveled, women followed. Groupies threw themselves at him, but he never let the situation get out of hand. He wasn't a saint—I knew there were flirtations—but he managed to avoid the bars and clubs that other players frequented and kept to himself most of the time. He was "a family man," he told everybody, and for his entire career he had a squeaky clean reputation. It wasn't until our relationship deteriorated and we stopped sleeping together that he started staying out late and coming home even later, and by then I didn't care what he did.

You may not have a job, but you're not a cheater, I thought as I waited for Dan to bring Buster over that Monday morning.

When he arrived, I invited him in for coffee, our new ritual.

"I've got some crumb cake too," I said. "I, um, made it." Evan had lent me his *Joy of Cooking,* and I actually followed the recipe in it. Hey, if Leah could cook, so could I.

Dan was disbelieving. "*You* baked?" he said with a good-natured laugh.

"*I* baked. Let me cut you a piece."

"I'm watching the calories these days, but there's no way I'm gonna miss this historic event. Besides, we've got something to celebrate."

"What now? An interview with another college?"

He put his hands on my shoulders and looked at me with the sky blue eyes that had made me weak in the knees the first time I saw them. "I got the L.I.U. job."

I shrieked with excitement, scaring Buster. "Oh my God, Dan! This is incredible!"

"I know. I'm still in a daze. They want me to coach the C.W. Post Pioneers in the fall. Me." He shook his head in amazement. "I'm employed. What do you think of that, huh?"

What did I think of it? Well, I was thrilled for him, of course, but also proud of him. I always knew he could find work if only he'd try, and now he'd tried and done it. He wasn't a bumbo anymore. He had pulled himself together, embraced life, taken charge of it, grown up. Everything I'd wanted for him. For us. But there was no "us." He belonged to Leah, and I was the genius who'd made it happen. Suddenly, I was more than confused. I was depressed.

"I think you'll make an outstanding coach," I said, forcing myself to sound upbeat. Like Leah. "I always told you that."

"You did, Mel." His hands were still on my shoulders, his gaze fixed on me. My knees weren't weak, but I felt my pulse race. "You told me over and over, but I was too—" He stopped himself and moved away from me, over to the sofa. "No point in dwelling on the past, right? I got the job. That's the important thing."

"Right. And this really does call for a celebration."

I served him the coffee and cake, sat next to him on the sofa, and watched intently as he took his first bite of what was basically a box worth of sugar held together by a tub worth of butter. "How is it?" I said as he was chewing.

"It's . . ."

"What?"

"Give me a second," he said with a mouth full.

I waited.

"It's . . . just like my mother's."

I smiled. "Give me a break. Your mother's a great cook. If this is even edible, I'll be happy."

"It's delicious. Honest. And I appreciate that you made it." He laughed. "Remember that time you tried to make a soufflé?"

I burst out laughing with the memory. The coach of the Giants and his wife came over for dinner a few months after Dan was drafted. Instead of having the party fully catered, I got ambitious and decided to make my own dessert—a type of dessert that's hard to pull off even if you know what you're doing in the kitchen. But during a dry run the night before, it became evident that I should leave the cooking to the pros. "My soufflé looked more like a Frisbee."

"And tasted just as good."

"Thank God you bought that apple tart as a backup."

We laughed some more about the incident, and the mood in the room was so relaxed, so totally different from those months and months of nastiness. Dan was appealing again, the way he used to be, and it was hard not to feel—

No. I wasn't supposed to feel anything. Sure, his new job impressed me, and there was no question that his new behavior was turning my head, making me think we might have had a second chance if Leah were out of the picture, but that wasn't the case. She was very much in the picture, and I was simply the ex.

I was about to offer him more coffee when my doorbell rang.

"Who is it?" I called out.

"Evan," he called back. "Glad I caught you before you left for work. I want to ask you something."

Evan. Talk about bad timing. Not that I wasn't always glad to see him. It was just that I only had Dan to myself once a week, and I didn't feel like sending him back to *her* so soon.

"I'm kind of busy," I said through the door.

"Who's Evan?" Dan asked with an odd expression, as if he couldn't imagine that I might have a life.

"My neighbor," I said.

"Kind of early in the day for a visit, isn't it?"

"He lives right—"

"Hey, Melanie," Evan said, ringing my bell again. "Open up. One question and I'm out of there, I promise."

"Sounds important," said Dan. "I should go."

He set his coffee down on the table, stood up, and headed for the door. I trailed after him.

"You can stay if you want," I told him and opened the door.

"Oh," said Evan when he saw Dan. "Sorry, Melanie. I didn't realize you had company."

"No problem," I said. "My ex-husband came to drop Buster off."

"Traffic Dan Swain." Evan, who was in his standard smock

and jeans, seemed startled by Dan's presence—not awestruck like a fan, because he didn't really follow sports; just surprised to be face-to-face with the man he'd heard me rant and rave about. "Great to meet you," he said. "I'm Evan Gillespie."

I expected Dan to give Evan the toothpaste-commercial smile that came naturally to him after all the years of being in the public eye, but he responded with a hint of a snarl. I'm not kidding; his upper lip sort of curled.

Either ignoring the chilly response or just determined to be friendly, Evan grabbed Dan's hand and shook it warmly.

"Nice to meet you too, pal," Dan finally managed. Pal? What was that about? It sounded so condescending and very un-Dan. He was the glad-hander who was always so cordial to strangers, so gracious and eager to put them at ease. But not this time. For some reason, he seemed to have taken an instant and inexplicable dislike to Evan.

"Evan's been an enormous help to me," I said, trying to smooth over the awkwardness. "He calls me his damsel in distress, and he's always there to rescue me when I do something stupid."

"And she's not the easiest person to rescue," Evan said jokingly. "She's pretty feisty, but then you already know that."

Dan tensed again—how odd!—and said, "She always seemed pretty capable to me. Aren't you, darlin'?" He put his arm around my shoulder, almost as if he were reclaiming his territory. I honest-to-God didn't know what to make of his behavior.

"Evan's a very gifted painter," I said, just keeping the conversation going.

"You do portraits or something?" said Dan in yet another condescending tone that was so unlike him.

"No. Mostly images of the sea," said Evan. "The water's magic for me."

"Then why would you live here?" asked Dan, suddenly the expert on painting. "The East River isn't the most inspiring body of water I can think of."

"New York's been my base," said Evan. "I go off to the islands for inspiration."

"You should see the painting he did in the Bahamas," I said to Dan, who was still holding on to me, still not the congenial guy he usually was with new people. "It's so realistic that you feel as if you're there."

Evan smiled at me. "I should hire you as my publicist. But instead I'll ask the question I came here to ask and then let you get on with your business. Are you and Buster free Wednesday night? I was planning another culinary extravaganza, Chez Gillespie."

I turned to Dan. "Evan's a fabulous cook too. He even feeds Buster."

Dan's response? "Sounds like you're taking care of everybody around here, pal."

The "pal" again! So bizarre!

I hoped that by plowing ahead and bringing Evan's visit to an end, the discomfort all three of us were experiencing would be over. "Dinner on Wednesday would be great," I said. "Thanks for the invitation."

"My pleasure," said Evan, who turned to Dan and grabbed his hand for a good-bye shake. "And a pleasure meeting you, pal." Obviously, it hadn't been a pleasure, but off he went, and the tension in the room eased.

Dan removed his arm from around my shoulder, checked his

watch, and announced that he had to get going too. I, of course, was already late for the office.

As he stepped across my threshold, he stopped and said, "The guy's got it bad for you, darlin'."

"Evan?" I said, bewildered by the remark. "What makes you say that?"

"What makes me say it?" He grinned, coming through with the toothpaste-commercial smile after the fact. "Because I've been there. Takes one to know one, right?"

After my ex walked out the door, I leaned against it, staring after him like one of his groupies, his parting words reverberating in my head. I had no sense of Evan's feelings for me, nor were they my focus then. What I wondered was whether Dan really did "have it bad for me." Present tense. And was that why he'd treated Evan with such disdain?

How else to explain what had just happened? How else to account for the climate change in my apartment after Evan showed up? Dan had been in a great mood—the best mood. We'd been celebrating, reminiscing, enjoying each other's company. And then along came Evan. Suddenly, Dan wasn't himself, speaking to my neighbor with near scorn, almost as if he were sizing him up like a rival.

A rival! That was it! Dan had never seen me with another man, and, given my workaholic tendencies and my professed disinterest in romance, he probably figured he never would. But there I was, first thing in the morning, with a very attractive guy at my door, and he was jealous!

I staggered into the apartment, sank onto the sofa, and let this revelation register. Dan was jealous. The idea of me moving on with someone else at some point in the distant future was one thing. But actually watching me interact with someone else—accept a date with someone else—was a very different reality. A reality for which he obviously wasn't prepared.

He's still in love with me, I thought with a jolt. He hasn't gotten me out of his system any more than I've been able to let him go.

It must be true. His relationship with Leah wasn't as solid as it appeared. She hadn't won his heart after all, not if he still cared for me.

And he did still care. Yes, my ex, who had gone out and gotten a fulfilling job and turned himself into the kind of man I'd hoped he'd be, still cared for me.

And so, knowing Leah was no longer blocking my path, knowing that nothing was blocking my path, I decided I wanted him back.

Chapter 22

"You're nuts," said Desiree. She shook her head so vehemently that her wig—a coal black curly one this time—nearly fell off. "You've only got thirty days to go before the alimony's over. Thirt-eee days. You're practically home free, Melanie."

"I don't want to be home free. I want to be home. Safe and secure in a stable environment. With Dan," I said as I sat across from her in her office only hours after I'd seen him. "I made a mistake, and now I need you to help me fix it."

"By convincing Leah to break up with him?" She scoffed. "I'm a heart hunter, not a heart breaker. Besides, you're paying me the second installment of my fee once I've kept her there for the full three months. I'm not giving that up."

"What if I paid you to get her out of the relationship instead?" I wheedled.

She took a few seconds to think about this. "Look, I love money more than anyone," she said finally, "but even I won't involve myself in something so crazy."

"It's not crazy," I protested. "Dan doesn't love Leah. He loves me. I don't want to hurt her, believe me, but you'd be doing her a favor by convincing her he's the wrong guy for her. It would be a mission from God."

"Okay. Enough with the 'mission from God' business. It's my slogan, not yours." She was testy. She'd been expecting praise for her handiwork, not a plea to undo it. "Besides, how do you know Dan loves you? Because he's been nice to you lately? Because he stays to drink your coffee? Because he acted macho when your eager-beaver neighbor dropped by?"

"All of the above, plus one more thing: he never stopped loving me."

"Then why is he still depositing your checks every month?"

"Because the justice system says he's entitled to them."

Her jaw dropped. "Are you on drugs?"

"No!" I really wished everybody would stop asking me that. "I'm still not wild about the alimony, but as soon as Dan starts his coaching job, he won't want the payments. He certainly won't need them if we're back together." I thought of the money I'd save once we *were* back together. One apartment instead of two. One set of utility bills instead of two. One everything instead of two. Heaven. "All you have to do is introduce Leah to one of your other male clients. If she's such a prize, it shouldn't be too hard to make another match for her."

She stared at me. "I won't do it. I have my scruples."

I returned her stare. "And *I* could rat you out to the Better Business Bureau about your new division, Desiree Klein Heart Hunting for Exes. I was here the day Lynda Fox, the golfer, showed up for her consultation, remember?"

"So? I could blab about the person who gave me the idea for the division. I don't think a hoity-toity place like Pierce, Shelley and Steinberg would be thrilled to hear that one of their VPs tried to scam her ex out of what was legally his and convince other women to do the same."

"Good point." I was never big on blackmail anyway. I too had my scruples. Well, I used to.

She leaned across her desk, her six thousand necklaces clanging against one another. "Listen to me, would you? Let the clock run out. Let the alimony terminate. Pay me what you owe me. And then go after Dan if you want to."

"Oh, like he'll even be speaking to me after he realizes what I did?"

"What's to realize?"

"That I set him up with Leah. That I tricked him into living with her. That I hired people to spy on them. That I exploited his lack of attention to the details of our divorce agreement. That I set him up so he'd invalidate the alimony without knowing it. You think he'll come rushing into my arms when he finds out I did all that?"

"He'll never find out. Yeah, he'll kick himself for not reading the fine print of the agreement, but why would he blame you? Who's gonna tell him you hustled him into losing his meal ticket *and* his girlfriend? Not me, that's for sure."

"But what if Leah doesn't want to leave? The longer she's living with him, the tougher it'll be to get her out of there."

"Hey, once the ninety days are up, I'm done with this." She waved her pudgy dumpling hands in the air to make her point. "You want him back after that? You and Leah can duke it out on your own."

I considered Desiree's advice and decided she was right. I would wait another month until I reclaimed Dan from Leah. Why not let the alimony terminate before moving in for the kill? It would be so much cleaner that way. He'd lose the support payments and I'd be all sweet and sympathetic about it and we'd live happily ever after. So Leah would get to stay there for another thirty days. So what? In the meantime, I'd lay the groundwork for my campaign to win him back. I would be subtle, careful not to scare him off. I would ease him into confessing his feelings for me, so it would be an effortless transition. By the time the thirty days were up, it would be clear to both of us that we'd needed the period apart but that we were better off together.

The laying of the groundwork began with my descent into a psychological condition I called Manchausen by Proxy. It pains me even to admit it, but I faked my dog's medical problems to get my man's attention.

On Tuesday, I called Dan and told him Buster didn't seem quite right.

"Leah said she thought he might have cataracts," he reminded me.

"I remember," I said, "but it's not his eyes. It's his balance, his gait. He sort of tips over when he walks."

"Did you take him to the vet?" he asked.

"I was going to, but I hate to be an alarmist. Could you possibly come over and check him out yourself? Maybe you'll think I'm overreacting, but I just want to be sure."

"No problem. I'll be right there."

Dan came over that night, took a look at Buster, pronounced him healthy as far as he could tell, and suggested we keep an eye on him.

"Next week, when he's with me, Leah can watch him closely too," he said.

Leah. Like I felt like hearing about her. "Wow. It's almost seven-thirty," I said before Dan started for the door. "Why don't we go out and grab a bite? There's the Hungarian place next door. You've never tried it."

He seemed surprised that I suggested dinner out together—*that* hadn't happened since we'd separated—but pleasantly surprised. "I'd really like to, but Leah's waiting for me. We're going out with a couple of her friends."

Leah had friends? Good, I thought. She'll need them to comfort her after Dan leaves her for me.

"I understand," I said breezily. "Maybe another time."

"Absolutely."

"Thanks for checking on Buster, Dan. Being a single parent can be tough at times like this."

"You're doing a great job." He patted me on the arm and took off.

On Wednesday afternoon, I called him from work and said I thought Buster might be worse. He volunteered to meet me at my apartment around six.

"See how his left leg sort of droops?" I said, lifting the dog's left leg and letting it, well, droop.

"Yeah, but he's walking okay," said Dan. "You know, he's not getting any younger, Mel. Maybe it's an age-related thing and he just can't jump around the way he used to."

"Maybe," I said.

And then the most amazing thing happened. Dan looked at his watch and said, "How about that dinner offer from last night? Is it still good?"

My insides did cartwheels. "Of course."

"Leah's got a seminar tonight, so why don't we try the Hungarian place?"

I was ecstatic, naturally, and was about to say yes when I remembered I'd made plans with Evan, who was probably slaving over his hot stove that very minute. There's no way you can cancel when somebody offers to cook for you *and* your dog. What's more, I was looking forward to seeing Evan as I always did and didn't really want to cancel. Still, it was tough to put Dan off while I was in the throes of trying to win him back.

"I can't," I said, not hiding my disappointment. "Buster and I are going over to Evan's for dinner."

At first, he pretended not to know whom I meant. "The guy who was over here the other day?"

"Yes, Dan." Who was he kidding.

"He seemed okay. Not a serial killer or anything."

I smiled. "He's very nice. You'd like him."

"Do you like him, Mel?"

There was no kidding in the question. His expression was serious. I half expected him to confess his feelings for me right then, given the way he was looking at me, but maybe he was just as confused as I'd been before I faced the truth. Maybe he feared my rejection and wasn't ready to admit it to himself. Or maybe it was his sense of obligation to Leah that was keeping him from revealing what was in his heart. Either way, I knew that I was the one who mattered to him. He just needed a little more time to get comfortable with the idea.

"I do like him," I answered. "He's a good friend."

"Then enjoy your evening," he said and proceeded to do something he hadn't done in over a year: he kissed me on the cheek. My skin was still tingling when I knocked on Evan's door a few minutes later, Buster in tow.

"I was worried you might stand me up," he said when he ushered us into his apartment, which smelled fragrant with herbs and spices. "You're late."

"Sorry. I got caught up with something and lost track of the time."

"That big project you're always working on?"

"Yes."

"I forgive you." He reached for my hand and walked me over to the small canvas in the corner of the living room. "I couldn't wait to show you this."

I peered at the oil painting on the easel. The scene was his favorite, the turquoise sea of the Bahamas, but unlike the stormy weather in *Summer Squall,* the sun was sparkling over calm surf and a cove with a sandy beach. And sticking his paw into the water was a pug, his tail curled tightly and high, just like Buster's; his face the same clownish mix of wrinkles and luminous round eyes. The image was so real, so lifelike, that I could almost feel the water making contact with my dog's fur.

I glanced at Evan with amazement. "This is incredible," I said. "You captured him perfectly. Whenever we go to the beach, he sticks his toe in the water, just the way you painted it, and then he runs like hell for dry land. He never goes in beyond that paw. Never!"

He laughed. "It was fun. Something different for me. And I thought you'd like it."

"Are you kidding? I love it. Is it finished? Can I buy it?"

"No, it's not finished, and we'll negotiate whether you can buy it. Right now, I've gotta concentrate on our dinner."

He took hold of my hand again and walked me into the kitchen. There was a large pot of water on the stove and another pot filled with an aromatic tomato sauce. "We're having pasta tonight. Hope that works for you."

I told him it worked beautifully and asked if I could help and continued to rave about the painting of Buster as I guzzled the pinot noir I'd brought. I wasn't the hardy drinker Weezie was, and even one glass of booze gave me more buzz than I could handle if I drank it fast, but I was anxious and jumpy that night, struggling to focus on my host instead of drifting back to thoughts of Dan. No matter how attractive and attentive Evan was, my mind was elsewhere, and I kept socking back the wine in a futile attempt to steady myself.

"Everything okay?" he said later, after we'd finished dinner and were sitting on the sofa. He was sipping decaf. I was polishing off what was left of the pinot.

"It was delicious," I said, slurring. I wasn't drunk, but my tongue was thick and my brain scrambled. Okay, so I was drunk.

"I'm not talking about the food," he said. "I'm talking about the mixed signals."

"Mixed signals?" It came out sounding like "missed" signals. Not too far off for a person whose mouth wasn't operating properly.

"Yeah. You told me you were in a snit about Dan and the alimony, yet there you two were on Monday morning, looking all chummy. What's going on?"

"Actually, we're getting along much better lately," I said.

He moved closer and put his arm around the back of my shoulders. "How much better?"

Evan was a perceptive person, at least where I was concerned. There was no point in being anything other than candid with him, I realized. He was the one I kept turning to when I needed help. Why not trust him with the truth? I had to talk to someone about it or I'd burst. Weezie had her own nightmare to deal with, so I didn't want to burden her further. Why not bare my soul to my neighbor and friend? Why? Because when you're drunk, you shouldn't bare your soul to anybody except a bartender.

"I like you, Evan," I said. "I wouldn't be here if I didn't."

"Like me how?" He leaned in, as if he was about to kiss me. I pulled away.

He nodded. "Yup. Mixed signals. You like me, but you're still into Traffic Jam, is that it?"

"I'm still into him," I confessed. "When we split up, all I cared about was getting back at him. Now, all I care about is getting him back."

Evan withdrew his arm from around my shoulders, his smile fading. "Wow. Okay. I'm disappointed." He paused, then moved away from me as if I had a contagious disease. "What changed?"

"He changed, Evan. He has a job now."

"Is that what a man has to do to win your heart? Have a job?"

"It helps. He also took a hard look at his life and went out and improved it. I respect that."

"So do I. But what about the alimony? It was the big sticking point for you."

"I won't be paying it much longer. In a month or so, it'll be a nonissue."

Evan looked confused. "What's happening in a month?"

I giggled. "You really wanna hear?" I should have shut my trap right then, but no. The wine had made me stupid.

"Hear what?" he said.

"Well, you know that project you keep asking me about?"

"Yeah."

"It's almost over."

"I'm not following you. How would a financial project relate to your relationship with Dan?"

More giggles. God, this is embarrassing to recount. "See, Dan and I have this cohabitation provision in our divorce agreement."

"Kaitlin and I put one of those in ours."

"Uh-oh. Better be careful." I wagged my finger at him. "Maybe she'll hire Desiree and you'll be out of luck."

"Who? You're not making sense." He picked up the wine bottle, saw that it was empty, and rolled his eyes.

"I am so making sense." I hiccuped. "In our agreement, it says Dan can't live with another woman for ninety days or else the alimony terminates. The project was to find him that woman. And I did it."

"You found him what woman?" He was totally baffled now.

"Leah Purcell. She's a vet and she's really, really in love with Dan. She's been living with him for sixty-two days! And I can prove it! I have my spies!" I kept punctuating each example of my treachery with an exclamation point, as if I expected Evan to pat me on the back for every single one, as if I deserved cheers instead of boos. (For the third time, I was drunk!)

His expression darkened. "Did you actually introduce him to this woman?"

"No, silly. I hired Desiree. She's expensive, but she's the best professional matchmaker in New York. She fixed up my friends Weezie and Nards, and they got married, although Nards is sleeping with the new doctor in his office, so it's not going too well."

Evan got up from the sofa and stood in front of me, his hands on his hips. "Dan doesn't remember about the cohabitation clause, does he?"

"Nope."

"Leah doesn't know anything about it either."

"Leah doesn't know anything about anything. She's too busy repainting *my* apartment."

"So he's living happily with this woman and has no clue that it'll mean the end of his support money?"

"He's not living happily with her. He loves me and I love him, and as soon as I tell him how I feel he'll tell her to move out."

Evan just stared at me for several seconds, as if I had six heads. And who could blame him? I'd never been a cruel person, but what I was admitting to him was unconscionable.

"You think I'm terrible," I said before he could.

"I think—" He stopped to collect himself. "I think that if what you're doing to Dan is your way of showing love, I'm glad I found out now."

"Oh, Evan. Come on. Don't be like that. It's only natural to try to get out of paying alimony. Men have been dreaming up schemes like mine for years. I bet Kaitlin's sitting at home right now, crossing her fingers that you'll violate your agreement."

"Not that it's any of your business, but Kaitlin isn't paying me a dime."

"She isn't?"

"No. I'm supporting myself."

"By selling your paintings?"

"Why not? You keep saying how talented I am."

"You are. It's just that—"

"Just that what? Being an artist won't make me rich? It paid for the meal you didn't hesitate to eat."

"But, Evan, you need more than food money."

"How much do I need?" he demanded. "Or I guess the better question is: How much do you need? Ask yourself: How much money does it take to make you happy?"

I didn't answer. My dinner was coming back up my throat. I was dying to ask if he had any Pepcid in his medicine cabinet but thought better of it.

"Look, I know you grew up poor," he said. "I know your father didn't work. I know how hard your life must have been and how much it distorted your reality. But I'll ask again: How much money does it take to make you happy?"

I shrugged. "Enough to feel secure. We all need a sense of security. Even you."

"Yeah, but mine is in here." He tapped his hand on his chest. "Not in a fancy title and not in a cushy corner office, but right here. It may sound New Agey, but when you believe in yourself, the money flows to you, Melanie. You don't have to scratch and claw for it. You don't have to manipulate people to get it. Maybe someday you'll learn that."

I sat there listening. I mean, I heard what he was saying. But it wasn't getting through. I wasn't letting it, and the wine didn't help.

Convinced that I was a lost cause, he called for Buster to come. "Time to go home, doggie."

"Wait, Evan," I said, panicking. "You're not throwing us out, are you? I value your opinion and I admire your convictions. I just—"

"I'm throwing *you* out," he said, helping me up from the sofa and sort of pushing me toward the door. "I have nothing against Buster."

"Couldn't you try to see things from my perspective?" I said. "I thought Dan had taken advantage of me, and I wanted to correct the injustice. That's the only reason I set him up with Leah."

"Did it ever occur to you that she's partially responsible for his new self-confidence? That it was her love and support that turned him into this person you think you want back?"

"Dan's told me she's had a positive influence on him, and I'm sure he's very grateful to her. But he's been in love with me since we were barely out of college and, deep down, he still is. I saw it on Monday when you stopped by. He was rude to you because he was jealous."

"Maybe he *was* jealous," said Evan, "but it could have been a knee-jerk reaction, an old impulse. It doesn't mean he still loves you."

"It does," I insisted.

"Melanie, listen to me. What if his definition of love changed along with his attitude toward life? What if, in the process of becoming a grown-up, he decided he's ready for a grown-up relationship?"

I didn't answer, because the room was starting to spin. And because I didn't have an answer.

Evan opened his door and motioned me out. “I’ve got dishes to wash.”

“Can we still be friends?” I asked like a fourteen-year-old as I stumbled over the threshold.

“Good night, Melanie.” He closed the door and locked it.

“I’ll take that as a no?” I said from the other side.

I waited in the hall for some reply—part of me fantasized that the door would swing back open and Evan would be standing there with a forgiving smile—but there was only silence.

“I wish he wasn’t so mad at Mommy, Buster,” I said as we trudged home. “I’d hate it if he didn’t like me anymore. But at least we can concentrate on getting Daddy back, right?”

My dog barked a short, muffled bark. At the time I thought that he’d heard somebody in the hall and was being protective. I realize now that he was being reproachful; he was as disgusted with me as Evan was.

Chapter 23

The next morning I called Evan and got his voice mail. I was about to leave a message saying I was sorry, embarrassed, hopeful that we could—No. I realized I had nothing of substance to convey and hung up. I regretted that I'd hurt him, disappointed him, even repulsed him, but I was who I was. Dan may have changed, but I hadn't.

I carried on with my ill-advised campaign. I told my ex that Buster's balance seemed shaky again (like I was one to talk), and he came rushing over. After determining that our dog was healthy, we kept each other company for a while. We found ourselves reminiscing again about the early years of our marriage. I brought up our trip to Bermuda, for example, and how it had rained the entire time we were there. He chimed in with how we'd draped ourselves in the bathroom's shower curtain whenever we'd ventured outside to the restaurant and how we'd gotten drenched anyway. I added how we'd towel dried each other off after every meal and stood next to the electric pants presser to get warm. He remembered how we'd run out of towels and ended up ordering room service for the next four days. I said I thought being stuck in the room was the best part of the vacation. He smiled and said he did too.

At one point, Dan put his hand on my knee as we sat on the sofa and said, "We had great times, didn't we, darlin.'" It wasn't a question.

As for Buster, he pranced around like a contented clown while his parents did all that reminiscing. I hated that I had used him in the service of my love life, but there was no doubt that the more time Dan and I spent together, the closer we were becoming.

Over the weekend, I hoped to run into Evan, just to try to smooth things over between us, but didn't. I did run into Patty, who was glowing—and not because of some new beauty product.

"Have you seen Evan?" I asked her as we chatted in the hall.

"No, but I met a guy on the Internet," she said, looking so happy. "It's only been a month, but it's the real deal."

"Gosh. Congratulations." This was a surprise. "How'd you get beyond the heartache of Jason and the alimony?"

"I just moved on," she said. "I think all those nights of sobbing my guts out helped. You should try it."

"Not me," I said, waving her off. "I never cry."

"Maybe that's why you're alone," she said and disappeared inside her apartment.

What did she know, I told myself. Besides, I wasn't going to be alone for long. There were only three weeks to go before Dan would lose the spousal support and I'd be there to comfort him and Desiree would be there to comfort Leah. A nice, tidy ending.

On Saturday night, I was home working when Mrs. Thornberg called. She asked why I hadn't come by to see her lately. She said she missed me.

"I miss you too," I said, because in a weird way I did. She was one of the few people I hadn't alienated, and stepping up and taking care of her when nobody else would mitigated how crappy I was feeling about myself.

"I'm about to make egg salad, and I always put a few secret ingredients into it," she said. "I could fix you a sandwich and we could eat and watch TV together."

Okay, maybe she *was* a mother figure. All I can say is I didn't hate being with her, so I took her up on her offer and went to her apartment.

She kissed me hello and told me I could afford to lose a few pounds and asked me to open the new jar of relish that she'd been struggling with for an hour. (The relish was one of her secret ingredients; the other was celery salt.) We ate the sandwiches on tray tables in front of her tiny television set.

"Your ex is still hot and heavy with the dope fiend," she said during a commercial. "I heard them go out a few hours ago. I thought about telling them to quit slamming the door every time they leave, but I was too tired."

"I have a feeling they won't last much longer," I said with a smug little smile.

She turned down the volume on the remote and looked at me. "What makes you say that?"

"Just a hunch." I wasn't about to blurt out the truth, given the negative reaction I'd gotten from Evan.

"I don't know that I agree with your hunch," she said, shaking her balding head. "They're still breaking the sound barrier at night, if you get my drift."

I laughed. "I get your drift, but I wouldn't put much stock in it," I said.

Of course he's still having sex with her, I thought. Guilty-conscious sex, because he'd rather be making love to me, given the choice. If he only knew how I felt—if I came right out and told him—he'd be overjoyed and we'd be back together and he wouldn't have to fake orgasms anymore.

Well, I just assumed that's what he was doing.

After Larry King's weekend show was over, Mrs. Thornberg's eyelids began to get heavy. I helped her up from her chair, eased her into her nightgown, tucked her under the covers, and plopped her dentures into the cleanser.

"You want to stay in the guest room again?" she gummed, gripping my hand so hard it hurt.

"I've got to get home to my dog," I said, "but I'll stay until you're asleep."

"You're a good girl."

I sat at her bedside for another fifteen minutes or so. By then she was off to dreamland and the circulation in my hand had returned.

I leaned over and adjusted the covers just the way she liked them, then tiptoed out of the bedroom, through the apartment into the foyer.

I had only opened her front door a crack when I heard Dan's voice.

"I've never had such a great time sitting in a dark movie theater," he said between laughs. "I didn't even mind that the movie stunk."

Leah responded with her own ha ha ha. "You didn't see the movie, Swainy. You were too busy making out with me."

The vein in my temple bulged—my Dan vein—and I felt a rush of jealousy until I persuaded myself that Dan had only engaged in guilty-conscious making out; that he would much rather have been making out with me, given the choice.

I opened the door a little wider so I could take a peek at my ex and his cohabitator. He was fumbling in his pocket for his keys while she was hanging all over him.

"I think we should plan to stay home every night next week," she said. "We'll have Buster, and I know how you value your time with him. Mel may leave him alone a lot, but we don't have to."

The nerve! Mel did not leave Buster alone a lot! Mel was not an unfit mother! Mel took better care of her dog than Leah ever could!

Okay, so I'd left him alone that night, but he was happy with his toys and his food and his comfy bed. And I was only gone a couple of hours. How dare she!

I waited until they were inside the apartment before scurrying out of Mrs. Thornberg's, into the elevator, down to the lobby. When I got home, I hugged Buster and gave him one of his favorite biscuit treats and told him how much I loved him no matter what anybody said. He responded by having a coughing fit. I asked his forgiveness for involving him in my devious plot to get Dan back, and the coughing subsided.

I woke up Sunday morning, went into the kitchen to make myself some coffee, and found Buster standing near his food bowl coughing again.

"Did something get caught in the old windpipe, Busty?"

Just as I kneeled down to check him, he collapsed. Collapsed! I swear to God, it was the most terrifying sight I'd ever witnessed, and I screamed like a person whose beloved dog had just died. As far as I knew, he had died.

I lay on the floor next to him and ran my hand along his chest, on his heart, feeling for a beat, a pulse, a breath, something.

Yes! There was a pulse! He was still breathing! But how could he have fainted? He was healthy. I'd only pretended he wasn't.

I called Dan, hysterical. He came over in a flash. By the time he arrived, Buster had revived but was still a little out of it.

"You probably don't believe me after all the false alarms," I said, "but he was coughing one minute and out cold the next." I was being punished for my Manchausen by Proxy, I just knew it. Watching my dog nearly die was my penance for all my misdeeds. My wake-up call. *I* should have been the one who was struck down, not poor, innocent Buster.

"Of course I believe you," said Dan, because I'd done such a good job of keeping him in the dark. "Let's get him examined."

When we brought Buster in, Patrick Kelly, our vet, was waiting for us, along with his wife, Olivia, his nurse and trusty right hand. It was heartening that there was at least one doctor in America who actually answered his pager on a weekend. Even more heartening was that he didn't treat me like the lying, scheming, wolf-crying psycho I was, but rather listened intently to my description of Buster's symptoms, nodding solemnly, and then assuring me he would run every relevant test.

"Can we be in there with Buster while you examine him?" I asked, clutching Dan's hand as fiercely as he was clutching mine.

"Why not let me have a look at him first," said Patrick. "He'll be okay, I promise. It may be a while, though, so try to relax. Both of you."

Dan and I sat alone in the waiting room, which was wall-papered with cartoonlike shapes of animals. There were no other anxious pet parents sitting beside us. Just us and the hum of the fluorescent lights overhead.

I turned to my ex. "I won't be able to handle it if I lose Buster."

He pulled me to him, wrapped me in his arms, and said very softly, "Neither will I, but we won't lose him. We can't."

We remained like that, holding each other, for what seemed like forever, the way it always does when you're waiting for word of a loved one's medical condition. As we sat in silence, I berated myself over and over for exploiting my dog. It was my fault that he was sick. I had caused him to collapse by my willful, selfish behavior. If I had just gone along with the divorce settlement as Robin had advised, if I had stopped being bitter and angry, if I had focused less on the money I was losing and more on the reasons my marriage had failed, Buster wouldn't have collapsed on my kitchen floor. *I* was to blame, but it was time to make things right.

I glanced at Dan as he continued to hold me and thought, If I'm truly sorry for what I've done, I need to tell him the truth.

No, not the truth about tricking him out of the alimony—I couldn't even contemplate losing him *and* Buster—but the truth about my feelings for him. I couldn't wait for the alimony to terminate. I didn't care if the alimony *did* terminate. All I wanted was my man—the first and only man I'd ever loved—and this was the moment to reclaim him; this moment when I needed to believe that my world wasn't crashing down around me.

"Dan?" I began. I pulled away so I could face him.

"I know," he said. "I'm scared shitless too."

I nodded. "But it helps to have each other to lean on, doesn't it? I mean, if you have to go through something like this, it's a little easier when you have history with the other person, right?"

He squeezed my hand. "No question. And we had some first-rate history, darlin'."

I smiled, hopeful. "The thing is, we've been getting along so well lately that I'm almost wondering why we ever split up."

"It *has* been nice these past couple of months. Can't argue with you there."

Okay, I told myself. He's clearly on the same page as I am. He's been burned by me in the past, so he's not about to come right out and tell me he still loves me. It's only natural that I'll have to be the one to reach out to him. Only fitting.

"Dan," I began again, "I hope you know how excited I am about the L.I.U. job and how proud I am of you for going after it."

"I've always wanted to make you proud of me. When we were married, that's practically all I thought about."

"What about now?" I said tentatively. I didn't realize how difficult it would be to just spit it out. I was more afraid of rejection than I realized.

"Now?"

"Do you think about me even though we're not married anymore?"

"Of course I do. You're the mother of my dog." He laughed. "And he's gonna be fine. I'm telling you."

"He is," I said. "But, Dan, I was referring to the two of us. I know

I was the one who walked out of the marriage and up until fairly recently I was very angry at you, but—"

"I gave you good reason to be angry."

"Yes, but I let my anger blind me to the amazing person you are. You had your problems, granted, but you also put me through school and took care of me and introduced me to potential clients."

"I did it out of love, Mel. Simple as that."

"Right. And while we're on the subject of love, there's something I need to say." My mouth was dry and my armpits were soaked. I was a nervous wreck. Not only was my dog's life hanging in the balance, but so was my own. Or so it felt.

"Say whatever's on your mind. You can tell me anything."

"Can I?"

"I'm still here for you, Mel. I always will be. Have I done and said hurtful things to you? Yeah. But underneath it all, I still care. Never doubt that."

He still cared. He said it. All I had to do was tell him I wanted him back and we'd live happily ever after.

"I still care too," I said.

He gave my hand another squeeze. "I'm glad. This is so much better than fighting."

"It is," I said, growing frustrated with all the buddy-buddy stuff, "but I'm not sure you understand what I mean."

"I think I do," he said. "We've got the history. We've got the bond. We've got Buster. So from now on, we're playing on the same team."

Nope. He didn't understand.

I took a huge breath, cleared my throat. "Okay, Dan. Here it is, in a nutshell: I want us to reconcile."

On the word *reconcile,* a fire truck came speeding past Dr. Kelly's ground-level office windows, its siren obliterating all other sound.

"You want us to *what*?" said Dan, cupping his ear and reminding me of Jed Ornbacher.

"I want us to get back together," I tried again. Louder. "I love you. Still. Now. Always. Please tell me you love me too, so we can rip up the divorce papers and start fresh."

He shook his head and shrugged helplessly. Two more fire trucks had whizzed by during my declaration, and he hadn't heard a single syllable I'd said.

I waited several seconds until I thought the coast might actually be clear, and tried yet again. "I want to be your—"

"Melanie. Dan." It was Patrick.

Dan and I jumped up. "How's Buster?" we asked in unison.

"Stable," he said. "I've got one more test to run. Then we'll talk. I just came out to make sure you were both okay."

We bombarded him with questions, all of which he promised to answer shortly. After he was gone, Dan and I sat back down. He turned to me. "You were about to tell me something."

"Right." I prepared myself for the big speech. Again. "I—"

"Mel." He took my hand in his. "I know what you're going to say."

"You do?"

"Sure. But you don't have to keep apologizing. The blame cuts both ways. We were a couple of crazy kids who didn't have a clue how to be in a marriage. We did the best we could."

Not exactly what I was going to say, but he did mention marriage, which was a place to start. "And now that we're older and wiser," I persevered, "we can have another crack at it."

He beamed. "Wow. You totally read my mind."

"Oh, Dan. Really?" Now it was my turn to beam.

"You bet. I've decided I *can* have another crack at it."

I lowered my eyes shyly.

"With Leah," he said.

My head jerked up. "*What?*"

"I wasn't planning on telling you today," he went on, "but maybe my good news will cheer you up."

"What good news? I'm not following you," was all I could manage. I was suddenly very cold. I felt my teeth begin to chatter.

He gave me another high-wattage grin while I started playing with my hair, twisting it, curling it, tying the ends in knots. "You know how you kept asking me if Leah and I were getting serious and I kept saying no way?"

Not only were my teeth chattering and my fingers getting tangled in my hair, but there was a stabbing pain above my right eye, sort of like an ice cream headache.

"Well, we *are* serious," he said, without waiting for me to respond. "So serious we're engaged."

"*Engaged?*" This wasn't happening. It simply wasn't happening. I had envisioned several scenarios but never this one.

He poked my arm. "I know what you're thinking, darlin'. I'll be giving up my legal right to the alimony by remarrying, but I figured you'd be happy about that."

I wasn't happy. I was the opposite of happy. But I sat there with this stupid stunned smile on my face.

"The truth is," he barreled ahead while I'd been rendered mute, "I could have kept on living with Leah and not gotten married and held on to those checks you've been writing every month. But number one, I never felt right about taking your money and throwing it away on stuff I didn't need or deserve, no matter what my lawyer said I was entitled to. With the coaching job, I'll be able to support myself. Not in the style of Traffic Dan Swain, but well enough."

I nodded, my mouth hanging open now, like a complete dim bulb.

"And number two," he continued, as if number one hadn't already done major damage, "I really do want to marry Leah. I want to marry her so much that we're gonna have the festivities at my folks' house in Minco. Her family's coming, plus a couple of friends, and we're doing it next month."

Next month. Probably on the very day the alimony was supposed to terminate. The very day I was planning to break out the champagne and celebrate with Desiree. The very day I would now flush my head down the toilet. God, did I hate irony.

From then on, I saw Dan's lips move but couldn't distinguish one word from another. I was too crushed to comprehend anything.

"Hey," he said at one point. "You listening?"

"Absolutely," I lied.

"Good, because you need to hear this. Once Leah and I are married, we'll be moving out of the apartment, probably into hers. You can have 32G back, Mel. No strings. I want you to have it back."

"Uh-huh," I said articulately.

"Regarding Buster, you can spend as much time with him as you want to. Now that we're not lunging for each other's throats, we can forget the legal bullshit. If Leah and I have him on a Wednesday and you want to see him that day, you can just come on over and see him. She's all about what's in his best interests. She loves him. She'll be as good for him as she's been for me."

Well, wasn't that touching. Wasn't that *sweet*. I got to move back into my apartment *and* stop supporting my ex, plus spend unlimited time with my dog. Everything I thought I wanted. As I said, irony sucks.

I made a feeble attempt at congratulating Dan and at thanking him for his various gestures of generosity. And then we kind of ran out of gas and just waited in awkward silence for Patrick to emerge from the examining room.

Eventually, he did emerge, a subdued Buster in his arms, and gave us the results of the tests, the most important of which was the ultrasound.

Buster, it seemed, had a faulty mitral valve, the valve located between the left atrium and the left ventricle of the heart. Very common in older dogs, said Patrick. Very often the cause of fainting, due to periods of inadequate oxygen flow to the brain. Very responsive to treatments.

He went on to discuss those treatments—a blood pressure medicine, less sodium in the diet, a diuretic to reduce blood volume—and he stressed that a faulty mitral valve wasn't a death sentence by any means.

"Buster will live a long time with the proper medications and good overall care," he said. "His ventricle will enlarge, but there's no real threat of a heart attack."

Thank God, I thought as Patrick went into greater detail about my dog's medical condition. He's going to be all right. I'll make sure he's all right. I'll give him whatever he needs and keep him away from whatever he doesn't need, and he'll thrive in spite of his newly discovered defect. Valves and ventricles are nothing to fool around with, but he isn't going to die. He's not.

I glanced over at Dan, who was listening intently to the vet, his expression one of enormous relief that Buster would survive. I was relieved too, of course. As deeply as I'd ever been relieved about anything in my life. But all it took was that one look at my golden boy ex-husband and my spirits went to hell again.

I couldn't escape the reality—the reality that *I* had brought about—that he was engaged; that he was having a quickie wedding in a month; that he was moving on with his life. However much he loved me, and I still believed he did, he now loved Leah too. Leah, who accepted him for who he was, encouraged him to be a better person, and had sex with him in the bathtub as well as in the bedroom. Leah, who was kind to animals. Leah, who had perfect hair and skin and breasts. Leah, who used the word *resonates*. Leah, for whom I had shelled out ten grand in order to plant her directly in my ex's path.

My brain caught the tail end of Patrick's findings and recommendations, and another irony struck me: he reiterated that Buster's heart wasn't in danger of rupturing, even as mine already had.

Chapter 24

Buster went to Dan's for the week. In a way, I was glad he wasn't with me. If anything happened to him, Leah was a vet. She'd know what to do.

Besides, I couldn't take care of myself during that period, let alone my dog. I had crashed after all the energy and emotion I'd expended on Dan, and now I was depressed. Not the kind of depressed where you pad around the house in your bathrobe and forget to brush your teeth and let the mail pile up without opening any of it. No, I was depressed in the sense that I cried. Yeah, me. All of a sudden, I was a crybaby. I boo-hooed when I got up in the morning and boo-hooed while I ate my breakfast and boo-hooed while I watched Katie Couric interview the author of a book about cliquish adolescent girls. It was as if the tears had multiplied during all those years of my repressing them, and now I couldn't hold them back. They just kept coming, no matter where I was or what I was doing. Some people have bladder control problems. I had tear duct control problems. What I needed was an adult diaper for my eyes.

At the office, the crying thing was particularly troubling. I teared up at my desk. I teared up in meetings. I teared up at lunch with Bernie, which was the proverbial last straw as far as he was concerned. When he asked me why I was crying all the time, I told him the truth.

"Because of Dan," I said over our orders of pasta puttanesca, the red sauce clashing with his red hair. "It finally hit me how much I love him, now that he's marrying someone else."

"Look, I'm sympathetic. Really," he said unsympathetically, "but you haven't been yourself for a long time. And now this . . . this—" He started biting a fingernail, not a good sign, especially since there was something much tastier to eat right there on his plate. "This . . . sobbing in front of clients. It can't happen."

"I'm thinking about going on Zoloft or Paxil or one of those," I said, wondering which medication Roberta Chapman, the woman he'd fired because of her divorce problems, had tried, assuming she'd tried any. "They take a few weeks to kick in, but if you'll just give me a chance to—"

He shook his head. "Can't. Too much at stake."

"Meaning?" Naturally, the tears began to plop down my cheeks at that moment, straight into my pasta. I could never tell when there would be "leakage," and it was very embarrassing.

"Meaning that we need to make a clean break."

"We do?"

"You do. I'm letting you go, Mel. I've stuck with you longer than I've ever stuck with anybody."

"Letting me—" I wiped my wet face with my napkin, but the tears were raining down harder now. "I'm a vice president, Bernie," I reminded him, as if he needed reminding. "Your top gun. Yes, I've been working on the smaller accounts lately, but as soon as I pull myself out of the situation with Dan, it'll be just the way it used to be. I'll handle the Jed Ornbachers of the world, and you can sit back and relax."

"I'm sorry. I've made my decision."

"But you can't fire me," I pleaded. "I mean, you'll never find anyone as good as I am to replace me."

He leaned forward and said, with not nearly enough sensitivity for someone who claimed to give a shit about me, "I already have."

"Who?"

"Steffi."

I was dumbstruck. "As in: my assistant?"

"She's been doing your work for months," he said, between chomps on his fingernail.

"Well, maybe," I conceded. "She's very efficient, but she's hardly ready for a promotion like that. Besides, she's loyal to me. She'd never overstep. If you offered her my job, she'd only—"

"She was the one who approached me," he said.

"What?"

"She did, Mel."

That traitorous little bitch! I was horrified. So horrified that I stopped crying for a second. Maybe that was the key—to scare my tears back wherever they came from.

Bernie went on to praise my dedication to the company and

my memorable years of service, and he offered me a generous severance package, which human resources would explain to me in greater detail.

"You'll land on your feet somewhere," he said in conclusion. "When you're ready, there'll be plenty of opportunities. You just have to get your priorities straight."

Bernie was right. I did have to get my priorities straight, and one of them was to work for someone who didn't bite his nails.

On my way home, I dialed Weezie on my cell phone. I hadn't spoken to her in, well, too long. I'd been busy suffering from Manchausen by Proxy.

"You won't believe this," I said when she answered. "Bernie just fired me."

I expected something along the lines of "Oh my God" or "Are you kidding?" or "What a bastard." Instead, Weezie said, "Like I'm supposed to care?"

Back came the tears. Luckily, I was in a cab, so no one could see me sponging them up with the sleeve of my sweater. "What's wrong?" I asked. "Are you mad at me?"

"I'm very mad at you," she said. "My marriage is falling apart and where's my best friend? Never around."

"Oh, Weezie," I said. "You know I've been all wrapped up in this mess with Dan and Leah, but I'm—"

"All wrapped up in your own problems, in other words," she said. "Did it ever occur to you that the world doesn't revolve around Melanie Banks?"

"I'm sorry," I said. "I should have paid more attention to what's been going on with you."

"You should have," she said. "But now that I think about it, you've always been a little self-involved. From the day we met, you've operated under the assumption that my life was perfect, which gave you a free pass to talk nonstop about *your* struggles, how tough everything has been for *you* all your life. Well, guess what? I'm finished with that kind of friendship. Done."

"Don't say that," I urged, completely taken aback by her outburst. And yet she was right. I hadn't been up to Connecticut to see her since the incident with Nards, and I hadn't called often enough to check on her. But she was my rock. I couldn't lose her now. Not when I had lost my job and Dan too. "I'll be a better friend, Weezie. You'll see."

"You need to get your priorities straight," she said, echoing Bernie. "Gotta go."

She hung up. I was crying so ferociously by then that my tears had wet the seat of the taxi. The driver yelled at me in a foreign language I couldn't identify, which made me cry harder. Ever since Dan had announced his engagement, it seemed there was more and more to cry about.

Back at the Heartbreak Hotel, I sobbed as I watched the news and sobbed as I ate baked beans out of the can and sobbed as I tried to find my résumé and realized I'd never written one. I'd never had to. I'd been recruited by Pierce, Shelley and Steinberg straight out of business school, thanks to the jock clients I'd been able to bring with me through my connection to Dan. It had been my employer for my entire adult life. Where else would I go?

Plenty of places, I thought as the tears kept coming. I'll find a new company and make new memories there—a company that will offer me a wonderful, stimulating, well-paying job. But what company will hire me once they hear I've been dumped by Pierce, Shelley?

Pierce, Shelley.

Sob sob sob.

I tried to think of other occupations I might investigate once I stopped crying. I did have an MBA. That had to count for something. Maybe I'd take the CPA exam and become an accountant.

An accountant.

Sob sob sob.

Or maybe I'd abandon my business expertise altogether and explore my creative side. I could design jewelry or knit trendy wool scarves or maybe even become a painter like Evan.

Evan.

Sob sob sob.

Maybe he's home tonight, I thought as I opened another box of Kleenex and blew my nose. And maybe he's calmed down since I last saw him. Maybe he'll listen to my tales of woe and offer some comfort, understanding, and advice. He'd referred to me as his damsel in distress, hadn't he? Well, I'd been mighty distressed for days.

I grabbed the Kleenex and my keys and trudged down the hall to his apartment. I was poised to ring the bell when I heard noises from inside. Somebody moving something? Dragging something along the floor? Rearranging furniture?

I rang the bell. When Evan didn't answer right away, I nearly lost my nerve and left, but I rang it again.

"Coming!" he yelled, sounding out of breath.

I waited another second or two, and then he opened the door.

He looked very surprised to see me. Or did he look surprised to see my red, swollen eyes and red, blotchy skin and red, swollen nose?

"Are you all right?" he said, studying my distorted features. "I mean, no one died or anything?"

"Buster has a faulty heart valve," I said. "He gave us quite a scare, but he'll be okay."

"You must be relieved." He exhaled heavily. "Sorry you had to go through that."

"Me too."

His hair had fallen across his forehead, and his face, as well as his T-shirt, were stained with perspiration. Clearly I had caught him in the middle of strenuous activity. He hadn't been painting, that much was clear.

"Can I come in?" I said. "I know I'm not your favorite person lately, but I really need someone to talk to."

"About Buster or lover boy?" he asked with a weary sigh.

"Lover boy," I admitted, my voice barely above a whisper. I was so choked up it was hard to speak.

"What have you done now? Talked him into walking down the aisle a second time?"

His question triggered another round of sobs. "Yes," I said. "With *her.*"

Evan rolled his eyes, opened the door wider, and pulled me inside. Apparently, he had thawed toward me. At least, enough to tolerate my presence. "The place is a mess, but the couch is safe. Have a seat."

"Thanks." As I sat I looked around his apartment and saw that there were a half-dozen cartons scattered around the room; some were sealed with packing tape and labeled in black marker, others still open. "What's with all the boxes?"

"Let's hear your story first. Can I get you something to drink? Something nonalcoholic, hopefully? I'm not interested in a replay of last time."

"No. I'm fine. Well, I'm not fine, obviously."

"Not with that face. I thought you said you never cry."

"I never did. But now Dan's marrying Leah. Next month. On top of that, my boss fired me, and my best friend isn't speaking to me."

He perched himself on the arm of the sofa. "So I'm your last shot at human contact?"

"Possibly."

"Okay, let's go back to lover boy. You told him you were still hot for him and he's marrying the girlfriend anyway?"

"I never told him. He dropped his bombshell first. There wasn't much point in revealing my innermost feelings after that."

"Not necessarily. Maybe he'd change his mind if he knew how you felt."

I shook my head. "He's crazy about her, Evan. Crazy enough to give up the alimony by marrying her."

He applauded. "Good for him. At least one of you has ethics."

"I deserve that, but it hurts. It hurts so damn much."

More tears. Tears on my face. Tears on my clothes. Tears on Evan's sofa, which was upholstered just like mine—in a fabric that was about as soft and comfy as steel wool.

"All right. All right. We get the point that you're upset," he said, then slid down next to me and put his arm around me. "So your plan ran amok, huh?"

"Big-time," I said, tilting my head back so it rested on him. "Dan's with Leah and I don't have a job and my life is one stupid suck-ass pit."

"Is that a technical term?"

"No." I turned and buried my face in his arm. There was more sobbing and choking and snarking, and most of it landed on his T-shirt.

"Look, I was serious about telling Traffic how you feel," he said, stroking my hair. "Maybe Leah's just a rebound thing. He might call off the wedding if you're honest with him for a change."

"I can't tell him about Desiree and the matchmaking."

"Why not?"

"You just said it yourself. He's got ethics. He'd never speak to me again. *You* didn't speak to me again after I told you about it."

"I'm here now, aren't I?"

I managed a smile. "And I'm very grateful."

I reached out to touch his face, but he stood up suddenly and began to stretch the muscles in his neck. "I think I pulled something," he said. "Must have been all the lifting."

"That's right, you never said. What are the boxes for?"

"Some are going into storage. Some I'm taking with me."

"Where?" I couldn't disguise my alarm. I didn't want Evan to move out of the Heartbreak Hotel in the worst way. Who would walk me around the neighborhood and show me where to eat the best pastrami? Who would surprise me with toys for Buster? Who would be there to set me straight?

"Now that the terms of the divorce are final, I'm heading down to the Bahamas."

"To paint?"

"And for some peace and quiet. I rented a bungalow in the Abacos on a month-to-month basis. No phone. No computer. Just the sound of the waves. There's nothing keeping me here at the moment, so it seemed like a good time to do it."

Tears again. Lots and lots of tears. "But you can't go. You can't."

He put his hands on his hips and looked at me. "And why's that?"

"Because you rescue me when I forget my key or spring a leak in my garbage bag or need a home-cooked meal."

"Hire yourself a nanny."

"But most of all," I said, ignoring his sarcasm, "you put up with me when I vent about Dan. You listen. You get me, Evan. I don't have to pretend with you."

He laughed ruefully. "Oh, I get you. But here's the thing: I'm kind of sick of hearing about Dan. And I'm not really interested in being your shoulder to cry on. What I want—wanted—was for us to start a relationship of our own, but you were too hung up on your ex to even think of me in those terms. So I'm off. Out of here. Gone."

What could I say? Or do? As much as I cared about Evan—as much as I was attracted to Evan—I wasn't ready for a new relationship. He was right: I *was* stuck in the old one.

"Maybe someday the fog will clear and you'll get your priorities straight," he said as he resumed packing. That made three people to harp on my priorities. A consensus. "You're just clinging to the past because it's familiar. You do have a fondness for security, Melanie."

"You think that's what this is about?" I said. "That I want Dan because he's familiar?"

"Could be. The devil you know, and all that. Remember my painting of Buster?"

"How could I forget it?"

"When you saw it, you said it was realistic; that he sticks his toe in the water, then runs for dry land. Maybe you stick your toe in the water and run too. Maybe you think it's safer on solid ground. But there's no such thing as 'safe.' I once told you that."

I shrugged. "I hear you and you're very wise, but it doesn't feel like I'm clinging to safety. It feels like I still love Dan."

"Well." He walked back over to the sofa and offered me his hand. I took it and he pulled me up to him. We stood face-to-face, our bodies so close I could smell his sweat, spot the tiny hole in his shirt, make out the pulse that was beating on the side of his neck. "Then you should tell the guy that. Don't hold anything back. Let him see you in all your misery, although I'd probably do something about the red nose if I were you. I've got white paint over there. It's waterproof, and you're welcome to use it."

"I wish you weren't going," I said, on the verge of another crying jag. "The Bahamas is a long way from New York."

"Nah. Only three hours."

"Can I visit? I won't have to worry about Pierce, Shelley giving me vacation time."

"Let's not be in touch," said Evan. "Not if you're still—"

Instead of finishing the sentence, he looked at me for a beat, then leaned in and kissed me on the mouth. It was the kiss we'd never managed to share until then, and it caught me utterly off guard. Or was it the exquisite sensations it set off that surprised me? Stirred me? All I know is that Evan Gillespie packed plenty of passion into that kiss, and I responded in kind, and my legs nearly buckled from the force of it.

"There," he said when he broke away. "I didn't want to leave town without doing that, Melanie."

"You know," I said, trying to catch my breath, regain my equilibrium, "all my friends call me Mel. The friends I have left, anyway."

"I'm interested in being more than your friend, in case I didn't make that plain."

Before I could respond, he put his arm around my waist and walked me to the door. "I do have one question before we call it a night," he said when we got to the threshold.

"I've already told you all my secrets," I said. "That's what's so amazing. You've seen the real me and you kissed me in spite of it."

"What a guy, huh? And they say chivalry isn't dead."

"That's funny. I said the exact same thing the night we met."

"What same thing?"

" 'And they say chivalry isn't dead.' You came to Patty's to replace the detergent she'd lent you. I had no idea you'd turn out to be the most chivalrous man I've ever known."

"Flattery won't get you anywhere. I still have to pack."

"Okay," I said, wishing he didn't. "But you said you had a question. Ask away."

"It's about the first time you were here for dinner. Your cell phone rang, you had a quick conversation, and then you left to go help some elderly woman."

"I remember."

"So does this woman really exist, or were you just blowing me off so you could go work with your coconspirators on the Dan plan?"

"Both," I said and gave him the whole story of my relationship with Mrs. Thornberg, including how much I'd grown to like her. "I actually enjoy being with her now, taking care of her, easing her loneliness, letting her ease mine. Does that mean there's hope for me and my priorities?"

"There's always hope."

He kissed me lightly, barely brushing my cheek with his lips, and sent me home.

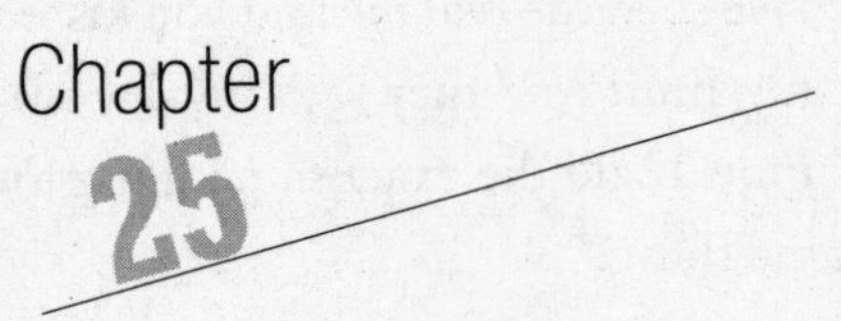

Chapter 25

"She'll be just a few more minutes," said Taylor, Desiree's assistant. It was eleven-thirty the next morning. I'd been waiting to see Madam Matchmaker since eleven and didn't appreciate having to sit there staring at the ceiling, but then I didn't exactly have anyplace else to go.

"Is there someone in her office or is she out buying more fuzzy slippers?" I said.

"Slippers? She's with a client," Taylor said indignantly. She, unlike Steffi, was loyal to her boss. "But I'm sure she'll—"

At that moment, Lynda Fox, queen of the LPGA tour and member of the Heart Hunting for Exes club, emerged from

Desiree's office looking a lot more upbeat than the last time I'd seen her. I figured she must have stopped by to leaf through the files of potential cohabitors and/or new spouses for her ex-husband.

I walked over to her as she was making her way toward the door and touched her forearm, which was the size of my thigh. Well, she was a professional athlete. It was her job to take steroids.

"Hey," she said, yanking the arm away, as if I were some toady autograph seeker. "What do you think you're doing?"

"Trying to save you from making a big mistake," I said, then lowered my voice. "Take it from me. You don't want to fix up your ex with one of Desiree's A-listers so you can dodge the alimony."

She raised her eyebrows. "Who said that's why I'm here?"

"Look, I'm the one who came up with the idea, okay? My ex is Traffic Dan Swain, the football player. I set him up with Desiree's A-plus client, and now I'm sorry I did, because he's marrying her."

Her brows relaxed, and she grinned, slapping me on the back with such force that I nearly fell over. "That's great. You screwed him on the money, so what the hell are you complaining about?"

"I still love him," I said, feeling the tears well up. I hadn't cried all morning, but I knew the dry spell wouldn't last. "I realized it after I'd already set him up."

"Too bad, but I don't love my ex, so I have nothing to worry about," she said. "I can't stand the sight of him, if you want the truth. Every time he shows up to visit the kids in his new clothes and new shoes and new car, I wanna strangle him."

"I used to feel that way, but I learned that money isn't everything."

Huh? Had I just said that? Or were my sinuses so blocked up with sob snot that I wasn't thinking straight?

"What planet have you been living on, honey?" said Lynda Fox. "Women didn't get this far only to hand over half of everything to men. That's not what Gloria Steinem fought for."

"Maybe it is," I said. "Maybe sexual equality means sexual equality for both sexes."

Had I really just said *that*?

She backed away from me as if I'd sprouted a penis. "You need to get your priorities straight," she said, joining the chorus.

"They're getting straighter all the time," I said. "You're the one who should rethink what you're doing. You could end up losing more than your tournament winnings."

"You remind me of my friend Margery Pinckney the way you're pining for your ex," she said. "She was married to a chiropractor—they had five kids, one of them a Rhodes scholar, another one doing ten years for armed robbery—and she divorced him. Mostly because of the problems with the kid who went to jail. Anyhow, her ex remarried and had a child with his new wife, and Margery was all by herself, regretting her decision to walk out. She was so depressed that she had her tongue pierced. A nice diamond stud, but still. It interfered with her ability to eat, and she became anorexic."

I stared at Lynda, amazed by her lack of sensitivity. Once again she had prattled on about people whose personal business was entirely their own. What a blabbermouth.

"So," she said, as if to sum up, "unlike you and Margery, I don't want my ex-husband back."

"I get it," I said and stepped aside so she could leave.

When it was my turn with Desiree, who was in a brunette wig

and weighed down by enough gold chokers to literally choke her, I told her about Dan's engagement. She'd already heard an earful about it from Leah, of course, but I put my own spin on the story by crying throughout it.

"Take it easy," she said as I reached into my purse for yet another pocket pack of Kleenex. I'd gone through a case of them. "I had a feeling this would happen."

"That they'd get married or that I'd want Dan back?"

"That they'd get married, that you'd want Dan back, and that you'd be stuck having to pay me even though you ended up miserable."

"Maybe you should have been a fortune-teller instead of a matchmaker," I said sourly.

"Can I make a suggestion?"

"If you're going to tell me to get my priorities straight, I'll scream."

"I was gonna tell you to wash your hair. You look like hell."

"It's been a tough time, Desiree. I'm deeply despondent."

"Then I'll give you the same advice I give all my clients. If you want to attract a member of the opposite sex, you have to take stock of your appearance."

My jaw dropped. Attract a member of the opposite sex? Hadn't she been listening? "I'm not one of your clients," I said. "Not like the others, anyway."

"Didn't you just tell me you wanted Dan back? It all starts with that first date. You have to look your best for it."

"What are you talking about?" I said. "He's engaged to Leah. Helloooo?"

"Melanie, Melanie, Melanie." She sighed. "Have you forgotten that one of the services Desiree Klein Heart Hunting provides is love coaching? I spent enough time coaching Leah in how to get Dan to commit, didn't I?"

"So?"

"So now you need coaching in how to get him to come back to you."

I blinked at her, hoping she'd disappear and that my entire experience with her would turn out to be a figment of my imagination, sort of like Dorothy in *The Wizard of Oz.* Desiree, it seemed to me then, was a cross between the wizard and the wicked witch, with a munchkin thrown in.

"You'd sell her out to help me?" I said.

"I'm not selling anybody out," she said. "I'm offering you the benefit of my years of love coaching, that's all. You want it or not?"

What did I have to lose? I was desperate. "Why not."

"Fine. Here it is. If Dan really loves Leah, then there's nothing you can do to change that. But if he's on the fence even just a little, you've got a shot."

"Asking her to marry him doesn't sound like he's on the fence," I said.

"You never heard of broken engagements?"

"Yes, but—"

" 'But' nothing. I'm not advising you to steal him from Leah. I'm not 'selling her out,' as you put it. I'm only telling you to see if there's any fence sitting going on—any window of opportunity."

"And how do I do that?"

"Knock on the window. See if anyone's home."

"Please." I rolled my eyes. She was as crazy as she was corrupt.

"Fight for him, Melanie. Stop all the hysterics and just go tell him how you feel. Even if he gives you the boot, you'll be no worse off than you are right now."

She did have a point. I couldn't sink any lower. Or so I thought.

"Go," she urged. "Play it out one last time. At least you'll know for sure where you stand."

I got up from my chair, dabbing at my eyes with the tissue. "Thanks, but I still wish I'd never met you."

"No one twisted your arm to walk in here and throw money at me," she pointed out. "It was your idea to play God with Dan's life, not mine."

"I just pray he never finds out," I said.

"Why should he? Who's gonna tell him?"

Who indeed.

I went home to wash my hair. Well, it wasn't the worst advice Desiree had given me, especially since I was competing with Leah, the hair goddess. I iced my face too, trying to deflate the tires I'd grown on my eyelids. And then I put on some jeans and a sweater and called Dan. I asked if I could come over and see Buster right away. He said I could. I asked if he would be there. He said he thought so but that Isa would let me in if he had to run out. I asked if he could make sure he'd be there, because I had something I wanted to discuss with him. He said it sounded serious. I said it was.

The stage was set. I gave myself one last check in my hall mirror and off I went, prepared to either win back my ex or accept my fate and concede victory to Leah.

"So, what do you think of the big news?" said Ricardo when I entered my old building. "Bet you never in a million years figured Mr. Swain would marry the caretaker."

"No, I never did," I said, stating the obvious.

"Guess the insurance company won't have to worry about her showing up every night." He laughed. "She took such good care of him that he can't live without her, huh?"

"Seems that way," I said. I had hoped to avoid having this conversation with Ricardo, but, as I knew all too well, he never left his post and, therefore, could never be avoided.

"Maybe I'll give them your notebook for a wedding present," he said. "As a token of how the romance began, you know?"

The notebook. Oh, God. It was incriminating evidence and could never fall into Dan's hands. I instructed Ricardo to hand it over to me immediately. I told him *I* would be giving it to the happy couple as a wedding present.

He went on for another minute or two about how many babes there were in the caretaker profession and explained that he, himself, was dating a nurse who was pregnant with his child. "Seven kids, I'll have," he said. "Incredible, right?"

"What would be incredible is if you made an honest woman of this one," I said. I had no further interest in sucking up to him, since he was no longer my accomplice. I just wanted to get upstairs and talk to Dan.

When Ricardo finally did buzz me up, I was met at the door by Isa, another former accomplice I would rather have avoided.

"Hello, *chérie,*" she said. "You hear the news?"

I took a deep breath and exhaled slowly. "Yes, Isa. Dan's engaged to Leah. I know all about it."

She beamed. "I'm the one who made it happen. I put a spell on them—her, so she'd sleep here for those ninety days you wanted, and him, so he'd stop making you pay him every month."

"Good job," I said. Did I ever deserve what I got.

"And I have all the pictures on that digital camera," she added with pride.

The photos. More evidence of my deceit. "I'd like the camera back, Isa."

"No problem, *chérie*. It's at my place. You could come by some night and pick it up."

Like that would happen. I had enough problems without running into crackhead sons and car thieves. "In that case, why don't you hang on to it for now. But don't bring it to work until I tell you, okay?"

Just then, Buster pranced into the foyer, followed by his master.

"Here's my sweetie boy," I said, referring to my dog, although the same sentiments applied to my ex. "You feeling okay, Busty? No more coughing?"

"He's done really well on the medicine," said Dan as Isa waved her cleaning rag at me and disappeared. "No coughing or fatigue or anything."

I looked at my ex more closely—he was wearing a cable-knit sweater I'd given him one Christmas, and it made me even more nostalgic for our happy days together. Unfortunately, nostalgia often elicits tears, and out popped mine. I was sick of crying, not to mention embarrassed that I was doing it in front of the man I was supposed to charm, but they dripped down my cheeks, onto my chin. Lovely.

"Hey, hey, hey," he said with genuine concern. "What's this?"

He pulled me up off the floor where I'd been hugging Buster and guided me over to the sofa. I sank down onto the soft cushion, put my head in my hands and sobbed my guts out. I wanted so badly to be as bright and perky as Leah, but there I was, an open wound.

"Buster will be fine," he said, rubbing my back. "You've got to believe that, Mel."

Sob sob sob.

"I've never seen you like this," he said. "Want some water?"

As he started for the kitchen, I mumbled, "I've cried enough water to fill your sink."

"Okay. No water." He sat beside me, waiting for me to come up for air. "I knew you were upset about Buster, but I didn't realize how upset. Leah agrees with Patrick about the treatment plan, by the way. She's been keeping a close eye on our Busty. He's very comfortable around her."

Sob sob sob.

"Mel, I'm worried about you," he said. "You've never been a crier. Where's the tough cookie I know so well?"

"Melted!" I picked up my head. Suddenly, I didn't care if he saw my swollen eyes and swollen nose and swollen lips. What difference did any of it make?

"What do you mean?" he said, looking bewildered.

"I've turned into this pathetic tear factory because you're marrying Leah." There. I said it.

"Come on," he said with a chuckle, as if he didn't understand that I was serious. "That doesn't make sense. Now you're off the hook for the alimony. You should be celebrating."

"I don't care about the alimony. I just want you."

"Me?" He stared at me, stunned. "Since when?"

"Since . . . since . . . you became the man I always hoped you'd become."

"Aw, now you're yanking my chain. You just need to calm down." He resumed the rubbing of my back.

"It's true, Dan. You're taking charge of your life and acting responsibly and proving that I was wrong to leave you, leave our marriage. I love you. I never stopped loving you, even though I said horrible, nasty things to you and you said horrible, nasty things to me. I want us to get back together."

Finally realizing that I meant what I was saying, he took his hand off my back, this time as if he was afraid he might have caught something by touching me. He looked that unnerved.

Sob sob sob.

He rose from the sofa and started pacing. "I didn't see this coming at all," he said.

"Neither did I," I said. "But the feelings are there, and I can't hold them in. I'm not trying to ruin your happiness, I swear I'm not. I just had to tell you. In case there's any chance you have feelings for me too."

He stopped pacing and stood there staring at me again. "But I love Leah."

"Do you?" I asked.

"And she loves me," he said instead of giving me a direct answer. "I'll always care about you, Mel. I told you that at Patrick's office. But getting back together?" He tugged on his earlobe, a sure sign that he was out of sorts, and returned to his pacing. I had clearly shaken him up. "When we split, you kept telling me there was no way you'd come back. And it wasn't like I didn't ask. And ask. Eventually, I believed you and stopped asking. And now this?"

"Okay, so my timing isn't the greatest. But what should I have done? *Not* come to you? Watch you marry Leah without ever letting you know what's in my heart?"

"Maybe."

"Why? Because you're having doubts about her?"

"No."

"You sure?"

"The person I'm having doubts about is you. If we got back together, what would be different? Yeah, I'd have a job, but you'd still be married to yours. I'd never see you."

"Bernie fired me. I'm not a VP at Pierce, Shelley anymore. He couldn't get past the fact that I was too busy moping around about you to concentrate on my clients."

"Oh, jeez. I'm sorry."

"Don't be. I'll find another job, and when I do I won't make it my life. I'm not as obsessed about security anymore. My security is in here now." I tapped on my chest, just the way Evan did when he had tried to make the same point to me.

Dan shook his head, confounded. "So you're gonna stop and smell the roses, is that it?"

"That's it. Overdue, but true. I just want to smell the roses with you, Dan. Please say you want that too?"

"I still don't get this. First, I was on your shit list. Now, I'm your candidate for man of the year?"

"I know it sounds unbelievable, but things change. People change."

Suddenly, his expression darkened and his eyes blazed. "I can't listen to this. I really can't. I love Leah and we're getting married next month and I think you should go."

He was angry—not the reaction I was expecting at all. I had anticipated that he would be surprised, flattered, and steadfast in his loyalty to Leah, but not angry.

"You want me to leave?"

"Yeah. You know why? Because you *are* yanking my chain and I'm tired of it."

My tears stopped immediately. I'm telling you, if you scare them, they'll scoot right back up where they came from.

"I never meant to do that," I said.

It occurred to me that if he thought I'd yanked his chain now, what would he think if he found out I'd hired a professional matchmaker and fixed him up with Leah? Well, that wouldn't happen. I wouldn't let it happen.

"Just go," he said. "Please."

"I'm going. I'm going." I went to kiss Buster good-bye, then gave Dan one last, longing look. It was inconceivable to me that we were really finished. But he had made it plain that he wanted no part of me.

"In some ways, it feels as if we've switched places," I said. "You're the one with the job and the bright future, while I'm the one who's vulnerable and alone." I moved toward the door. "But you know what? It's not a bad thing to be in your shoes. I have insight into what you must have gone through when we were together. I understand now what it's like to lose everything."

While he watched silently—jaw set, lips pursed, the picture of a man who was struggling to rein in his emotions—I opened the door, walked out, and closed it behind me.

Chapter 26

I stopped at Mrs. Thornberg's instead of going straight home. She took one look at the sad, bedraggled spectacle I was and opened her arms to me. I rushed at her and let her hold me. Her bones were so frail I was afraid I'd break them.

"I know," she said as she rocked me. Her breath smelled of dill pickles, which, together with the odor of mothballs in the apartment, made for a pretty rank combination, but I cared more about the affection she was showing me. Never had I needed it so much. "He's marrying the dope fiend and you're worried how your poor little doggie will take it?"

"No. That's not it," I said. "That's never been it."

"What do you mean?" she asked.

"You always say I'm a good girl, but I've been a bad, bad girl." There was something about my odd, yet habit-forming relationship with Antoinette Thornberg—about the fact that she kept reaching out to me and I kept being there for her and the whole thing made me feel better about myself—that allowed me to tell her my story.

Yes, I confessed it all, including the part about using her to spy on Dan and Leah, and when I was done she sat quietly for several minutes before saying, "I've got turkey from the deli. I could make you a sandwich. Mayo. Mustard. Russian dressing. Even sauerkraut."

I was stunned. Where was the outrage? The scolding? The finger-pointing? Why wasn't she exploding at me the way she did at her noisy neighbors? Surely, my offenses were more serious than playing loud music after 9 P.M.

"Thanks, but I'm not hungry," I said. "I'm more interested in hearing you convince me that I'm not an awful person."

"Misguided, but not awful," she said. "I played a trick on Mr. Thornberg and I didn't beat myself over the head about it."

"Really? What was the trick?" I said, conjuring up the man with the bad toupee and the defective testicles.

"I sold my clothes so I'd have my own money," she said, then cackled at the memory. "I've given you a hard time about being a career girl, but the truth is I envy you. In my day, we had to get allowances from our husbands. Since Mr. Thornberg was a tightwad, I had to be creative about it."

"What'd you do?" I said.

"Every few months I took my fancy stuff to a high-end consignment shop on Sixty-fifth and Lex," she said. "They'd sell the clothes, pay me the money, and I'd spend it on whatever I felt like—movies, museums, more clothes, the racetrack."

"The racetrack?"

"You have a problem with that?"

"No." I squelched a laugh. "Didn't Mr. Thornberg ever catch on? He must have wondered what happened to your clothes."

"Did the football star next door ever notice if you stopped wearing a particular dress?"

"Not that I can remember."

"There you go. Men never notice those things. They're too busy noticing our breasts."

I couldn't squelch that one. Mrs. Thornberg was as flat-chested as the slices of turkey she had in her refrigerator. "My trick on Dan was worse though, don't you think?"

"Probably. But look at it this way, dear. You did him a huge favor by introducing him to Leah. If it weren't for you and this Desiree person, he wouldn't be walking around with that big smile on his face. When you love someone, it can be enough just to see them happy."

"Even if it's not with me?"

"Exactly. You gave him a gift. An anonymous gift. Put it in that context and you'll be able to dry your tears and get on with your life."

I stayed with Mrs. Thornberg for a couple of hours, during which she talked and I listened and we ate. Well, I ate and she picked.

I felt better after the visit. As a result of her soothing words, I had vowed to accept the idea that I'd lost Dan, and that I did do him a favor by setting him up with Leah. I was planning to move on. I was.

■ ■ ■

Over the weekend, I worked on my résumé and cleaned my apartment and, on Sunday, drove up to Connecticut to see Weezie. I threw myself on her mercy and begged her to forgive me and pledged that I would be a more attentive friend. She agreed to give me another chance and conceded that I wasn't the only one to blame; she hadn't been forthcoming about her problems with Nards, which had started long before Dr. Corbett complicated her marriage, because she couldn't bring herself to admit failure. She said that he had seemed restless ever since they'd had their second child. She was convinced that once she'd given up her career to raise their kids, he'd lost interest in her.

"He totally changed," she said as we sat together on a park bench near her house. Spring was finally around the corner, and it felt good to be outdoors, good to be with her, mostly. "He was the one who wanted a stay-at-home wife, remember?"

"I do, but is it possible that you changed once you did stay home?" I asked. "I mean, did you become more about the kids and less about him? Do you think he misses the part of you that enjoyed making out in hotel restaurants, for example?"

"Oh, now you're taking his side?"

"No. I'm just trying to see both sides. I never used to do that, Weezie. I never stopped to consider what men want or need or are entitled to. But lately I've come to realize that they're more like us than they are different from us, despite all the Mars-Venus crap. We all want to feel supported, championed, fussed over. We all need to feel sexy and desirable too. And we're all entitled to be respected for who we are, not how much money we bring home."

"Nards doesn't complain about my not bringing money home," she said. "That's not the issue."

"No, but you complain that he's so busy bringing money home that he's not helping you with the kids. Maybe you can't have it both ways. I tried to have it both ways with Dan, and look how that turned out. I wanted him to get out there and find a job, but I was too consumed with my own to understand what he needed from me to bolster his self-confidence. And then along came Leah, who was everything I wasn't: sweet, encouraging, nurturing, patient. No wonder he fell for her."

"You *were* all of those things, Mel. Don't sell yourself short."

"I was in the beginning," I said. "But it's easy to be encouraging to the golden boy wide receiver of the New York Giants. What was there to nurture?"

We talked and talked and talked, and it was cathartic for both of us. By the time I drove back to the city, she had promised she would get together with Nards and try to find common ground with him. I promised I would stop obsessing about Dan and focus on my future without him.

One of us broke our promise.

I was sitting on my bed on Sunday night, eating a gooey, microwaved Milky Way and studying the *New York Times*'s classified section, when the doorbell rang, startling me. I checked the clock on the night table. It was ten-fifteen. I wasn't expecting anybody at that hour obviously.

My first thought was that it must be Patty. Then I remembered she had pretty much abandoned the Heartbreak Hotel and was spending almost every night at her new boyfriend's place.

And then I thought it might be Evan, who wasn't leaving for the Bahamas for at least another few days.

I chuckled as I padded to the door, thinking of all the times he'd seen me when I wasn't exactly looking my best. This time I was wearing grungy sweatpants and an even grungier sweatshirt, and I had creamy nougat all over me. Poor guy.

I peered through the peephole just to make sure it was Evan, not one of America's Most Wanted, and staggered back when I caught a glimpse of the guy outside my door: Dan.

Great, I thought, frantically licking the candy bar off my fingers. What's he doing here and why do I have to be dressed like a slob?

I fluffed my hair, pinched my cheeks (actually, I sort of slapped them), and told myself to calm down. He was my ex-husband, for God's sake. He was marrying a babe in a matter of weeks. What difference did it make how I looked? He had probably only come to berate me for "yanking his chain."

"Dan," I said after I opened the door and watched him charge past me into the room. "If you're here about the other day—"

"Damn right I'm here about the other day," he said, clearly distressed. "You came over to the apartment and cried your heart out and showed me a side of you that I—" He stopped to collect himself. "That I hadn't seen in a long time. You were vulnerable, open, honest. No criticizing. No judging. Just loving. All of a sudden, you were my college girl again, the one who used to make me feel like a million bucks. I started reliving how it used to be with us." He threw his hands up in the air as if he couldn't believe what he was saying. "Would you listen to me? I'm engaged to Leah. We're getting married in Minco. This makes no sense."

I shouldn't have worried about how I looked. He looked worse. He hadn't shaved. He had dark circles under his eyes. And his hair—Well, let's just say I wasn't the only one who needed a shampoo.

"It makes perfect sense. I reminded you of the girl you loved," I said, my hopes growing. Was it possible that I hadn't lost him? That I'd been too hasty in admitting defeat? "The question is: Do you still love her?"

"I never stopped loving *her*," he said, planting himself in front of me. "But how am I supposed to know what it all means? How do I tell if these feelings I'm having are real or just leftovers from the past?"

"You've got to explore them, Dan. Running from them won't do any of us any good."

He took my face in his hands. "Explore them?"

"Yes."

"Like this?"

He lowered his face tantalizingly close to mine and whispered my name. My immediate thought was: oh my God. I'm not dreaming this. It's not some lame fantasy. He's not finished with me any more than I'm finished with him.

"Yes."

He pressed his lips against mine and kissed me. The kiss began tentatively, even clumsily, as if we were rusty at knowing how to please the very mate with whom we'd once been so intimate. But gradually it built into an embrace that quickened and deepened and propelled us from our standing position in the middle of the room over to the sofa. When we finally broke apart minutes later, breathless with the unexpectedness of the physical contact, neither of us spoke. We just looked at each other, took a gulp of air, and went back at it. For two solid hours we kissed and groped and humped, fully clothed, like teenagers on a first date. Or, more accurately, like ex-spouses on a reconnaissance mission.

What we discovered during those two hours was that the magic between us was still there. We weren't wrong about that. Maybe it was the kind of magic that can only ignite between two former lovers, because it feels forbidden and familiar simultaneously, but we were definitely in the throes of it, neither of us wanting or even able to stop.

"This is trouble for me, darlin'," he murmured at one point. "I'm not some sleazeball who asks women to marry him and then goes out and makes it with his ex-wife."

"Of course you're not," I said, my mouth wonderfully raw. "But let's take this one step at a time."

He nodded and took the next step, which was to kiss me again.

Chapter 27

Dan and I didn't sleep together, if that's what you're thinking. It was just a kiss fest at my place that Sunday night. A big, fat, juicy kiss fest. When he finally pulled himself up off the sofa, it was nearly midnight. I asked him if he'd told Leah where he was. He said he'd lied and told her he was out with an old college buddy. I said he hadn't lied, not entirely, because I was an old college buddy. He said he hated that he'd sneaked out of the apartment to see me. I said he wasn't a sneak and never had been; that these were extremely trying circumstances and there were no rules for how to handle them. He said he didn't want to hurt Leah under any circumstances, because he loved her. I said I thought he loved me. He said he did love me. What we had, ladies and gentlemen, was a man in conflict.

He came back Monday morning to bring Buster to me, and the kissing started all over again. We couldn't keep our hands off each other, couldn't get a sense of perspective. It was just like the old days, when reality was not on our radar. Neither of us had jobs to run off to (well, he had one, but it wasn't full-time yet), so we tuned the world out and let the Heartbreak Hotel become our hermetically sealed trysting place.

There was still no real sex, mind you. Dan was insistent that we shouldn't "do it." As long as we remained dressed, albeit with zippers unzipped and buttons unbuttoned, he rationalized that he wasn't really cheating on Leah. And yet he was riddled with guilt, confusion, and indecision.

"I understand that you're torn," I said during a break in the action. "But maybe if we play this out, if you see how right we are together, if you get more comfortable with the idea of me being back in your life, you'll have the courage, the conviction, to tell her it's over between you."

"I don't know," he said. "I don't even understand how this could be happening."

It went on like that—intense passion interrupted by concerns about Leah—for the rest of the week. Since I didn't have any work to do, other than trying to find work, I allowed myself to daydream freely.

I envisioned Dan having The Talk with Leah and, though she would be devastated, she would find solace in her thriving veterinary practice and eventually attract many new suitors, due to her sweetness, pluck, and bodiliciousness.

I envisioned Dan and me getting remarried. We would not

have the ceremony and reception at his parents' house in Minco but rather at a tasteful venue in Manhattan, one of the spots recommended in a recent cover story in *New York* magazine. I would wear an off-white suit, something in the ecru/eggshell/oatmeal family, and he would wear a crisp dark suit, something that suggested formality without being formal, if you know what I mean. His parents and siblings would be only too happy to fly in and welcome me back into the family with the sincerity for which Oklahomans are famous. Weezie and Nards would be newly reconciled and serve as our matron of honor and best man, respectively, their two children contributing to the occasion by strewing rose petals from straw baskets as they preceded us down the aisle. Dan and I would write and recite our own vows; they would, of course, refer to our "time-out" from each other and be both witty and poignant. When the justice of the peace pronounced us "husband and wife," someone in the audience would shout "Again?" and everyone would laugh and cheer, especially Robin, my divorce lawyer.

I envisioned Dan and me honeymooning in Paris or, perhaps, Rome, where we would sightsee and take lots of photographs and eat expensive, once-in-a-lifetime meals before repairing to the sea (Cap d'Antibes or Positano, depending) for a truly picturesque commemoration of our remarriage.

And I envisioned Dan and me returning to New York, to our old apartment, and resuming our life together. He would coach the C.W. Post Pioneers to a conference championship in his very first season with them while I, in addition to basking in his reflected glory as a coach's wife, would start a small business. An antiques shop. Or maybe a chain of Vietnamese nail salons. We would have babies—perfect, well-behaved little towheads who looked just like Dan. He would want four and I would opt for two, but in the spirit of compromise we would have three. Mrs. Thornberg would be their surrogate grandmother; they would beg her to babysit for them, and she would be only too happy to oblige. She would let them sleep over in her guest room whenever Dan and I went away. She would make them egg salad sandwiches using her secret ingredients. They would call her "Nana."

These reveries reassured me, entertained me, kept me in a constant state of anticipation for Dan's daily visits. And then a development. On Thursday of that week, he said his conscience was killing him; that he couldn't lead a double life anymore.

I tensed as I lay next to him on my bed. We'd spent the afternoon together, kissing and holding each other and playing with Buster, our little family intact. His announcement put a pin in my bubble of domestic bliss.

"What are you saying?" I asked. "That you're ready to make a choice?"

"No. I'm not ready. That's the point."

"Then what?"

"I need more time with you. And I don't mean the hours we grab when nobody's looking for us, holed up here at your place. I mean free. Out in the open. Doing the kinds of things couples do. Taking it slow."

"Fine with me," I said, extremely relieved, "but what about Leah? And, more importantly, what about your wedding?"

"I guess I've gotta postpone it or cancel it or whatever it is people do," he said with real anguish. "I'll tell her I'm having second thoughts about making a commitment to her so soon. We've only known each other, like, three months. We fell in love, she moved into my apartment, we got engaged. Bam bam bam.

It all happened so fast. I'm gonna say I need some space, to figure out if I'm sure about everything. What else can I do? I can't go ahead and marry her. Not when I'm feeling the way I do about you."

I kissed him, stroked his forehead, told him I loved him. "When are you planning to deliver this news bulletin?"

He shrugged. "Next couple of days, probably. Leah's an amazing woman. She doesn't deserve to be jerked around."

The way I'd jerked Dan around. Another irony: my ex, whom I'd once cast as the villain, turned out to be a much better person than I was. "I'm sorry," I said. "It was never my intention to hurt her."

"Of course it wasn't. You didn't even know her."

"Right."

I didn't know her. I just knew her medical history, her educational background, her height and weight, and every other scrap of personal data about her. God, did I hate myself.

"The main thing," said Dan, "is that the pressure will be off once I put the wedding on hold. You and I can have all the time we need to find out if we're the real deal."

"Do you really doubt it?"

"I thought Leah was the real deal. Maybe she still is, and I'm just living in the past. It wouldn't be the first time I've done that, according to you."

I leaned over and kissed him again. He pulled me closer and kissed me back.

"Did that feel like the past?" I asked.

He shrugged. "Too hard to tell. We'd better do it some more."

■ ■ ■

Later that night, Evan came over. He was leaving in the morning and wanted to say good-bye.

I was very glad he'd stopped by. Buster was too. I still dreaded the thought of not having him right down the hall, not seeing him, not being able to get to know him better, but he was doing what he needed to do, and I couldn't stand in his way. It wasn't my place.

"I brought a going-away present for you and Buster," he said and handed me a flat package wrapped in brown shipping paper.

"Oh, Evan. You didn't have to do that. You're the one who's going away," I said, thinking again how much I would miss him. It seemed as if no matter what dumb-ass thing I did or how badly I screwed up my life, he kept showing up, either to rescue me or to try to talk some sense into me. If it hadn't been for Dan, I suspected that he and I would have—Well. There was no point in speculating. I *was* with Dan, and that was that.

"Open it," he said, his eyes shining with the enthusiasm of a kid at Christmas.

"Yes, sir." I ripped the paper apart to find two paintings. The first was the one Evan had done of Buster at the water's edge, the one of him sticking his toe in the water. "You finished it!"

"All done. My first canine painting ever." He laughed. "And probably my last. One of them, anyway."

"Are you kidding? It's great." I loved it even more than the earlier version. He had added colors, shading, and texture to the painting, as well as fine-tuned Buster's face to make it look even more realistic.

I turned my attention back to the package and studied the second painting. It was of the same scene—a sandy cove with calm seas and blue skies overhead—but the dog had actually ventured into the water, his head bobbing above the light waves, the sun reflecting down on him, sparkling on him.

"I decided to do another one," said Evan. "This time he makes the choice not to run for dry land. He's swimming, paddling along without a care in the world. See how liberated he is? How daring? He's not worrying about his security. He's enjoying the moment."

"I do see," I said. Intellectually, I understood the message of the painting, of course, but I was still clinging to Dan and couldn't identify. Not emotionally. Not yet. "It's beautiful. Both paintings are."

"They're all yours."

"Wait. You can't just give them to me," I protested. "I want to buy them."

"No way. They're parting gifts," he said. "Hang them somewhere and think of me."

I hugged Evan. His body was lean and rangy compared to Dan's more beefy football player physique. And he was dark—hair, eyes, complexion—while Dan was fair. The contrast between them was striking, and I couldn't have gotten involved with two more different-looking men. But then I wasn't *involved* with Evan, so why was I comparing them in the first place?

"What's the latest with you and lover boy?" he said as he took a seat on my sofa.

"I followed your advice and told him how I feel."

"And?"

"He's postponing his wedding."

Evan didn't react right away. He just looked at me with this disapproving expression, almost as if he felt sorry for me.

"This is a *good* thing," I said, plopping down next to him. "Dan and I are meant to be together."

"I don't think Leah would agree with that," he said.

"No, but isn't it better for Dan to let her down now instead of after they're married?"

"Look, I don't know Dan or Leah, and none of this is any of my business as I've said a thousand times. But has he flat out told you he doesn't love her?"

"He said he's confused and doesn't want to make a mistake."

"I repeat: has he told you he doesn't love her?"

"No. But he told me he loves me."

He sighed. "Melanie, it isn't possible to love two women. Not in the same way at the same time. I'll always love Kaitlin, no matter how badly she hurt me, because she was my first real love and we share so much history. But then I realized that I was starting to fall in love with you and it's a whole other—"

He stopped midsentence when he grasped what he'd just allowed to slip out. We both sort of sat there in stunned silence.

"I had no idea," I said finally. "I mean, I knew we were getting closer, but love?"

"Maybe," he said. "If you'd have let it happen. Right now it's all hypothetical, because you chose someone else. But, yeah, I thought we were headed there." He laughed. "I think it was the night you locked yourself out of this place. You came knocking and seduced me with the T-shirt and bare ass."

"Seriously, Evan. When did you start to have feelings for me?"

"When I figured out that you were this competent, I-can-do-everything-myself woman who'd been forced to grow up much too fast. You never had a childhood, Melanie. You never got time off to experience the joy of trying new things, of doing things just for the sheer fun of it. Maybe it was watching you bite into that pastrami sandwich and seeing the goofy look on your face that did it, but I loved being the one to experience those new things with you."

"That's a lovely sentiment," I said, filled with emotion I didn't fully understand.

"I think we could have had something special," he said, his eyes so black, so beguiling. "I'll never know for sure, but it seemed like we had a shot at a grown-up love. The kind of love that accepts weaknesses as well as strengths."

"How could you love me when you know how shabbily I've treated people?"

He shrugged. "That's what acceptance is. I don't believe you meant to hurt anybody. I believe you were afraid and went into survival mode."

"You *are* accepting," I said with a shake of my head.

"Is that the kind of love you have for Dan? Or do you just love him when he's behaving himself?"

"It's not that he's *behaving* himself," I said. "It's that he's acting like he used to, when we were happy together. His self-confidence has really gone up, and it's changed everything."

"Leah gave him that self-confidence. She's responsible for the change in him. She supported him unconditionally, loving him even when he was down. Can you say that about yourself?"

"Not exactly, but he does love me, Evan."

"I'm sure he does, and that love will never really die. But you're his past, Melanie. Leah's his future. If you really loved him, you'd see that and let him go."

"Is it possible you're just saying that because you have a vested interest in what happens?"

He smiled ruefully. "I'm saying it because it's true. When you love someone, you want them to be happy, even if it's not with you."

I rolled my eyes. "You must have talked to Mrs. Thornberg. She force-fed me the same speech, word for word."

"Good. Maybe it'll sink in now that you've heard it twice. But here's another one I'd like you to remember: what makes ordinary people heroic is when they give up the thing they want most."

"So that's why you're leaving?" I teased, trying not to face the fact that he *was* leaving. "So you can give me up and play the hero?"

"Nope. I'm no hero. Just an ex–book editor with some heavy quotations still floating in his head." He rose from the sofa. "I'm leaving because the weather in the Bahamas is pretty damn fine. I'm gonna soak up the sun, read a lot of books, and paint my heart out."

"Sounds like paradise. What if you never come back?"

"Then you won't have to listen to my lectures anymore."

I walked him to the door. "Paradise aside, when will I see you again?"

"I scribbled down my address on a piece of paper. It's in there with the paintings." He stood straighter, threw his shoulders back, as if he were marshaling his strength. "But promise me something. Don't write until this Dan situation is resolved."

"I promise."

"And one more favor."

"Sure."

"If he ever finds out that you were the one who set him up with Leah, don't duck it. Admit it. If your relationship can withstand the truth, maybe it's stronger than I thought."

“He’s not going to find out.”

“But if he does, Melanie? If he finds out and confronts you, be heroic. Be prepared to give up the thing you want most.”

“Okay, okay. I promise that too. Anything else?”

“Yeah.” He put his arms around me and started to lower his head toward mine, as if he were about to kiss me, then changed his mind and gave me a quick hug instead. “Take good care of Buster,” he whispered.

“I will,” I said and felt a hard lump in my throat as I watched him go.

Chapter 28

I didn't hear from Dan for twenty-four hours. I figured he was dealing with Leah, sitting her down and breaking the news, arranging for her to move out, offering to buy her a ring as sort of a consolation prize. And I remembered he was supposed to appear at some sports function where pro athletes were signing autographs to be auctioned off for charity. I knew how much he enjoyed those events, so I was happy for him even though he wasn't with me. See how unselfish I had become?

I went about my business on Tuesday, calling Pierce, Shelley's competitors who'd once tried to woo me to their companies. I announced that I was finally ready to join them and to apply my considerable skills on their behalf. None of them wanted me.

Apparently, word had traveled fast: Melanie Banks was talented but unemployable. There'd been rumblings about my erratic work schedule. There'd been rumblings about my getting tossed off the Jed Ornbacher account. And, of course, there'd been rumblings about my drug use, which, though utterly without merit, had become as good as true. As one former colleague put it, "You'd be coming in with baggage, and no one needs another corporate executive with baggage right now."

Baggage. Who didn't have that, for God's sake? We were all a product of our past, of our mistakes and miscalculations. If I hadn't been raised by a father who barely scraped together a living, would I have made the choices I made? If I hadn't worked three jobs as a teenager, would I have learned to manage personal relationships as well as I managed investment portfolios? If I hadn't lived with the fear of never having enough money, would I have grown up to be such a relentless striver for whom security was everything? Probably not, as Evan had pointed out. But what is baggage if not a series of defining moments in life? Besides, we're stuck with it and there's no sense in making excuses for it. The trick is to overcome it and change, and I felt that I *had* changed. I was the new and improved Melanie—at the precise time that nobody wanted her.

Well, nobody except Dan, I thought, as I waited for him to call.

By Wednesday afternoon, I still hadn't heard from him, and I was starting to worry. Had Leah managed to talk him out of postponing their marriage? Had she seduced him with her shampoo-commercial hair and saccharine personality and steady, well-paying job and convinced him that he was only having wedding jitters, not actual doubts about their love?

I was about to cave in to my insecurities and call him at home, when there was a knock on my door. Actually, a pounding. I couldn't imagine why anyone wouldn't use the bell, given the option.

"Dan!" I said after I swung open the door and found my ex standing there, looking rumpled and sullen. I wrapped my arms around his waist. "I'm so glad you're here. I've been dying to know what's going on."

Instead of returning my hug, he removed my arms as if he couldn't bear me near him. Even Buster could feel the chill in the air and abandoned his usual animated Daddy greeting for the safety of his bed. People always say that dogs can anticipate a thunderstorm, and my boy was no exception.

"What's wrong?" I said as Dan took a slow walk inside my apartment. His posture was slumped, sagging, almost as if he'd been kicked in the stomach or had the wind knocked out of him. I wondered if he'd been in a fight but didn't see signs of bruising. "Did things go badly with Leah?"

He threw back his head and laughed, but he wasn't smiling. "You could say that."

"Oh. So she flipped out when you told her you were postponing the wedding?"

"You could say that too." He walked away from me and ambled around the room, picking up a pencil here, a newspaper there, and then setting them back down where they belonged. Odd behavior, to say the least.

"Dan," I said. "Could you focus for a second and fill me in?"

The question caused him to pivot and glower at me. "*I* should fill *you* in?"

"You're very upset," I said. "Why don't you sit down and I'll make you some coffee."

He pointed his finger at me, jabbed it in my direction. "You stay right where you are, *darlin'*."

His tone was sarcastic, mocking, toxic. I couldn't imagine what might have set him off. "Fine," I said. "Why don't we both sit down?" I sat on the sofa and patted the cushion next to me.

"Why don't you stop trying to control me?" he said. "If I wanna stand, I'll stand."

Uh-oh. "Then stand," I said. "Just tell me why you're upset, okay?"

"You already know."

"No, I don't. As a matter of fact, you've been AWOL since Monday. I would have thought you'd call and tell me what happened. How did Leah react to everything?"

"Leah." More mirthless laughter. "She claims she really loves me."

"I'm sure she does," I said. "But you and I have the kind of long-term—"

"She even pretended she wasn't in on it."

"In on what?"

He cupped his hands around his mouth and whispered, "The big plot."

The big plot. What the hell was he talking about? "I'm trying to follow you, Dan, but maybe you're just tired. Why don't you stretch out on the bed and take a quick nap? How does that sound?"

"Like something you would say. Jeez, do I hate you."

I felt as if he'd just kicked *me* in the stomach. "Hate me?"

"Hey, skip the amnesia, okay? You set me up. You wanted out of the alimony so much that you hired Leah to play my girlfriend. I know the whole sick story. You're so busted, baby."

Oh, God. Oh, God. Oh, God. I couldn't breathe, and my heart dropped down to my feet. He knew. Or at least he sort of knew. But how? Who told him? Oh, God. Oh, God, Oh, God.

If he finds out what you did, don't duck it. That's what Evan had made me promise. But I couldn't lose Dan. Not when we'd only just rediscovered each other.

"Say it, damn it," he shouted, startling Buster enough to trigger a bark. "You conned me. You and Leah both conned me. I've gotta be the dumbest sonofabitch that ever walked the face of the earth."

If he finds out what you did, don't duck it. I wanted to be heroic. Really, I did. But I couldn't coax the truth out of my mouth.

"I didn't con anyone," I said. "Whatever you think you know must be some silly misunderstanding."

He stormed over to me and stabbed another finger at me. "Leah already admitted it! When I told her what I heard, she admitted that the matchmaker put her together with me in Central Park the day she and I met. Naturally, she denied knowing anything about your part in it. You women take care of each other, I guess. Does she get a cut of the money you're gonna save on the alimony now that she lived with me for ninety days? Is that how it works?"

So he thought Leah and I were in cahoots? No wonder he was as furious at her as he was at me.

"How could you pay someone to trick me out of what was legally mine?" he said, shaking his head, as bewildered as he was enraged. "And how could you fuck around with my emotions like that? You said you loved me. What a joke! What a goddamn joke!"

If he finds out what you did, don't duck it. The words kept reverberating in my brain. *If your relationship can withstand the truth, maybe it's stronger than I thought.* All right, Evan. You made me promise and I did promise, so here goes.

"It's not what you think, Dan," I began.

"Oh, please," he snapped. "That's what every liar says."

"I meant that it's *worse* than you think. I didn't just con you. I conned Leah too."

"Like I believe that," he scoffed. "If you're gonna confess, then confess."

"Well, believe this: I love you. I'll tell you everything—the whole horrible truth—but whatever you may think of me at the end, don't you dare think I was conning you about my feelings."

"You don't have feelings, Melanie. I finally get that."

The tears started to come then, but I flicked them away. I had to stay strong, had to recount the story without breaking down, had to make him understand why I'd done what I'd done and how I'd do anything to atone for it.

And so I told him how angry I'd been about getting stuck with the spousal support and how his lavish spending had infuriated me all the more.

"You didn't make a secret of that, honey bunch," he taunted.

"I know," I conceded. "But Robin Baylor reminded me that we had a ninety-day cohabitation provision in our settlement. She explained that if you lived with a woman for that period of time, the spousal support would terminate automatically."

"I bet you were licking your lips when you heard that."

"I was. But you kept saying how you weren't interested in committing to another woman, so I forgot about it."

"What was it that changed your mind? A dip in the bond

market? A bad day on the Dow? Or was it just too weird to have to turn your money over to a *man*?"

"Maybe all of the above. I don't know," I said. "But you didn't help the situation by chartering private planes and buying expensive clothes and drinking the finest champagne—and rubbing it all in my face."

"I've already said I was sorry about that. We're talking about what *you* did."

"Right. I'm just trying to put it in context."

"Fuck the context and tell me about this matchmaker."

"Okay, okay. She was the one who introduced Weezie and Nards. They suggested that I talk to her about setting you up with someone."

"Nice. And I thought they liked me."

"They did. But you lost a lot of goodwill the way you were acting, Dan. I wasn't the only one who was pissed off at you."

He didn't say anything, so I kept going.

"I went to see this matchmaker and looked through the files of her clients and, to make a long story short, I picked Leah to meet you in Central Park that day." Why complicate things by telling him about Jelly and Rochelle?

"The idea being that she would be so pretty and sweet that I wouldn't be able to resist her?"

"Yes. But she wasn't in on the plan. All she knew was that there was this newly divorced ex–football player who was too proud to hire a matchmaker, so she wasn't supposed to say anything to you about it."

"Then she did lie to me."

"Only about why she was in the park that day. She had no idea that I was behind the plan or that I wanted out of the alimony or any of it."

He narrowed his eyes. "So what you're saying is that she's only a little less of a schemer than you are."

"She's not a schemer." I gulped back another threat of tears. "She's just a woman who loves you."

"Bullshit." He waved me off. "When did you two decide to fight over me? I mean, you set me up with her and then all of a sudden you wanted me to break it off with her. Was that a little twist in the plan? Does she get a bigger piece of the action for bowing out?"

"Of course not. When you started to change, when Leah's love started to change you, I couldn't help noticing. You went from being this guy who hid from life to a man who embraced it. You stopped showing up late when it was your turn to bring Buster over. You went on job interviews instead of hanging out in strip clubs. You got hired as a college coach, the very thing you swore you'd never do. And when I saw that, when I realized how you were facing up to your responsibilities, I loved you all over again and no one was more surprised about it than I was."

"Don't give me that crap. You loved me all over again because you knew you were home free on the alimony."

"Wrong. I didn't begrudge you one cent of the support after I saw how you'd pulled your life together. The money didn't matter to me anymore. I only wanted you back."

"So you figured you'd pay Leah to go away, and then you and I would walk off into the sunset, huh?"

"Leah has nothing to do with my wanting you for myself."

"Sure, she does. You didn't want me for yourself until it looked like I was falling for her." He exhaled loudly. "This is so nuts. And I'm so out of here."

He wheeled around and headed for the door.

"Wait!" I said as I trailed after him. "You have to believe how sorry I am."

"Come on. You're only sorry I found out."

I barred the door, splaying myself against it. "You're wrong." I paused. "By the way, how *did* you find out?"

While he stood there scowling at me, I ran down my list of accomplices and speculated about which of them could have ratted me out.

Was it Desiree? Had she intervened on behalf of Leah, her A-list client, when Dan tried to postpone their wedding? That didn't seem plausible, since it implicated Leah and made Dan even less inclined to marry her.

Was it Ricardo? Had he dropped some dumb comment about my interest in keeping a record of Dan's sleepovers with his "caretaker"? He didn't even know about Desiree. It was unlikely he was the culprit.

Was it Isa? Had she blurted out something about me and the digital camera? Had she brought the camera to work and shown Dan the photographs she'd taken? She was a loose cannon, but she too was in the dark about Desiree. She couldn't have been the one to spill the beans.

Was it Mrs. Thornberg? She did know about the Desiree connection, but she was my mother figure! She was totally on my side! There was no way she would have breathed a word about my evil deeds to my ex!

Was it Weezie? She was the architect of the plan, but she was also my best friend. Yes, she'd been miffed at me for a while there, but we'd mended our fences. We were fine now. Besides, her mind was on her own marriage, not mine. With two kids and a wandering husband, she had her hands full.

Was it Nards? He was the co-architect of the plan. Did he suddenly feel the need to unburden himself to Dan, in an attempt at male solidarity? Nah. He was far too busy with his practice and his affair to bond with a man he hadn't seen in two years.

Was it— Of course not. It couldn't be. Yes, Evan knew everything, but he would never have sabotaged my relationship with Dan. *When you love someone, you want them to be happy, even if it's not with you.* That's what he'd said. But had he taken it upon himself to speak to Dan before leaving for the Bahamas? Had he written him a note? No. Not possible.

"I found out yesterday," said Dan. "At the event where I was signing autographs."

"What? How?"

"They mix it up at those things. They put everybody at one long signing table. A baseball guy sits next to a tennis player and the tennis player sits next to a hockey guy and the hockey guy sits next to a figure skater. Guess who I sat next to?"

"Dan, I have no idea," I said, knowing my whole world was seconds away from shattering. "Just tell me."

"A golfer by the name of Lynda Fox."

My mouth fell open. "Lynda Fox?"

"The woman didn't shut up for a second. I had totally tuned her out while the signing was going on. But then, after the event, we were shaking hands and out popped the juicy tidbit about you and the matchmaker. It sure ruined my day."

Lynda Fox? I never dreamed that the one, brief interaction I'd had with her at Desiree's—one stupid, stupid conversation where I'd let it slip who my ex was—would come back to haunt me. But Dan was right: she didn't shut up. It must not have occurred to her that by spilling my story, she was spilling her own.

"What did Lynda say?" I asked as calmly as I could.

"She told me all about Destiny."

"Desiree."

"Whatever. She said you were the one who came up with the brilliant idea of using a matchmaker to screw ex-spouses on their alimony. Once I heard that, I went straight to Leah, who filled in the blanks."

I couldn't get over it. I'd been undone by a player on the LPGA tour? Don't those women seem fairly harmless?

"Leah didn't fill in all the blanks," I said, continuing to block Dan's exit. He weighed many, many more pounds than I did and could easily have lifted me up and hauled me away from the door, but he was a gentleman, even then. "She didn't tell you how much I regret what I did. Oh, Dan. If I had it all to do over again, I'd never have interfered with your life or tried to worm my way out of my financial obligation to you. The only thing I'm not sorry about are these past few days we had together. They were amazing."

"You know what I think about these past few days?"

"No."

"That they were about the *past*."

"Dan."

"It's true. Every time I pictured telling Leah the wedding was off, I couldn't do it. It finally hit me that she was the one I wanted to spend the rest of my life with and that you were an old habit I was having trouble breaking."

"You're just saying that because you're hurt and angry and—"

"But now I've told her to move out of the apartment and I'm telling you to move away from the door. I'm done with both of you. Let me out of here."

I didn't budge.

"Get away from that door," he said again.

"You didn't say good-bye to Buster," I reminded him. Feeble, I know, but I was desperate.

He turned toward our dog and said, "See you Monday, Busty," then stared me down again. "Call before you drop him off, so I can make sure Isa will be there to let you in."

"Where will you be?"

"Out. As for 32G, as soon as I start the day-to-day coaching and draw a regular salary, I'll find my own place and vacate. See that? You won the game, darlin'. You got your money. You got your apartment. You scored big time. Congratulations."

I stepped aside and let him leave. There was nothing more I could say or do, no point in prolonging his misery or mine. He was right. I'd won the game. Woo-hoo for me.

Chapter 29

I took Buster up to Connecticut for the weekend, so I could pour my heart out to Weezie and he could play with the kids. It was a balmy, blue-sky day when we arrived, with spring flowers in bloom and birds chirping and the lawn green and fragrant, and I was grateful to be out of Manhattan, away from the scene of the crime. Of all my crimes.

To my surprise, Nards was there when I pulled into the driveway. He hadn't moved back into the house permanently, but he and Weezie were spending the occasional night together, working things out, taking it one day at a time. Or, in this case, one weekend at a time.

"I hope you don't mind that he's staying over too," she whispered as we were unloading my car.

"Mind?" I said. "You've got a huge smile on your face. I'm thrilled."

"He and I realized we both made mistakes," she said. "This marriage business isn't easy."

"But the divorce business is worse. So whatever you guys are doing to stay together, keep it up."

We went inside, and there was Nards, looking contrite but pleased to be back home, even temporarily. He bounded over to me and hugged me like my long-lost brother.

"Before another minute goes by, I need to tell you how ashamed I am for what I did," he said sheepishly. "If I can restore even half of Weezie's trust in me, I'll be happy. Your trust too, Mel. You saw me in the restaurant that night. You must—"

"I'm hardly in a position to judge others," I said, cutting him off, wanting to lessen his load. "Not after the fiasco with Dan."

"That's another thing," he said. "I feel guilty about encouraging you to hire Desiree. If there's any way I can make it up to you or help you repair your relationship with Dan, please tell me."

"Thanks, but he and I are beyond repair."

"Don't say that. He has his weaknesses, but he never struck me as a guy who holds a grudge."

"Yeah, well he's holding one now. Two, actually."

Weezie joined us, and we all sat in their cozy den. "Two what?" she asked with her usual cut-to-the-chase curiosity.

"Grudges," I said. "Dan's holding one against me and one against Leah."

"I can't believe he thinks she was in on your plan," she said. "She was just another single woman in the city, looking for love."

"And she found it," I said. "She adored him. She was good for him. She was everything to him that I wasn't."

"Would you stop putting yourself down?" she said. "Let's concentrate on how you're going to get him back."

"I'm not," I said. "It's Leah who has to get him back, and I'm going to help her do it."

"*What?*" said Weezie and Nards at the same time.

As soon as the pronouncement was out of my mouth, I knew I meant it. Dan told me he'd chosen Leah; that she was the one he wanted to spend the rest of his life with. I was his past, and she was his future. *When you love someone, you want them to be happy, even if it's not with you.* Yes, there it was again. Evan's voice. Mrs. Thornberg's too. But for the first time their words weren't empty rhetoric. They felt right to me. *What makes an ordinary person heroic is when they give up the thing they want most.* Maybe I was getting in touch with my inner heroine after all.

"It's true. I've been mulling this over for the past few days and now I'm sure about it."

"Sure about what?" Weezie said, still confused.

"I'm going to find Leah, talk to her, and help her win him back," I reiterated. "It's the only way I can really make amends to him."

"Very generous of you," said Nards, regarding me with new respect. He had always been the pontificator. I never expected him to look up to me as his shining moral example.

"He was generous to me once," I said. "It's time I returned the favor."

We discussed how I might accomplish bringing together two people who no longer trusted each other. We all agreed that hiring Desiree to help with the matchmaking wasn't an option.

I was done with her, besides which I wasn't in a position to hire anybody now that I was jobless.

"We're strategizers," said Weezie. "We'll come up with something by the end of the weekend."

But we never did.

On Monday morning, I brought Buster over to Dan's, afraid he'd be home, afraid he wouldn't be. True to his word, he'd made himself scarce. It was Isa who answered the door and explained that he was out running errands, then driving to a meeting at L.I.U.

"As for her, she cleared out of here and took all her things," she added, referring to Leah. "No more marriage."

"Is Dan very depressed?" I asked, sickened by this latest irony. I'd told Ricardo that Mr. Swain was so depressed that he needed Leah to care for him. Now Mr. Swain really was depressed and needed Leah to care for him. What had I done? And how could I have done it?

"He is, *chérie*. He keeps her picture on the dresser in the bedroom."

"He always did hang on to his glory days, those times when he was happiest," I said. "Keeping a picture of her proves he still loves her."

"If he still loves her, then why is she gone?"

I sighed. "He's convinced that she wasn't honest with him about why she was living here. He thinks she was part of my plan. He thinks she tricked him too."

"But she didn't know anything about your plan. I took those pictures of her personal items behind her back. I could show them to him, so he could see for himself that she was innocent in all this."

I considered the idea, because it would probably help Leah's cause, but I ultimately rejected it. Dan was upset enough that I'd hired Desiree to trick him. He'd go ballistic if he found out about Isa's involvement and would surely fire her. I couldn't let that happen. She had Reggie to feed. No small thing. Literally.

I went into the bedroom and looked at Leah's photograph. It was a color shot of her with Buster, which surprised me. (I'd expected a picture of her alone, the breeze blowing through her mink coat hair.) She was down on the floor with him, her face cheek to cheek with his, and she was beaming. I had no emotional attachment to her, obviously, but even I couldn't help but be moved by her obvious affection for my dog.

"Isn't that a nice picture?" Isa said, coming into the room behind me. "She was crazy about Buster, and Dan loved that about her."

No, I didn't know Leah, but if she was crazy about Buster, she couldn't be all bad.

As was my custom now, I stopped over at Mrs. Thornberg's before heading back downtown. She had just spent over an hour wrestling with her TV remote—it needed new batteries and she couldn't pry the battery door open, not with a fingernail or a bobby pin or even a key—so I was glad I came. Thanks to my Swiss army knife, I was able to solve the problem in time for her to watch Larry King later that night.

"What's the latest?" she said as we sat in her kitchen munching on dill pickles. I felt so at home that I didn't even notice their smell anymore. Same with the mothballs. And I was relieved that her dentures were holding up well enough for her to keep biting into them. (The pickles, not the mothballs.)

"I'm taking your advice and throwing myself into getting Dan and Leah back together," I announced.

"I gave you that advice?"

"You told me that if I loved Dan, I should want to see him happy, even if it wasn't with me."

"Glad you listened."

"I listen to everything you say."

She clucked with pleasure. "Most young people today think we *seniors*—such a stupid word—don't know what we're talking about. Like we all have Alzheimer's or something. Some of us still have our marbles, you know?"

"I do know. And I'm taking your advice, as I said. The question is: How do I get Dan to let Leah back into his life? And how do I get Leah to forgive Dan for not trusting her? How do I even get them to tolerate being in each other's company for five minutes, not to mention decide to go through with their wedding after all?"

"That's a tough one," she acknowledged, "but not insurmountable."

"Really?"

"Sure. Mr. Thornberg and I had a tiff before we got married and we ended up together," she said.

"What was the tiff about, if you don't mind my asking?"

"Remember when I told you he was a tightwad?"

I couldn't help laughing. "Yes."

"I wasn't kidding. He gave me an engagement ring with a diamond the size of a pea. No, half a pea. His parents were big shots in the brassiere business. I thought, They couldn't afford better?"

"What did you do?"

"I gave the ring back to him. I thought money was everything then, because I was such an ignorant, willful girl. I accused him of being a cheapskate, and he accused me of being a gold digger. We were both sorry, naturally, but were too pigheaded to admit it. Such fools."

"So you broke up, and the engagement was off?"

"Yes. And it took Mr. Thornberg's brother, Harry, to bring us back together. I didn't think it was possible, because nobody was speaking to anybody at that point."

"How did Harry get you and Mr. Thornberg to kiss and make up?"

She scratched her chin, as if to jog her memory. I noticed she had a single hair there. A whisker. "Harry knew we shared a love of music."

"Classical?"

"No, dance music. The jitterbug. There was a band that was popular in that era—the Jack Gordon Band, I think they were called—and we used to dance to their records. So Harry bought each of us their latest hit. He told me that mine was a gift from his brother, who was 'too remorseful' to give it to me himself, and he told his brother that his was a gift from me, because I was 'too remorseful' to give it to him myself. On top of that, he finagled it so we both showed up at this dance hall where the band was playing. Well, given that we each thought the other was apologizing, we fell right into the trap and got back together. The rest, as they say, is history."

"I'm trying to figure out what the lesson is here."

"The lesson is this: if you want them back together, you've got to appeal to their mutual interest in something."

I shrugged. "Dan likes football, but I don't even know Leah, let alone what she's interested in."

"You're not a dummy. You'll think of it."

"I feel like a dummy these days. I don't have a job and nobody will hire me and the Heartbreak Hotel is starting to look like a palace compared to living out of my car."

"I thought you were moving in next door once he starts coaching. Isn't that what you said?"

"He offered. I haven't decided."

She put down her pickle and went for her purse. After rummaging around for her wallet, she pulled it out and handed me a roll of bills.

"Take it," she said. "It's all the cash I've got on me."

"Oh, no," I protested. "I couldn't."

"Fine," she said, continuing to shove the money at me. "Call it a loan if it'll make you feel like Miss Businesswoman."

I didn't take it. I couldn't believe she'd even offered it. I was the one who was always handing out cash, or so it seemed. "I'm very touched," I said. "More than you'll ever know. But I'll be okay. Once I get my self-respect back and can look at myself in the mirror without flinching, the career stuff will fall into place."

Mrs. Thornberg patted my head. "You're my good girl. You'll find a way to make things right between the lovebirds. But in the meantime, my bad arm is killing me. I think I strained it trying to get the batteries into that remote. Could you help me clean my refrigerator?"

I helped her clean her refrigerator. I helped her reorganize her pantry. I helped her wash her kitchen floor. And as I did, she reminisced about the story she'd just told me, about Harry bridging the gap between her and Mr. Thornberg and getting them to the altar.

"Remember," she said. "He appealed to our common interest in something and then put us at the same place at the same time. That's what did it."

As I alphabetized her spices and scrubbed her fridge and mopped her floor, I wondered how I could replicate her brother-in-law's feat. It wasn't until I got home and started thinking about Evan—about how I missed him and wished he were there to guide me—that an idea broke through.

Chapter 30

I didn't know where Leah lived, so I looked her address up in the phone book. Not listed. Then I called information to get her phone number. Unpublished. Apparently, she was yet another single woman who didn't want to be hassled by perverts. I couldn't blame her there, but I'd hoped to speak to her in the privacy of her apartment.

Moving on to Plan B, I was heartened that her veterinary practice *was* listed in the phone book. I guess she wasn't worried about perverts as long as they had pets.

On a Tuesday afternoon, I walked through the door of Purcell Veterinary Medicine, which was located in the East Eighties. I did not go there empty-handed.

"May I help you?" asked a young, sort of effeminate male receptionist, who sat behind a glass partition that he pulled open after I'd tapped on it a couple of times.

"I'm here to see Dr. Purcell," I said.

The receptionist, whose name tag identified him as Adam, gave me a puzzled look, probably because I was not accompanied by an animal. The office was packed with them, most of them dogs and cats, along with a ferret and the usual parakeet or two. "Do you have an appointment?"

"No," I said.

"She's completely booked," he said.

"No need to try to squeeze me in," I said. "I'm fine with waiting until Dr. Purcell is finished at the end of the day. There's a personal matter I'd like to discuss with her."

"Oh?" Adam seemed intrigued. "Can I get your name?"

"Sissy."

He recoiled as if I'd slapped him. "That could be construed as a hate crime in this state."

"You don't understand," I said, not wanting my goodwill mission to get off to a bad start. "I'm not gay bashing you. I'm telling you my name. It's Sissy. Sissy Swain." Hey, it wasn't my fault that everybody in Dan's family called his sister Susanna that. Maybe it was an Oklahoma thing. And yes, I was hoping that pretending to be related to Dan would get me an audience with Leah. I was sure she wasn't interested in seeing *me.*

"I'll let the doctor know you're here," said Adam, who got up in a huff and closed the glass window with more attitude than was necessary.

I took a seat between a woman with her snarly Doberman pinscher and a man with his even snarlier German shepherd.

I wasn't a masochist, but we were talking about a full house, and seating was at a premium.

At some point, Adam motioned me over and said, "Dr. Purcell has agreed to meet with you, but only because she knows you've traveled a long way."

"I appreciate that," I told him, putting a little southern twang on the sentence. It was probable that she'd throw me out once she realized I wasn't Dan's sister, but I was willing to chance it. The first step was to wedge my foot in the door.

I endured the growling, teeth-baring, generally unsociable temperaments of the dogs to my left and right for well over an hour. After they'd been treated by Leah and sent home with their owners, after all the patients had been treated by Leah and sent home with their owners, Adam escorted me from the waiting room into her office, closed the door behind him, and left me alone with her.

When I entered, she was standing beside a bookcase, flipping through a heavy volume, her back to me. Even in her white lab coat, her lustrous hair piled haphazardly on top of her head, she was a babe. I cleared my throat to make my presence known.

She turned to face me and began to sputter. If smoke really came out of people's ears, it would have come out of hers. "You? Adam told me it was Dan's . . . You? How could you use his—"

"Leah," I said. "Please calm down." Like I would have calmed down if I were in her shoes. I would have slugged me.

"You pretended to be Dan's sister!" She slammed the reference book onto her desk. We both jumped when it went *bang!*

"I didn't think you'd let me in otherwise," I said, speaking in a soft voice so as not to excite her further. "I had to find a way to talk to you."

"Talk to me? You tried to steal Dan away from me! Why should I let *you* in here?"

"Because you're a nice person," I said. "Dan always bragged about how nice you are. You're the one he loves, Leah. I should never have tried to come between you."

"Then why did you?" she demanded. "And why did you play that dirty trick on him? It's disgraceful how you hired Desiree so you could cheat him out of the money."

"You're right," I said. "What I did is disgraceful and I'll regret it for the rest of my life. But my poor judgment doesn't have to ruin your chances with him."

"You say that, now that he's rejected both of us." She sank down in her desk chair, utterly depleted, as if the positive spirit he had found so inspiring had been drained out of her.

"I want to undo the damage I caused," I said, sitting opposite her. "I want to help you and Dan get back together."

"Oh, spare me."

"I mean it, Leah. I want him to be happy, and you make him happy."

She turned her head away, biting her lip. "Even if I believed you, it'll never happen. He thinks I was partners with you. He thinks I'm just as dishonest as you are."

"No, he doesn't," I lied. I had promised myself I was finished with the lying and the scheming and the conniving, but the sort of lying I was currently doing was benevolent lying. Its purpose was to help two decent, well-intentioned individuals find true love. That couldn't be bad, right? "I spoke to him and told him everything and he understands now. He doesn't think we were partners anymore. He knows I duped you the same way I duped him."

She looked at me, her eyes filling with hope. "He doesn't blame me?"

"No. He still wants to marry you, Leah. He's so sorry he ever doubted you."

She arched one of her perfectly plucked eyebrows at me. "Then why hasn't he called?"

"Because he's too ashamed. He thinks you'd never hear him out."

"He *should* be ashamed," she said with a pout. "He hurt me so much the way he tossed me onto the street. And now he can't even pick up the phone and tell me he's sorry?"

"Sad, isn't it? I was married to the guy for thirteen years. He has wonderful qualities, but he's a little macho, you know? He's dying to apologize to you, to make things right with you, to marry you in Oklahoma if you'll still have him. He's just too proud to walk in here with his tail between his legs and beg."

"So he sent you?" she said skeptically.

"Yes, because I'm the one who's responsible for this whole mess," I lied some more. "After I told him he was wrong to punish *you* for *my* mistake, he asked me to be his emissary. He said I owed him a favor and I do." I held up the package I'd brought with me. "He insisted that I give you this."

"What is it?" she said, eyeing it as if it were about to detonate.

"Something that celebrates a mutual interest of yours—a love you both share."

I reached across her desk and handed her the package. She unwrapped it carefully and looked perplexed when she saw what it was.

"An oil painting?" she said.

"Of Buster," I said. "Dan had it commissioned for you as a wedding present. He knows how important Buster is to you, to both of you, so he thought it would be the ideal gift."

She studied the painting for a minute or two. "It's really, really beautiful," she said finally, smiling for the first time since I'd arrived. I was encouraged. I was really, really encouraged.

"Do you see the way the dog has ventured into the sea? How he's swimming along without a care in the world?" I pointed out. "Buster is afraid of the water. He sticks his toe in it and runs for dry land. So the symbolism here is that the dog in the painting is willing to take a risk, which is what Dan hoped you would do by flying off to Minco to marry him."

As she glanced up at me, a single tear rolled down her cheek. "I can't believe he had an artist paint this for me. Nobody's ever painted anything just for me. It really resonates."

"That's wonderful," I said, "but has it convinced you to forgive him? Will you let go of your pain and loss and suffering and accept his gift as an invitation to venture into the sea of life with him?" I know, I know. I even made myself nauseated. But hyperbole or not, my spiel was working. I could tell. Harry Thornberg had nothing on me.

"How can I not forgive him after this?" she said, gazing at the gift Evan had intended for me. "A painting of Buster. It just proves how well he knows me."

"Exactly."

"Well, now that he's shown remorse for how he treated me, maybe we do have a future after all."

"Oh, Leah. I'm so thrilled to hear that." I clapped for joy until I saw her grab the phone and start dialing. "What are you doing?"

"Calling Dan," she said. "He made the first move. Now it's my turn."

"No!" I snatched the phone out of her hand and placed it back in its cradle. "I mean, it's not a good idea."

"Why not?"

"As I said, Dan is kind of old school when it comes to things like *feelings*." I rolled my eyes to underscore that my ex had caveman tendencies. "You can't just go gushing about the painting to him. He'll die of embarrassment. He's not ready to talk to you. He couldn't even come here himself, remember?"

"But if he wants us to get back together—"

"He does want that, but his ego is bruised. He needs to feel comfortable in his own skin before he talks to you." God, I hated that expression. "Did you know that his favorite memory of you is the day you met, in the North Meadow in Central Park? He was playing football, and you walked by and stole his heart."

"Wow. It's my favorite memory too," she said after a lovesick sigh.

"Excellent, because that's where he wants you to meet him next Wednesday afternoon at two o'clock. At the football field in the North Meadow at Ninety-seventh Street."

"Next Wednesday?" she said. "Why not tomorrow?"

Because it's not going to be easy to get him there at all, I thought, and I'd better give myself at least a week to pull it off. "He specifically mentioned that day. It must have sentimental value for the two of you."

"Not that I'm aware of."

"Look, he asked me to persuade you to be there, so I'm doing my best," I said more firmly than I meant to. I counted to ten and began again. "Will you meet him at the place where destiny intervened, where you spoke your first words to each other, where your love blossomed? Will you take the leap of faith and reclaim your man?" Yikes. I wondered suddenly if I might have a career as a writer of country and western songs.

She pondered Dan's proposition. My proposition. "How do I know he'll show up?" she asked. "He might get cold feet."

"It was his idea," I reminded her.

"But still," she said. "If his ego is so bruised . . ."

"He'll show up," I said. "If he doesn't, then he isn't the guy we both think he is."

More pondering, accompanied by a narrowing of her eyes. "This could be another one of your schemes, Melanie. Another way to trick me."

"Fine. Don't trust me," I said. "Trust love." Forget the country and western songs, I thought. Maybe I should write Hallmark cards.

" 'Trust love,' " she said, nodding. "I really, really like that. It reminds me of romance novels."

Okay, so I'd write those. As soon as I figured out how to get Dan to trust love too.

Chapter 31

Yes, of course I felt awful about handing over Evan's painting to Leah. He'd *given* it to me instead of trying to sell it and make money from it, and it was a piece of art, not some cheesy knickknack you pawn off on somebody you hardly know.

What's more, it had personal significance for me, not only because Buster was in it but because Evan had cared enough about me to teach me a life lesson with it. I wouldn't have dreamed of parting with it—or the painting where Buster doesn't venture into the water—if Mrs. Thornberg hadn't told me the story of her brother-in-law and the dance records that brought her and Mr. Thornberg back together. Leah honestly believed that the painting was a conciliatory gesture from Dan, and now I would convince him that the other painting was a conciliatory gesture from her, and their relationship would be repaired just as the Thornbergs' had been. I hoped that Evan would be proud of me, as opposed to disappointed in me.

The only hitch was that Dan had frozen me out to the extent that delivering the second painting to him was a major challenge. In the days following my visit with Leah, I'd tried calling him but never reached a live human being, only his voice mail. I'd tried going over to the apartment, but he'd instructed Ricardo not to buzz me up unless he was out and Isa was there by herself. I'd tried ambushing him at his old haunts—the places to which Desiree had dispatched Jelly and Rochelle—but he no longer frequented them. He wasn't an idle, aimless, unemployed bumbo anymore. He was a college coach now, and he was busy with a full slate of preseason activities. Or so Isa told me.

Yet again it was Mrs. Thornberg who offered the solution to my problem after I'd presented it to her. At her insistence, I brought the painting over to her apartment and stayed overnight in her guest room. The next morning we camped out in her foyer, our ears practically Velcroed to the wall, and lay in wait for Dan to emerge from 32G. When he did, she opened her door, wished him good morning, and asked if he could help her open the jar of honey she was hoping to dribble over her oatmeal.

"I've got a bad arm," she told him. "It's never been right since I slipped on a wet spot in the lobby. I'm still looking into who was at fault."

There was a brief back-and-forth—Dan said he had a meeting to attend; Mrs. Thornberg said her arm hurt so badly she was contemplating taking dope. Ultimately, he said he'd be glad to be of service, and before I knew it they were walking in the door. I swallowed hard and prepared myself for his reaction when he saw me.

"Oh, jeez," he said when he did, his eyes flashing with anger. "If you think you're cornering me, you've got another thing coming." He was wearing a business suit, so he must have been on the level about the meeting. But if I had my way he wasn't going anywhere, no matter how many times he spun around and threatened to storm out. When he finally stopped huffing and puffing and tugging on his earlobe, I stood face-to-face with him.

"Dan, you have to listen," I said. My impulse was to reach for him, to touch him, but I knew that any demonstration of affection would not be welcome.

"And you have to stop stalking me," he snapped.

"Now, now, Mr. Swain," interjected Mrs. Thornberg, who placed herself between us like a referee. "Melanie is my guest. I'd appreciate it if you'd treat her with respect."

"Then you'll have to find someone else to help you open your jar," he said. "You can't treat people with respect if you don't respect them."

"I just need a few minutes with you," I told him. "It's not about us. It's about you and Leah. She asked me to give you something. Something important."

He tensed, working his jaw muscles at the mention of her name. "So you two are still bosom buddies?"

"Oh, give that a rest." Suddenly, I was emboldened by his stubbornness. I had planned to be gentle with him, as I'd been with Leah, but the tough love approach seemed more appropriate. He was macho? I'd be macho right back at him. "We were never buddies. I met her twice. Maybe three times. With *you* there. She didn't know anything about the alimony plot. You should believe that, if you know what's good for you."

"Why?" he demanded.

"Because she loves you and you love her. You're just too much of a Neanderthal to admit it."

"Would either of you like some oatmeal?" asked Mrs. Thornberg. "It's supposed to lower the blood pressure."

"No oatmeal, thanks," I said with a wink. "Just a little private time with my ex-husband."

"Of course," she said and dashed into the kitchen, out of sight, the model of circumspection.

"Now," I said when Dan and I were alone. "Would you let me give you Leah's gift?"

He had his arms crossed over his chest, and he was tapping his toe, impatient and unyielding. "If you're not buddies, why would she entrust you with this *gift*?"

"Because she's so upset about what happened that she was afraid to come to you herself," I said. "She thinks you hate her. God knows, you've shut us both out of your life. I guess she just figured I'd be the more persistent one."

"That you are, Melanie." It was not meant as a compliment.

"She said I owed her a favor after what I'd done," I continued. "So when she asked me to be her emissary, I agreed."

Aware that he might bolt at any second, I quickly ran over to the wrapped painting and brought it over to him. "Before I give this to you, I just want to say again how sorry I am for trying to steal the money that was rightfully yours."

"Not interested. Tell it to someone who cares."

"But mostly," I went on, ignoring his dismissal, "I want to say how sorry I am for messing things up between you and Leah.

She's so good for you, Dan. Much too good to let me or anyone else come between you. She fell in love with you when you were down, stood by you as you made your way back up, and helped you change from the boy I married into the man you've become—and in just a few short months. *She* did that. *She* was your champion. *She* loved you unconditionally. Never forget that."

"What I can't forget is that she was fixed up with me by *your* matchmaker."

"She was a client of Desiree's. So what?"

"She didn't tell me. She let me think we met by chance."

"Oh, come on! She didn't commit a murder! Get over this, would you please?"

He smiled just a tiny half-smile. "Did Leah ask you to give me a tongue lashing along with whatever you've got in that package?"

"No. She's much nicer than I am."

"No argument there."

"Then open her gift."

I handed him the package.

He shook it. "You sure it won't blow me to pieces?"

"Just open it already. It's something that celebrates a mutual interest of yours—a love you both share."

He unwrapped it carefully and was instantly delighted by its contents, smiling in earnest now. "Jeez. It's a beautiful painting of Buster."

"Leah had it commissioned for you as a wedding present," I said. "She knows how much you love our dog. She thought it would have special meaning for you."

"She did that?" he said, his expression one of genuine awe.

"She did," I confirmed.

"It's amazingly realistic," he said, studying the painting.

"The artist captured our Busty to a tee. See how the dog will only stick his paw in the water instead of jumping right in? You must have told her Buster does that," I said with the beatific smile of a nun. A macho nun. "The symbolism she intended is that the dog in the painting wouldn't take a risk but that *she* would—by marrying you after only three months of living with you."

He glanced up at me. "You're telling me she had this made for me? Really?"

"Yes, for the second time."

"Then I've got to tip my hat to her. It was a great idea for a wedding present," he acknowledged.

"Yes, but now it's more than that. It's her way of saying she wants *you* to take a risk and go forward with your relationship."

He ran his fingers over the dog in the painting and heaved a heavy sigh.

Smelling victory, I stepped up the attack. "So will you stop hanging on to your pride and anger and resentment? Will you accept this painting as proof that she loves you in spite of how cruelly you cast her aside? Will you melt your hardened heart and venture into the sea of life with her?" Yeah, yeah. It was even more over the top than the speech I gave Leah, but I was starting to enjoy myself.

"So she thinks we can make it work?"

"Absolutely."

"Even after all that harsh stuff I said to her?"

"That's what 'unconditional' means, Dan."

There were a few beats, then: "I don't know if I can handle a relationship yet. You knocked the crap out of me emotionally, Mel, and I'm just getting back on my feet. I'd rather concentrate on the new job for now."

"Concentrate on the new job? Leah was the one who urged you to go out and get that job!"

"She did, but I—"

"Just talk to her."

"All right, all right. I'll call her sometime."

"Too noncommittal. Go see her."

He squirmed as he stood there in Mrs. Thornberg's living room. "I'm not ready to see her."

God, he was uncooperative. "Listen, she made another request when she asked me to bring you the painting. She wants you to meet her at the football field in Central Park on Wednesday afternoon at two—the place where you and she met. It's her way of trying to rekindle what you had, I guess. If you get there and decide you don't love her as much as I think you do, so be it. But go. See her. Just this one time."

"I can't. I've got a meeting on Wednesday at two."

"Then reschedule it. You used to tell me how I made my work a higher priority than I made us. How about practicing what you preach?"

He hesitated. "I'd hate to lead her on. If I show up, she might mistake—"

"If you show up, she'll be thrilled, trust me."

"Trust you?" He laughed. "Why should I? All you've done is manipulate me."

And I wasn't about to stop manipulating him until I made sure he was happy, even if it wasn't with me. "Fine," I said. "Don't trust me. Trust love."

I know, I know. Dan's a guy, and guys don't normally fall for treacle like that, especially caveman types, but I had the routine down. Macho was fine at first. But treacle was better for the big finish.

"'Trust love?'" he said derisively. "Sounds like you've been watching chick flicks."

"It does," I agreed, thinking perhaps I would write those instead of country and western songs, Hallmark cards, or romance novels. "But that doesn't mean you shouldn't do it."

"You never let up, do you, darlin'?"

"That's what they tell me."

"Did they also tell you I could bring legal action against you if I wanted to?"

"Do you want to?"

"No, but only because I'd rather get past this nightmare."

"Good choice. So will you trust your love for Leah and hers for you and meet her in the park?" I said, staring intently at the man who'd aroused every imaginable feeling in me over the years, the man who would always own a piece of my heart, the man who was better off with someone else. "Will you forgive her, Dan?"

"Am I supposed to forgive you too?"

"I would like that, yes."

"I'll give them both some thought," he said.

And just like that, he walked out of the apartment, Evan's painting under his arm and an inscrutable look on his face.

After the door closed, Mrs. Thornberg came scurrying out of the kitchen, fluttering her hands in excitement.

"How'd it go?" she said.

"I'm not sure," I said.

"Did he say he'll meet her on Wednesday?"

"He didn't say he wouldn't."

"Men." She shrugged. "You career girls made them scared to cross the street. In my day, they knew who they were."

I put my arm around her bony shoulder. "In your day, we didn't know who *we* were. That wasn't so great either."

"Maybe the next generation will even things out."

We both knew that was unlikely, and so we changed the subject.

Chapter 32

On Wednesday afternoon at one-forty-five, Weezie and I were huddled together behind a clump of trees and shrubs in Central Park. The dirt football field where Leah and Dan were supposed to rendezvous was a hundred yards from our lookout point—close enough for us to follow the action through the binoculars I'd brought and far enough away for us not to get caught.

There was a game in progress, just a bunch of kids as opposed to the guys Dan used to play with, but it was Leah we were watching. She'd arrived early, right after we had, and she was looking eager, anxious, and very sexy in her miniskirt and boob-hugging top.

"You weren't kidding. She *is* a babe," Weezie remarked, having never seen her before.

"And sweet," I said. "Not the sharpest knife in the drawer, but Dan would be nuts to let her go."

"He *had* the sharpest knife in the drawer for thirteen years," she said, giving me an affectionate pat on the arm.

"Thanks, but I could have used more of the 'sweet.' "

"Maybe, but look what you're doing for him today. For both of them. In case I haven't told you, you've turned into a very generous person, my friend. Watching your guy hook up with someone else isn't easy. I know from experience."

"It's easier than I expected," I said. "Dan wasn't the only one who needed to grow up."

She was about to say something in response when I spotted a blond man walking toward Leah and shushed her.

"There he is!" I said, my hopes soaring.

"There he isn't," she said, my hopes plunging. She was the one with the binoculars at that moment and had a better view.

"Then where is he?" I said.

"Relax," she said, trying to be the voice of reason. "It's not even two yet. You said he loves her. He'll come."

"I also said he wouldn't commit to coming," I reminded her. "He didn't want to lead her on."

"I'm betting he'll come," said Weezie.

"It better be soon. I'm getting cold without a sweater or jacket." The mild spring weather had teased me into wearing a sleeveless shirt with my jeans. But now a breeze had kicked up, and the temperature had dropped and my arms had goose bumps.

"You'll warm up as soon as you see the fruits of your labor," she said.

And so we waited for Dan to join Leah. Two o'clock came and went. Five-after-two. Two-ten. Two-fifteen.

"Okay, where the hell is he?" I groaned. "Leah's standing there looking like her heart is breaking. I'm gonna kill him if he doesn't show up."

"How long should we give him?" said Weezie, who seemed less sure of the outcome now.

"As long as she gives him, I guess."

Two-twenty came and went. Two-twenty-five. Two-thirty. Two-thirty-five.

"I think she's crying," I said, peering at Leah through the binoculars.

"Who can blame her?" said Weezie. "She's been here for forty-five minutes."

"I can't believe he stood us up," I said.

"I really thought he'd show," she said, nodding.

"Could the whole deal with Desiree have traumatized him that much? Enough to swear off women forever? Even the one he wanted to marry?"

"Who knows." She sighed. "I've said it before and I'll say it again: men are the weaker, more fragile sex. They die before we do. They smoke and drink more. They crack themselves up in cars. They flunk out of—"

"Weezie, give me the glasses." I grabbed the binoculars and squinted at the field. As I narrowed my eyes, I could see that Leah had left her post beside the field and was taking a slow, resigned stroll around the area. She looked like a lost soul in search of her lost soul mate. "If he doesn't show in the next five minutes, she'll leave, and there won't be anything I can do about it."

I handed the binoculars back to her, frustrated that my plan didn't seem to be working.

"Oh, God," she said suddenly as she peered through the lenses.

"What?"

"Leah just looked over here. Get down!"

Weezie tugged on my shirt and pulled me down into the bushes with her. We hid there like soldiers in an enemy camp, squatting in the brush, willing ourselves not to move a muscle.

"Oh, no. She's seen us," I said after peeking. "She's heading in our direction and she's not happy."

"What do we tell her?" said Weezie. "That we're soaking up the afternoon sun?"

I ran through other possible excuses for being in the park at precisely the same time that Leah and Dan were scheduled to reunite: bird-watching; practicing tai chi; snipping specimens for our horticultural group. But, hey, we'd been caught.

"And I was feeling so good about this," I said, closing my eyes so I wouldn't have to watch Leah storm over to us and rant. I know I was being a coward, but I couldn't bear her anger and disappointment, both of which would be targeted at me and with good reason.

"Wait," said Weezie. "She just turned around and went back down to the field. And now she's running."

I opened my eyes. "Running?"

"Yeah, look." She passed me the binoculars. Sure enough, Leah had switched course and was now rushing toward the dirt field where a blond man—a handsome blond man who could only have been Dan—was rushing toward her.

"He came!" I said, dying to shout but muzzling myself. "If this were in slow motion, it would definitely be a shampoo commercial. Her hair. His hair. It's a beautiful thing."

Weezie and I watched like a couple of hard-core voyeurs as the two of them embraced. He kissed her. She kissed him. There were tears. There were hugs. There was love. There was so much love down on that field that we felt it all those yards away. But you know what? I barely flinched during their emotional reunion, only registered a minor tremor as it began to sink in that it was Leah Dan was kissing and not me. I was finally letting him go. I was not only letting him go, but I was deriving actual pleasure from seeing him so joyful. I even felt less antagonistic toward Desiree. She wasn't the most principled person I'd ever met, but she brought people together as a result of her matchmaking, and until then I didn't understand the satisfaction in that.

"Why do you think he took so long to show?" Weezie asked.

"Who knows?" I said. "Maybe he couldn't resolve his feelings. Maybe he was so ambivalent that it paralyzed him for a while."

"Men really are the weaker sex."

"And I'm too weak to discuss gender issues. I need food. Pizza. Beer. Lots of beer, as a matter of fact."

"Are you drowning your sorrows?" she asked, patting my arm with concern.

"No way. I'm having a victory party. You in?"

She smiled. "I'm not only in. I'm buying."

We stealthily abandoned our base and then made a mad dash for Fifth Avenue, where we jumped into a cab and rode down to Hell's Kitchen.

When we got to the neighborhood, I bought the pizza and Weezie bought the six-pack, and our party-of-two was soon under way at the Heartbreak Hotel. We were in the process of gorging ourselves on slices of pepperoni with mushrooms and onions when the phone rang. It was Leah.

I braced myself for her accusations. She had spotted me hiding in the bushes and I was sure she wasn't going to be pleased. "If you're going to yell at me for spying on you and Dan, I just want to say that it wasn't because—"

"I'm not going to yell at you," she interrupted. "I know you had my best interests at heart. You really, really wanted to make sure he showed up."

I was stunned. I was sure she'd think I had a more sinister motive for being in the park. "I did want to make sure he'd show up," I said, continually amazed by her forgiving nature. "Did he explain why he was late? I assume it was because he was wrestling with his emotions, still brooding about the terrible things I did to him."

She laughed. "It wasn't that at all. It turns out that Traffic Dan Swain gets stuck in traffic just like the rest of us."

"What?"

"There was a fire on the side street his taxi took across town, and everything was at a standstill. He was so fed up that he got out of the cab and ran the rest of the way to the park."

"So Traffic got stuck in traffic," I repeated, realizing that Dan would have been on time if not for the fire, which meant that he hadn't wrestled with his emotions; that he'd had every intention of meeting Leah at two o'clock; that he'd only left me hanging at Mrs. Thornberg's to "yank my chain."

She went on to thank me for making it possible for her to get together with him.

"You two are solid again?" I asked, hopeful that my staged reunion had set them back on course.

"Very. We're rescheduling the wedding and having it in Minco after all."

Her announcement triggered only a tiny flutter in my stomach, not the lurching I'd felt when I'd first heard they were getting married. "I'm very happy for you. And for Dan."

"It wouldn't have happened without you. We both know that."

"Don't be silly. If you're talking about the paintings, they were just my way of making amends."

"The paintings were an inspired idea," she said. "And now that we've figured out that they're yours, we'll return them to you as soon as possible. No, I'm talking about how you hired Desiree to find Dan a live-in."

"I'll say it again. I'm sorry I—"

"I'm serious! If you hadn't picked me, I would never have met him. So thank you."

"Oh. Well, then you're welcome."

She hung up. I turned to Weezie. "That was bizarre. Leah actually thanked me for playing matchmaker. I was expecting a hissy fit, and instead I got a pat on the back."

"Hey, she reconciled with her guy. Why shouldn't she be grateful?" She sipped her beer. Some of the foam clung to her top lip. "So now that she and Dan are squared away and Nards and I are growing closer, that leaves you."

"What about me?"

"Men, Mel. You remember them. When are you gonna let yourself have one?"

"*Have one.* Like they're fattening or something."

"Come on, pay attention. Have you heard from Evan?"

Evan. I'd been so focused on getting Leah and Dan together that I hadn't thought about him. Well, not in the past twenty-four hours. "No, and he said I shouldn't get in touch with him until the Dan situation was resolved."

"Presto! It's resolved. What are you waiting for? Call him."

Easy for her to say. She was married. She didn't have to put herself back out into the singles world, where there was never any certainty, never any security. It was only about "Will he like me?" and "Did I remind him too much of his last girlfriend?" and "Can I lay my heart on the line one more time?" It all seemed so daunting. Who needed it?

"Are you gonna call him?" she prodded.

"He doesn't have a phone. He's renting a bungalow in the Abacos so he can paint in peace. I told you that."

"Then visit him. 'It's better in the Bahamas.' Isn't that their slogan?"

"Oh, Weezie. Getting on a plane and just going there seems like—"

"Like Leah and Dan showing up in Central Park, not knowing if the other was going to show up too? Yeah, it's called taking a leap of faith. You've been telling everybody else to do it. Now it's your turn."

"Leah and Dan had already said the *L* word to each other by the time they took that leap of faith," I pointed out.

"Evan has already said it to you."

"Not exactly. He said he was *starting* to fall in love with me."

"Honey, he fell." She smiled. "You know he did. The question is how do you feel about him?"

I waited before answering. I wanted to be honest, straightforward, the way Evan always was. "Okay. How I feel is that I'd really like a chance to be with him without the complication of Dan," I replied. "I'm very attracted to him, that much I know, and I admire his values and his way of viewing the world. And, of course, I think he's talented. Oh, and he's also responsible; he doesn't shut everybody out just because he's passionate about his art. I guess what I'm saying is that it would be wonderful if we could have a future together."

Weezie shot me a devilish grin. "Yeah, you need to go to the Bahamas. And soon."

"But what if he's found somebody else by now? There must be a zillion women running around in their bikinis, tempting him."

She cast her eyes heavenward, as if I were too dense to understand. "If you learned anything from this debacle, it should be that people don't turn love on and off like a faucet. It lasts. It lasts through arguments, financial setbacks, infidelities, and, yes, divorces."

I nodded. She and Nards were living proof of that. Dan and I were too.

"Which means that if Evan loves you, he loves you," she said.

"A big 'if.' "

"*If* you went to visit him, you'd find out," she persisted. "You'd be doing exactly what he has Buster doing in the second painting: chancing it instead of playing it safe."

"What about money? I can't just fly off to paradise. I have to get a job."

"Oh, Mel. Mel." Another heavenward glance. "You have plenty of money. Pierce, Shelley gave you a very substantial severance package. You could take a whole year off and still be okay. I thought you'd gotten over your debtors' prison demons."

"I have, but I still need to find work at some point."

"At some point." She polished off her beer and looked at me. "Actually, I've been thinking about going back to work myself."

"You have? I had no idea." She had always maintained how content she was to stay home and raise her children.

"The kids are in school, and we have people to take care of the house," she said. "What I'd like to do is ease myself back into the workforce, but not at a hornets' nest like Pierce, Shelley."

"So you're thinking of changing careers?" I asked.

"No. I'm thinking of starting my own financial planning company." She smiled. "And I could really use a partner."

My eyes widened. "Me?"

"Who else?"

"Oh, Weezie! That would be fantastic. The best! But how would we swing it?"

While I listened raptly, she laid out her ideas for a financial consulting business. *Our* financial consulting business. We would start small, renting modest office space in the city, and expand as the need arose. Two star strategists together again, only this time with plenty of flexibility in terms of our schedules and no Bernie types looking nervously over our shoulders.

"With e-mail, fax, and teleconferencing, we can service clients from anywhere," said Weezie, her excitement growing. "I can work out of my house a couple days a week, and you can work out of—" She giggled. "Your bungalow in the Abacos."

It sounded like a dream come true. Doing what I was trained to do. Partnering with my best friend. Earning a living without sacrificing my personal life. A lot to consider but no downside, as far as I could tell.

"Why don't I figure out the numbers while you're gone?" she suggested. "By the time you're back, I'll have a budget and a business plan for you to look at."

"While I'm gone?" I said with a laugh. "You have me out the door already!"

"Out the door and on the beach with Evan."

"When am I making this trip, by the way?"

"Tomorrow," she said. "Dan's got Buster for the rest of the week, so you could stay until Sunday night. All we have to do is book your flights, pick out some sexy bathing suits for you to pack, and send you off to be with Picasso."

I sighed as I thought about Evan. I closed my eyes, sat back in my chair, and pictured myself surprising him at his bungalow—without a cheese booger dangling from my nose; without a grungy T-shirt riding up my chest; without a red, swollen face resembling a parade float; without old feelings for an ex-husband clouding my new feelings for him. I pictured us without encumbrances. It was a lovely picture.

"Earth to Melanie," Weezie said, shaking my foot. "Where's your head right this minute?"

I opened my eyes. "I was thinking that I might just do it."

"Which?" she said. "Working with me or going to see Evan?"

"Both," I said.

Weezie jumped out of her chair and hugged me. "I'll get the airlines on the phone. You start packing."

I smiled. "Who made you the boss? I thought we were partners."

"You can be the boss when you come home. We'll trade off as the situations warrant."

I started to say something—to thank her for being a constant in my life, for teaching me about friendship, for being such a great sounding board—but she held her hand up.

"Go pack," she said.

"Yes, boss," I said.

Chapter 33

The next morning at seven-forty-five, I was on a 757 bound for Fort Lauderdale. From there, I would board a nineteen-seat turbo prop for Treasure Cay, one of the more developed islands in the Abaco chain. And from there, I would hop a ferry over to Green Turtle Cay, the tiny island where Evan was renting his cottage.

I make this sound very carefree and no-big-deal-ish with all my flying and hopping and ferrying. But I wasn't a relaxed traveler, to put it mildly. I was terrified of even slight airplane turbulence and made a point of avoiding turboprops, which were SUVs with wings, as far as I was concerned. Still, Evan was worth my death-defying acts, I'd decided. If I was brave enough to go to him without an invitation, I was brave enough to go to him propping and hopping.

Actually, I was lucky to get a coach seat on the New York–to–Florida flight on such short notice, given all the snowbirds and second homers who commute back and forth regularly, and even luckier to get a seat in the "two" section next to the window. As I soared over the eastern seaboard, about twenty minutes into the flight, I turned to the passenger next to me, as I always do, seeking reassurance. If he or she didn't seem anxious whenever the plane dipped or shook or shimmied, I would take it as a positive sign.

The man next to me on this particular flight was in his sixties, I guessed, wearing a navy blue blazer, kelly green slacks, a pink sweater, and white shoes. Which is another way of saying he had shed his Manhattan black for South Florida's all-colors-all-the-time. He was buried in a book—it was one of those evangelical novels theorizing that God lets some people into heaven but leaves others behind—and he seemed fairly engrossed in it, perhaps wondering if he would be in the former group or the latter.

Pumped up with the thrill and uncertainty about my adventure, I was dying to talk. And so I interrupted his reading and made chitchat. He put down his book without annoyance and made chitchat back, which hinted at his goodness and led me to believe that he would, indeed, make God's cut.

Our conversation was superficial at first. His name was Charles, although his friends called him Chuck. He was married with two children and three grandchildren. He was a dermatologist with a private practice in Fort Lauderdale, and he'd been visiting his grandkids in Long Island. That sort of stuff.

Then, as often happens between airline passengers who know they'll never see each other again once they get where they're going, the chitchat became more personal. At least, mine did. I was pretty keyed up, as I said, and couldn't stop talking.

I told Chuck all about Evan, about how he'd supported me during an exceptionally difficult period in my life; about how he was tackling a career as an artist after being squeezed out of the publishing business; about how excited/nervous I was about my spontaneous decision to visit him; and about how he and I would finally be able to be intimate now that we had put our pasts behind us. (I really couldn't shut up.)

Chuck asked me if it was commonplace for me to break out in hives whenever I was excited/nervous. I asked him why he was asking. He said, "You've been scratching the daylights out of that left arm of yours. It's dotted with lesions."

I looked down at my arm, where there *was* an unsightly rash. I must have been so focused on Evan that I hadn't realized I'd been tearing at my own skin. "Now that you mention it, it does itch," I said.

He took a closer look at the source of the itching and asked me to show him my other arm, which I did. To my horror, it had similar *lesions* on it.

"I've never had hives before," I said.

"They're not hives," he said, after examining both arms as well as my hands, my fingers, my neck, and a small patch behind one ear. There were rashes everywhere. "Have you spent any time in the woods over the past twenty-four hours?"

I said I hadn't. He asked me if I was sure. I said sure I was sure. Then I flashed back on my Central Park experience.

"But I wasn't in the woods, exactly," I said. "It was just a clump of bushes, and I was only in them for a few minutes."

He nodded, chuckling.

I asked him what was so funny. He said people often mistake poison ivy for less benign plants.

"*Poison ivy?*" I yelped. I'd had it twice after weekend jaunts to the country with Dan and had wanted to kill myself both times. Never had I itched so much. Never had my skin turned the color of raspberries with the bumpy texture to match. Never had I been forced to wear only a bedsheet for an entire week until the rash began to dry up and I could tolerate having clothes touch it. Never had I gone through a vat of calamine lotion.

I told Chuck I couldn't possibly have poison ivy. Not now, of all times. He said he was sorry but that he would stake his thirty years as a doctor on it.

"Try not to scratch," he cautioned. "Oh, and stay out of the sun, don't bathe or shower, and avoid physical contact with others. It'll make it spread."

After his diagnosis sunk in, I considered smashing the window next to me and leaping out of the plane. I mean, this guy had basically just taken away any expectation I had of being at my best for Evan, who had seen enough of me at my worst. Never mind that I also felt guilty about Weezie; since I'd dragged her along on my spy mission, she must have gotten The Crud too.

But, of course, I didn't smash the window or leap out of the plane. Instead, I spent several minutes in quiet contemplation, remembering not only what Weezie had said about love (that it doesn't waver) but what Evan had said about love (that it was about accepting weaknesses as well as strengths), and I decided to go for another kind of flying leap.

When you get right down to it, what *is* a leap of faith if not appearing at your beloved's doorstep, not only uninvited but letting him see you for who you really are?

My arms started to itch in earnest then, driving me insane. It was as if the rash, having now been identified by a professional, was free to run rampant.

As I battled the urge to rip my skin to shreds, a question suddenly popped into my head and ended up steering this story right back to its beginning.

"Just curious," I said to Chuck, who'd retreated into his book. "Do men and women come down with poison ivy with the same frequency?"

"Now that you mention it, I *have* seen a rise in the number of women who come down with it," he said, looking up. "It's probably because you're doing your own yard work now, along with hiking and hunting and fishing—activities that used to be considered 'male.'" He chuckled. "Hey, you women wanted sexual equality? You've got it."

Yes, I thought, as he went back to his reading. We have it and we're better for it. But it does have its occasional drawbacks.

When I landed in Fort Lauderdale, I stopped at an airport sundries shop during the layover and bought some cortisone cream and some Benadryl. Then I went to the ladies' room, took the pill, and applied the cream, which, unlike the pink calamine lotion, was a pasty white. As I peered at myself in the mirror over the sink, I noticed that the poison ivy had surfaced on my face; there was one patch on my chin and another on my left cheek and a third on the tip of my nose, so I put the cream there too.

Are you getting this? I looked like a monster. Or like those people who paint their faces to support their teams at sporting events.

Two hours later, I made it through the turboprop flight and its attendant turbulence with relative ease. Thanks to the Benadryl, I was pretty much knocked out from takeoff to landing, and the only bumps I felt were on my skin.

But it was on the fifteen-minute ferry ride that I really began to loosen up. It suddenly dawned on me that I was in paradise. I mean, like utopia. I'd been to the Caribbean and I'd been to Bermuda and I'd been to Hawaii, and they were each stunningly beautiful in their own way, but the Abacos had a more quiet, less showy allure. No giant hotels. No giant fast-food restaurants. No giant tourists with video cameras. (Okay, there were a few, but they stayed in Treasure Cay to play golf.)

As the boat carried me along to Green Turtle, I sat and watched nature go by: the water, which was the sort of turquoise/aqua/teal you only see in either movie swimming pools or your dreams; the soft sandy beaches that make you want to bury your toes in them; the lush, tropical landscape with its swaying palms and trees laden with coconuts, grapefruits, and berries; the afternoon sky, which was blue but dotted with big, puffy clouds that felt low enough to touch. And I listened, both to the excited chatter of visitors like me and to the natives, whose melodious voices were singing to one another about their workday.

"Excuse me. Is there a city on Green Turtle?" I said to one of the locals. I asked this, not because I was hankering for a city. God, no. I just wondered if civilization had encroached on all this beauty.

The Bahamian woman, who was with her three young children, smiled and said, "New Plymouth, you mean?"

"I guess so," I said, picturing paved roads, traffic congestion, and everything else I'd left behind.

"*This* is our settlement," she said, gesturing past the dock where our ferry was about to tie up.

Her settlement. I looked around and sighed with relief. Along with secluded inlets and gently sloping hills and green forests, there was, at this southern tip of the cay, a little village with the flavor of an eighteenth-century New England harbor. Clapboard houses with gingerbread trim lined its narrow streets, which weren't clogged with honking cars but were quiet and pristine, except for a couple of clucking hens. No wonder they call the Abacos the "out islands," I thought. And no wonder Evan loves them.

"New Plymouth is very small," said the woman almost apologetically, mistaking my expression for disappointment. "Only about four hundred people live here."

About half the population of Minco, I thought, remembering how afraid I'd been of small places, of not being able to succeed in small places. No more.

As we disembarked from the ferry, I reached into my pocket and pulled out the piece of paper with Evan's address on it. "Excuse me again," I said to the woman. "I'm sorry to bother you, but could you tell me how to get to this address?" I showed her the paper.

She laughed. Laughed! Not knowing that people in the Abacos are generally happier than people anywhere else in the world and that they laugh simply *because* they're happy, I was convinced that she was laughing at me.

"Don't tell me," I said, rolling my eyes. "I've gotten off at the wrong island or something." I sighed. "I've been so preoccupied with my poison ivy and my boyfriend—well, he's not my boyfriend yet. Not until I find him and tell him I'm ready to be with him. I was so excited about seeing him that maybe I wasn't as careful as I should have been when I made the reservations yesterday. I kind of rushed—"

I stopped when she started shaking her head at me.

"No," she said, continuing to laugh. What a jolly person! What a jolly country! "I was trying to explain that the place you're going to is just up the street—a two-minute walk."

"Really?" I said. "I didn't screw up?"

She grinned the widest grin I'd ever seen. "Not at all," she said. "You're right where you want to be."

So, there you have it. I was right where I wanted to be. What I hoped—well, "hope" is an understatement—was that Evan would be there waiting for me; to accept me, welts and all.

Want More?

Turn the page to enter
Avon's Little Black Book —

the dish, the scoop and the
cherry on top from
JANE HELLER

Dear Reader,

First, let me say a heartfelt thanks for picking up *An Ex to Grind.* I mean, wow. Seriously. You could have picked up *The Da Vinci Code* or *War and Peace* or anything by Nora Roberts, and yet you chose my book. Again: wow. Was it the cute artwork on the cover that pulled you in? The subject matter of the novel? The fact that you'd enjoyed my books in the past? Oh, who cares. The important thing is that you're holding *An Ex to Grind* in your hands right this very minute, and it's a beautiful thing. I'm honored and flattered and I owe you for giving me your attention when there were so many other ways you could have spent your leisure time. Yes, I owe you. So what I'm going to propose is that I submit to a no-holds-barred interview with you for a few pages. Sounds like fun, doesn't it? How often do you get to interview the author of the book you've just read! You'll ask me questions—*grill* me, if you must—and I'll answer every one. Are you ready?

Reader: Wait. Wait. I've never interviewed an author before. Am I supposed to pretend I'm Barbara Walters or something?

Jane: Sure. You're in charge. As I said, I owe you.

Reader: Okay. I guess I should start by telling you that I really did enjoy the book. It made me laugh out loud.

Jane: I'm glad. That's always been my goal as a writer—to make you laugh, take you away from the daily grind, spin a tale that has some contemporary social relevance but is accessible enough to escape into.

Reader: How did you get the idea for a book about a woman who schemes her way out of writing alimony checks to her ex-husband? Are we talking autobiographical here?

Jane: No, thank God. The idea first percolated after I read a statistic that stunned me: in a third of American households where both partners work, *she* earns more than *he* does. That's a lot of females bringing home the bacon in this country! Then I read an article in *New York Magazine* called "Power Wives," in which women were resentful that their husbands were not pulling their weight in the career department—a gender switch if ever there was one. And then I went to a luncheon attended by women in media. I was surrounded by the sort of alpha babes in the *New York Magazine* story—heavy hitters in their power suits and power haircuts and power attitudes. At one point during a conversation with the woman seated next to me, I said, "What does your husband do?" She rolled her eyes and said, "Nothing—well, besides play golf and poker." Just as her reply was registering with me, the woman on my other side piped up, "My husband doesn't have a job either. He claims to be an artist, but I'm still waiting for his first painting." And just as *her* words were sinking in, a third woman at the table groaned, "I put mine through graduate school. Now that we're divorced, he's got four degrees but I'm stuck paying him alimony." I remember thinking, There really has been a shift in our culture; maybe there's a comic side to all of this and I should write about it. And then came the final trigger: a close friend decided to divorce her husband and discovered, much to her dismay, that she would have to pay him alimony—for *ten years*. She was extremely bitter because her ex wasn't even trying to support himself. She said to me on the phone one day, "I would do anything to get out of writing those checks to him every month." *Anything?* Hmm. My mind starting spinning and, after consoling my friend, I hung up the phone and went to my desk and made notes. There had been plenty of revenge comedies about men who would do anything to wriggle out of having to pay their exes alimony, but I couldn't remember any about women doing the same thing. I figured my novel would be the first—a funny cautionary tale about this latest skirmish in the battle of the sexes.

Reader: Um, no offense, but weren't you sort of exploiting your friend's misery for your own purposes?

Jane: Actually, my friend encouraged me to write the book. She loved the idea of seeing the ex-husband in the story go down. She'd call me and suggest ways to make him suffer.

Reader: Melanie Banks, the heroine, is good at making Dan, her ex, suffer. Didn't you worry that people wouldn't like her for being such a manipulator?

Jane: It's true that Melanie's not warm and fuzzy like some of my other heroines and we don't root for her right from the get-go. But I thought it would be interesting to write about a woman who makes mistakes, who has rough edges, whose personal issues about money cloud her judgment. Melanie feels real to me because of her flaws. I wanted to slap her at times, but she does learn and grow over the course of the book and by the end, she's ready to put her past behind her and start over, no longer the bitter divorcée. I've always been a fan of redemption stories where people make questionable choices, are brought to their knees by those choices, and are better for it in the end.

Reader: Speaking of the end, you don't actually show Melanie living happily ever after. She goes off to the Bahamas to be with Evan, the painter, but we don't see his reaction to her choosing him over Dan. Did you mean to leave us hanging? Because if you did, that's not very nice.

Jane: I'm sorry you feel that way.

Reader: Well, *did* you mean to leave us hanging?

Jane: Not in the way you're suggesting. Anyone who's ever read my novels knows that I usually tie everything up into a neat and tidy package at the end. I love happy endings because they're so uplifting. As a matter of fact, one reader told me my books are better for depression than Prozac.

Reader: I'm on Zoloft.

Jane: Ah, well the point I was about to make is that with *An Ex to Grind* I just decided to deviate from my formula a bit. Not to leave you hanging, just to leave something to your imagination. So you're right. It's not perfectly clear what will happen with Melanie and Evan once she arrives in the Bahamas. But my hunch is that they'll have a wonderful life together. Melanie has finally let go of Dan and their turbulent relationship and has declared herself open to loving someone else. As for Evan, he told Melanie over and over that love is unconditional, that when you really care about someone, you're there for them in good times and bad. So they'll have a blast in the Bahamas and then fly back to New York, where she'll launch a successful consulting firm with her best friend Weezie and he'll sell enough of his paintings to contribute to their financial stability. Oh, and everybody will share custody of Buster, the pug. A happy ending indeed.

Reader: I love dogs. Will your next book have a dog in it too?

Jane: No dog, sorry. But I hope you'll be on the lookout for the book anyway. It's called *Some Nerve*, and it's about a celebrity journalist named Ann Roth, a very ethical reporter who tries to prove to her demanding boss that she'll do whatever it takes to score the big interview. There's just one problem: she's got a major fear of flying. When the mediaphobic actor she's been assigned to interview decides he'll only talk to her while he's piloting his Cessna, she panics, loses her job, and goes home to her small town in Missouri, determined to get her career back. And then a lucky break . . . The mediaphobic actor lands in her local hospital with a heart ailment (he thinks he'll avoid media scrutiny by hiding in the middle of the country), and Ann finds out. She volunteers at the hospital hoping to pry an interview out of him, but she winds up with much more than she bargained for.

Reader: My aunt Doris volunteers at a hospital. She could have helped you with the research.

Jane: Thanks, but I researched *Some Nerve* myself by signing up as a volunteer at Cedars-Sinai Medical Center in Los Angeles, and the experience changed my life. Now I volunteer every Thursday afternoon and I really look forward to it. I never realized how rewarding it could be to work with patients. I urge everyone to donate their time to helping out. Hospitals are always looking for people to pitch in—from providing the nurses with an extra pair of hands to handling administrative duties.

Reader: So you volunteer once a week *and* you write a book a year. Busy, busy, huh?

Jane: Volunteering is a great break from writing. And I do my best brainstorming about the books while I'm driving to and from the hospital. We have lots of traffic in L.A.

Reader: So I've heard. How do you keep coming up with ideas for your books?

Jane: I read a ton of newspapers and magazines and am always clipping interesting articles and stuffing them into my "Ideas" file. I also get out and talk to women to find out what's on their minds. And—this goes without saying for a writer—I eavesdrop. Whether I'm eating at a restaurant or standing in a crowd, if I overhear a juicy conversation you can bet it'll find its way into one of my novels.

Reader: For instance?

Jane: *Female Intelligence*, a book I wrote a few years ago, is about a female linguist who teaches men how to communicate better with the women in their lives. The idea came to me while I was walking out of a movie theater. I overheard a wife ask her husband, "So, Harry, what did you think of the movie?" Harry's response? A grunt. The wife tried again. "I asked you, what did you think of the movie?" Harry's response? A shrug. The wife, clearly frustrated, said, "Harry, why won't you ever talk to me?" Harry's response? "About what?" I remember laughing after that exchange, but I also remember rushing home to my computer with the germ of a story.

Reader: Just wondering. Would you call the type of books you write "chick-lit?"

Jane: I'm not a big fan of that label. I mean, do people refer to John Grisham's novels as "dude-lit?" No, they don't. What I write are novels with female protagonists and plots that involve relationships of all kinds—man/woman, mother/daughter, sister/sister. They're comedies about ordinary women who find themselves in extraordinary circumstances, often of their own making, and during the course of solving their problem they find love, happiness, self-confidence, and an inner bravery they didn't know they had. I don't write stories about how to get a fabulous guy. I write stories about how to have a fulfilling life. The chick-lit thing bothers me. It's so dismissive.

Reader: Okay. I hear you. No need to have a hissy fit.

Jane: I'm not having a hissy— Do you have any more questions?

Reader: Yes. I read on your web site that you used to work as a publicist at different publishing houses in New York. Did you become a writer because you were around writers all the time?

Jane: Just the opposite. Working closely with writers gave me a very real understanding of how difficult the job of being a writer is. You sit in a room alone, day after day, staring at a computer screen, never knowing if what you're doing has any merit at all. It's lonely and isolating and requires incredible focus and concentration. It's not the profession to go into if you're looking for a good time. One very prestigious novelist told me the only thing he enjoys about being a writer is typing in the words "The End" when he finishes a manuscript. No, I became a writer because I had an idea for a story. It was that simple. I was living in Connecticut in the 1980s and the stock market crashed. Suddenly, everybody was trying to unload their McMansions before the bank foreclosed on them. Suddenly, people were trying to reinvent themselves after being laid off from their jobs. Suddenly, even members of the moneyed set were scrambling. I had the notion: what if a suburban princess who's never worked a day in her life loses all her money in the stock market crash, is dumped by her husband, and is forced to go to work as a maid to support herself? And what if her employer gets murdered and she becomes the prime suspect? Those "what ifs" were the basis for *Cha Cha Cha*, my first novel. It was published in 1994. It was translated into over a dozen languages, was a Literary Guild selection, and was optioned for a TV movie. I felt very, very lucky.

Reader: You've had a bunch of your books optioned by Hollywood, according to your site. When will we see one of them on the screen?

Jane: Eight out of my twelve published novels have sold to Hollywood and producers keep telling me what great movies they'd make. Meanwhile, I'm still waiting for one of these projects to happen. I think we're inching closer, but let's just say I haven't bought my dress for any premieres.

Reader: If you were to buy a dress, would it be one of those strapless gowns that are all about showing cleavage?

Jane: You should go back and check out my jacket photo. You pretty much need cleavage to show cleavage.

Reader: Good point. What do you do when you're not writing? Besides volunteering?

Jane: I'm hardly ever not writing. Just ask my husband, who is positive that my fingers are glued permanently to my keyboard. But we all have our passions and mine is baseball. I grew up in New York and my father and grandfather were Yankees fans, and I've been devoted to the team for as long as I can remember. Since I usually deliver my manuscripts in the spring or summer of each year, I have more time to watch the games during the season and I seize it. I was supposed to take a trip to Europe last summer but it coincided with a Yankees-Red Sox series so I rescheduled. Someone asked me the other day: "If you could have dinner with any person, living or dead, who would it be?" I answered quickly and with conviction: "Derek Jeter."

Reader: He's a hunk. And single. I'd have dinner with him too.

Jane: He *is* a hunk, but I'm interested in talking to him strictly for research. I'm dying to write a novel with a baseball backdrop, even though the conventional wisdom is that women don't buy books about sports. I'm also dying for the Yankees to invite me to throw out the first pitch before a game, the way Stephen King did it at a Red Sox game.

Reader: Stephen King's more famous than you are.

Jane: He is, but after you tell all your friends how much you enjoyed *An Ex to Grind*, maybe that'll change.

Reader: I'll do what I can. So how do you find the discipline to write a book a year?

Jane: I'm someone who works well within a routine. There may be writers who can take a laptop to the beach, wait until the muse strikes, and feel a burst of creativity. But I need structure. I get up in the morning, have breakfast, head for my office, and start writing. I take a short break for lunch, then work until dinnertime. When I'm into the last third of a book and nearing the finish line, I work nights too. There's such an adrenaline rush when you're racing toward the end, because you want to see how it all turns out.

Reader: Come on. You don't already know how it turns out?

Jane: I know in a general way, but the specifics—the plot twists and the reactions of the characters and the words of dialogue—become clear to me as I'm writing.

Reader: Your books are very realistic about falling in love, falling out of love, and finding new love. Do you write from personal experience?

Jane: Absolutely. I'm on my third marriage, which doesn't exactly make me Elizabeth Taylor but does make me familiar with love—finding it, losing it, divorcing it, being heartsick over it. I'm a cynic about love, but I'm also the biggest romantic sap in the world. Every time I watch the movie *The Way We Were* and see Barbra Streisand standing in front of the Plaza Hotel, running her fingers through Robert Redford's hair, I start sobbing. Those two still love each other! They had a child together! Why can't they work it out? That scene makes me so mad I want to throw something at the TV! What I'm saying is that I believe in true love even as I poke fun at it. I embarked on each of my first two marriages with the expectation that I'd live happily ever after. But the reality is that things happen and feelings change and relationships don't always work out. I wish I'd been better equipped to be a wife my first two times out, but hopefully I'm wiser now. They say the third time's the charm, right?

Reader: They also say three strikes and you're out. Isn't that a baseball expression—ha ha?

Jane: It is, but I prefer to look on the bright side.

Reader: Must be expensive to get married over and over. Did you have big weddings each time?

Jane: That's sort of a personal question, isn't it? I think you're warming to this interview thing.

Reader: You promised: "no-holds-barred."

Jane: Right. The first wedding was lovely and traditional and, yes, expensive. It was in a tent on my parents' lawn, complete with bridesmaids and bridegrooms, a live band, and a cake several layers high. The bad omen was the skunk that crawled out from under the dance floor and sprayed the waiters.

Reader: How about the second wedding?

Jane: It was a festive but less extravagant occasion at my sister's apartment, and the person who officiated was the therapist my fiancé and I had been going to so we could iron out our issues.

Reader: You're kidding me.

Jane: Nope. We didn't want some generic Justice of the

Peace to marry us. We wanted someone who'd really know us. And who knows you better than your shrink?

Reader: Another bad omen if you ask me. How about the third one?

Jane: The wedding was at a charming country inn on a crisp fall afternoon. I don't remember how much it cost. What I remember is that as I watched my husband reciting his vows I kept thinking to myself, I'm madly in love with this man. Thirteen years later I feel the same way, even through the ups and downs that come with marriage.

Reader: You really *are* a romantic sap. Is your husband supportive of your work?

Jane: Very. He's not only my first reader and the one who takes my jacket photos, but he also comes with me on my book tours. I'll be up at some podium telling my same, stale jokes and he laughs at them as if he's heard them for the first time. That's support.

Reader: He sounds like a keeper. Does he have a brother?

Jane: He does. I'll have him call you.

Reader: Great. Listen, I've got to wrap this up—a dentist appointment, sorry—so I'll just ask one more question. What's the best part of being a writer?

Jane: That's easy: the mail from readers. When I get letters and e-mails telling me that my novels keep people smiling in tough times, I feel fabulous. The books are fast-paced and breezy, so I never think of them as being *meaningful*—until the mail comes. I'll never forget one letter in particular. A woman wrote to me that her husband was in the hospital, having been diagnosed with terminal cancer, and that she had to leave her two young children with a relative to be at his side. The situation was grim for her. Then one day she was standing at the nurses' station when she spotted a copy of one of my books and started reading it, just as a diversion. The next thing she knew she was laughing! She hurried into her husband's room with the book and began to read whole paragraphs aloud to him. And *he* laughed too. She was so encouraged by his change in mood that she went out and bought all of my books and established a ritual at the hospital: she would read to him from a Jane Heller novel every day and they would laugh together. "My husband's been gone awhile and I'm still grieving," she wrote in her letter, "but I wanted to thank you for giving us some light-hearted moments. Now, whenever I read your books, I think of them as my friends. They seem to be published just when I need a boost the most. I'm very grateful to you." Well, I'm the one who's grateful, of course. Whenever I wonder if I should keep on writing, I remind myself of her words. And back to the computer I go.

Reader: Thanks, Jane. This was fun.

Jane: No, thank you. And good luck at the dentist.

JANE HELLER

Michael Forester

JANE HELLER is the author of eleven previous novels: *Cha Cha Cha, The Club, Infernal Affairs, Princess Charming, Crystal Clear, Sis Boom Bah, Name Dropping, Female Intelligence, The Secret Ingredient, Lucky Stars,* and *Best Enemies*. Her thirteenth novel, *Some Nerve*, is soon to be released by William Morrow. Visit her at *www.janeheller.com*.